Below, Peter scr

"Peter?"

Her gaze darted around the room: everything in place. Coffee table, modular sofa and loveseat, brown. Files on the armchair, where she'd left them. There was that sensation-mongering newspaper too, the one with the front-page story about some reporter from *Idol Magazine* found horribly murdered on her way to interview Timmy Valentine.

"Peter, what's happening?"

She took a few more steps down the staircase and slipped in something. She lurched, sprawled, stabbed her nose into something squishy—

Oh God

Another scream tore from her as blood and rheum squirted into her face.

An eye stared at her, lifeless.

Also by S.P. Somtow in Gollancz Horror

MOON DANCE

S.P. SOMTOW
VAMPIRE JUNCTION

GOLLANCZ HORROR

To Lydia,
who accidentally gave me this title
and to Thaithow,
who imbued in me an undying
love of horror

Gollancz Horror is an imprint of Victor Gollancz Ltd
14 Henrietta Street, London WC2E 8QJ

First published in Great Britain 1985
by Futura Publications

First Gollancz Horror edition 1992

Copyright © 1984 by Somtow Sucharitkul

A catalogue record for this book is
available from the British Library

ISBN 0-575-05057-8

Printed and bound in Great Britain
by Cox & Wyman Ltd, Reading

CONTENTS

SPRING:
The Red King's Dream 1

SUMMER:
The Gods of Chaos 105

AUTUMN:
Bluebeard's Castle 197

WINTER:
I Am the Darkness 315

SPRING

The Red King's Dream

I'll hop on the train in Kansas
You change at Santa Fe.
We'll cross tracks at the Vampire Junction
that sucks our souls away.
—Timmy Valentine

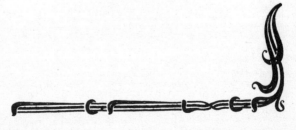

1

fire: A.D. 79

. . . brimstone . . . a child's footsteps patter on a splintering mosaic, bittertoast smell of charring feet . . . fleeing, mountain thunder, then. . . .

. . . blood, *spatter spatter spatter* bursting *spatter spatter spatter* boiling on the hot stones *spatter spatter spatter*

. . . marble columns snapping like bones over the screaming and . . .

. . . blood *spatter spatter spatter*

. . . bloodgutted eyes through the sulphur-haze and the screaming and . . .

. . . through the ash-hail, fangs glitter blood *spatter* glitter *spatter* glitter *spatter* glitter

dissolve: the present

I'm scared.

Why?

Don't you feel anything? I'm cold. Hold me.

All right.

No don't. Your hands are so cold. It's nothing, I guess. *Brrr.* Ever since I got into the car though. Maybe I'm not as blasé about the very rich as I'd like to be, huh? You *are* very rich, aren't you? I mean, like you're only a kid, but you must be one of the richest people on earth, what with that new album and everything. *Vampire Junction.* Yeah. Am I talking

3

too much? I'm nervous. Where was I? Yeah, money. They want to know about money. Tell me all about your money.

FDR Drive, Rudy.

I've interviewed lots of people before, you know. You name 'em. But you, like you're so mysterious. Is this really the first time you're going to be on TV? Of course it must be. You know you're even shorter than in those photos. How old are you? Twelve? But cute. *I'm* . . . twenty-nine. I don't look it, right? They always say I don't look it. Now I want to do a huge feature for the magazine, understand, *huge*. You don't have to say anything at all though, frankly I'm just going to make most of it up, like who gives a shit about those weeny-boppers anyway, huh? Oh sorry, maybe I shouldn't have said shit. They're your fans after all.

Well . . .

Hey, like this is some limousine you got. Two phones! I guess the driver picks it up and then just intercoms it back to you? Ritzy. Look, here's the toll booth. Nice night, huh? Traffic's not too bad either. Sometimes it can take hours to get to mid-town from LaGuardia.

I've done it before.

Huh? Yeah, of course. You know you got beautiful eyes . . . so *sexy* . . . if I were a weeny-bopper I'd go for you in spades. How do you like New York?

Well enough.

I guess you've seen the whole world though, even if you're just a kid. Huh?

Probably.

Where do you get those cute cloaks from, by the way, the ones you do the concerts in?

In Europe. I have them sent.

Oh.

I love the night.

What? Oh yeah, really, like I love the way you talk, you know, really compact, like those songs of yours. There's never been a teen star like you before, never in my ten years of working for *Idol Magazine*. But if I'm going to interview you you'll have to tell me more about yourself, I mean like what you like to eat and drink, your views on teen sex, your—

. . . .

Anything wrong?

No. Just . . . memories.

What kind of memories? That's just the kind of thing the fans want to know, like how you grew up and stuff and—look, the Big Apple already! I know how I'm going to describe it in the article: "rearing up over the water like a giant graveyard in the moonlight."

Pretentious.

They love shit.

I can see that.

Huh? Oh, yeah. Back to you, Timmy—can I call you that? You and your memories—

(spatter spatter spatter) You wouldn't want to know.

Bad childhood, huh?

Very bad. I've forgotten it all.

There you go, looking at me with those haunting eyes. I'd swear they shine in the dark. There now. It's not often I get to hold the hand of a million-dollar property—oh, I don't mean to hurt your feelings—

?

It's all right. They're like ice, your hands! Your metabolism must be weird or something. You should try more organic foods, you know? Here, I'll warm them. Better? Hey, this is sort of a turn-on, you know, I . . . oh, your hand, it's *burning* my breast, I mean *burning*, and . . . why're you smiling at me like that? Oh, let me hug you, let me . . . don't think I'm kinky now. You're a sophisticated kid, but I don't like little boys, you know, I'm all of . . . twenty-nine . . . want to see them? Here, look, I keep in shape, you know, I . . . how am I going to explain this rip? You like my breasts? Here . . . ouch! Like glaciers, your fingers, like glaciers, and *here, don't scratch* you've drawn blood it's running down my Izod sweater don't think I'm into this stuff now but you're so famous and all and ow! Let go of it! What are you doing? Don't bare your teeth, you animal, you little bastard, you—

I grieve for you. You should not have awakened my memories. I've known . . . someone like you . . . before.

Let me go you're so strong your teeth the moonlight don't bite! don't bite! it hurts it hurts it hurts oh oh oh

Rudy, not this exit yet. If we go into mid-town they'll see us. I hate it when they scream and struggle. It attracts too much attention. I'm so hungry, it hurts so! The breasts are all ripped up. She'll die in a minute or two. Oh, the fresh blood . . .

warming . . . easy . . . easy . . . shall I kill you permanently? Shall I? If I did not you would wake up to a terrible solitude . . . poor creature. I've yanked her heart out, Rudy. That should save her from the great loneliness. There it is, on the seat, going *pit-a-pat* as it seeps into the upholstery . . . easy . . . still now, heart . . . look, her lifeless eyes . . . I'll close them . . . there, she's dead. The seat's all bloody now. Tell Maria to clean it up. My concert's in an hour.
. . .

I'm sorry, Rudy! I was angry, she plucked such vivid memories from me. . . .
Forget, master Timothy.
How can I?

memory: 1918

He has slipped through the railings, this child of darkness, and is standing in a pool of moonlight by the quadrangle's edge, his thin pale face striped by the shadows of the iron bars. He feels the hunger a little, like a rodent scurrying in the pit of his stomach. But it is not hunger that has drawn him out of his hiding place. It is the sound of children singing. It has touched him in his dreamless sleep; he has followed it blindly, as a bloodhound follows a scent, many days' walk from London, leaving behind the house on Fitzroy Square and the old woman who took him in.

For a few moments he watches the stained glass windows, lit from within, of the massive fifteenth-century chapel. It must be an evening choir practice. The building is one of the Cambridge colleges with its own choirschool where young boys are trained for chapel services. He hears the children's voices, cool as the wind.

"What are you doing here, boy?" He averts his eyes, catching a glimpse of the Cambridge don's face, then looking down at the mirror-polished boots and the edge of the gown. "Answer me. Are you lost?" The hunger stirs in him for a moment. "Are you late for practice?" The don indicates the chapel. "No, you're too scruffy to be one of the choristers. Go away, it's out of bounds here."

He stares at the man's eyes, stung by his rebuff. He thinks of feeding for a moment. The pickings have been slim since he left the city. The young men have gone to the war, the women have latched their doors, and there are only tramps, whose blood is bitter with methylated spirits. He is about to spring—

But no. The don rubs his eyes and sees only a black animal, perhaps a cat, dark silver slicing the gloom.

The boy comes to in the nave. Soft light on the Rubens over the altar in the distance. A few seconds of memory surface; he has been here centuries before, and there are dead men, dust now, whose memories still touch him through the warm earth and the cold stone. He longs to join them. In the dark the fan vaulting is shadowed, and there appears to be no ceiling. The boy crouches in a pew as the singing dies away in the musty stillness. It is Purcell's *Funeral Music*: the boy remembers it from long ago, a king's funeral.

For a moment peace steals into his haunted eyes, for he has always loved music.

The voices have allayed his hunger for now. It is at such times that he wishes he could weep. . . .

He hears voices. "Perfect, chaps. But Miles, don't attack that top B flat so viciously in your solo. Just let it grow naturally from the phrase. It's a nuisance, I know, having all these extra choir practices, but with all these chaps dying in the war, and all these memorial services, what can you do? Damn the Kaiser! Very well, that's all for tonight."

The boys troop out, passing under the ornate archway of dark, oily wood that splits the nave. They are giggling, irreverent. The Organ Scholar has come down from the loft and is discussing something with the director; childish laughter and old men's whispers blend into cavernous echoing.

The lights go out. The boy is alone. The dark is kind to his eyes. He must feed now.

He rises, making no noise.

He crosses the aisle, soundless as shadow.

He freezes. Somewhere hinges creak. He hears distant clattering. He dissolves behind the altar's long shadow. Once, the cross, boy-tall, silver, crusted with amethysts, would have caused him grief, but it is not a fervent age, and the symbols are losing their power.

Now he sees tiny lights, dancing, flickering, casting shadow-giants on the walls. An old verger is leading a grotesque processional of men with black robes on which are embroidered stars and moons and cabalistic signs and hieroglyphs, holding candles and staves. The boy smells terror.

It comes from a young woman, bound and gagged, whom they are dragging behind them. Two young acolytes, mere boys, bring up the rear, swinging censers that exude a stench of perfume and charred flesh.

The boy remembers such things from a past better forgotten. He peers from the pool of darkness.

The celebrants are giggling. This is no genuine rite of the old ones, but some game they are playing. The young boys run in front now, scattering the foul smoke everywhere.

"Thank you, Sullivan," says one of the robed ones. He appears to be tipping the verger, who slinks away, leering at the woman.

"You're sure she can't be traced?" says a plump Asian man.

"A waitress at the Copper Kettle," says the first, the tall one with a paper mitre on which is painted a crude skull and other sigils. The girl flails about helplessly as they bind her to the altar. Her arm has almost brushed the boy; his hand has stolen the warmth from hers. He is invisible to them, for he has cloaked himself in darkness.

They are all laughing now. "Be solemn for a moment, won't you!" the leader cries. "This is serious business." Laughter breaks out again, stifles itself.

"What a nuisance the incense was! Are you sure this nauseating concoction is quite necessary?"

"The Book of the Order of the Gods of Chaos absolutely specifies that the frankincense be mixed with the caul of an unborn child," the leader says sternly. "I had little enough trouble with our friends in the medical laboratory." The boys are running gleefully about now, and the fumes are thick and pungent. The girl coughs through the gag.

"Perhaps we shouldn't really—"

"Silence, novice!" says the leader. He pulls a knife from his robe. Now the boy senses the terror in all of them. "This is serious, I tell you, the summoning of a presence—"

Inside, the boy laughs bitterly. He knows that the presences are long dead, if they ever existed. Only their shadows have survived the dark times. They are hypocrites, these humans, they know nothing of my bitterness, my grief. And now the girl will die for it.

The leader has stalked to the altar, knife upraised, the blade catching the candlelight. Quicky the young vampire blends into the shadows.

There is a sudden gasp from the celebrants; the girl, bound too tightly to move, has begun to urinate in her terror. It trickles onto the stone.

Delicately the leader slices into her, reddening the crease between her breasts and drawing a thin line down to her pubes. The stench of fear is overwhelming now, drowning out the incense and the smoking flesh.

The boy feels the madness within; fear has always been an intoxicant for him. But he is angry, and he struggles to quell the hunger.

A robed man begins to draw the girl's blood into a chalice. Her eyes widen. Her scream, through the gag, sounds immeasurably far away. The leader begins to improvise, carving patterned slits into her abdomen. The boy sees his crazed face, implacable.

Anger rises deep inside the boy, rage at this senseless slaughter. And with the bloodsmell comes the ancient hunger, leaping, bursting. He leaps—

He is a wild thing now, pouncing—

The knife clangs on the steps. The leader shouts: "The presence! I didn't know—only a game—!" He sees what he has done. He runs. For a moment, he has seen a wolf, others a panther, others a monster from their own nightmares. They scatter, screaming, their footsteps tiny in the echo-rich vastness—

But there is still one. A small boy, his censer smashed . . . the vampire sees him in a cloud of smoke. Their eyes meet. "Wait," the boy vampire says, "I do not mean to harm—"

They stare into each other's eyes. The vampire sees what he has always seen: terror, naked, crystalline. Has the child seen him in his true shape? Has the borrowed form slipped for an instant?

And now the vampire recognizes the child. It is Miles, the chorister. Only an hour ago he heard the boy pluck that high B flat from the air. It was *his* ethereal singing that he heard in London, singling it out from the millions of voices that assailed his inhumanly acute ears, troubling his not-sleep with its loveliness.

"Miles," he says. His voice is low, half-taunting, half-seductive. But the child is gone.

Then comes the smell of blood, overwhelming his senses. He goes up the steps to the altar where the girl lies bleeding, dying. "I do not want to feed," he says to her; yet, his hunger pounds like an ocean wave. He removes her bonds; she does not struggle now. "You are a virgin, of course," he says, remembering. "They use virgins." She only stares at him, awed, fascinated. "Now I will love you as only the dead can love." He sips the life from her. Warmth shoots into his veins, tingling, soothing. His eyes redden. She stirs, moans, is gone.

Tomorrow, as soon as the light begins to fade, he will seek out a doorstep, a kindly face, another surrogate mother. He will stay here a while because of that child's voice. There is music here, music to warm the millennial ice within him. . . .

dissolve: the present

They looked alike, Rudy. The two women. Do you believe in reincarnation? Or the recurrence of certain somas, perhaps?

I don't know, master Timothy.

It's tempting for me to believe in cycles. They relieve the monotony of immortality.

Yes.

I believe its Thirty-fourth Street. I'll expect the remains to be gone by the time the concert's over.

Of course.

Stop now.

Of course, master Timothy.

fire

Stephen Miles was in his hotel room watching the blaze that reddened the distant skyline. His tailcoat lay abandoned on the floor; the television had been on all day, even though he had been out, first at rehearsal, then at a formal, pretentious cocktail party, then at the final performance of *Göt-terdämmerung* and then at a bloody reception afterwards. Thank God he was still spry at almost seventy.

The fire danced. Smoke-clouds billowed across the night, and he thought he could almost smell it. He had always loved fire, ever since he was a child . . . fire awakened madness in him.

The phone rang. He cursed.

"Stephen Miles," he said.

"Eva Weiss. I call you too late? The time is different here." A faint voice, a transatlantic call.

"Weiss? Oh, from the Goethe-Haus. Munich." Quickly he placed her. "How on earth did you get my number?"

"From your agent. We had . . . an understanding. Listen, when you are coming this summer to do *Tristan* in Winterthurm, do you want a Mahler Nine in Munich thrown in? Hans Schick is very ill, they think he may go by then actually, you need in any case a live German Mahler to complement the record series they're reissuing—"

"They're reissuing it? I seem to remember stepping in for Schick then, too. We'll see." He slammed the phone down and ignored it when it began to ring again at once. His arms ached. He should have given up the five-hour operas ten years ago, but what could he do? It was the history of his life . . . the endless circuit of mediocre opera houses and concert halls, now and then stepping in for some indisposed Big Name ("Miles coped splendidly, despite the short notice") and basking in borrowed glory.

And the breakdowns, the blackouts. And the terrifying memory that would not be dredged from his mind. "I'm a flake," he whispered. "Flake, flake." Americanisms still had a vibrancy for him, even though he had been in America for much of his life.

He leaned against the pillows. Sirens moaned far away. And then he chanced to glance at the television set.

The local news. The same fire, close up. Some office buildings. An announcer was dryly cataloging six deaths.

Miles stared at the screen now. He saw the flames flicker in the windows, saw a charred child plummeting, the firemen wielding their serpentine hoses. He was excited. He wanted to make a little fire himself, to watch it dance . . . easing the bedside ashtray onto the bed, he tore the room service menu into neat strips, groped for a match, lit the paper scraps, extinguished the match and the room lights. . . .

The little fire fizzed for a moment and died. When he turned to the television again they were relating some dull news item, some minor public figure's assassination. He tapped impatiently at the remote control, switching to channel after channel—

A boy's voice was singing in the dark room.

Stephen stopped. He *knew* that voice. But not singing this
... this. . . .

It was one of those sugary crooning songs that preteen girls
listened to; unremarkable enough, especially after a night
of Wagner. But the voice . . . the tone was pure, true, like a
trained choirboy's, inhumanly beautiful. The accompaniment
was tawdry; tinkling, hackneyed piano figures and syrupy
string chords pitted against a rhythm dull and incessant as
Chinese water torture. But still that voice soared free above it.
It stirred troubled memories: the choir school, England, so
many years ago.

The words were sophisticated; lovers were like trains in the
night, crossing at a vampire junction that sucked away their
souls . . . a clever conceit in a song of alienation, of despair.
Surely a child had not written the lyrics. Yet the boy sang with
such wounded innocence, such ancient grief. And now as he
watched, the camera panned the audience, the band, alighted
on the singer's face—

He gasped. He *had* seen this child before—thirty-five years
ago! And even then he had thought him a face from the past, a
dream-face out of his childhood.

He was trembling. Outside, the fire was dead now, and the
sirens silenced.

The face—

Pale, pale as snow. The long hair swirling like a flock of
ravens. The thin mouth, a crease of crimson. And the dark
eyes, hunter's eyes, haunting.

It couldn't be. The boy had been dead for years. That
dreadful first summer on the European opera circuit, taking
over from Karlheinz von Hahn. He'd gone to the funeral, for
Christ's sake, and sent the mother a garland! The mother who
never cried, who'd ordered a coffin with steel bands, welded
shut, weighted down with boulders . . . madwoman, madwoman.

And now here was the same boy. The same voice. Un-
changed.

I'm dreaming, I'm going mad again, he thought, remembering the "rest home" where he had first met Carla Rubens.

He wanted to call her now.

Four rings. "Carla. . . ."

"*Stephen?* What *is* this? I'm asleep." She sounded perfectly
composed. He knew she was only pretending sleepiness.

"I'm sorry."

"Where the hell are you?"

"Arragon, Kentucky. That Wagner festival."

"Yes, I've seen the junk mail for it. Now get off the phone and leave me alone! I haven't heard from you in two years, and I can do without you now, Stephen."

Images flooded his mind: the hideous rest home, the therapy, the marriage, the divorce, Carla still trim and beautiful at forty-five and thirsting for younger men. How he hated being old. . . .

"I have to see you. I mean professionally. I mean—"

"Professionally! I do have a secretary, you know. And office hours."

"I know, I know, I—"

"There was a fire in Arragon, wasn't there? I saw it on the late-late-late news." She had given it away now, she hadn't been sleeping at all. The years since the divorce seemed to dissolve to nothing. They were still playing the same games; she lying blatantly, not caring that he knew.

"I know you think it's the old trouble." He guessed what she would have surmised. After all, he had been under treatment for pyromania, and he had felt a twinge of the old firelust tonight. "But no, it's not that. I'm still in control of that."

"What then?"

"I've seen the boy, Carla, the dead boy! On TV. Tonight. Now."

Silence. Then, "What channel?"

"It's ZQR here, but—"

"Hold on . . . why that's Timmy Valentine, the latest weeny-bopper idol. You called me at two in the morning just to—"

"But it's him! The thing from my nightmares at the rest home, the wolf-thing, the boy with the dead eyes—"

"Come now, Stephen. What did you *really* call about?"

"Nothing! I mean . . . this is what I called about, and—"

"Imagine being frightened by a child star. Poor kid, probably being exploited to death by his parents and his agents. He's one of my patients, you know."

"What!"

"No, I haven't seen him yet. His agent's made an appointment for tomorrow, while he's still in New York."

"Don't see him! Don't see him!"

The phone dropped from his hand. Despair gripped him; he sweated, shook, banged at the television remote control. The screen went black. He found an uneasy sleep, tingling with terror.

2

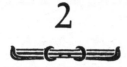

night child

"How did you get in here?" Carla said, panicking because nothing was supposed to be out of place in her Park Avenue office.

"Your door was ajar." A soft voice, an unusual lilt, perhaps even a trace of some European accent. And there he was, leaning against the sill of the panoramic casement, against the jagged skyline—a starscape of lit windows, glittering.

Carla sat down in her worn plaid armchair in front of the eerie monochrome mandala—blowup of a patient's work—that filled half the wall farthest from the window.

"You insisted on an evening appointment," Carla said, "not backing off when I named an outrageous fee." She didn't want to like the kid. She looked at him, not inviting him to sit as yet.

He was beautiful, certainly. The way he looked on TV wasn't due to makeup. His hair, fastidiously unkempt (one knew that not a strand was where it wasn't supposed to be) was so black that it glinted ultramarine in the subdued light. His face was pale, almost anemic. His eyes were dark, wide, captivating. His expression seemed both surly and innocent. She stored all these features in the back of her mind; she'd been taking notes, too, on the songs of his she'd heard. Apparently he *had* written them himself. If he had, you could certainly see the seeds of psychosis . . . if you looked hard

15

enough, and if that was how you made a living.

"Won't you sit down, Timmy? Wherever you want—the couch, the chair, the floor cushions." He selected the couch. His eyes never left her. She sensed something lascivious about the way he fixed his stare on her. "Your agent seems to have gone to great lengths to get you a *Jungian* analyst. . . ."

"It's fashionable."

"I'm all ears."

"At a hundred an hour, you should be."

"You have only fifty-one minutes left."

A brief silence. Timmy seemed to relax a little. Carla fiddled with a notepad, with the concealed controls of a tape recorder in the arm of her chair, with a twist of her hair. Stephen's call had distressed her more than she cared to admit, and she had to remind herself that she was not paid to think of her own problems, nor of those of an estranged husband who might set fire to something if provoked.

"Because you deal with archetypes." Abruptly, the boy had answered her question.

A well-read child. Precocious, even. "Yes."

"But can an archetype itself be susceptible to analysis? This is what I've come to ask." He sounded so serious, yet so childish, too.

"What do you mean?" Was he mocking her?

"I mean," he went on earnestly, "what if some force, some image out of the collective unconscious, could become focused somehow, be born as a living entity?"

I can't believe a little boy is talking like this, she thought. A sliver of dread pierced her thoughts, but she made herself ignore it.

"I want to understand myself," the boy said. "And especially to live with my loneliness."

Now they were on safer ground. Clearly, being catapulted into fame had made him paranoid, awakened old insecurities. She listened, not prompting him.

"What are your feelings about the soul?"

"Well, *I'm* the analyst."

"The soul."

"In a religious sense?"

"Do you have a soul?"

"In a sense . . . Carl Jung believed in the soul. . . ."

"Can you prove it? If I slit you open will it come gushing out, woman?"

. . . Her instincts had been right. There *was* something there after all. She sat quietly, not wanting to interrupt his train of thought.

"I am, in a sense, archetypal, you see," he said. "I have no soul. I am animated only by your fears, your private terrors. It is this that gives me my terrible aloneness."

"I don't understand."

"I am a vampire."

No emotion, she told herself, don't betray yourself . . . "Then the song, *Vampire Junction*—"

"A conceit, nothing more. You see, I like model trains . . . you should see my collection at home." He smiled disarmingly and shook back his dark hair. But for a second Carla had seen another look: eyes sparkling crystal-cold, terrifying her. *Terrifying!*

"Do you dream, then? I get a lot of mileage out of dream analysis, you know," she said, trying to draw him out, humoring him.

"Never."

"And the appurtenances . . . the garlic, the crucifixes, the nighttime appearances, the native earth, the running water?"

He laughed: a high-pitched, silvery laugh, a child's laugh. "Who am I? Lugosi, Lee, Langella?"

"You tell me."

"It is not an age of faith. As the power of symbols crumbles, so their effect on me dwindles."

Outside, in the waiting room, a phone began ringing. Oh, Christ, she thought. I'll ignore it.

Timmy said, "Those movies that so fascinate you mortals only touch on the myths. I am not a myth, Ms. Rubens. I am a distillation of men's most secret terrors, a summary of their million shapes of alienation. That is why I am more real than I ever was, why I am hungrier than ever before"—she shuddered—"why for the first time I am being seen by millions, worshipped by children, lusted after by adults."

The goddam phone!

"Look at me, woman!" The child's voice was so compelling . . . "You *do* believe me! You must believe me because your own unconscious is a shard of that which shaped me—"

. . . ring . . . ring

"Excuse me," Carla said. She ran to the reception desk outside, slamming the door, seizing the phone. "Hello, hello." She was panting. This kid was more than she'd ever bargained for. A flake she'd expected, but a schizophrenic . . . "Hello!" She calmed herself now, carefully masking her unease.

dissolve

Seated alone in his dressing room, he had started to dial several times during the rehearsal, but he would get halfway through his exwife's phone number and then fear would freeze his fingers and he would have to shut it out by playing the anvil music from *Rheingold* over and over in his mind: *dum-di-dum da-da-da dum-di-dum dum-di-dum da-da-da dum-di-dum. . . .*

But later, in another hotel room in yet another city, he got out his memory book and his old clippings and began sorting through them. He had long since stopped collecting clippings, but these, from his first few years, he had always carried around on tour as a kind of lucky charm.

He found what he had been looking for among the yellowing papers, stared disconsolately at them for a long while, and then ordered a half bottle of vodka from room service. He thought of setting the whole sheaf on fire. He could turn out the lights and watch it sparkle . . . instead he picked up the phone and dialed.

"Carla?"

"Damn you, I'm with a patient!"

"*Him*." Nervously he fumbled with the phone before wedging it carefully between ear and shoulder.

". . . listen, this one's a real basket case . . . or a brilliant actor . . . but it's really very interesting, and I want to get back to—"

"I want to see him, Carla. Can you arrange it?"

"What? You're calling up and demanding to see a patient, one you don't even know?"

"You sound anxious. Unnerving, isn't it? The way he half hypnotizes you with those eyes, that voice."

"How do you know?" She breathed uneasily.

"Fix an appointment."

"Call his agent! I'm not your slave. I've kicked you out of my life before—" *Click*. He replaced the receiver and turned the lights off, thinking.

The room was dark; on the TV screen, Christopher Lee was being solemnly impaled by Peter Cushing to ominous music, but he had turned the volume down to a whisper.

There was a knock. Startled, he sat up on the pillows.

"Room service."

He switched the light back on.

After the man left he poured himself a tumbler and spread the old papers out on the bed.

There they were—all the programs of his first tour of the small German opera house circuit; it had been not long after the war. He hadn't been back to Europe since childhood, since his parents had died in a fire and he had been packed off to his American relatives. All those tiny towns, each with its own shoestring *opernhaus*.

There it was.

Opernhaus Thauberg, Wolfgasse 13. He'd done three weeks of repertory there: *Zauberflöte, Fidelio, Tosca* (in German, of course), and others. There were the cast lists. The names meant little now, except for a few: Rothstein, Della Strada, who'd made it relatively big . . . and then, singing the young shepherd boy in *Tosca* and one of the three supernatural boys in *The Magic Flute*, the name of Konrad Stolz.

There were a few press photos, including one that showed the three boys leading Prince Tamino to the castle of Sarastro the sorceror. The children wore frock coats and powdered wigs and waved little wands with stars—an extraordinarily kitschy production.

He held the photo up to the bedside lamp. No, there was no mistake. And when he recalled the child's superbly eerie voice, touching the highest tones without a strain, never seeming to draw breath for any of the broad, soaring phrases, he was sure. A musician couldn't forget such an unusual voice.

The child in front . . . with the clear dark eyes and rapt expression, the boy they'd taken on a last-minute audition because the original singer had died in a bizarre accident, whom he had hired as much because his face reminded him uncannily of some forgotten event in his childhood as because of his voice, had returned.

As Timmy Valentine.

Miles turned the lights off again and tried to get some sleep. As he closed his eyes, the sun rose on the TV screen and Dracula crumbled horribly to dust. . . .

night-child

Damn Stephen! Carla slammed the phone down and returned to her office.

The boy hadn't moved a muscle. She was sure of it. Uncanny.

What could Stephen have meant about Timmy Valentine? She went back to her plaid armchair, shaken.

"You don't believe me," Timmy said.

"Of course I do."

"No, you're just saying that, humoring me until you can learn more about my psychosis. There may be a psychosis, Ms. Rubens, but it is not one of identity. But right now you probably think I'm . . . shitting you."

"It had occurred to me." From the other room, a grandfather clock, a wedding gift from Stephen, began to strike twelve. Timmy waited for the sounds to die away completely.

"The witching hour," he said. "Shall I turn into a bat for you?"

He dissolved. Leather flapped in her face. She shrieked, fangs flashed in the dim light—

And he was sitting on the couch again, twiddling his thumbs. "I didn't see that," Carla said slowly.

"Got a mirror?"

She got up, not taking her eyes off him, found her pocketbook, took out the compact, opened it. She caught a glimpse of herself: sagging in the cheeks, she thought. Crows' feet. But my hair's still pretty. Self-consciously she fussed with it for a moment, and then she turned the little mirror on the boy.

It splintered. Glass shards streamed down onto the carpet. "My mind did that," she said half-aloud. "Or yours. We see what we want to see."

"And touch what we want to touch," the child said. And he rose and went to her and caressed her cheek, once, slowly, his slender fingers like icicles.

"If it's true that you're a vampire," she said, and those eyes were on her, inescapable, "created out of the Collective Unconscious, from our hate and longing and despair . . . then why are you here? What do you want of me?"

"Have you read Petronius?"

The question startled her. She shrank back in her chair. "I can't say I have."

"In the *Satyricon* he talks of visiting the immortal Sibyl at Cumae, a shriveled crone hanging in a bottle, attended by a host of young boys; and the boys were saying to her in Greek, *'c Sibyla, ti theleis?*—Sibyl, what is it you desire?' And she answered, *'Apothanein thelo*. I want to die.' "

"You're immortal then? And you want to die?"

"I don't know!" he cried out. At last he seems moved, she thought, anguished. "All I remember is the outrage on her face, the anger of eternity."

"You remember?"

"Before I became a vampire," he said, "I served the Sibyl of Cumae."

She didn't know whether she should believe. But she found herself yearning for it to be real. It was as if she had never been truly awake before, all through her years of listening to the rich regurgitate their souls, all through her brief, stagnant marriage with Stephen, stranded and isolated by a private fantasy . . . in a way that both moved and frightened her, she was falling in love with this child of the night.

hunger

Rudy, look, Times Square. Slow down. People everywhere, scuttling through their tiny lives. I'm hungry, Rudy. Shall I feed now? See the garish lights. Perhaps there will be someone here. But we'll have to be careful; some of them have drugs in their blood, sickening chemicals. Slow, slow. . . .

Was I right to see that woman, Rudy? It may be that what I am is some disease, something they can take from me. Look, two old women with little paper bags of trash. Look there, they're showing a vampire movie. Look, leering men haunting the street lamps, smelling out their prey. In our soundproof limousine you cannot hear the blare of intermingling Muzaks, but I can, I who can never shut out the sounds of the world.

Hungry?

Yes. Ravenous.

You should be able to find something here.

Yes. Yes. Slower, slower, skim the sidewalks by the porn

shops and the skinflick houses. Before I met you I drank a
woman dry in Cambridge, Rudy; she was a human sacrifice.
She looked just like the woman I drank from the night of the
concert. I was angry at her, Rudy, because she thought she
knew me to the core, thought I was there to be exploited and
to exploit other children in their turn . . . otherwise I wouldn't
have. But then I was sorry for her, so I plucked her heart out
and snapped her neck, just enough so that she will not wake to
this eternal cold. But the one in Cambridge . . . I just left her
there. How terrible it must have been for her, waking to
unlife, not knowing herself to be dead, not understanding the
driving thirst that growled within her . . . I was confused then,
angry at the senseless way these humans kill one another . . .
they do not feed on blood! *They* only do it because they have
no compassion!

. . . .

Wait. Stop, Rudy, stop . . . she's there! Sitting astride the
fire hydrant—

Surely, master, there've been so many girls—

It's her . . . I cannot forget her. We are so few now, so desolate . . . she's leaving the street corner, look how she melts into
the shadow, she must be shadowstuff herself, like me. . . .

. . . .

All right, Rudy. Pick me up at this corner an hour before
sunrise. Don't worry about me. If they look they will see only
a lost dog sniffing the sidewalk.

nightmare

The crude skull, crayoned on a paper crown . . . the falling
knife, the spurting blood . . . the stench of incense . . . the wolf
springing from the altar, the wolf with a child's face. . . .

"No!" Stephen was screaming, his baton was flying from
his hand; the orchestra was braking itself in a flurry of
cacophonies, the soprano's high A wilted into a gurgle—

Got to keep calm, he thought. "Joan, you really must count
that entrance," he said to the first bassoon. "I simply can't
give the cue, you see, I'm doing too much here, with the harps
and the offstage semichorus and so on."

He didn't dare close his eyes, if he closed them again he
would see the skull and smell the burning incense—

"Are you all right, Mr. Miles?" someone in the second fiddles was asking.

"Quite all right," he snapped. "Take five, will you?" He stumbled into the wings, brushing off the young violist who had extended an arm. "I'm not a geriatric patient, you know," he snarled.

After sixty years—

It had finally returned to him in a nightmare, that scene from his childhood. It had really happened. It wasn't some dream or fantasy for Carla to take to pieces and go hunting for archetypal situations in!

He found a phone booth behind the heavy blue velvet side curtains. What was the name of the man? What were all their names? The Gods of Chaos . . . the Gods of Chaos. . . .

Carla's not going to deal with my so-called madness again, he thought. But there *is* someone who will know I'm telling the truth. But what was his name? The leader of the Gods of Chaos, who had blackmailed him into being an acolyte at their unholy games sixty years ago, when he was in the choirschool at Saint Cecilia's, Cambridge. . . .

"Directory assistance. England. Not *New* England, England! Sir Francis Locke, Waldrop, Cheshire."

A moment later: "I want to make a credit card call, operator: country code 44, city code—"

After a static-filled pause: "Jeremy Locke speaking. What the bloody hell do you mean, ringing us up in the middle of the night?" A middle-aged voice, an Old Etonian accent, very irritable.

"I'm sorry. I'm calling from America, you know. For your . . . father."

"Good heavens." The voice paused. "Well, he hasn't lived here for forty years. Got a flat in London now. In any case, he's gone to Thailand to visit his old friend Prince Prathna." Yes, Miles remembered, one of the Gods of Chaos had been an Asian prince. "Couple of octogenarians, you know, having a fling, reliving their old Cambridge days."

"Have they got a phone there? It's an emergency."

"Yes, let me see. . . ."

The young violist was beside him again, brandishing his instrument. "Are you OK, really? Maybe Yermakova should take over for a while."

"Yes. Yes. Leave me alone for a bit. Olga can handle this scene very nicely." Olga Yermakova was concertmistress. "Now, please, I want to be alone."

Presently he heard the vengeful trio of Brünnhilde, Gunther, and Hagen start up again; in a few minutes the chorus would burst onto the stage bearing Siegfried and Gutrune on their shoulders. This was a silly *Götterdämmerung*, preposterously artsy-fartsy—they had a motorcycle instead of Brunnhilde's horse, and the River Rhine was spanned by a papier-mâché reproduction of the Brooklyn Bridge. Well, this summer he would get Bayreuth; he was standing in for Karel Gruner one night and for Hans Ackerwald another. It was almost as good as being invited.

He stared dully at the phone number he had just scrawled on a scrap of score-paper. Did he dare telephone a man whom he had last seen as a bully, tormenting a frightened child, as a gruesome murderer, as a man driven mad with terror?

But only Locke would understand about the boy.

Gingerly he picked up the receiver and asked for a second credit card call, this time to Thailand.

It rang a very long time.

"Sawàddi, krai phûd kráb?" said a faint voice in a melodic, alien tongue.

"I want to speak to Sir Francis Locke."

The connection crackled. Someone else was on the line now.

"Locke? It's Miles here—"

The sizzling sound was cut short. The voice that came on now was crystal clear, as if it were in the same room. It was a raspy, croaking voice. It frightened Stephen just as it had the first time he'd heard it, watching the fire ravage the old house, sixty years before.

"Stephen Miles," it said, chuckling like a stage evil scientist. "Prathna and I were wondering when you'd ring us up."

3

huntress

His slender form shimmers, whirlpools into the shadow of a newsstand; when he emerges he is at her heels, slipping into the sea of legs. Brown legs, pale legs, withered legs, legs checkered like lizard-skins, legs aswirl with silk and damask, legs smelling of soap, of sweat, of Givenchy, of dried piss. Legs shoed and shoeless, knock-kneed and muscly, shambling and mincing through the patchwork of shadow and sodium glare.

When they do not look too closely, they see a little dog, black-furred, wagging its tail. If they look too long an unease comes over them and they glance away, drowning their dread in a sea of inconsequential thoughts.

She turns. She looks at him; she gazes long and longingly. It is her. He cannot forget her. Her face freezes at the junction of joy and terror; in a second she has turned away, hurrying East down Forty-third Street.

He pursues.

Calls out to her in the language of night, a howl that pierces the sleetlike chatter of the crowd.

There are fewer people on this street; when they look they are startled. Two dogs are chasing each other, paws pattering on the pavement, snarling, baring their tiny fangs. They dash between an old pimp's legs, their attenuated senses catching a

25

mingled whiff of crotch and cologne. He shoos them away, cursing in jive.

"Wait!" Timmy is calling.

"Why? Why?" she answers, and her words can be heard, like the whimper of a bitch in heat. "Why do you come now, after sixty years?"

He growls his atonement, and they race around a corner, down the grassy islands that divide Park Avenue, again across town, down Lexington, dead after midnight, down past shuttered shop windows and small trash heaps up the broken steps of a seedy hotel.

A closet of a room, dingy, laced with a perfume of decay.

He sees her: through the shoddy makeup shines the luminescense of their kind. The cheeks are gaunt. Once golden, the hair is matted, mousy, streaking the pallid face. The lips are blood-red, not from feeding, but from a cheap lipstick that suggests seductiveness without seduction. She has been doused with a dimestore scent. She wears tight jeans, Calvins, and a crimson top with a little white alligator perched on one tiny breast.

"Forget your bitterness," he says. "There are so few of us now. I've been alone so long. . . ."

She never smiles, but says, "So you too are in America. The land of opportunity." She has a bitter laugh.

"Yes, I came here in the sixties, in the time of the flower children." He sees the grubby drapes, the left one floral, the right one with a children's bedroom design of whooshing starships and fuzzy aliens.

"I make a good living," she says. "When I was killed, when you made me . . . what I am, I was only seventeen. I had a good body. I can make money, and when I feed, my sources are never traced. Who checks on the patrons of street whores? You should join me. There are boys here too, you know. Have you seen Playland, where johns hover over the video games? You could make enough to live on, and you would never hunger."

"I'm . . . well off. I sang before my changing. I melted Emperors' hearts. I still sing."

She scoffs. His glance wanders. A cockroach crawls on the handle of a yellow refrigerator. From under the bed a hand emerges, limp, drained.

She reaches down and pulls out the hand; it is some days old, and gray with mold. She squeezes it absently, hoping to pump out a drop or two of blood; then she throws it angrily into the trash. He sees a garbage pail, from which a dirty foot protrudes, half cased in a scruffy black sock.

"You don't have to live like this," Timmy says. "I have money. I need . . . a friend."

"*Live?*"

"You know what I mean," he says testily.

"You are so late, so late." He feels a sadness emanate from her; he has felt such sadness even in living whores. "Are you, of all people, trying to buy me? You, one of my own kind?"

He says nothing.

"You're hungry, perhaps." He hears the moaning of hurried copulations; for this is a hotel of furtive encounters, where love comes at the clink of coins, like a can of soda from a vending machine. She reaches across to the refrigerator—in this apartment one hardly need walk anywhere—and pulls out a platter containing a fresh human head garnished with severed fingers, floating in a pool of blood.

He is sickened. But his hunger rises, implacable.

It is an older man with wisps of hair. Black dye is running into the blood. His staring eyes are covered with a pair of hornrimmed spectacles. The huntress falls to, lapping greedily at the platter; presently Timmy cannot help himself, he gorges on the icecold blood, licking at the stump of neck where puddles have collected, sucking on the fingers. . . .

Now they are sated. They watch one another, and he sees her sunken eyes, red with pleasure and repleteness.

She says, "You know, we have never been properly introduced. I am Kitty Burns."

"And I . . . you would not be able to pronounce my original name, but today they call me Timmy Valentine, and I still sing." He is repelled by this creature. How could I have let her come into being? he thinks. He cries out: "How can you live in such degradation, like a hyena, like a vulture?"

"How dare you accuse me, you who sucked away my life?"

He cannot answer.

"Besides," she says, "one must take advantage of the conveniences of science. This way I needn't keep a lover in tow, feeding on him slowly until he dies; I can kill quickly, store the diced corpse for as much as a week—"

"You're monstrous! You kill without passion, without emotion!"

"You sound like a human being. I don't need emotions—I only need food!"

He thinks: I could have been like her. He feels pity for her. "This little hell," he says, "is over. Come with me, Kitty. We are kin, after all, you and I. One day, when you have faced the loneliness as long as I, perhaps you will learn compassion."

As bats they fly into the early dawn, racing the hurtful sun. The light no longer pains him much, but he sees that she still dreads it, that she still suffers from the superstitions that she carried to her grave. At the corner of Forty-second and Broadway the black limousine pulls up; they circle the car, and then they are in the capacious back seat and the shutters have been drawn, closing out the day.

labyrinth

Two very old men were drinking tea in an eighteenth-century pavilion of sandalwood, sculpted with a frieze of *thepanoms*, praying angels, that jutted over an almond-shaped lake carpeted with lotus pads and freckles of light green algae. There was a breeze; a scent of jasmine filled the air. The pavilion was not native to this city; it had been taken apart, plank by plank, and brought from an ancient city far upcountry, lovingly reconstituted. They were watching the dawn, enjoying the hour or so of cool before the stifling heat-haze of a Bangkok summer.

"Oh," the prince rhapsodized, "times were good then. Do you like the celadon tea-things, Francis, what? I'll have them make you up a set. Yes, we've all turned potters and business-men, we old aristocrats . . . my nephew's dealing with the Americans now; got an office in Los Angeles or one of those places." As Locke remembered, Prince Prathna spoke English like any other Cantabrigian, without any trace of accent.

"So why am I here, Prathna? You're far too devious a man to invite me here for nothing. After all, I've not heard from you for sixty years, old thing." He sipped his tea. The dazzling Hawaiian-style shirt of Thai silk he had found lying gift-wrapped on his bedspread fit perfectly, but he felt uncomfortable. One felt naked without a tie.

The prince didn't answer directly; instead, he went on with his paean to the vanished past. "Why, in those days, before they did away with the absolute monarchy and all that, we could have anyone on the estate clapped in chains or flogged . . . the country has certainly gone to seed. Trade unions, my goodness! Freedom of the press! Whatever will they think of next?" He shuddered. Locke could not tell if the man was joking.

In some ways Prathna looked no different from the Cambridge days or even the old Eton days, when they had slipped off into the graveyard by College Chapel in the dead of night to tell ghost stories or dissect cats . . . a childhood memory surfaced.

. . . leaning on a headstone, and he saw the boy prince's eyes in the moonlight, glittercrazed, and they had smeared blood on their faces and sworn fealty to each other, giggling nervously. The prince had been too short for the regulation tailcoat, and was ignominiously forced to wear bumfreezers—a monkey jacket with a large, stiff, white collar— and his round head poked out like a jaundiced crystal ball. Was he balding even then? Certainly he was not quite so roundly Buddha-like . . . Locke's memory was cloudy . . . but now the prince's pate was quite bare.

He's not very wrinkled, though, and Locke ruefully rubbed the furrows on his face; he knew that he had not aged gracefully, that he was shriveled and toothless and pockcheeked and that his hands were mottled like dead leaves.

"What was I saying?" Prathna went on. "Ah yes. Why I've invited you here, gone so far as to send you a ticket and so on . . . not terribly hard to arrange, mind you, since my cousin is chairman of Siam International Airways. But you will have guessed. It's the Gods of Chaos, Francis."

Locke started. "I'm afraid I don't remember."

"Of course you do."

Memories surged, confusing him. There had been rites, initiations, often involving cruelty or depravity, and then—that girl from the Copper Kettle. Charmed out of her menial job into the lair of a dashing young student, dragged into the chapel, killed; then the leaping wolf-thing—

"I'll have nothing to do with the Gods of Chaos. I don't know why you'd even mention our youthful . . . ah . . . indiscretions. I've led a decent life, I have grown children now—"

"Who have tossed you off the estate like the ingrates all you Westerners are!" The prince's hand reached across the table to grip Locke's. "Your life has been empty, hasn't it? Tell me the truth. Empty. Nothing has ever come close to the thrill of those days, the carousing, the toying with the flames of darkness . . . such a closeness we had, we Gods of Chaos! Such mayhem we wreaked! And that final evening, when the terrible thing attacked us . . . you have not forgotten. It was your idea, Francis. You, old thing, wanted to kill someone."

"Yes! Yes! But that was sixty years ago, and I'm old now."

"Empty. Spent. Your soul charred like a cinder."

"How can you know these things?"

"Because I too suffer from them!" The prince's face betrayed nothing. He clapped his hands. Servants in white blouses and navy sarongs came in on their hands and knees and began inconspicuously to clear the table. Locke had been amazed at first by all the ceremonial bowing and crawling, but he had soon learned that such things were mere common courtesy to persons of Prathna's rank and were hardly to be considered demeaning. The prince himself was occasionally summoned to court (although the present rulers had a tendency to ignore, as much as possible, their embarrassingly wayward relative) and there were plenty there to whom *he* must crawl. He would always groan about breaking his spine or getting a hernia, but custom prevailed.

When will the man get to the point? Locke wondered. It had been two weeks since he had arrived at Don Muang airport, been whisked into a custom gold Mercedes blazoned with Prathna's personal crest, and taken past pagodas; carcrammed streets like syrup streams around an anthill; grimeblack canals and sprawling complexes; temples, shiny and faded, gaudy and drab, monumental and seedy; and finally to this palace, an island of tranquility in this city of spectacle and bewilderment.

"Surely," Locke said, "the Gods of Chaos can't touch us now, across all these years. We've lived respectable lives, haven't we?"

"On the surface."

Prince Prathna rose. Locke followed him into the garden. There were hedges sculpted into mermaids, diving and surfacing out of a rosebush sea; artificial hillocks concealed most of the wall of concrete crowned with sharp shards of glass. The heat was insufferable. "I, alas, continue with my libertine's life, pursuing pleasure after pleasure. Look!"

There was a fence of woven wood, and a padlocked gate. "A garden within my garden. . . ." Although he had uttered no command, an old attendant, stooping so as not to raise his head higher than the prince's, stepped out of the bushes with a key; Locke and Prathna stepped in.

It was cooler here. The garden was roofed with the interwoven branches of misshapen trees imported from Japan, and the paths were walled with man-tall bushes from which hung rattan baskets of orchids: purple, mauve, lavender, dazzling white. Stoneware jars, shoulder-high, glazed black, their bases reliefed with furiously mating dragons, stood at forks in the path. Prince Prathna strode, puffing a little, while Locke lagged. "Here we are," said Prathna. "My private labyrinth of sensuality."

As they penetrated deeper into the maze, Locke saw leafy rooms opening to left and right; their floors were polished teak or the skins of tigers or Persian carpets, and in each room sat a beautiful woman or two. Some were naked; one, petite and golden haired, smiled quickly at him before she averted her eyes.

"I'm lost," Locke said. "Where are we, what is all this?"

As he spoke a naked dwarf ran by, intent on some errand. In another room, lesbians made love; in yet another, four or five men and women wove shifting patterns with their copulations. The prince looked a minute, smiled a little. Locke felt the sadness behind the smile. They passed more rooms, all canopied with green: darker fantasies now. In one room, the platform boasted only a gilded sarcophagus. In another, scourges hung from orchid-baskets. And finally—at what seemed to be the very center of Prathna's creation—there was a circular chamber walled and floored and roofed with greenery, and at its center, marked out with lines of shrubbery, was a design that Locke remembered inscribed with chalkdust on the floor of a Cambridge room: a pentagram.

"Ha!" said the prince. "You do feel its dread, don't you, old thing? Well, here we are. Step in." He gingerly stepped over a bush and was at the heart of the pentagram. "And now I can tell you why I have invited you here."

"Very well," Locke said dubiously.

"Do you believe in . . . karmic nexuses? Turning points,

junctions where people's lives must inevitably meet?"

"No."

"What a wretched liar you are. Come on, step into the forbidden circle." Locke found himself obeying. He fought his
fear; curiosity proved stronger. "There," said Prathna. "I
knew you wouldn't be afraid. After all, it was you who were
brave enough to kill a woman, bound, in cold blood."

"Don't you dare mention that again!" said Locke. The
prince cackled like a demon.

"My astrologer tells me," he began, and Locke remembered that this was how their games had always begun, sixty
years ago, "that it is time for a reunion. They're all coming:
Terrence, Strathon, even Muriel Hykes-Bailey. All the ones
that aren't dead, that is. As you and I soon will be. I'll even be
inviting the old acolytes, Miles and Owlswick."

"I understand that Miles is a half-famous conductor," said
Sir Francis. "Not half bad. But Owlswick is dead." He would
never have admitted it, but he had assiduously kept dossiers
on all the members of the Gods of Chaos. As if he had always
known this moment would come. "But I still don't understand
the necessity for—"

"Look around you. Haven't you noticed something a
little—halfhearted about this garden of delights?"

"Well, I daresay it's all very decadent, old chap, but you
don't seem to be enjoying it at all much, what."

"I'm jaded. Frankly, I haven't even had an erection in ten
years."

"Good heavens!" said Sir Francis, mildly miffed at this
vulgarity.

"No. It takes darker things to arouse me now. Deformity.
Disease. Oh, I am glutted with beauty, glutted, glutted. I'm
practically a corpse myself. Perhaps it's only appropriate that
I have recently felt the desire to . . . have carnal knowledge
of. . . ."

"Good heavens, old chap!"

"Well, I'm sure you haven't done much better. And now
we're old, old, old! We'll all die soon. I haven't the patience to
bridle my tongue anymore. I want it all to be—like when we
were children!"

In the pause, an albino woman with African features
walked through the inner room; pink eyes glanced casually at
them. Then she was gone. "That's Lola," said Prathna. "My

latest. I've tried them all! Girls, boys, cats and dogs, dwarfs, giants and deformed horrors, whippings and chainings—the lot! Desire stirs sometimes for a second or two, then I feel nothing at all. Once we were something important! In the days of the Gods of Chaos, we were like kings!''

It was true. He knew it. Where his emotions, his loves, his terrors had once lived there was a void, a gnawing coldness. Locke knew he was an ugly old man the world had passed by. He hated himself now, even as he realized how Prathna was using that hatred to twist him into obedience . . . nothing had ever changed, nothing, nothing.

He waited.

"In any case . . . my astrologer says that the time is ripe. And here's another thing. My granddaugher Premchitra goes to boarding school in America; I got a letter from her last week. All the girls there are talking about this new singing idol, this young boy Timmy Valentine; they're all madly in love with him. Well, children must have their idols. But she also sent me the words of his latest, what do they call them, *hit*. The song says this: that human beings are like trains, their lives are railway tracks crisscrossing time, and sometimes, when their paths cross in the night, there is a vampire junction that sucks away their souls. Is that not beautiful?''

"The way you phrase it," said Locke, "it is certainly an intriguing conceit . . . especially for one of those"—he wrinkled his nose in distaste—"pop songs. But what possible relevance—''

"You don't hear what I'm telling you, old thing. Are you senile? I have been talking of karmic junctions . . . we are near death, all of us, and I want to bring the paths of our lives together in one final intertwining before our souls are sucked away . . . there is no afterlife! My astrologer hopes in vain. One day I shall lie on a pyre and a bored royal personage will set a torch to it, and thousands of sycophants will prostrate themselves for the last time, already in their minds dividing my estate, my collections, even this little palace. I don't want to sit here waiting for that. I want a spectacle! And I want it now, while I'm still breathing!''

"Surely this very garden is enough of one."

"Oh, Francis, you are so terribly prosaic . . . has all your wildness left you? Cast your mind back. To the last spectacle. *Your* idea, may I remind you.''

The plunging knife . . . the trickling blood and urine . . . the burning flesh and frankincense . . . the ceremony pieced together from half a dozen old manuscripts from the university library . . . and the wolf-thing springing from the darkness.

"The presence we summoned up," the prince prompted.

"There was no presence!" Locke whispered. "It was all our imagination! I remember nothing at all!"

"You remember everything, Francis. It haunts your dreams. In the middle of the night it curdles your blood, and you wake up screaming."

"No!"

"Listen, Francis. Do you remember the oath we swore in the graveyard beside the college chapel at Eton where the moon was full, and we were both fourteen? I do. It was the Summer Half. We were both drybobs, and it took forever for the sun to go down, and my house was Jourdelays with its cobbled alleyway and plaster Greek frieze facade, so I just crossed the street to wait for you, but you were a tug and had to slip past the cloisters, past the green Founder, past the steps where we played fives, to meet me. You took out a rusty penknife and cut your finger and we swore—"

It came flooding back. All at once Locke was sobbing, burying his face in his hands. It was all true. For sixty years he had seen the wolf-creature in his nightmares. They were two spent old men, weeping in each other's arms; the one uncontrollably, helpless as a child, the other quietly, as if even weeping were an act of labyrinthine calculation.

"The presence we released . . . whatever it was . . . by our rite," said the prince, dry-eyed now. "I want to hunt it down. It exists somewhere. It must exist if it can still exert such terrible power over us. Perhaps I shall kill it. Perhaps I shall love it, learn from it, become its slave rather than endure this life of fantasies, of shadows. . . ."

Somewhere very far away Locke heard a phone ringing.

"Dear me," said Prathna. "Well, life goes on, I suppose. Let's go back to the house."

Locke dried his eyes on a fold of the silk shirt. In sixty years he had not felt such delicious terror. Perhaps he was still alive after all.

"By the way," Prathna said, "feel free to use my garden of

delights whenever you want. Or to have someone sent up to
your room. Anyone."

"Yes, I prefer that, rather. At my age, one can't be too
finicky about copulating in comfort." He could hardly admit
that his amorous adventures had been confined to fantasy for
some years now, with only occasional recourse to a discreet,
overpriced London agency. Quickly, he added, trying to make
it sound an afterthought, "Might I . . . the albino. . . ."

"Certainly, old chap." The prince's lips twisted in a wry
smile. "And now . . . oh, heavens, the bloody phone!"

As he followed the prince through the maze of verdure, a
different path from the way they had come, the phone's ringing grew louder. Sir Francis wondered which member of the
Gods of Chaos it would be.

4

night-child

Moonlight . . . a tap on the window of a store, a converted brownstone on a side street, tucked between rival undertakers.

Phil Preis had been dozing at the counter. Now he jerked awake, in time to see a dark limousine pull away. And a pale boy with dark eyes. A red neon sign flashed somewhere down the street, bloodying the kid's face, on-off, on-off. He looked again to make sure who it was. Then he grinned.

"Why, it's Timmy." He hurried to the door and undid half a dozen bolts and locks. "Come in, come in! I just saw you on TV, kid, my best customer and all. You brought a friend?"

He glanced at the mousy, unattractive teenage girl who had come in with Timmy. She didn't say anything. Made him uneasy, this one. If she weren't with young Valentine, he'd have pegged her for a hooker. Or a pusher. Or a pickpocket . . . Forget it. . . .

He hobbled over to the counter. Dozens of switches dangled from a nest of wiring. "Are you ready?" he whispered. "There, there, one, two, three—" His hand glissandoed over a rank of switches.

The shop whirred to life. Lights twinkled, model trains lurched, clacked on tracks that swerved and crisscrossed and figure-eighted from countertop to countertop. Glass cases crowded the narrow shop walls, packed with engines of all periods and tiny trees and houses and little men and women in fancy dress. Little colored lights twinkled onto boxes

37

crammed with track in odd lengths and stashes—bridges and crossings and used boxcars and tunnels stuffed one inside another—and catalogs: Bachman, TYCO, Märklin—

"Welcome," he said in mock stentorian tones, "to the Magical Greenwich Village Junction! The station where all times and all locomotives meet!" The boy laughed.

The girl was still silent. When Phil looked at her she stared him down. There was something about her . . . as if she wanted to eat him alive. Phil shuddered involuntarily, and then went on with his performance.

"My package? You have my package?" said Timmy Valentine. He reached out eagerly.

"Success ain't spoiled you at all, kid," said Phil. He bent down and fished out something.

"The engines? The forest? The castle?"

More packages. Phil piled them up on the counter. "Cash or charge?"

"Oh, Phil—" The boy's eyes sparkled.

How long had he been buying here? Three years? Strange, Phil thought, how he's never grown taller. He seems frozen in the moment between childhood and puberty, like Peter Pan. No wonder all those little girls raved about him. He'd made the cover of *Idol Magazine*. Phil had seen it at the drugstore, but didn't want to be seen buying such junk.

"American Express," Timmy said. He pulled the card from a pocket of his black cords and handed it over.

"They sign you up for that commercial yet?" Phil said, taking the card and thinking how *he* was past middle age and still couldn't get one of those things.

"As a matter of fact . . . " Timmy giggled again. "No, of course not, I'm just kidding."

The girl glared at them during this whole exchange. He saw her snarl. For a second he thought he had seen an animal there, a black panther, a she-wolf . . . a trick of the light. Gotta stop working late. It's past midnight.

"Ain't you going to open the boxes?"

"Not yet. I'm too excited," Timmy said solemnly.

"Wait, I'll see you to the door."

"Yeah. Come on, Kitty." He cradled the packages—they must have been heavy for the youngster—and made for the door. Phil limped over and pulled it open with a flourish. Then he produced another little package from a shelf and said, "Here. On the house."

"Phil!"

"Go on. Merry Christmas."

"But it's April!"

"So? I'm a Jew."

The girl was behind him. Close behind him. But he couldn't hear her breathe. Outside the street was empty, quiet for a whisper of distant disco music. "Anything wrong?"

Panic, flooding dread and *Shit she ain't breathed once since she came in she's dead she's dead—*

All at once he was sweating, icewater soaking his hair. He whirled around and saw—

Fangs glittering red in the slow strobe of neons, feral eyes narrowing, taut body surprised in mid-pounce—

Shit she's dead she ain't breathing she's a corpse a walking corpse a corpse a corpse—

A hungry rasp of a howl bursting from her mouth, alien counterpoint to the bop-bop-bopping from a far-off bar room—

In the second before the scream tore loose from him—

"Kitty, Kitty. . . ." Timmy spoke, quietly, commandingly.

Before Phil's eyes the moon-spattered form quivered, shivered into the shape she had come in.

He stood, gaping, looking into Timmy's eyes. Eyes like polished black sapphires, their stars an endless spiraling . . . "It is nothing," Timmy whispered. "Nothing. You were just seeing things." The voice was so soothing. . . .

"Don't forget . . . the last box . . . Merry Christmas," Phil found himself saying, handing it over to the boy. A couple of blocks ahead he saw the limousine, turning at the corner of Bleecker and Sullivan. He smiled vacuously. They were gone.

Two sleek animals, cats perhaps, were slinking toward the corner, slithering into a pool of darkness.

He shook his hand. A conversation-fragment played over and over in his mind like a stuck record.

(He was just standing there! Easy prey! And you warned him!)

(He is my friend. . . .)

(How can you say that? We are far apart, we are the hunters, they the prey, how can you dare befriend them?)

(He is my friend. . . .)

Where did I hear that? Phil thought. Gotta stop working late. Does crazy things to your mind. Or maybe it's the kid's new song. Stuck in my head: *Va-a-ampire junction, va-a-*

ampire junction. Life ain't a movie. Shit.

He stood for a while as though stoned.

Timmy's my best customer. He's a sweet kid. Not at all snooty, though he's famous. But those groupies—hell, that one had me scared for a minute. Imagine being scared of a teenage girl! It's late. You never stop being a child. I mean, about things that jump you in the night. You never stop being afraid of the dark. Oh, shit.

Phil laughed, a big hearty chuckle, to scare away the terror. The disco music died. The city was a silence punctuated by random tumults: here a siren, here a screech of tires, a lovers' caterwauling, a shout. Whistling the obnoxiously catchy song, Phil went on inside, shutting it all out.

He touched switches, one by one. Trains halted. A draw-bridge stood half-open. On a papier-mâché mountain that overlooked an elaborate junction, one by one, the lights in a fairytale castle were winking out.

fire

Stephen wanted to cancel the rehearsal and rush back to the hotel as soon as he'd put the phone down. But professionalism prevailed.

He put the soprano through her paces, making her stop marking and sing full voice even though the evening would kill her. Let her sweat. He took the immolation scene at breakneck speed, slowing it down only when calculating stage managers remonstrated, pointing out that they couldn't wheel on the motorbike-horse in the time provided, they didn't have time to set fire to the pyre, the sound-effects tape didn't synchronize, Valhalla couldn't collapse properly in only three point seven minutes—

At this point he threw the baton to Olga Yermakova, stalked out of the theater, summoned a taxi, and returned to the standard suite in the standard Sheraton.

He lay down on the bed. Pain pounded at the base of his skull. It was one of those migraines he always used to get just before the urge would come. The urge to burn something.

The first time he'd had the urge—

It had been a perfect day in June. Only a few weeks left before the summer holidays, and he had the day off after the morning choir practice. His parents had met him in the nave.

They'd gone punting along the Backs, Father at the oar, Stevie helping sometimes, mostly hindering; then Mum dismissed him to the back, and he lazed in the sun, not really listening to their idle nattering, not really seeing the colleges go by on the right, a hazy procession of spires and crooked walls and gates blazoned with coats of arms all veined with vines . . . and later meadows, weeping willows, all the way up to Granchester. They had tea there—with all the strawberries and cream a ten-year-old boy could imagine—then went home for the night. He had dreamed for weeks of a warm bed in Warkworth Street instead of sharing a dormitory that reeked of old socks and farts and echoed all night with childish secrets.

For supper there was shepherd's pie and more nattering, and Father made a fire in the grate. He loved his parents, but they never talked to him, they talked right through him. Stephen never made it into the cosy little bed; he fell asleep in a crook of a leather armchair, spellbound by the flickering flames.

When he woke, the house was very quiet. And then he heard them arguing upstairs.

"Send the little bastard to your mum, that's what we ought to do! How much d'you think I make anyway as Head Porter at Saint Cecilia's. And to waste it all on some bleeding boy what ain't mine—"

"Shush, Jim, you'll wake him. And you know very well it's the choir school what's praying for his upkeep and that."

"Send him to your mum's what I say."

"It's the least you can do, is look after him. He's never been no trouble. He won that scholarship to the school, and he's got a precious little voice."

"As precious as Bill Thornton's voice? Was it his voice he used to snare you, you hussy?"

"Can't you forget a bloody thing, after eleven years? You owe me. You're just a coward, putting on that limp just to get out of fighting the Germans and that, like an honest English-man—"

"Why you—"

"Lay off me or I'll yell bloody murder—"

Please God, Stevie thought, squeezing his palms together in prayer, let it stop let it stop—

He saw the fire. It danced in his eyes.

Let it stop let it stop don't let me be a bastard let it stop—

He got up. He kicked at the fire. A coal fell out. Hit the rug. Smoke tendriled slowly, and then—

Stephen was angry. He took the poker and banged on the grate, over and over, and then the divan caught fire and they were still arguing up there—

Let it stop—

Flames were spurting from the couch, the carpet. He stared at them. They were beautiful. He yearned to be like them, to consume the world, to dance out his anger on the shadow world, to roar. He stared until his eyes watered, and then—

"What's going on?" A voice from above.

The flames were hissing up the stairs now.

They'll die, he thought, they'll die—

The smoke choked him. Cough-spasms racked his body. I can't let them catch me, I've got to run away. He dashed for the door, unlatched it, ran out into the street. Behind him there was a roar as sagging wood cracked. He whipped around to see his silhouetted parents banging on the window, and then he screamed and screamed and ran—

Smack into a man's rough arms. New Harris tweed against his face, prickly, leather-smelling.

"Please, please, I didn't mean to—"

"So *you* did it, eh, little fellow?" Stephen couldn't see who it was. He fought. The man slapped his face, twisted him around so he could see the burning house. He squealed. His cheeks stung. Pain darted up his arm.

"Let's watch together," said the stranger in a whining, drawling voice.

"But aren't you going to save them? To get help?"

Flames lit up the man's face. A young man with a beaklike nose and squinting eyes. He looked cruel. "They'll die, you know, before they can put it out."

Above, he saw a window smash open, he saw a man in flames, falling—

He couldn't scream. For in that moment, frozen out of time, he perceived the beauty of that falling, that fiery arc that leapt from death to death. His heart soared, fueled by the joy and the terror.

"Shall I tell them?" the young man was saying quietly. "The police. They'll hang you. You don't believe little boys can be hanged, what?" He laughed.

"Please, sir. . . ."

"You'll do everything I say then! Everything!"

"Y-yes."

"Or I'll tell."

"Or you'll tell."

"Tomorrow you'll come to my rooms at College. In the Andrews Building. The name is Locke." The boy nodded.

Father's body splatted onto the pavement. And then came his mother, sizzling rainbow of fire. Stephen was numb now. There was no grief here, only the dance of flickerlight in the night.

They came then, too late, and put it out, and the constable drove him to the choir school in his shiny motor car. The headmaster made him sleep in his own private chambers.

In the morning the boys looked at him with an awe that bordered on hero-worship. All summer he stayed at Cambridge at the headmaster's home; he remained until the end of the Michaelmas term, and then, in midwinter, the war only briefly over, they put him on the ship alone, to America.

But not before Locke and the others had drawn him into their circle of terror, always threatening to reveal how he'd killed his parents.

And now, after sixty years, he had spoken to Locke again. Again he had come under the spell of that whining voice. He had told Locke about the boy.

There'd been a long pause. He could hear them conferring in whispers through the buzzing.

And then, just like that, Prince Prathna came on the phone and invited him to Thailand.

"A reunion, old chap, nothing more."

But he knew he was being sucked into something huge and frightening.

He didn't want to resist.

He wanted the fire to come back!

Slam down the phone, he had thought, run away, hide . . . but when he heard their voices he was a little boy again, utterly in their power, luxuriating in their scorn, for it was at least a kind of attention. . . .

"Late summer," he found himself saying. "After Bayreuth. I wouldn't want to cancel Bayreuth."

And as soon as he hung up the headache had come, raging, burning up his brain.

5

night-child

Carla stirred. "Stevie? Steve?" She snuggled up to the body in the bed.

"I'm not Steve. Remember me? Peter. Peter DuPertuis. From the party at the Moyers'."

"Oh." She felt a pang of disappointment. She'd been dreaming of the day she first met Stephen, in a snack bar near Carnegie Hall. She'd been putting herself through school by ushering, he was the conductor with all the prospects; she was just gaping at him, he smiling urbanely as he held out a chocolate cream doughnut . . . he hadn't even remembered her ten years later, when he came as a patient to the rest home, shrunken, pitiable. . . .

"No," she said sleepily. "You're not Stephen."

The covers were half off. A breeze drifted in from the half-open French windows; velvet drapes rustled, fell deathly calm. It was good to have moved out here to Larchmont, in spite of the morning commute and the huge redecorated rambler that was meant for a whole family and housed only her, and memories, and resentments.

She clasped him to her now. Please don't let me be too old, she thought. He thrust perfunctorily; she moaned, trying to convince herself. Then he shuddered, slid off, and was still. "Sorry. I'm not up to it right now."

"Yes." It was all right. She had only gone to the party

45

because of that Valentine boy. She'd dealt with certified
loonies before; they often gave her the creeps, at least for a
moment or two before her training took over, but . . . the bat
thing. And the breaking mirror. Was menopause like adoles-
cence, then, sparking off poltergeist phonemena and
hallucinations and things? She wondered if there was any
literature on it, and made a mental note to look it up. She'd
have to see her own analyst, who was one of those dismal
Freudians; an hour of reliving your potty training could sober
anyone up. But for the past couple of nights she hadn't been
able to sleep alone.

That's my prerogative, isn't it? she thought, angry at having
to justify it to herself. She sat up against the pillows. She was
just reaching for the light, when she thought: I don't want him
to see me. Idly she mopped the sweat from her neck with the
bedsheet. "Go fix yourself a drink, downstairs."

"Yeah."

Outside, in the night, a howl.

"What was that, Peter?"

Stillness.

"Nothing. I'll go down to the kitchen now."

The howling again, rending the hush of darkness like a child
in pain. Carla sat bolt upright. The room chilled a notch.
"Listen. Listen."

Stillness: the breeze, a twig falling.

And then the howling: shrill, desolate.

The drapes moved; moonlight rippled on the pile carpet;
leafshadows crawled against the floral wallpaper.

"Hey, Carla, the neighbors are probably into something
kinky."

"Not the Lechners. No way. Forget it." She closed her eyes.
But she couldn't forget the sound. Eerie. What kind of animal
was it?

"It's gone now."

Purr of a passing car. "Someone's out late. . . ."

The car slowing to a stealthy crawl, coming to a stop.
"They're coming *here!*" she said, alarmed suddenly. "But it's
three in the morning . . . Peter, honey, go take a look. . . ."

Peter sprang from the bed, macho man, potbelly belying the
image. Flung wide the curtains. A darkstreaked moonbeam on
the wall. "Nothing," he said. "Just a black limousine. Pulling
away now. Probably drunk as shit, came to the wrong house.

There, it's turned up Chatsworth now."

rat-tat-tat-tat

"What's that?" She clutched the bedsheet.

"I'll go see."

"No, don't go—"

He drew the curtains. Darkness zippered out the lightpatch on the wall. Carla shivered, though she knew it wasn't cold.

"It's nothing, woman! Jesus, I'm the one who ought to be nervous, I'm married, for God's sake. I'll go downstairs and check it out."

A tiny cry died on her lips. He was gone.

"Where are you now?" she shouted, too loud, making herself jump.

rat-tat-tat

"I'm just letting your cat in. It's mewing like crazy."

rat-tat-tat-tat

Cat? *Cat?*

tat-tat

"I don't have a cat!"

Oh my God

Terror seized her. She flew out of bed naked. She groped for the doorknob. Too dark, got to find the light switch. She clawed the wall. Struggled with the door. It yawned open. She stumbled out, grasping at shadows. Can't see. Find the banister. Feel along it. A splinter. Easy, one foot in front of the other, one step at a time . . . damn it's so dark so dark—

Below, Peter screamed.

She screamed too, panicking, clambered down the stairs, banged at the wall for the light the light—

Glare hit her, blinding. A dark form whirlpooling into the shadow of an armchair.

"Peter?"

Her gaze darted around the room: everything in place. Coffee table, modular sofa and loveseat, brown. Files on the armchair, where she'd left them. There was that sensation-mongering newspaper too, the one with the front-page story about some reporter from *Idol Magazine* found horribly murdered on her way to interview Timmy Valentine.

"Peter, what's happening?"

She took a few more steps down the staircase and slipped in something. She lurched, sprawled, stabbed her nose into something squishy—

Oh God

Another scream tore from her as blood and rheum squirted into her face.

An eye stared at her, lifeless.

His neck had been broken. The body stretched from the steps half into the kitchen; the head dangled. She pulled herself up by the banister and looked at him, half fascinated . . . blood oozed from a dozen bitemarks on his chest, his face, his neck. When she rubbed herself she found her breasts and belly smeared with it. She spat on her hands and scrubbed frantically at her pubic hair, matted with crimson.

A wild thought struck her. Maybe *I* did this! Maybe I blacked out and did it, like one of the cases you read about in the literature, the cases you dream of dealing with except you know they can never afford fifty, a hundred bucks an hour. She started to giggle uncontrollably, then she threw up. Vomit hit the corpse and marbled into the bloodstains.

All right. Enough screaming for now.

"Timmy. I know you're here somehow. You broke in or something. Timmy, I'll listen to you, I won't harm you . . . Timmy. . . ."

Shadows swirling . . . whirling . . . first came the eyes, resolving out of the dimness behind the armchair. Then the rest of him. A small boy, red-eyed as though he'd stayed up too late, in neat black parachutes and a black T-shirt. Over his lips, a blood-mustache; on them, a thin wry smile.

Easy now. Keep cool. "Timmy—"

Fuck professionalism! Rage broke out in her. "Damn it, you killed him, you killed him, you fucking psycho kid, they fed you too much junk TV and horror movies and violence so you can sit there taking it all casually you think you can get away with it because you're a goddamn millionaire—"

"Carla."

Her hysteria was subsiding now. I must look preposterous, standing here all withered and in the nude and covered with blood.

"Carla." Such authority in his voice. Such calm.

"Get out," she whispered.

"I was invited."

"So you can't come in unless you've been asked? I thought you said all those myths had lost their power."

"Of course I was invited! My very existence is born out

of your longings, hidden, inadmissible to your conscious minds." The answer came glibly; the boy had the madman's gift of casuistry, of warping words to his twisted logic.

"And the cat? You released a cat at the back door, to complete the image?"

For a split second his shape shimmered, and she couldn't be sure if he wasn't a sleek black cat—

"You cheated . . . pretending to be a cat. . . ."

"He did not invite me in. *You* did." He looked her full in the eye. "You wanted him to die, didn't you? You hate him. And yourself. For wanting him. I smelled your hatred. It was like jasmine on a tropical evening, like distant music."

"That's absurd."

"Perhaps you'd rather think of it as some primal jealousy, sexual or even Oedipal." He avoided her eyes.

"It's true," she said, making nervous conversation, trying to hold down the scream that was building inside her again, "that the patient often falls in love with the analyst; it's been argued that this is essential to Jungian analysis, and—"

From a few blocks away a car hummed. "Good," said the boy, listening. "Rudy can help me clean up this mess." He wiped his face with his hand, as if he'd just been eating a bowl of cornflakes.

"Rudy?"

"My chauffeur. And, for tax and legal purposes, my guardian."

She stepped carefully over the corpse, willing herself not to look, covering her crotch with one hand.

The boy said, "But I didn't really come to feed. I'm not, you notice, attacking *you* . . . mainly because I would like you to be my friend. I have a proposition to make."

Play for time, she thought, then call the police . . . "Let me put on my robe. And fix myself a stiff drink. I've a little wine I filched from the Moyers' party . . . er, care for some?"

"I never drink. . . ."

"Wine. Right."

"I'm underage." His eyes twinkled, but he didn't smile. "Sorry, but these old jokes get to one after a while."

"You old ham, you." Why did I say that? Because he *is* a child still, even if he's so ancient. How terrible. How lonely . . . why am I believing this bullshit anyway? She tried to quell an onrush of sympathy for him. Then panic again. She ran up-

stairs, threw on a kimono, returned. At the head of the staircase she thought she saw a black kitten, lapping at the
corpse's wounds. How ugly Peter looked. I wish I'd seen him
in the light, she thought coolly, thinking of the smoky, dopey
party, the sweaty night. She looked away quickly, not wanting
to admit to herself that there had been not one shred of emotion between them. When she reached the living room Timmy
was lounging on the couch, reading the article about the
woman from *Idol*.

"I didn't mean to do it," he was murmuring, for himself
alone.

"Sit down," he said at last.

Slowly, she sat down facing him.

"I think," he said, "that I really do need an analyst."

"Well, you've . . . come to the right place." She wished she
had that drink in front of her now. But somehow the thought
kept flicking through her mind: must maintain rapport with
the patient . . . it was ludicrous, but she found herself falling,
as though preordained, into place.

"Listen to me," he said. "The past, the past . . . it is burning inside me. I need someone who will listen, someone with
the skill to probe down deep, into the parts I've forgotten . . .
my memory has gaps, you know. Once, a hundred, two hundred years ago, I don't know . . . I lost the power of speech. I
roamed the woods like an animal, living off the blood of hares
and squirrels. They brought me back to the town and taught
me to speak."

"I've seen the movie," Carla said, suspicious suddenly. The
spell that he had worked on her was not complete. She still
doubted. "*The Wild Child*. Truffaut."

"Yeah, something like that. Perhaps it was me. Before that,
I don't remember much, except that crucifixes used to hurt me
and now they don't much anymore . . . hardly at all. I
remember the face of the Sibyl . . . that's all I can see, of my
life before the changing. But that was a thousand years before.
Oh, and the fire."

"Fire?"

"Fire and brimstone. Something terrible. It has to do with
. . . how I became the way I am."

Fire! He was somehow like Stephen then; for fire had
shaped Stephen's life too. There was something in Timmy's
song about the way lifelines crossed one another. *The vampire*

junction that sucks our souls. . . .

She collected herself. She had always faked it pretty well when she was working for the home. Her trained detachment took over.

"This is what I want," he said. "Next week I'll be going back west, back to my nifty mansion, to retrench, write a few more silly songs, cut another record maybe. Will you come?"

Carla waited.

"It would be an adventure, such an adventure, for us both," Timmy said. His voice was pure melody now, spellbinding, hypnotic. "You would discover things no mortal has ever known. You would understand me, a creature alien yet plucked from the very souls of men. And I would understand too. I feared the light once, and the cross; now I feel nothing, though Kitty, my companion in loneliness, suffers badly if she cannot hide by sunrise. Wouldn't you like to understand why? Wouldn't you like to interview an archetype made flesh? Think of how Carl Jung would have felt. You would come as a guest of my estate, and nothing would be barred from you."

"But what about my practice? I can't give up treating scores of the New York nouveau riche overnight."

"You'll figure out something." And indeed she was already sorting out, in her mind, how she might split up her clients between Drs. Denton and Trautmann, and claim to be on vacation. The eyes were fixed on her. She couldn't avoid them.

"You seem pretty damn confident." A token resistance.

"You will come," said the boy, grinning now, "because you love me. As much as you love yourself. Because I am in some real sense a fragment of your deepest self . . . your death wish, Carla Rubens."

6

dissolve

Slow down, Rudy.

Yes, master Timothy. But do you really want to feed now?
You will be home in only a few minutes. Miss Rubens has
already gone ahead.

But can't you see her? By the side of the freeway. A girl crying, clutching a suitcase, in the shadow of the North Hollywood exit ramp.

No.

Slow down, Rudy! Your eyes are misty with old age, but
mine are clear as eternity. There she is. You can't see her
because the ramps, crisscrossing overhead, have cut out a cleft
of shadow from the wash of sunlight. Don't you see her? Her
face is dirty; the tears have streaked it. Her hair is bedraggled,
and she is wearing braces; in that band of dark they have
caught the sun, and they glitter like a star. . . .

It's not natural for you to feed in broad daylight, master
Timothy. You want Maria to be seen outside, swabbing at the
blood with an old washcloth? In ten minutes we'll be there.
That analyst woman has probably arrived already and they'll
be busy unpacking your Kitty's coffin.

Coffin, Rudy?

She insisted on a coffin . . . and a little pouch of English
soil.

Absurd. She still has so much to unlearn.

53

How so? Does the light not pain you even slightly, master?

No. No. Know your place, Rudy. Stop the car.

Of course.

See, she is hitchiking. Let her in. How far are you going? And why are you crying?

I'm lost I'm lost I'm lost—

Be calm. Be still. I can let you off about ten miles further down the Ventura freeway. Now, hold my hand.

Who are you? Your hands are so cold! I'm lost. I've been on the road for two weeks. I hitched from . . . from Phoenix. I'm lost. Who are you? Who are you? I'm lost. I'm lost. Help me. Don't let him find me.

Who?

Uncle Brian. He'll send me home. I don't want home. I want to be lost. Lost. Run away. Hollywood. He's coming like a . . . shark! In the . . . cold water . . . Hi, I'm Lisa. I'm lost. Lisa Zottoli.

Why did you run away?

I don't know. Saw a movie. Girl ran away. Hollywood. But . . . shark! Eating machine. In the . . . cold . . . Hi. I'm Lisa. I'm lost.

Are you mad? You're talking in a closed loop. Will you calm down, Lisa? Look at me.

Phone home . . . then a . . . shark! In the cold, I'm lost, I'm Lisa.

Poor girl. I'm lost too. Can you understand that? You have to break out of the circle. You can, you know. I can't. I've been lost far longer than you have. Can you say something that's not out of a movie, Lisa? It's OK. You can clutch my hands hard. It's OK. You won't hurt me. Look at me.

You're . . . you're . . .

Look at me.

You're . . . eating machine phone home in the cold, lost, lost, lost Lisa . . . you're . . . oh, you're Timmy Valentine, you're the star the star, saw a movie girl ran away Hollywood Hollywood in the cold phone home. . . .

Yes. I'm Timmy. I'm real. Why are you running? What is your uncle's phone number? We could find him for you—

No! No! Saw a movie girl ran—

Be calm. Little pills? Thought so. Slow. You ran away from home? Why? Not the movie now, Lisa, the reality.

. . . .

You don't have to talk.

You're Timmy Valentine! A girl ran away met star rich and famous—

It's not like that. I won't take you in. I won't make you rich and famous. You should call your uncle and go home.

I want to stay, let me stay, I'm lost, lost—

No! Are you crazy? Do you want to die? How can you possibly understand the raging hunger . . . I'm saying too much. Rudy, the exit. Drop her off. Now, Rudy, don't let her see the turning for my house . . . too late . . . Stop clawing at me, girl! Don't you understand what you're doing to me, don't you understand? Don't even look at me.

. . . .

Rudy's letting you out now. Glad I could help.

You're Timmy Valentine—

Yes. Write me, I'll send you an autographed picture.

But wait, but wait, can't you see I'm lost, in the cold, scared, scared, the shark! . . . eating machine . . . phone home . . .

There she goes now. Houses cluster on the foothills like mushrooms. You were right, Rudy. I should not have picked up the girl. But you're wrong too. You think I just toy with these mortals, but that is not true. I am linked to them, because it was their collective shadow that gave birth to me. I hope I don't see her again, though. Her blood must be full of strange drugs, foul-tasting, nightmare-inducing. I would not have touched her, Rudy, but I had hoped to show . . . compassion!

Why?

Why? You never used to say *why* to me before. What are you anyway, Rudy?

I cannot say, master Timothy.

I hope I don't see the girl again.

So do I.

She only believed in me because she saw me on television. She's scared of sharks because she saw *Jaws*. She's surrounded herself with illusion to escape . . . what? And I too am illusion, illusion made real by the likes of her. . . .

Don't think of these things, master Timothy.

Is it long till evening?

An hour.

Yet it is still so light out. Kitty will want to prowl around as soon as it's dark. I don't know what to do about it, Rudy. Should I have left her in New York, opening her legs all day long for men who never knew that they were practicing necrophilia?

You are the same kind, master Timothy. It would seem to be only a matter of degree.

I'm afraid of her.

Nonsense, master! You do not possess fear, or understand it, except to feed on the fear of humans. You, master Timothy, are dead.

night-child

On the plane, the dread deepened in her all the way to Los Angeles. She had flown first class at the insistence of Timmy's agent, and even as she luxuriated in the width and softness of her seat she could not avoid a twinge of guilt. When they came around to offer her a movie headset she had refused out of habit, even though she knew it was free. It was the Langella *Dracula*, and the soundless images of cobwebbed baroque mansions and of bats and wolves did little to alleviate her discomfiture.

At the airport she had been met by a dour, prim woman in black; she spoke little, in a generalized European accent of such impenetrability that it appeared to have been manufactured in Hollywood. She looked a hundred years old. Carla had to laugh. When she stepped out of the terminal and saw the brilliant sky, she smiled. Maria, the woman in black, soon reappeared at the wheel of a lime-colored Cadillac convertible, and Carla laughed out loud again at the incongruity.

She started to get in the front, but Maria gestured majestically at the back. "Would not be seemly," she declared, "for master Timothy's guests to sit beside the house domestics."

"Oh." She got in and relaxed. Maria began to drive ridiculously fast. "Where are we going?"

"The Valentine mansion, madame. Quarters have been prepared for you there."

"And Timmy?"

"He is coming later. On another flight. When he flies, he takes whole compartment of aeroplane, you see. He must be alone. You meet him at home." Maria turned a sharp corner with a screech, her expression never changing. "You stay long?"

"As long as he needs me, and is willing to pay for this foolery. I'm his analyst."

"Bah! He don't need analyst."

This sounded interesting. "What does he need?" she said. "I presume you know him far better than most people." She paused as Maria careened onto the Ventura freeway. The warm wind roared in her ears. Maria didn't answer. Perhaps she should try another tack. "What's the house like?" she said.

"You expect what? Bavarian schloss towering from mountaintop, thunder and lightning? Coffins and tied-up naked virgins and dust and cobwebs? I am not go for dust, madame, I am good housekeeper."

"Yes." The old woman had lurched into the fast lane at a forty-five degree angle, and had just overtaken two hulking semis. "But are you a good driver?"

"You are dead?"

"No."

"But master Timothy is. So you see, not necessary I can drive."

About twenty minutes later Maria abruptly cut across four lanes to an exit ramp, and they began the climb uphill. And then, with a stomach-turning halt, they arrived. A man came for Carla's baggage. She stood for a moment, toying with a fold of her conservative tweed suit, wishing that she had picked out something less conspicuous at Bloomingdale's the day before. Then she turned.

Behind her, wrought-iron gates and a low brown-brick wall; in front, a sprawling house that melded with the hillside, a surreal hodgepodge of architectural styles; orange-pink Spanish portico, an imitation Tudor wing smothered in vines and creepers, a clear plastic dome through which she could see a large swimming pool. And strangest of all, in various niches of the portico, and standing here and there on the lawn, statues: one or two, like the Venus de Milo, she recognized, and so realized they were imitations.

She did not go toward the house yet; her mind was swamped by its monumental tackiness. Surely this was not the residence of a vampire.

She wandered out onto the lawn. There were flowerbeds there, and a gravel path. She followed it, feeling a sudden chill. In her excitement she had not noticed until then that the sun was going down. The path ran through a clump of trees; true New Yorker that she was, Carla couldn't identify them. But the setting sun shone through them, and leaf-shaped shadows, each bordered with wine-red, made dapple-patterns on the gravel. There was a little fountain there, and behind it a gravestone.

On the stone perched a marble choirboy in cassock and surplice, holding open a piece of music, his mouth open in song. The gravestone read *Konrad Stolz, 1935–1947*. At first she thought it was another of the collection of inferior marbles that lined the portico and dotted the lawn. But there was something familiar about the name . . . wasn't there? Wasn't it one of the names Stephen had called out in his delirium, at the rest home, years ago? Wasn't it, though? Surely a coincidence. But the choirboy's face. The shadows were deepening. She reached out to touch the little statue. Just then a shaft of dying sunlight touched the face, painting it pink for a second. She jumped. For an instant it had seemed to come to life. She recognized the face at once.

Timmy's face.

"Carla?"

She started. Don't panic, she told herself, and slowly turned around. "Oh, Timmy. You startled me. I was just looking around."

"Of course." The boy was standing on the gravel path, his pale skin crimsoned by the sunset. "You may look anywhere you like, Carla. I can't conceal anything from you, if you are to pry from me my hidden past."

"I was afraid for a moment."

"I won't harm you." Strange that a little boy would say that to me, she thought. "Do you like this house?"

"It's . . . not like New York!"

"Very tacky, isn't it? I bought it from some Arabs who had to go home to assume the throne or something. It's even stranger inside."

She followed him, keeping her distance. A black limousine was parked behind the convertible; a tall man in a dark uniform and cap stood at attention beside it.

"Thank you, Rudy," the boy said. They stepped into the portico, and then into the house proper. They were in an antechamber dominated by a maroon velvet sofa. In a corner of it sat Maria. When she saw them she burst into a raucous cackling, like a cartoon evil witch.

Suddenly, inexplicably, Timmy too began to laugh at her. It was too much, too frustrating! First the trip, the ludicrous mansion, and now these shrieking mad people—

"I'm going home!"

As suddenly as they had started, they stopped; and then Timmy said to Maria, very seriously, "Did you manage it?"

"Oh, completely," Maria said. Not a trace of the accent remained.

"What's going on?" said Carla.

"Oh, just a little joke," Timmy said. "Carla, meet Maria— actually Mary Karney—my housekeeper, my fan-mail answerer, my know-it-all."

"We've spoken on the phone," Maria said.

"We have?"

"Yes. I'm also his social secretary."

"But why . . . the accent, the sepulchral black dress, the grand prix antics?"

"Hee! Master Timothy wanted your arrival to be suitably . . . archetypal."

"She loves to act," Timmy said. "Used to be in silent movies, you know; they ditched her when the talkies started because her moan wasn't sexy enough."

"We are serve dinner now," Maria said, returning to her bizarre accent, in which Carla could now discern a trace of Lugosi's peculiar mode of speech. "Come."

"You eat?" she said to Timmy. Maybe if she caught him eating she would know for sure that the rest was all imagination.

Timmy only smiled weakly. "One man's meat," he said. "But I'm not coming to dinner. I'm going upstairs to open my boxes."

"Boxes?"

"My new trains. And my castle. I can't wait any longer." His eyes twinkled, little-boylike.

"My sweet Timmy," said Maria, patting his head fondly. And the boy dashed into the next room. She heard the sound of feet pattering up a heavily carpeted staircase. "Come, Miss Rubens, you and I will dine alone; you must be famished after your journey. And then I'll show you to your room."

"Yes, of course," Carla said, uneasy again.

"But listen, Miss Rubens. You are a fancy analyst from New York, and Timmy's convinced that you can do something for him, but I doubt it. I and Rudy can take perfectly good care of him. Even if he does drink—"

Carla studied the woman's face. She seemed on the verge of tears. "You love him," she said, knowing it for the first time.

"If I didn't," Maria whispered fiercely, "would I mop the blood from the upholstery of his car? Would I take the trouble to dispose of the bodies?"

"So you know about him." Or was it another trap? "But he kills people!"

"Not if he can help it," said the old woman. "But when the hunger seizes him, there's not much he can do about it."

"Does the name Konrad Stolz mean anything to you?"

"One of his old aliases."

"Oh?"

"Do you think it's easy to be twelve years old for almost two thousand years, Miss Rubens?"

"Call me Carla."

"I think not."

"Why do you hate me?"

"I don't. But I don't like this new craze of Timmy's one little bit. I've taken good care of him. No one has ever found out anything, you understand! But now you are here to dig up the past. Who will come next? Witch doctors? Peasants with torches? Van Helsings with stakes and crucifixes?

"He told me that stuff doesn't work anymore."

"Perhaps not. But even he is not utterly without superstitions, Miss Rubens."

Carla shuddered. Once more she wanted to flee. She'd been safe in New York, with all those nice big buildings. She'd been safe in Larchmont . . . but a man had been killed in her very living room and drained of blood. The memory surfaced.

She said, "Maria, I wish I could go back, too. Please understand me. I was safe once, but I never will be again."

"You are safe here," Maria said grimly. "From him at least, if not from yourself." She was not comforting.

mother-image

Maria knocked softly at the door: heavy teakwood, inlaid
with an oriental frieze. It was dark. He's been gone so long,
she thought. He needs me. I must go to him. She rubbed at the
heavy white makeup she had plastered over her wrinkled face.
She caressed the sequins on her black gown. Delicately, with
the tip of a long fingernail, she adjusted her lipstick. Then she
knocked again, her fist thudding lightly on the wing of an
engraved phoenix. When there was no answer she pushed to
the door lightly; it gave, and she was in Timmy's room.

A four-poster bed; a French window opening onto a balcony. At her feet, untidily piled up, a dozen issues of *Model
Railroader*.

"Timmy? Timmy, dear?"

He didn't answer, but looked up from the floor where he'd
been sitting, unwrapping the packages. There was a heap of
boxes against the wall, taller than Timmy. He was unpacking a
locomotive. Some lengths of track, hastily put together, surrounded him. Gingerly she stepped over the track, a small
clump of bushes, and a drawbridge, and came to him.

"Mommy," he said, almost inaudibly, thus fulfilling her
fantasy, as she knew he would.

"What a mess your room is!" she said in mock anger. "I'll
have to spend all day straightening it up."

"Sorry."

Children, children, children! she thought, this woman who
had never borne any. But now she had one without going
through childbirth. And this one was immortal. As she too
would be, one day.

"Look what I got!" Timmy cried. A castle was emerging
from the wrappings. "All spires and turrets and . . . do you
know what this is?"

"No, Timmy." Children always liked to show off, tell you
things.

"It's a scale model of the castle of Ludwig the Mad, in
Bavaria."

"That poor analyst woman!" She couldn't resist a little dig.
"She actually thought *you* might live in one of those things."

Timmy set the castle down beside the bushes and the
drawbridge. "One day I'll put it all together. Everything that's

in storage and in this house and in all the other houses. It'll fill the whole room." He hummed an old tune to himself in his eerily pretty voice.

Maria walked to the window. It's the big night, she thought. I'm going to tell him. I'm going to fulfill his dream.

"Look," she said. From the French window you could see the wrought-iron gates of the mansion, hugging the hillside. There was someone standing there. "Can you see? A girl." Timmy was beside her now. He touched her arm; cold, deliciously cold.

They saw a young girl in the moonlight peering through the gates. She wore jeans. Even at this distance, Maria could see the girl's braces; they glittered in the moonlight like fangs. The girl tossed her long mousy hair back and began embracing the railings of the gate.

"Oh, no," Timmy said. "That's the girl I picked up in the car. Why has she decided to haunt my house?"

"Groupie? I'll have Rudy dispose of her," said Maria, anxious that nothing should get in the way of her revelation. "But then again, maybe it won't be necessary."

For a large animal, perhaps a she-wolf, was bounding across the lawn, fur silvered by the leaf-dappled moonlight, and they could hear a howling, compounded of both beauty and anguish, shattering the night's silence.

"No!" Timmy said. "She was to be good! I didn't invite Kitty here to pursue her victims at my very doorstep—"

"How can she help her nature? Timmy, my baby, don't pay her any heed. Rudy and I will take care of any mess."

"I could have found her someone willing, someone who might love her—"

"Don't let it trouble you. Come, let's look at your new toys."

"I'm going to warn her." He closed his eyes. And he was gone. For a moment she waited. Then, in the crossing of the shadows of bed and rococo dressing table, he took shape once again.

"Should you be fighting your own kind?" Maria said.

"I knew the girl . . . lost in fantasy . . . a runaway . . . she only knew me for real because she had seen me on television."

"If she continues to hover around the house, Kitty will find her. I do not like this Kitty. Just because she is a vampire

doesn't give her the right to take over my household. I live for
you, my little Timmy, not for anyone else.'' She played with
his hair. Its coldness shot through her arthritic fingers.

"Do as you're told,'' he said curtly, breaking out of their
game.

"Oh, I'm sorry, my Timmy, my dear little boy. . . .''

"You are too jealous.'' But he spoke gently now. "But you
take good care of me.''

"Yes. That is why we should play the map game now. There
is a special reason why we must play it.''

"The map game?'' Timmy dragged a huge leatherbound
atlas from under the bed and opened it, fastidiously moving
the train accessories out of the way so that it would lie flat.

She squatted beside him. She turned the pages to the index.

"Junction," said Timmy in a faraway voice. "Junction.''

She began to read the names. "Junction, Kansas,'' she said.
They turned to the page on the map. "B17. I found it.''

"Too flat. My trains won't like it there.''

"Junction, Massachusetts.''

"Too la-di-da.''

"There are *two* Junctions in—''

"Yeah. But one's on the sea. What kind of Junction is
that?''

"Idaho.''

"That's it. Idaho.'' Suddenly he smiled broadly.

"While you were away in New York, Timmy, I bought it for
you.''

"You're not joking, are you?'' Oh, he was so close to her,
so achingly close . . . I could have had a baby once, she
thought abruptly.

But I had a career. I had a five-year contract. Fifty dollars a
week. The abortion. In 1925. The dirty abortion. I'm barren
now, barren. They ripped my womb up. My child is dead.
Here is my dead child. Timmy, Timmy, dead and not dead,
my dead child. . . .

"I'm not joking,'' she said. "While you were gone your
agents scouted it out. It's a sleepy, lonely town with a railway
station no one uses anymore. And a vast abandoned house. I
took the liberty of buying the house.''

"Oh, Maria, you're the greatest!'' He kissed her cheek. The
burning cold stung. But it was sensuous. How else but with

frozen lips could a dead child kiss? "For a long time I've dreamt of such a place. I'll be far from the publicity. I'll sing and play with my trains, and Carla will wring the truth from me and redeem me."

"You don't need an analyst. You're supernatural, Timmy!" She was momentarily annoyed; how could he mention Carla in that very moment?"

"Yet I exist." He looked away. With a finger he traced a spiral round and round Idaho, narrowing until it reached the little town of Junction. "But I've got to open this . . . Phil gave it to me."

He tore at another package. "Oh, Phil. . . ." he said. "If I could only weep." It was a model of a row of brownstones. On the corner, to the left, was Phil Preis's train store. The sign in the window had been lovingly painted in with a tiny brush. "Look! He made it! He wants to be in my landscape, see, he wants to be in my vision." He fumbled with it. Maria lost interest. But she started when he touched a lever in the back of the brownstone and a melody tinkled forth. It was *Vampire Junction*. The boy's eyes shone. Children, children! she thought. My broken nest. But my child is dead, is dead, and this dead child found me, sixty years old and dead drunk, in a gutter, and claimed to remember seeing me in *Furnace of Passion*, 1926, and I laughed at him but I found out he was dead and a child and mine to take care of, and he never grew older in fifteen years. . . .

"Hungry? You haven't fed," she said. "You must be hungry, darling."

"Yes, Mommy," he whispered, feeding her fantasy as she would feed his life force.

He touched her throat and slid his finger down, pausing on every wrinkle. She loosened the dress, loosened the yellowing bra to reveal a withered breast. "Drink me," she said hoarsely.

She felt the touch of the icy lips. The steely prick of animal fangs. She felt the oozing of the warm blood, the tingling of their perverse communication. She was drunk with it. I am feeding my child, my dead child, she thought, closing her eyes in the only ecstasy she was still capable of feeling.

labyrinth

That howl! What was that howl?

Carla sat up in her bed. Palms swayed in the bay window; through them shone the full moon. The palm leaves' shadows fell on the red satin sheets like sharp black teeth. The howling came again, menacing. *Children of the night.* That silly horror movie cliché, but she felt its dread. Carefully she got out of bed and reached for the blue Yves Saint Laurent bathrobe draped over a wicker chair.

She went to the window.

Was that a wolf, running across the lawn? Was that a young girl, running in the moonlight, beyond the railings and the spear-capped brick walls of Timmy's domain?

Quickly she turned away. I am safe from him, she thought, remembering Maria's words. Maria! There was a woman whose hold on reality must be tenuous at best. They were all loonies here. At dinner, the waiters had hovered over them like vultures.

She drew the curtains.

Now the shadow-jaws of the palms were painted against the ripple of silk curtains.

Like being a kid and seeing monsters at night in every shadow, closing her eyes, not daring to peep—

I am well over forty years old, she told herself. I have treated schizophrenics, psychopaths, and even a multiple personality. I will deal with my fear. The shadow is a very powerful archetype, but I've helped a hundred people face and conquer their shadows. Why am I so daunted by *my* personal shadow?

She tried to sleep again but could not, though the howling had ceased. After an hour she decided to go outside.

"He said he would conceal nothing, right?" she said to herself, aloud, grateful for the sound of any voice. She opened the door.

She was on a railinged landing, thickly carpeted. She reached along the wall but found no lightswitch; there was a little light coming from downstairs, moonlight no doubt, leaking in through windows or through that plastic dome thing.

She inched her way along the wall. She could see several more doors. From somewhere far away she could hear music,

too. A child's voice. Was it Timmy? Perhaps it was a recording.

Bolder now, she tried the first door. It was locked. So was
another, and another. The singing seemed to be coming from
above. Was there another floor? Yes. There was the staircase,
she could see it through a half-open doorway at the end of the
landing. She tiptoed there; the deep carpet sucked away all
sound. She felt as if she were floating.

Maybe I'm dreaming.

The singing came again; even further away, the howling.
She found the first step. Its creak made her start, but she put
her foot down more firmly, wincing at the high-pitched
squeak of old wood. It was darker here. The steps must lead to
an attic, she thought.

Dank smell now. A chill in the musty air. As her eyes grew
used to the darkness, she saw that she was at the crossroads
of several corridors. Surely this house, big though it was,
couldn't contain all these corridors. She tripped—

A broken doll, ivory-faced, with one eye permanently shut.
Almost reverently she set it to rest against one plaster-cracked
wall.

Louder now, the music . . . one corridor was brighter than
the others; electric candlebranches were set into the walls.
Grimy wallpaper: yellow flowers, crudely drawn humming-
birds darting. The music: a piano, stopping and starting, high,
tinkly arpeggios; Timmy's voice soaring eerily above it. Creeping toward the end of the hall, where there was a doorway cur-
tained off with heavy brocade, she drew the curtain aside a
little and peered through.

Gleaming electronic equipment littering the floor. One wall
—a poster of Timmy in a Dracula cape, blowup of an album
cover. Wooden floor, dark varnish, and a white concert Stein-
way towering over an assemblage of electronic keyboards and
tombstone speakers. Brilliant light from overhead fluorescent
lamps. . . .

Timmy was sitting at the piano. He didn't see her. She saw
that his eyes were bloodshot, and that a red stain dripped from
one corner of his mouth and had spattered his cornflower-blue
pajamas. He was strumming at the piano, singing along now
and then. His left hand was outlining a rather dull rock
rhythm; his right was doing the saccharine-laden arpeggiated

harmonies. His singing was dreamy, detached. What were the words? She only caught a few, couldn't make much sense of them.

Then, almost imperceptibly, he began to shift harmonies, blending the arpeggios until they had become a sequence of throbbing, repetitive chords. The left hand suddenly broke into an articulated melody, and then Timmy began to sing a song she knew, a song she had heard often when she was married to Stephen . . . Schubert. *An die Musik. "Du holde Kunst,"* he sang, "O beautiful Art". . . .

She gasped. He must have heard her, surely, but he didn't stop. As far as she could tell, his German was flawless. And the strained purity of his voice, its unearthly luminosity—

What was this? She, Carla Rubens, was crying? It was because she remembered Stephen. Stephen dashing home from rehearsal so wrapped up in the transcendence of his music, so entranced by the fire, that he seemed to see right through her—

The song ended, and Timmy looked up. He must have seen her. But she couldn't talk to him. She ran down the corridor, the artifical candlelight streaking in her teary vision. She could hardly see. Where was she? She was lost. The junction of the seven corridors . . . where was it? Left, no, right, no, this way . . . she ran into darkness now. The corridors themselves —they were shifting, transforming, they were all in the mind, in Timmy's mind—

Another staircase, spiraling, upward, upward—but there's no turret here what is this some medieval castle? she was thinking as she ran, the unfinished wood scraping her feet raw—

Another room. Stone walls. A tower room. Rapunzel's room or something. An open window. Bitingly cold, the wind, and outside stark mountains and rings of crenellated walls and the dragon's breath in the sky and—

A bat. Circling. A vulture—a bat? Shifting constantly from one to the other, a black splotch against the bright moon's face, and she turned around and her hand brushed against the wood of an open coffin and—

Stop. Breathe deeply. This is not reality, she told herself. It is a reenactment of an archetypal situation. Individuation. The conquest of the shadow, the confrontation with the anima

. . . words from the Jungian texts unreeling, unreeling, and
. . . stop. Stop. Breathe deeply.

She stood up and leaned over the coffin.

It was empty. Someone had sprinkled a little soil on it. Its
lid lay against the wall. Polished oak. She ran her hand along
the coffin's side: smooth, so smooth, so cold. The wind roared
outside.

Then came a screeching, and she saw the bat-vulture swooping out of the black sky and—

At the window. An adolescent girl with too much makeup,
her face caked white, her eyes coal-bright, the full overpainted
lips parting in a sinister smile and the fangs glittering. Carla
couldn't move. She was pinned to the side of the coffin, her
fingers squeaking frantically against the silksmooth polish,
and the vampire girl was coming, coming, and she knew it
wasn't Timmy, she didn't know who it was, maybe it was a
dream it was herself plucked from inside herself and she
couldn't close her eyes and shut it out and it still came and
now came thundercrack laughter from its lips and new blood
still clotting against the teeth and Carla screamed then,
screamed wildly, screamed her throat raw, and—

"How dare you!" A bellowing woman's voice, raspy, aged.
The vampire girl hesitated for a moment. A snarl burst from
her bloody mouth.

"Aieee—" A cry of pain, terrible, eternal pain . . . the spell
was broken. Carla whipped around to see an old woman in a
black dress holding aloft a silver cross, advancing firmly
toward the vampire.

"This is one of master Timothy's guests!" the old woman
shrieked. "How dare you abuse his hospitality! How dare you
attack one of his own? Now get into that coffin, whore, before
I burn this cross on your forehead!"

The vampire whimpered, protested in a submissive whine,
"Only feed-animals . . . how can Timothy . . . treat them as if
. . . they had true identities . . . they're nothing but . . . animals . . . animals . . . so hungry, so hungry . . . he wouldn't let
me devour the girl either, the girl that was watching by the
gate, just dying to die, I smelled her deathwish on the wind . . .
no, don't hurt me, Maria, don't hurt me, Maria, no, no. . . ."

"Maria!" Carla cried. "Oh, thank God, thank God—"

"Not yet, Miss Rubens. You, Kitty, back into your coffin.

Dawn is coming! You'll shrivel up, you hear, if I don't tuck you in.''

Cowering, the girl crept into her coffin. "Help me now," said Maria. "I'm too old to lift the damn lid."

Carla was too numbed to react for a moment. Then she and Maria hefted the coffin cover up and slammed it down over Kitty's face. Carla was sobbing.

"Where is this place? Why couldn't I see it from outside?"

"It is all right. The mind has a thousand landscapes, does it not, analyst? You above all should know. Once there has been a tiny crack in the armoured walls that separate the conscious from the unconscious . . . could not pandemonium break loose? We, Miss Rubens, are the horror. We. Accept that. It will set you free."

Carla stared at the old woman for a long time. Then she crumpled sobbing hysterically, into her arms, and fell into a thick darkness.

7

It's May, I've been here for three days. I'm confused.

The house is here and it's not here.

Question: if Timmy is (as it were) a solidified illusion, what are *his* illusions? Do illusions, in turn, create their own reality?

Parts of the house: forbidden pathways in my own mind. Never liked vampires when I was a kid. Who's being analyzed? Ask him in session, try to keep him on track of himself, not me.

Watch Maria. She's weird.

Maybe Stephen does know something about Konrad Stolz. This means there's a great deal more at work here than I think. Junctions. A town in Idaho, too, Timmy tells me. He dreams of it, he says.

The dreamworld is the archetype's home turf. How, then, can an archetype dream? What does it dream of? Are the worlds reversed? Am I the concretization of his dream, as he is of mine? And if so, are Rudy and Maria illusory (i.e. manufactured by the realization of the illusion's illusions), existing only as projections of his desires-fears-traumas? Possible hypothesis: a dualism. Mirror-image worlds.

Think of *Through the Looking-Glass*; the Red King's dream. . . .

What I mean is this. What if, rather than vampires and other realized archetypes being "sorts of things in our dreams," what if *we* were only a concretization of *his*? What if the sole purpose of our existence was to provide the physical corollary of Timmy's mythic nature? If the need for creatures to feed upon and spear carriers in the private drama of his existence were so powerful a force as to generate my entire universe?

The Red King's dream—

(Red, rose, blood.)

Who is the Red King?

seeker

A small town; a bar; a phone booth. Brian Zottoli fumbled in his pockets for a dime, then cursed to discover it cost twenty cents here. Oh, there was a quarter. God damn it, he thought, I'm on this wild goose chase and I don't even have change to play Pac-Man.

"Collect. To Phoenix. The number is—"

The quarter came back. Thank God! His ten-minute video-therapy session was safe.

"Hello. Mark?"

A gruff voice: "Brian. You got news?"

"A lead. Someone here thinks they saw her. Heading west, hitching."

"God damn it, Brian, you gotta find her. Will you go west for me?"

"Find her yourself."

"She's probably gone to Los Angeles. She's probably in some godforsaken unchristian whorehouse right now, turning her face away from the Lord."

"What about you, Mark?" Brian Zottoli couldn't listen to his brother long without repugnance. Religious nuts always made him uneasy. If only Mark hadn't met Heather and her goggled-eyed crowd of Jesus freaks. Brian listened to his brother babble on about how they'd always loved and cherished little Lisa.

Right. Locking her into a closet of a room for days on end with nothing but a cable TV for company until she'd mind their God-inspired words. He should have kidnapped the kid years ago. Only a few more months and he could have figured out a plan, but now it was all fucked up.

He couldn't stand his brother's self-righteous barking anymore. "Listen, you hypocrite," he said. "You treated her like an animal. You fed her TV movies until she thinks they're real. And you raped her, God damn it!"

"I—she teased me! She tempted me! It was for her own good, teach her a lesson—"

Brian hung up, walked slowly away from the phone booth. There were a couple of arcade machines in one corner of the bar. He made toward one. A woman in a bright red wig and a tight T-shirt looked up and grinned at him. "Hi, stranger."

"I have to get away from here."

"Hey, talk to me! I like guys with dark hair. Your nose is sexy. Your mouth is full and big, too. Betcha you're a real good kisser."

"I have to go."

"What do you do? Reporter or something? That was some heavy conversation you were having on that phone."

"I'm an out-of-work writer. Leave me alone."

"No kidding! Writer, huh? Give me a ride to the next town?"

"I—" What the hell? He was lonely. He'd been on the road for two weeks now. He'd only agreed to go looking for Lisa because he didn't want his brother to do it. "OK." She got up to follow him. They stepped out into dazzling light, mountains overshadowing the plastic cube blocks of a sleazy town.

As he opened the door of his old station wagon to let her in, he asked her name.

"I'm Rita." In the sunlight she was even less attractive than she'd seemed in the bar. She seemed a bit older than Brian's thirty-five. Her makeup, he couldn't help noticing, was unevenly streaked. But it would be good to have someone to talk to. Anyone.

I'll unload her in the next town, he thought, and said aloud, "There's beer in the cooler on the back seat."

night-child

The last time Carla had been in a recording studio had been fifteen years before, in London, to see Stephen inaugurate his Mahler cycle for Diadem Records with the Cambridge Symphonica. There'd been over a hundred players there, and the producer had sat in the little cubicle like a king, bringing the whole thing to a shuddering stop if the violins weren't together, changing his mind about cross-miking or boom placement, and with one hand scrawling on a notepad, juggling the union scale overtime with the budget sheet.

Rudy took Carla with her to pick Timmy up at Stupendous Sounds Systems; he waited decorously in the car while she went inside. It was nothing like the London studio. Behind a reception hall of shopping mall-like decor and proportions, she found a catacomb of corridors; at every intersection a bewildering array of color-coded arrows pointed the way. Finally she was admitted into a control room by a cadaverous man in a dark suit, who sported extravagant dark glasses and a razor blade dangling from one ear as his grudging concessions to the punk sensibility.

"Who are you?"

"Carla Rubens," she said timidly as the man towered over her.

"My name is Blade. Siddown and keep out of the way, OK?"

She looked about her. The banks of mixers, noise reduction units, special effects boxes and one-inch tape recorders were familiar to her. A couple of technicians were manipulating the machines; one was splicing the wide tape. Cartons of tape sprawled on one shelf. Over the equipment consoles, a glass wall allowed them to view the studio.

But there was no huge orchestra here, no rows of music stands and black instrument cases. In the large chamber, whose walls and ceiling were completely covered in a garish red plush material, Timmy stood alone. He wore very faded jeans, leather Nikes, and an old T-shirt that advertised an obscure brand of beer. He could not have looked more ordinary, more like a typical suburban kid.

Then he looked up and saw her. He smiled a little, and she remembered what he was. How could she have forgotten?

His voice came, muffled, distant. "We're running late," he said, "and my analyst wants me."

"Come on," Blade said. "Another go at the bridge. I wanna try something."

"Again? Do I have to?"

"Yeah."

"Are you just going to mess with the echo again?"

"No. Listen to this, we just respliced it."

As music poured from tall speakers in the control room,

Carla realized that Timmy's accompaniment had been put together, track by track, like a jigsaw puzzle. Carla moved to the glass barrier, pressed her face against it. The boy listened, frozen in concentration.

"OK," he said. His voice was distanced by glass and by electronics. He picked up some headphones from the floor and put them on. Now he looked like some antennaed little alien creature. He turned to Carla. Something passed between them, she didn't know what.

"Insert one, take five," said Blade behind her. There came commingled sounds: strings, piano, celesta, electronic sounds, hard percussion.

Suddenly she realized that it was the song she had heard him singing upstairs, in the attic that went on forever, that reached into the mind itself . . . then, plucking the notes from the emptiness that engulfed him, he started to sing, full voice. What were those trashy words, empty clichés about love and violence? He was staring her full in the face now; it was as if he sang for her alone. A veiled, breathy quality corrupted the purity of his voice; it conveyed a sense of lost innocence that belied the vacuous lyrics. And beneath the syrupy harmonies and tinkling keyboard figures she heard another rhythm . . . the heartthrob of Schubert's *An die Musik* . . . how had he woven it into the texture? The text was trite, uninspiring; the harmonic subtext revealed hidden exaltations, dark eroticisms . . . the song was its own surface, concealing completely its bitter core . . . and when she stared into Timmy's eyes she seemed to see within them once more corridors intersecting, widening, dividing, pulsing, doors within doors, the gateways of eternity . . . could he have this effect even on strangers? Even on the millions of screaming little girls who clutched his photograph in *Idol Magazine* and yearned, secretly and not so secretly? Could they all be made to glimpse the nightmare labyrinth of the soul?

Abruptly, the music stopped. The song had not yet ended, but the take was complete. And Carla stood, shivering, not noticing the chattering of the technicians, until Timmy came to her and announced that he was ready to leave.

Outside, it was already dark.

They sat in silence as Rudy drove them back to the house. There, Maria gave Carla the key to one of the locked rooms on the landing, the one next to her own. Timmy went in ahead of her, turning to dismiss Maria; when Carla followed she saw that the room was bare, except for a couch in the middle of the wooden floor, and a plaid armchair much like the one she had used in her New York office. Without a word, Timmy went and lay down on the couch. The lights were dim. Windows opened out into the garden, admitting the night breeze.

"Let's start," said Timmy.

"Who is she?" she cried. She had been clenching back that question since the night of endless corridors. "I didn't bargain for any vampire mindgames when I agreed to come, Timmy. Be straight with me!"

"The woman in the coffin?"

"What does it mean? Are you trying to scare me with references to my shadow self, are you trying to drag *me* down into the murky unconscious too?"

"Quiet, quiet. I am not playing with you. That's what Rudy and Maria think. There is another vampire here. Her name is Kitty Burns. She is only sixty years undead, though, and she fears crosses and garlic and all that nonsense. Hang garlic in your room. Get crucifixes. What can I say? I will not allow her to harm you."

"I didn't bargain for two patients!"

"She is not to be your patient. But you see, it is I who made her what she is, and I suffer a certain . . . guilt. I cannot dismiss her. You cannot know the degradation she once endured.

"And her victims?"

"We're arguing in a circle again, Carla. Sit down. Help me. That's why you have come, isn't it?"

"Yes." She sat on the armchair; it was amazingly like her own, and this comforted her. "But how shall we begin? With dreams? Tell me what you dream."

"I am in a white room playing a white piano. I have gone to escape the ape who pursues the woman in red. I always play in the key of F sharp. It is an L-shaped house. It is on stilts. There is a long spiral staircase of wood. The house rises up, up, up, far above the true world. One leg of the L is the white room with the white piano. The other is the toilet. The ape has pursued the woman in red into it. She has locked herself in. The ape bangs, thundering. I play to drown out the sound. I play only in F sharp, a key that is almost all black keys, yet the black keys too are white."

Carla sighed. "It sounds like one of your songs. What is F

sharp to you?'' Though she had learned much from Stephen, she was not really a musician.

The boy continued in a dreamy voice: "C major is the most basic key, the one every child learns first. F sharp is the most remote key from it. It's a key of alienation, you see. I have that figured out quite easily.''

A little warning sounded in her mind. How easily the dream fell into place as a classical sending from the collective unconscious! The woman in red would be the anima, the soul-thing, always the sexual opposite of the subject. And the ape was the shadow, the dark side. It was a dream of splintered self, one whose different aspects could not admit each other's existence. Timmy was in flight, finding refuge in the shut room, the remote key of F sharp. It was so perfect that Carla found it suspect.

"What does the dream mean?" Timmy said, all sweetness.

"I think you stole the dream.''

"Of course! I don't dream. I *am* a dream.''

"No dreams within dreams?''

Timmy went on, more slowly, "I am on a train. On the other side of the dark tunnel is the junction. I can see the other passengers with my night-piercing eyesight, but I am invisible to them. I see a girl in a cage. She is naked. She is beautiful. I want to release her. I break the cage bars. She runs with me through the train-labyrinth. She is soon gone. There is darkness. The tunnel goes on forever. I cry, 'Let there be light!' and I see that the lights have come on in the train, running down its corridors. But she is gone. I will never find her, and the tunnel may never end.''

"Who is she?''

"I don't know.''

"Tell me about the dark forest.'' She was searching frantically for a correct methodology for dealing with Timmy, but none presented itself. "The forest where you lost the power of speech.''

"I hardly remember. Animals. A squirrel's blood, dark, rank. Not like a human's. The blood of carnivores, foul, oozing; rabbit's blood, cloying-sweet; birds' blood, hot, like thin gruel. And always the darkness. It was then that I stopped fearing the light. In the daytime I would stumble on clearings, patches of brilliance erupting from the dark; but I found out that the fact of day, in itself, could not kill me. Gradually I accustomed myself to more light, though I think that at first it burned me too much, it dulled my intellect, it drowned my memories, it made me more an animal than a sapient being.''

Carla paused, overwhelmed by his intensity. In those moments she had felt his savagery. It seemed that a remembrance came to her of hunting side by side with him, skimming the smooth darkness, hugging the ground, the nose keen for the minutest bloodscent . . . I've never done that! she told herself, angry that she had allowed herself to sink into her patient's universe.

She said, "How long ago?"

"A hundred years, two hundred."

I'll let him go on talking, she thought. Be supportive; alleviate any guilt feelings. Accept the utter reality of his fantasy. She said, "And since that time?"

"They found me finally. I don't remember clearly. A gray period now: I see no colors at all, and I cannot distinguish words very well. Smell and hearing are still acute, but nothing else. I walk through Europe. Slowly I rediscover song. I remember some things. Like the fire."

"Fire?"

"Fire gave me birth."

Perhaps I should not delve so deep so soon, she thought. Perhaps we should work backwards from the present. Perhaps we will use hypnosis. She was improvising now. The image of the dark forest frightened her more than she wanted to admit. In the symbology of the collective unconscious, the dark forest was a very potent image, but for Timmy it was more than symbol; it was experience itself. More and more she was beginning to believe the words she had briefly scrawled in her notebook that morning: that in Timmy's universe, *we* were the dream, and the artifacts of our dreamworlds his reality.

Now came another symbol: the firebirth.

Why am I so reluctant to probe further? she asked herself. Her hands were shaking now. She realized that she needed more time; for now the depths were too terrifying. To start from the present and work back was as much for her own peace of mind as for any analytic pupose.

"No more dreams," she said, filing away his two dreams for later study. "Give me memories, Timmy, memories. You must have had many sets of parents, for example. Who were the last ones?" With an effort of will she conquered her anxiety and managed to speak in the reassuring, motherly voice that usually managed to bring out the child in all her patients. But even as Timmy began to speak, she questioned herself. In the few hours they had spent together it seemed that it was *her* traumas, *her* childhood horrors, that had come spurting to the surface, while Timmy remained untouched. She no longer knew why she was the analyst and he the patient. In this room, between the two of them, it scarcely mattered.

memory: 1967

In the moonstriped dark, he hears sheets rustling. A hand tugs at his arm; it recoils momentarily from the coldness, then tugs again. He has not been asleep, of course. "Hey, wake up, sucker!" comes an adolescent whisper. "Wake up!"

He sits up on the lower bunk, his head colliding with the legs of a boy who is climbing down from above. "What's wrong?" he says. There is no drowsiness in his voice. The hunger, never absent, gnaws at him a little, sharpening his senses. "Is it a fire drill or something?"

"No, dummy!" a surly voice says. He can see the other boy quite clearly in the dark; it is Jake Phillips, a tall twelve-year-old whose voice has already changed. "Don't you remember? Tonight's the night we're sneaking over to Camp Stroke 'n' Poke to spy on the girls! Come on!"

He hears other voices now. Even in the middle of the night, the heat is stifling. The boy wonders why he agreed to be sent to this summer camp. He should just have disappeared when his surrogate parents suggested it, slipped away, found another town and another identity. What is the attraction? An oppressive stillness fills the dark dormitory, and he smells young boy-sweat, a faint whiff of urine, and beneath it the acrid tang of young blood, heated to a maddeningly tempting savor by the feverish metabolism of childhood. He cannot feed, though. He has long learned that he cannot choose victims blindly, without fear of discovery. Only anger can release that feeding frenzy.

He must go with them, or they will taunt him. "Don't say anything!" Jake says. Another kid, the grotesque Morty Rooster, farts resoundingly as he oozes into a pair of shorts. "Get up, Alvarez!"

Who is Alvarez? For a moment he is confused. Then the boy remembers that it is his own name. He has had a hundred names; at night, when the hunger is strongest, things like names tend to fade from his consciousness. Alvarez. Wally Alvarez, that's me. He remembers now: the house in a Washington suburb, the smiling television parents. A name, a set of parents—nothing at all, really. More like a suit of clothes. They do not touch him.

He slips out of bed, so soundlessly that even Jake gasps for a moment. He is already wearing some old cutoffs and a detergent-fresh T-shirt with the Camp Siena Rapids logo blazoned across it.

He hears more voices: "Did you see the bazongas on that Harriet Lipschitz?" Rooster is opining to mumurous approbation. "I'm gonna stick it up her."

"Groovy!" says a distant voice.

"Sure you will, fatso," Jake scoffs.

"Fatty, fatty, two-by-four, couldn't get through the bathroom door," says another voice.

"So he did it on the floor, licked it up and did some more," the dormitory choruses.

"Aw, fuck off," Jakes says. "Let's go."

The vampire—Wally, he must remember to answer to Wally —falls in with them. A single window is open; they climb out, one by one, and drop down on the grass. The cabin is surrounded by pines; in the distance there are mountains. The air is dense, muggy, and spangled with fireflies. The boy does not bother to climb; some of the children, staring upwards at the window, have seen a black cat leap the impossible distance, the moonlight lending a glossy sheen to its fur. One of the boys stifles a little cry, but dares not reveal that he is afraid; only the boy-cat, sniffing the rancid fear-sweat, knows the truth.

Jake insists on melodrama. So they keep low as they skirt the hedges that separate the cabins and slink into the forest.

As they enter the darkness, the boy senses the primal awe. But he knows they cannot show their fear to each other. They begin to whoop gleefully, to run along the forest path, to tell exaggerated tales of sexual exploits. But Wally remembers a different forest . . . a forest with no end, whose dark heart was conjoined directly with a forest of the soul . . . he remembers, and the memories suffuse this children's forest with an ancient dread. He knows that the others have felt it; they speak too loudly now, and the big darkness swallows up their shouts, deadens them, turns them to silence. An owl hoots: Davie Ehrlich, the littlest, cannot hold back a little scream.

Far away, the sound of running water.

"What if they're not there?" says one of them.

"They're always there on Thursday nights," says Jake.

"You ain't seen nothing till you've seen Harriet's knockers," says Morty Rooster in a superior tone.

"Listen!" Davie says.

Morty farts again. It is his specialty, and the only socially redeeming asset he possesses.

"Shut up, fatso," someone says. "I'm trying to listen."

"Over there. On the left," Jake says.

But of course the vampire has heard it long before, has heard it even as they lay sleeping. It is the sound of young girls' laughter and the rippling of stream water.

In a moment they have reached the brook. They hide in a clump of bushes, five or six pubescent boys and a vampire, dressed in identical shorts and camp T-shirts.

"Wow," says Jake, his jaw dropping. His macho pretense leaves him as he peers at the dark water. Wally looks too, and he sees three teenage girls in the stream, giggling and splashing water on each other. They are naked. "Look at that one!"

"Told ya about Harriet's headlights," says Morty portentously. "Bet she uses a 38D. And she's only fifteen."

"Wow," says Jake. "I got a hard-on."

"Let's steal their clothes," Davie pipes up. Wally looks at him. His blond hair is trimmed in a perfect Beatle haircut, and he has a string of tiny puka shells around his neck. His parents must be liberals.

Jake says, "I got a better idea. Let's get closer. See, if we creep up along this rock—"

The girls bob up and down, unsuspecting. The boys move slowly away from the bushes toward a closer clump. Wally has already beat them to it, for he has assumed the shadows of the trees as his own shadow.

"How'd you get there so fast?" Jake whispers urgently.

Wally smiles. Again comes the hunger. Children's blood is the sweetest. He quells his frustration, reminding himself that he must cause no incident. If he can get away for a while, he can catch a rabbit or a frog; their dark, mealy blood must suffice. But the smell of so much blood, laced as it is with childish eroticism, maddens him. Control, control! he tells himself fiercely. Has he let go of himself? Has his form shimmered, has he slipped into some monstrous shape plucked from the hidden horror in their hearts? For just a second they are watching him with a strange awe . . . a presentiment? He cannot tell. The moment of unease passes. He turns to watch the girls, laughing with the others, blending in. Camouflage is *his* specialty.

"Oh, I want her, I want her," Morty says, letting out what he imagines to be a moan of erotic passion. "I could fuck her right now. Oh, oh—"

"So go and do it!" says another kid.

"Look at them bulge out," says Davie, impressed at the magnitude of Harriet's endowments.

"Must weigh more'n you do," says Jake.

Morty pulls off his shorts and begins to masturbate. The smell of blood intensifies. Hearts are beating faster, the vampire feels the pounding, the gushing of fresh adrenalin. The hunger seizes him. He is shaking.

"You're sick, fatso!" says Jake, still staring at the nymphs of the stream. One has got up now and is lying on a rock, letting the wind dry her; she is breathing in little spasms, rubbing herself . . . "Sick, sick, sick!" Jake says, but as he stares at this new spectacle he himself cannot resist prying his own penis free and squeezing it. "OK, now I'm beating off," he says, "so you all got to do it too, you hear?"

They are giggling nervously now, but one by one they are obeying. The vampire does not know what to do. He cannot do this. He will not. He is not a human. They are all scrunched together now, their faces competing for the gaps in the bush, their hands furiously working their genitals, when Jake notices the boy vampire sitting alone, a little way off, trembling with repressed hunger. . . .

"Hey, you little shit!" Jake says. "I said everyone."

"Don't feel like it."

"You wanna wake up with shaving cream in your pants, asshole?"

"Don't feel like it!"

Morty has ejaculated and is wiping his hands on his T-shirt. "Betcha ain't even *got* no dick!" he says. "Betcha you're a girl!"

"Girl, girl, girl!" the others whisper threateningly.

Suddenly, the girl on the rock turns over. She sees Jake without his shorts on, but she does not cry out. Instead, she hisses, mocking, "Hey, little boy! Take it all off! Wanna have a good time, honey?"

Jake stammers for a moment. He is confused. He turns on the vampire shouting "Girl, girl, girl!" with the others—

The hunger bursts out, uncontrollable. The boy leaps. A howl of anguish and bloodlust rends the air. He is on Morty, who has no time to scream before the blood erupts from his jugular and splatters the other boys' faces. A final fart tears from his loosened sphincter. The boys are so confused that they begin to laugh, an automatic response to Morty's antics. Then Davie yells out: "He's a killer—a—killer—a—"

Wolfjaws slaver in the moonlight. The naked girl screams. Wolfclaws rend her. Her cheek rips open. The beast roars with anger and desire. The other two girls have begun running; one clutches Davie, whose bloodied shorts still hang from a twig like a flag of truce. Again come the fangs, the yellow slitted eyes. Jake has backed against the tree, terror-frozen. The vampire toys with the fat boy's guts for a moment, tossing a slippery liver into the stream. He watches Jake, circles him . . . he understands these boys, understands their casual cruelty, their petty lusts . . . he could feed again now, he could shred the boy who has unknowingly just made fun of what he was . . . the hunger and the anger subside at once. He is left only with despair.

Jake has still not moved. Slowly, deliberately, the boy who has called himself Wally Alvarez reaches down to clasp the fat boy's head in his hands. With a single twist he severs the spinal cord. It is the only mercy he can give now, to deny this unhappy child an even more dismal future.

He looks at Jake. Their eyes meet. The rest have all fled. He cannot be Wally Alvarez again; it is time for a new identity. He says to Jake: "You cannot understand what has happened tonight. I know it was not really your doing. You could not know that what you said would awaken my anger. . . ."

"Will you kill me?" Jake says in a tiny little-boy voice.

"No. My hunger has gone."

As he watches Jake's face, unblinking, he sees the tears slowly forming in his eyes and begin to stream down his cheeks.

The vampire says: "You were set upon by . . . by a big, tall man. A maniac. Do you understand? You don't know what happened to Alvarez. Maybe he was kidnapped. You don't even want to think about what might have been done to him."

Tonelessly, Jake repeats the story.

"You have forgotten me now. You have forgotten what I am," says the vampire. He touched a bloodstained hand to the boy's cheek. The cold burns, and Jake cries out. "You have forgotten." And he thinks to himself: I'm never going to let myself be sent somewhere like this again. I'm never going to have parents again. I'm going to find a way to become self-sufficient, to survive alone in the adult world. . . .

He seizes a strand of the forest darkness and clothes himself in it . . . when Jake looks up he sees a soaring hawk silhouetted against the moon.

"It was a maniac," Jake whispers, robotlike. "Like I said, it was a maniac. The other kids, they're just hysterical. But I'm older. They didn't see no wolf, sir. It was a maniac. Like I said."

8

I dream the scent of blood on my nostrils, paws scraping the damp earth, the spoor of my prey clinging to the moist dead leaves. . . .

I wake; the forest's intoxicating odor is slipping away, but I know it was more than dream, it was remembrance. It is Timmy's forest. My forest.

Why do I report *my* dreams in this notebook? I am not the patient. Somehow it's important, though. I have to call my own analyst on this. There's nothing like a strict Freudian to set you straight.

I do remember it! I'm an animal. I don't have a quest. I don't have a vision. I just am. I exult in the darkness that hides me from my victim. I revel in its death-throes, I am drunk on the taste of its blood. . . .

This isn't me! This isn't a part of me! I have to reject it. I am the analyst. The analyst!

I am not the darkness.

So saying, I'm going to turn the page and strike a line through all the preceding, and go on.

There was a kind of breakthrough at that. There's some kind of sexual anxiety. Is it because Timmy has remained in the prepubertal stage for two thousand years (by Maria's reckoning)? The incident in the summer camp he told me about: gruesome though it was, what was it *really* about? The other

boys, flaunting their rampant sexuality, are mocking him . . .
for what? They have hurt him enough to make him respond
with the most primal level of infantile rage . . . why?

Can Timmy, archetypal creature, boy vampire, possess anything so prosaic as penis envy, when he's not even human, let
alone a girl? Or a castration complex?

Explore further.

Note that the vampire legend is sublimated necrophilia.

And still I smell the victim's blood and feel fear flood the
forest and touch the impenetrable darkness—

Whom do I pursue?

Note: Timmy seems to have a strong ability to infect me
with his fantasy world. Beware. Beware.

I think the forest is in the house, too.

fire

"So you see, Stephen," Therese Benzineau was saying as
she ushered him into the back seat of her capacious Rolls-
Royce, "there's very little point in continuing with the Mahler
series."

Stephen Miles was too nonplussed to say anything for a moment. There was jet lag, for one thing. And then there was
that boy's voice, still ringing in his ears, not letting him think.
The driver eased out onto the M1, and soon Heathrow Airport
was behind them.

"Will you be in London long?" said Therese, a middle-aged
recording executive who chainsmoked as they talked. Clearly
she had not been looking forward to telling Stephen that
Diadem Records wasn't renewing their option to the Mahler
series.

"Three or four days," Stephen said. "You know, rest up a
little before my rehearsals start over in Germany."

"Ah, Munich, is it?"

"And Bayreuth. I'm substituting for . . . oh, what do you
care. You're just a glorified accountant anyway."

Therese Benzineau looked away, staring at the countryside.
It was, of course, raining. "I don't suppose this rain will last
all through your stay, though," she said. "We wouldn't want
to ruin your rest, would we?"

"I think you already have."

"Oh, don't worry about it. We'll get you something else.

There's no one yet for that Szymanowski opera project, for instance, since poor old Lord Slatterworth had his heart attack."

"Szymanowski? I can't believe my ears! What you mean, my dear Miss Benzineau, is that no one else can be bothered to learn an entire opera on six months' notice for the sort of money you're paying."

"But you're so reliable!"

"I am almost seventy years old," Stephen said, "and I want to conduct Mahler's Eighth."

"Well, frankly, we've the Solti, the Morris, the Haitink, the Levine, the . . . and sales figures on your recordings of Two and Five have been a little . . . disappointing, and the Eighth is, of course, the most expensive to put on, and. . . ."

"I see. You've given up throwing good money after bad," Stephen said sullenly. They had come off the motorway now, and had entered one of London's seamier sections, made even grayer by the endless drizzle.

"I don't want you to see it that way, Stephen, really, but we at Diadem feel that you should consider yourself lucky to have a five-year recording contract at all."

He stopped listening to her. He closed his eyes and began resolutely to whistle the tune of *Vampire Junction*.

"Heavens, Stephen! I didn't know you listened to such junk."

"You recognize the tune, you self-righteous bitch?" Stephen said, abandoning all decorum as he realized that his most treasured dream was slipping through his fingers.

"Well, actually, my daughter plays the record a lot. Such trash these young things get addicted to!"

The car stopped.

Stephen looked up to find that this was not the Palace Hotel on Oxford Street, next to the EMI Record Shop, where Diadem Records had always put him up before. Instead, a doorman wearing a uniform of ludicrous elegance was opening the car door. His cap read *Savoy*.

"What's this then?" he said to Therese, who still would not meet his eyes. "Why the royal treatment all of a sudden? I never merited the Savoy Hotel before."

She said nothing.

It dawned on Stephen at last. "You really are getting rid of me," he said.

He turned his back on her and stalked past the doorman into the lobby.

He stopped at the desk, picked up a few messages, and then found his room. His luggage was already there. He sat down on the bed, threw off his raincoat, and stared at the messages.

A letter from Diadem, spelling out in black and white the bad news that he had just heard. He found an ashtray, pulled out his gold Dunhill lighter, and set the note on fire. For a second he felt the thrill of burning, but it was soon extinguished.

He burned one message after another.

The last one was sealed in a lavender Basildon Bond envelope. He tore it open, and there came a smell from it, a fragrance of crushed sweet and bitter herbs. The past was in that smell. It leaped up at him, this past he had been fleeing all his life.

He took out the note. The writing was spiky, nervous, as if by an arthritic hand.

It said simply: *Muriel Hykes-Bailey. Tea? Today?* There was an address in Mayfair.

Did he dare go? He had spoken to Locke and Prathna, and now . . . he remembered her now. A redhead from Girton, one of the few women's colleges at Cambridge, and the only female member of the Gods of Chaos. She claimed to be a witch in those days. She had been there too, that night in the chapel of Saint Cecilia's.

I'm going to burn this note, he thought, like the others. I'm going to burn it, and I'm not going to go to Thailand. I'm going to Bayreuth to stand in for a few conductors even more ancient than me, and maybe a critic will even notice. . . .

In an hour he had dressed himself; he had taken from his attaché case a number of old opera house program books featuring the dead boy Konrad Stolz and a fresh clipping from *TV Guide* with a photo of Timmy Valentine; and he was walking out of the Savoy, waving for a taxi.

little lost girl

A lot going on today at the wrought-iron gates. Clanging, clanging, and the sun hardly down.

Lisa crept alongside the brick walls. She had to get inside. Rich and famous was waiting for her. My head's clear now, she thought. Haven't had a pill in a week. I'm hungry.

The hunger was making her dizzy. Once a man bought her dinner, then she had to do the daddy thing with him. Men are all alike, she thought. I gotta go in there so I'll get rich and famous.

Another car pulled up. She peeked through the gates. The driveway was full. A tall nasty-looking man in a uniform directed the new car to park outside. It was sleek, shiny. Lisa could see herself in the car door. It was a rich and famous car like on TV. She missed TV. She liked shark movies best. They'd had a run of them on cable all week. She liked it when the shark ate everybody.

Maybe a shark should come to their house, she thought. A shark in Arizona! But if it ate me, I wouldn't have to do the daddy thing.

Some people got out of the car. A man in a tuxedo like at the Oscars, a woman in fur, so soft, so soft oh she wanted to touch, and perfume, like on TV the perfume was there too, they never transmitted it properly but that was because they had lousy reception and she was being punished anyway for not doing it with daddy but it hurt so bad you know maybe with a rich and famous like Timmy Valentine it wouldn't hurt, nothing on TV could really hurt, the shark ate people but they came right back didn't they, when they always show the movie more than once on cable anyways.

She half listened to the people talking, more fancy people came walking up the slope, chattering. "What's he going to do now that he's finished making this album? . . . I hear they've signed him for a nationwide tour and . . . talk show guest and he . . . so adorable, my daughter just creams in her jeans whenever he. . . ."

That was rich and famous talk.

Uncle Brian, now he didn't believe in anything; he didn't believe in TV and he didn't believe in the daddy thing either but he loved her somehow even without those things, he was probably looking for her now because Daddy wouldn't come look, he'd be too ashamed what would the neighbours think couldn't take off work anyway and he'd say Brian's just a good for nothing shit-eating atheist writer anyway let him go look let him go look.

She stared at herself in the car door a long time. When the next car pulled up there was a large group of people. They had crates on a trolley. They were pushing it in, and when the gates opened she stood right next to it and walked right alongside and she thought: can't see me, and there are lights on all over the house like a big Christmas tree, and all I have to do is see Timmy Valentine and be rich and famous too, and as she started to spring across the dark lawn, she thought of Daddy praying all the time and talking about sin and forgiveness and redemption and she thought about the daddy thing and all his special words he wouldn't say in front of anyone like *fuck you whore bitch fuck you flaunting your pussy in my face I'm a godfearing man you cunt you tease it's all your fucking fault bitch bitch bitch* but it's all over now because I'm going to be rich and famous and I'm not going to let you do it, just Timmy, so there, and I'm going to send a great big shark after you it's going to come right out of the TV set at you so don't you even turn it on—

witch

As soon as he stepped into the hallway he smelled it again, that faint odor of crushed herbs. He parked his umbrella and raincoat and waited for someone to come out and greet him. Instead, there came a voice from an inner room: "Miles, Miles."

He drew aside blue velvet curtains; he was in a room covered with a Chinese carpet at whose center was a dragon swallowing its own tail . . . at the other end of the room was an ivory screen with a relief of pagodas, rivers, mountains, bamboo groves, highlighted in peeling pastel paints. On the walls were masks: African tribal masks, Balinese Rangda masks with bulging eyes and long hair, Siamese opera masks with their tiers of crowned heads, carnival masks from Spain and South America . . . all were in poor condition, dusty, scratched, their paint worn.

Behind the screen, an old woman's cackle.

"Muriel?"

"After all these years, Stephen Miles!" the voice croaked. "Why am I behind this screen, you wonder. Am I afraid you'll see me as I am now? My once luxuriant red hair reduced to wisps, my face like a mottled old rag?"

"I really don't know. Why did you ask me to tea? How did you even know I'd be in London?"

"I am, Stephen, a practicing witch. Or had you forgotten?

What can I do for you in the eye-of-newt line, eh? A love-philtre, perhaps? Or you want me to put a hex on some enemy . . . Therese Benzineau, perhaps?"

Stephen Miles stood, shifting his weight from one foot to the other. Why do I feel like a little boy? She's a foolish old woman now. She's no longer pushing a frightened ten-year-old around. I've worked out all my guilt. She and Sir Francis Locke and Prince Prathna . . . they've no power over me now.

"Very well," she said. "Let us open up the mystic veils. Let us see the high priestess."

Stephen walked up and folded the screen in a single motion.

Staring up at him was a tiny woman in a wheelchair, tending a brazier on which a pot of liquid bubbled—the source of the unsettling odor in the apartment. She was in the process of sprinkling some dark powder into the pot. Behind her was an etagère stacked with parchments; yellowing skulls lined the top shelf and peered down at him. At eye level was a most curious thing: half a statue of some oriental idol. Just half, because it had been split, from head to toe, in a clean zigzag as if by symbolic lightning. The figure stood about six inches tall; the arm was outstretched in a posture of benediction, and the half-face was angelic, serene.

"What is that?" he said.

Muriel Hykes-Bailey cackled again. "We shall find out soon enough. I intend to find the other half, you know. It's from Southeast Asia, and it's extremely old indeed."

"Southeast Asia?" said Stephen. "It doesn't look Southeast Asian."

"It did not necessarily come from there originally," Muriel said. "The man I bought it from had some fanciful notion of its having originated in Persia, something to do with the dualistic fire-cult of Ahura-Mazda. Know anything about that?"

"Only that they worshipped fire," said Stephen, who had learned a great deal about the subject he feared and loved the most.

"It could have come to Asia with the soldiers of Alexander the Great . . . I think that if its missing half were restored it would be a source of great power. Real power. If you know what I mean. Though judging from your conducting—"

"I take it, then, that you're accepting Prathna's invitation."

"I am a witch, Stephen. I am dying. I sit in a wheelchair all day, mixing herbs. You'd be surprised at my customers. That Mademoiselle Benzineau, for instance—"

"What?"

"I do everything, my dear boy. I am . . . a charlatan, of course. But my dead husband's pension isn't quite enough, you know, with the cost of things in England. So I fiddle with ancient formulas to fool rich idiots. I do love-potions, as it happens. I also scry, prophesy—"

"What did you tell her?" Stephen shouted, as he began to suspect that he was the victim of a plot.

"Nothing she didn't know already. Listen!"

She pushed a button on her wheelchair. Music filled the room. Mahler Two. His own recording. "Don't you hear it? It's lifeless, Stephen, it's flabby . . . it has no fire, no fire! Fire! Fire! Ah, Stephen, have I said the magic word at last?"

It's true, thought Stephen. I'm not a great musician, am I? The Mahler welled up. He could hear now what he should have done. Here a little more urgency in the strings. Here a tiny rubato to let the melody breathe. Not this stiffness. I can't bear it, he thought. After all this time. They know it. They're pulling me into their trap.

"The pictures," said Muriel, holding out a skeletal hand.

He showed her Konrad Stolz and Timmy Valentine. She did not seem surprised at all.

"I'm afraid to go to see the Gods of Chaos again," he said.

"We are all afraid. But you must go. Because of this. And I must seek my idol. And we all, Stephen, must rekindle our hearts' fire once before we die."

He embraced her then, a cold, comfortless embrace.

huntress

From the mansion, music throbbed. Maria went outside to find Rudy. He was standing, as was his custom, beside the black limousine in the driveway. His shoes and his cap's peak were so polished that they flashed blue and red in time to the music and the light show in the house. Guests were chattering everywhere; one or two had come out onto the lawn. Tuxedos and new-wavers walked arm in arm, quaffing, smoking, and snorting.

"Rudy," she whispered. "Follow me. In the grove with the gravestone." He went with her.

"Perhaps you should have this." He fished in his cummerbund for a crucifix and handed it to her.

"Yes, of course. Quickly now! The guests aren't to see us."

The two hurried out to the center of the lawn. There were the trees that sheltered the Stolz grave marker with its statue of the singing angel. A ray of moonlight, piercing the foliage, had lit up—

"I knew it," Maria whispered. She held the small crucifix in front of her.

Sprawled against the gravestone was an obese man in a tuxedo. His collar had been loosened and his bow tie hung down on his shirt. A dribble of blood ran down his neck and onto the stiff shirt.

"We must act right away," Rudy said.

"Wait!" Maria went and touched the face, the body. "Come on, help me with the body."

Rudy was beside her. Together they began to tug the body into a manageable position.

A fat hand suddenly clawed at Maria's throat—

"My God! He's alive."

"He's drunk," Rudy said. In the moonlight, she could see the abstracted smile flit across his face.

"What are we going to do? Kitty's been at him."

"Not enough to change him, though. If she doesn't attack him again, he'll probably be all right. Come on, help me drag him back to this house."

"Will she go back to her coffin now?"

"I imagine she's sated for the night. A lot of alcohol in the bloodstream, though. She may not have liked the taste. That may be why he's—"

"Still alive?" How lucky I am, Maria thought, that my dead son is so considerate. He leaves messes for me to clean up, but not where other people might stumble on them. That's a good son for you. This Kitty Burns girl, now, she has no breeding. She's a slob. I wish Timmy had never brought her into the house, but, well, a mother suffers. . . .

"Well, woman," Rudy said, "help me. While no one's looking."

little lost girl

Look, Lisa thought, look, they're all around me, I'm actu-

ally inside a TV set now. . . . She was in a large reception hall,
no one shooed her away or told her to behave or threatened
her, a nice man gave her a drink from a tray, another nice man
gave her a puff of his funny cigarette—

She walked about in a daze. At the other end of the room,
Timmy was standing, so serious, only half-smiling, while
people crushed around him. She wondered if he could see her,
if he knew she was there and how they were going to be rich
and famous together. Many people were dressed really fancy,
but some of them were as scruffy as she was, like all the different TV people but all together, in one show, at once . . . she
saw someone who'd been in that shark movie and you see it
was true, she hadn't really been eaten up at all. Lisa went up
and smiled really widely at her, she didn't care about showing
her braces at all. She wondered if the woman remembered her,
because she'd watched the movie every time it came on so
maybe she saw her when she turned her back on the shark, she
would have had to see out the TV set, wouldn't she?

But the shark woman didn't say anything to her; her eyes
were real puffy like she'd had one of those pills.

Everyone looked so happy, they were laughing, and finally
she saw Timmy laugh too. . . .

There was another girl now, a bit older than her, dressed
real nice, an evening gown like the girls in the coffins in
Dracula movies, but she didn't recognize this one from a
movie. This one came up to her and touched her very gently on
the hand . . . her hand was cold, like the TV set when it hadn't
been turned on yet.

"I'm Kitty," the girl said. And she smiled. And Lisa saw
that it was a Dracula movie girl after all, because she had the
vampire teeth. So it must be all right. Lisa just hadn't remembered her because there were so many to remember.

The Dracula girl took her hand and wanted to take her
somewhere. But Lisa didn't want to go, she wanted to look at
Timmy.

"No," she said. "I think I'll stay here with all these happy
people."

The vampire girl didn't want her to stay. She said, "But I
want to show you something. Something really pretty. You
like pretty things, don't you?"

Oh, Jesus, she thought, that's what Daddy used to say when
he wanted to do it. Lisa knew you couldn't do that with

another girl, that was sinful and you'd go to hell for a million years. I'll keep myself for Timmy, she thought, I'll be a pure and good godfearing girl.

She knew it wasn't very nice to say no to the vampire girl, but she was very brave and said it anyway.

The vampire girl turned into a black cat and ran away into the garden. It was a neat trick but Lisa had seen it on TV, and she wasn't impressed.

huntress

Eric "Blade" Kendall wormed his way through the throng with a champagne glass in one hand and an album cover proof in the other. He found Timmy on a loveseat in one of the living rooms, flanked by starlets and groupies.

"I wanted to show you this," he said, affecting an easy manner although he felt distinctly uncomfortable around these people. He held out the cover; one of the girls oohed resoundingly.

Timmy took it from him and said, "Why do they always make me look like a vampire?"

"Well, the market experts say we should capitalize on that big hit of yours, you know. They think we can milk it for another album or two."

"What bloodsuckers!" said Timmy. A chorus of sycophantic giggles echoed him. Blade pushed some of the girls out of the way and sat down beside Timmy.

"I feel good about the summer," he said, idly fingering the razor blade in his ear, almost invisible against the splendor of his garb: blue velvet smoking jacket, wildly psychedelic cummerbund, and comic opera bow tie. "You'll start your tour in a couple of weeks, and then *this*'ll hit the stands, right at the climax, and we've got you on six talk shows."

"Oh, but I hate being on television. Some people think television is reality, you know," Timmy said abstractedly, as if he were remembering someone who wasn't in the room right then. "Of course I'll do it," he added quickly.

"Great. I'll tell them."

Blade hated kids. Especially kids with power over him like this. Pretty, androgynous-looking kids with pretty, androgynous voices . . . but there was no denying this one was different. He didn't know of another kid who would come right out and say he hated television. And there were times, too, when he seemed just so old. Made you nervous. But Blade knew what was hot, and he intended to climb to the top of Stupendous Sounds Systems by always knowing what was hot.

"Hey, Timmy, have a drink or a drag or something!" one of the girls said. "You haven't had anything all evening."

"I couldn't," Timmy said. "I'm just too excited, is all."

"What about?" Blade said.

"About my train. It just came UPS this morning. It's a Yamanote line local, from Japan."

"What are you talking about? . . . Oh, a toy train."

"Yeah."

What an enigma. Blade decided he'd had enough of Timmy Valentine. He got up; the bevy of interchangeable beauties closed in around Timmy again, hiding him from view. He turned his back on the giggling and started back toward the crowd, when a small cold hand tugged at his sleeve.

"I'm busy. Leave me alone. Wha. . . ?" He saw the girl suddenly. About sixteen or seventeen, shapely, and not at all interested in joining the cluster that surrounded Timmy.

"You're not . . . ah . . . a groupie?"

"No. I'm Kitty Burns. I like your razor blade. It's cute."

"Want to see more?" said Blade, who had been divorced twice and who never exercised his visitation rights.

"You're quick!" said Kitty. "Upstairs? I know a room—"

"Well, it's his house—"

"I live here."

"Oh. That's why you're not a groupie. Get you a drink?"

"I had something a little more exciting in mind."

She looked him in the eye. She wasn't that pretty, but she had a good body and he liked her insolence. The way she acted, she could have been plucked from the Boulevard or Times Square. Her small breasts positively jutted at him through a white Ralph Lauren shirt about a size too small. Her lipstick was an electrifying red.

"Well, I do have a lot to celebrate," he said. "Timmy's going to make me a fuck of a lot of money."

"Come on then."

"Where?"

"Upstairs. Do you dare?"

"Of course I dare! Tonight, anything."

She led him up some stairs. She held onto his hand; there

was something . . . creepy about the way she held it, and her hand was cold. Probably some kind of synesthesia, he told himself, from something I took tonight.

Then: a small closetlike room. Stone walls. Almost medieval-looking. A narrow bed . . . it almost looked like a coffin.

"Are you into anything . . . kinky?" said Kitty Burns, carefully unbuttoning her shirt and tugging at his bow tie.

"Like what?"

"I could bite you."

"Wait a minute."

Her jeans peeled slowly down her legs into a heap on the floor. She stepped out of them. She hadn't been wearing any underwear. Through the fog of drink and drugs, he was aware of his burgeoning erection. He touched her with the tip of his finger, as if afraid of electric shock. Cold. As if she were made of moonlight itself.

"Let me bite you!" she hissed, passionate.

"I can see it's going to be a tussle," he said, whistling as he threw off his jacket and tore at his evening shirt.

She touched his face. His cheek. His hair. She toyed with the razor blade that dangled from his ear.

"Hey, don't touch that," he said, starting. "You could cut yourself."

"I could cut you."

And she did.

And she put her lips to his neck and began to lick at the wound. Wow, he was thinking, what a kinky one! She was sucking harder now. This didn't seem like a game anymore. He was getting drowsier, drowsier . . . they sank down on the bed . . . the lights flickered . . . my god, are those fangs, are those . . . drowsier . . . drowsier. . . .

"Hey, I'm getting kind of sleepy, I'm not really *into* S&M, you know?" he was saying, but she went on lapping at him, and now he felt claws circling his nipples, carving concentric rings in his flesh, he was too dizzy to scream, he was getting drowsier and drowsier, like sinking into a coffin into earth into deep sleep. . . .

Later, at the limits of consciousness, he heard voices: "I think he'll live." "Well, Rudy, if he doesn't we'll just have to lay it down to an overdose of something." "That stupid, tactless girl!" the voices drifted out of his hearing. For a while longer he heard the sounds of the party, the clinking of glasses, the squeals of young women, a few dying strains of some repetitive minimalist new wave song. Then a lone voice: "Well, if he doesn't pull through, at least it'll make press, and it'll make Timmy some more press, and it'll sell more records than ever...."

lost little girl

The party is over. They have shown him the body of Blade Kendall. He has been very angry. He has wanted to drive a stake through Kitty's heart; he knows that this will kill her, because she is still young enough to believe. The belief in the stake, Timmy realizes, is like mortal children's belief in Santa Claus; it is a magic vampires cling to as long as they can, as if to keep at bay the bitter cynicism of immortality.

He has agonized over whether to allow Blade to reawaken. As far as he knows, the yanked-out heart, the severed spinal column, have always succeeded in allaying immortality where devices born of superstition have failed. He does not know. Can he live without Blade? Stupendous Sounds Systems can surely produce another executive.

He stands in the garden now. One by one they are turning off the lights in the house; though that makes no difference to him, who can see through the thickest darkness.

Rudy and Maria have brought him the body. They stand before him, their arms sagging from the weight. I am like a king now, he thinks, I can give this man death or undeath.

He shakes his head.

The body falls into the gravel of the driveway. Rudy goes away and returns with an axe. He hacks at Blade's head, but it is dark and the head obstinate. Blood is everywhere; seeping into the gravel. Maria has run into the house for a mop. Finally the head comes off. It rolls a little way onto the grass. Timmy stares at its eyes, glistening and lifeless as marbles. He is angry. If only Carla were awake, so he could pour out his anxieties to her. But she has long gone to bed; the party did not appeal to her.

Sickened, he walks back into the house. It is completely dark. He prowls about the living room, picking up a cigarette butt here, a spilled glass there, all in the utter darkness.

He hears a noise. He thinks it is a crying child. Where is it coming from?

Melding catlike with the darkness, he spirits himself past the two living rooms, through the capacious kitchen from which he has never fed, across a little covered walkway to the pool area. That was where it was coming from. Is it Kitty? He needs to reason with her, to persuade her that the household killings cannot go on.

No. He is under the dome of the swimming pool now. The water ripples a little, as if someone were stirring it with his feet. Far above, a shifting of clouds; there is a pallid moonlight now, and he sees the young girl sitting by the swimming pool, the girl he picked up in his car before, the girl who could not distinguish reality from movies.

"What are you doing here?" he says.

"Oh . . . " She looks up at him. He sees the adoration in her eyes, and is irritated by it. "I've been waiting, Timmy. I've been waiting, oh waiting, waiting. Oh, Timmy, I love you."

"Go away," he says. "Please."

"But you're going to make me rich and famous, aren't you, I mean after we do the daddy thing?"

"The daddy thing?"

"I mean," she says sweetly, *"fuck you bitch you tease you flaming pussy it's all your fault I'm a godfearing man but you'll lead me straight to hell flaunting your pussy at me you fucking bitch you fucking bitch—"* She utters the words without malice, without bitterness . . . she does not seem to understand them. But Timmy knows what has happened to her, what has driven her to this madness.

Compassion and hunger war in his mind.

"You have to go," he says gently. "You don't belong here, you see?"

The girl gets up and walks toward him. Timmy sees that she is sifting, in her mind, through the repertoire of scenes from movies that she knows, to try to find one that covers this eventuality.

"Take me," she says finally. "I'm yours."

"Please, no."

Suddenly, in a childish parody of a sexy voice, she says: "Look, here's the beach, here's the sea, let's go skinny-dipping, then the shark'll come, see? Look, the water. . . ."

"What are you talking about?"

"Come on, water's fine! Are you scared or something? Don't worry about the shark, it'll just be for a while, I'll be right back at midnight for the next showing now, won't I? Come on, come on. . . ." She is tossing her clothes away now. He sees her, pitifully thin. There is a scar across one of her breasts, as if from a belt buckle or a penknife; the moonlight has lit it up, and it wriggles, like a worm, as her breast moves. Her hips are thin; her pubic hair is sparse and uneven, as if someone had tried to hack at it with a knife. But she comes toward him grotesquely mocking some film star, undulating her hips and whispering . . . "Don't you want to? Come on, Timmy, come on, but you've got to take your clothes off too. . . ."

He balks at this. He remembers the summer camp, a dozen years ago, when he dared not expose himself to the boys, dared not risk their taunts . . . and yet he feels a strange kinship with her. Perhaps, perhaps. . . .

The moonlight brightens as the clouds drift farther apart.

Slowly he takes off his stiff white shirt and his dark striped pants. He turns to her, smiling a little. She has already slipped down the ladder into the deep end as he removes his underpants and folds them in a neat pile with the other clothes.

He knows what she will see. A slender, very pale body, not yet stretched out to awkwardness by puberty, the musculature only hinted at. Her gaze will fall from the haunting eyes down the smooth curve of throat and the line of chest to the firm, flat pubis, and—

She is laughing at him. He knows that she has seen—

"You've got no balls!" She is shouting. "I can't do it with you 'cause you've got no balls!"

Again the ganger. And remembered pain, pain from long before his changing, pain that has had two thousand years to grow in the remembrance. . . . "Yes. I am a eunuch."

"You're not really Timmy Valentine, Timmy's got balls, you're just a trick, I know because Timmy's going to do it to me so I'll get rich and famous, you've got no balls you squeaky you're like a girl where are your balls did someone cut them off?"

He cannot bear it. He leaps.

She is still screeching her taunts as he hits the water. Then she looks at him and sees him. She cries out "Oh, I'm sorry, it's the shark, the shark, oh, come to me, come to me—"

He bursts through the water toward her. He knows what she

has seen: a killer shark from a movie she has watched a hundred times. He feels his form shift, pliant in the power of the girl's terror. He is a force now. He cannot control it. It is she who controls him, who embraces him in a watery lovedeath fashioned from her most private fantasies.

His jaws open wide now, he has two hundred knifeteeth, she thrashes in the water, teasing his hunger and passion, and as she screams out in terror and desire he embraces her in his jaws. His teeth find a hundred soft openings in her flesh, the smell of chlorine is transmuted into salt and sea wind, her body twists again and again in a frenzy that feeds his bloodlust even more—

It is over. She shudders and grows still in his arms. The water is cold. It laps away the blood from his face, his lips. I should bequeath her life, he thinks. She has always been more part of this dreamworld than of her own. She belongs here. It was no accident that she found me, but a necessary conjunction of our universes.

He leaves the pool. He is still naked.

I must tell Carla about this, he thinks, before she concocts some outlandish complex from my summer-camp story.

He looks down at himself. The scars of castration are almost invisible now.

He feels pain. Once, he thought that the changing would drive away the memory, that he would never feel such pain again. But it returns to him, vivid. He tells himself: I have rejected mortality. That pain is no longer a part of me. I am the darkness now, only the darkness.

He covers his mutilated genitals with one hand, surprised that he can still feel this shame. Is he too much like the humans now? Was Kitty right?

Once more pain swoops down on him. It is no pain of eternity. It is a pain he never sought to remember. It is the pain and outrage of a human child, tied down to a table while a butcher hunkers over him with a paring knife.

No. Eternity is a slow, constant pain, a cold burning. This is a stab, overwhelming for a moment, then gone. Its transience mystifies him. But then he remembers that this is how humans always perceive their little pains.

For a single second, for the first time since his fiery death and undeath, Timmy Valentine has felt alive again.

analyst's notebook

I dreamed again. My nose was to the ground. I ran swiftly, knowing the patterns of fallen leaves, knowing the texture of rich dirt—

He has told me he is a eunuch.

I dreamed of—

He has told me that his castration was long ago, before he woke to the dark immortality.

I know the forest too well.

How can it be my own forest?

I am the analyst!

I am not the darkness—

little girl lost

Maria and Rudy stood at the pool area. The dawnlight fell through the glass roof on the water. Maria saw the body first: a young girl, naked, pale, floating face up. From her head a few streaks of blood, faint from the bleaching of the chlorine, radiated. In the faint light, it seemed like a soft pink halo around her face.

The corpse was smiling.

"Help me," Rudy said wearily.

"Yes."

They were both dressed in black.

"Shall I wade out, or will you?" Maria said.

"I will." Rudy started toward the shallow end of the pool.

They stopped.

A spasm racked the corpse's face.

"No!" Maria said.

A hand twitched.

"I have always told master Timothy that he should not have come here, should not have made himself so visible, so vulnerable," Rudy said evenly.

The whole body shuddered now. The mouth jerked open as if to utter a scream, but only a harsh whistle came forth, as though from a broken flute.

"What should we do?" said Maria.

"Tell the master."

"He is asleep. I've only just put him to bed. He is bloated and must rest."

Slowly, in an agony of rebirth, the corpse's eyes came open.

labyrinth

I am not the darkness!

little girl lost

. . . and came the hunger, ravening, blood-red, death-cold . . .

night-child

. . . and Timmy, open eyes bloodshot, lying alone in his mansion with his toy trains scattered on the floor around the four-poster bed . . .

fire

. . . and Stephen, in his hotel room, having fallen asleep over many glasses of vodka . . .

dissolve

. . . dream of fire.

dissolve

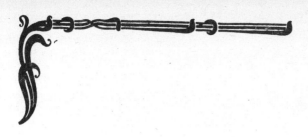

SUMMER

The Gods of Chaos

*I'll get on at the dark castle
You get on at the sea;
We'll crash headlong in the tunnel of love
And then there'll only be me. . . .*

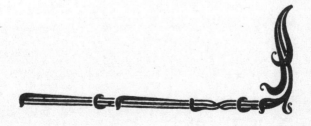

9

seeker

Around midnight, Brian Zottoli came down to the lobby of the motel. Rita was sleeping upstairs. He still hadn't had the heart to unload her, but he would once they got to L.A. Brian changed a dollar bill for four quarters at the desk and went to the tiny gameroom. There were only four machines, nothing really new either. He picked Defender at random, slid in the coin, and was just about to press the one-player-selection button, when he heard a noise.

There was a glass door that opened onto the pool area. Yellow light played over the water. Brian heard the noise again; like the crashing of giant waves, like the night wind from the ocean slapping against rows of empty deck chairs and unoccupied vending stands.

"What?" Brian said aloud.

He must be getting tired. Too long he'd been driving from town to town, flashing Lisa's picture, calling up his bastard of a brother with depressing news. He wished he didn't have to think at all. In a month his advance would run out and he'd have to write the fucking book and turn it in. He didn't need this. He decided to go back upstairs. He gave the arcade machine a friendly kick and started to turn away, when the noise started up again, louder . . . he went to the glass door. Was this a hurricane? Then why was the pool so still, why weren't the palm trees bending, why weren't there any sounds

107

of panicking people? Now the wind was whining. I should get
to the room, he thought. But he stood in place.

Slowly the pool parted. Veils of spray swirled above it. A
figure was rising up, moist, bathed in the cold chlorinated
light. A young girl, her wet hair plastering her sunken skull-
like face, her eyes catching the blue-green glow of antiseptic
water. She was naked but for wisps of seaweed draped about
her pubic area. One breast had an old white scar. Across the
whole chest was a row of gaping punctures, as though the girl
had been held in the jaws of some monstrous creature, and
each wound wept a dark reddish rheum, and blood-tears
spurted too from the crystal eyes. And the girl began to walk
to him across the flagstones, her hair streamed behind her in
that same wind that howled in Brian's ears.

"Lisa!" Brian whispered.

She did not seem to hear him. She came ever closer. He saw
that she was not really walking, she was drifting. Who had
done this to her? All his rage burst out. He'd always hated his
brother, even before his weird conversion and his kidbeating
and kidfucking, and look what had happened to the girl, his
own flesh and blood . . . Brian tried to open the glass door, to
go out to her, but he still couldn't move, the force still gripped
him.

Lisa was so close now. Why wasn't she breathing?

Her eyes turned on him at last. The muddy tears oozed on.
She did not blink at all. The gaping holes in her chest were bite
marks, he saw now, from a massive set of teeth. He'd seen
such a thing only once, in a movie on television. A shark
movie. Lisa couldn't *really* look like this and still be alive. . . .

The Lisa-thing's lips moved, strained themselves into a
rictus of a smile. And Brian saw that, in the bluish light, in the
unsettling immobility of her features, she had acquired a certain beauty; he had not remembered it in her before. Her skin
shone like the walls of phosphorescent caves, pallid, cold.

He opened the glass door.

A sweet-putrid odor in the air, like rotting oranges. . . .

"Lisa, what's happened to you? I've got to take you home
now, honey. I'm not going to let your father touch you again.
You can live with me if you want to."

"Back," came her voice; but not her voice, for her lips
hardly moved, and the voice was like wind that mimicked a
human voice. "Back, Uncle Brian. Don't ask me in, don't in-

vite me, don't . . . stay away . . . stay away . . . if you invite me I'll have to feed on you, Uncle Brian, don't you see I've become . . . a vampire girl like on TV . . . the shark came for me eating machine like I always said he would . . . Valentine Valentine . . . don't ask me in, Uncle, Uncle—"

"Of course I've got to ask you in." Brian thought: it's happened, she's finally been driven over the brink, she's mad at last. It had to happen. I have to take her upstairs, feed her, keep her warm, take her to a clinic or something. . . .

"Don't say the words!"

"Calm down, kid. I'm your Uncle Brian. I won't hurt you, Lisa. Remember, I'm the one who never hurt you before. Come on and—"

"Don't say the words!" The wind roared and he did not feel it.

He reached out to take her hand. Snatched it back. Icecold. A blanket. Kid needed a blanket.

"Uncle Brian. . . ." The voice was more rasping now, less human. "Leave, get out of this motel, go home, go home, don't you see, the only way . . . or get a stake, a sharp, pointy wooden stake and drive it through my heart and then it'll be OK and I'll come back and I'll be little Lisa again, I'll come out of the TV set and be normal Uncle Brian normal, find me at Valentine's, you know, like the song on the TV set?"

"No."

"I'm a vampire girl like on TV. I'm a vampire girl like on TV."

And Brian saw that from where she had emerged from the pool to where she stood there was a trail of blood, and that blood clung to her lips, and at the corners of her mouth there were sharp fangs, silvery, bloodstained. . . .

"I'm a vampire girl like on TV."

"I've got to help you, kid. . . ."

"Oh, help me, it burns, it burns, help me . . . oh, stab me, stake me, make me crumble, or I'll drink your blood . . . oh, Uncle Brian, I still love you for a few more days, I'm not all vampire yet, a little bit's little Lisa and Lisa's holding down the vampire girl, she's holding the fangs in, she's holding the hunger, don't you see, it burns, it burns, oh, stab me, stake me. . . ."

The stench of decay welled up—

Brian ran from the gameroom, ran to the elevator, fumbled

with the key, flicked on the light to see Rita lying on the bed—
Dead.

She was naked. She'd been waiting for him to come back so
they could make love again. Seaweed was stuffed into her
mouth, her ears, her nostrils, her vagina. Slimy, stinking
seaweed. Her neck had been torn open and a piece of windpipe
hung out of the wound like a tube from a vacuum cleaner. She
had no eyes; more hunks of seaweed clustered the bloody
sockets. Water streamed down the window that led onto the
balcony. He heard the wind again; then he saw Lisa standing
outside the window. She opened her mouth wide as if in
laughter, extruding an endless tongue of seawood that writhed
about her breasts like a nest of green snakes.

He knew better than to open the door this time.

"What am I going to do?" he shouted. "Christ, they'll
think *I* fucking did this!"

Salt water splashed his face. Where was it coming from? As
he looked at her she seemed to drift in and out of her familiar
shape . . . Jesus fucking Christ, was that a shark at the window, were they underwater, was he drowning? He stepped
back . . . dry land now.

"You *are* dead," he said. "And you've come back. With
your death still clinging to you. You're standing there in a
bubble of your private fucking reality, and you think you're a
vampire and a TV show and you're really nothing at all,
you're dead, you're dead—"

"The woman's dead too," Lisa said, "I'm sorry, Uncle
Brian, don't tell Daddy, I don't want him to hit me, Uncle
Brian, please don't tell on me."

"No. You're my niece. You're my blood, Lisa. I'll never
tell."

"Oh, and I'll help you. I'll clean away all the mess. Just run
away in the night, I promise there won't be anything here
that'll give you away . . . I'll protect you . . . just don't tell
Daddy, don't tell him . . . don't let anyone find me until I've
. . . come back through the TV screen, see, till I'm rich and
famous. . . ."

Brian found himself crying. He was surprised at himself. He
didn't know he could still cry.

"But you've got to promise me, you'll get the sharp stake
and you'll stop me going on and on and on forever, before the
vampire girl snuffs out little Lisa, you understand, Uncle

Brian? She didn't get killed enough, and she's scared, she's scared. . . ."

"Where will you be?" Brian cried out.

"Castle Valentine—"

"Where the fuck is that?"

"I love you, Uncle Brian—"

And she faded from the balcony. In a moment he saw a black panther spring from the shadow of the open bathroom door and begin to lap at the bloodstains on the bedsheets; then the creature bit firmly on Rita's wrist and tugged the corpse onto the floor and out onto the balcony and then . . . as he watched, terror-still, the black cat thing and the dead body began to shimmer against the yellow light of the atrium below, and Brian saw right through them, the chlorine-green of the pool rippling through Lisa's cadaver features, and then a fine mist that somehow still contained the twin points of burning, sunken eyes, and then . . . night.

Brian fled down the stairs, down to the parking lot, and drove away, tires shrieking.

dissolve

Sever the head, girl! Don't be all night about it, or she'll wake to the eternal cold. . . .

But she'll die, she'll never come back.

You stupid girl! In this new life you are an infant. You must learn, you must learn. Seize the neck, so. See how strong you are now. Twist it. Twist. Snap. A spine a twig, it'll all one.

It burns so . . . it burns so. . . .

The cold?

Yes.

That is eternity girl. You must not fear it. You must revel in it. You are forever dead, girl, and the cold is all you will ever possess . . . the blood will seem to give warmth, but only for an instant, and it will be but a dream of the remembered warmth, a ghost, a shadowlife . . . one day you will forget even why you hunger.

I'm scared.

I know. I am sorry I made you what you are. But even in the world of the living you belonged to fantasies, to dreams.

I don't like what I am!

I know. Look at you. Those wounds. You dreamed them up, you know. Will you need a coffin? I'll make sure and keep crucifixes away from you. . . .

It burns—

Holy water, too, I presume? If you could let Maria know precisely which horror movies you were exposed to, she can protect you from your own warped perception! She will help you now.

Uncle Brian—

He is a human, girl. Don't think of him. It will pass. But you mustn't attack people so viciously, just because they happen to have been sleeping with people whom, in your former life, you may have loved. That is vindictive, girl, and we don't do things that way here. Not in my house. Understand?

Yes, Timmy.

Good. Rudy will measure you for a coffin.

bluebeard's wife

When Stephen Miles drove into Thauberg it was already night. He had left Munich immediately after the Mahler rehearsal; though it was less than a hundred kilometers, the car soon left the Autobahn and made its tortuous way down country roads.

He parked on a cobblestoned sidestreet and crossed the Regentropfstrasse to the Wolfgasse, hardly more than an alley, where the Opernhaus stood. It had not changed in over thirty years. There was the genteelly baroque facade, the gold faded from the crowns of the Corinthian columns.

He pushed the heavy door open. Soft music . . . what was it now? Ah yes. Bela Bartok's one-act opera *Bluebeard's Castle.* He had conducted it himself back in America, both in English and the original Hungarian; here the words were German. He recognized the voice, even before he saw the playbill in the foyer: Amelia Rothstein. Yes. She had never deserted her home town, though she had become moderately famous. She sang in the Opernhaus Thauberg every summer. She had been here that summer . . . young then, voluptuous even.

Why did I come back? he thought. *She* of all people, *she* will remember Konrad Stolz, and I do not want to remember.

A wizened man in evening dress had emerged from a side room and was trying to attract his attention. *"Was machen Sie hier? Darf ich Ihnen helfen?"* he said. Stephen started. Were even the ushers still here after all this time?

"Wolfgang!" he cried. In the theater, strings murmured and woodwinds sounded the ominous minor seconds that symbolized the blood that ran through Bluebeard's castle, and he heard Amelia's voice, softly demanding of her husband the keys to his secret rooms, still innocent of the wonders and horrors they contained.

He dropped his voice, not wanting to disturb the performance. *"Wolfgang, kennst du mich nicht?"* he said in the German, flawed but tolerable, which he had picked up from his experiences conducting European orchestras.

The old man crowed in delight: *"Herr Miles! Herr Stephen Miles!"* I am so sorry, of course you must be seated, we have by chance a box empty, if you would follow me. . . ."

Wolfgang led him up, by a secret and circuitous route, to a box that overlooked the stage and afforded a good view of the prompter's box. Stephen looked about; the Opernhaus had changed very little. The blue velvet drapes were tattered as ever, and the main chandelier still swung precariously and seemed to have several bulbs missing. Only the audience was different, he thought, as he glanced across the orchestra seats and up the two tiers and the deserted standing room area. Most were in evening clothes, but some sported jeans and straggly beards, and in the front row there even sat two middle-aged punks with elaborate leather ensembles and huge earrings, avidly following a copy of the score with a flashlight.

It was . . . what was it, the fifth door? Light flooded the stage, and a verdant, mist-clouded landscape appeared by back-projection. Not a very sophisticated staging, Stephen thought. He decided to page through the program book. There were biographies of Amelia and of von Schlueck, the bass-baritone, with whom Stephen was not familiar. And . . . oh, an interesting newfangled touch: a Freudian analysis of the opera's approach to the Bluebeard myth, and . . . a note on Gilles de Rais, the historical Bluebeard—

. . . he distinguished himself at the side of Joan of Arc during the wars with the English . . . it was only after Saint Joan's burning at the stake that he became totally unrestrained in the practice of his perversions . . . he is thought to have killed at least two hundred children, mostly boys, in his castle, and in statements made to the Inquisition before he was himself burned at the stake he confessed to having masturbated while

*decapitating children, often while arguing with his compan-
ions and assistants as to which of the heads was the more
beautiful . . . he repented and was allowed the luxury of being
strangled before his burning . . . the tale of Bluebeard and the
murdered wives appears to be a fabrication or myth grafted
onto the historical figure. . . .*

Heavens, Stephen thought, opera program notes have certainly come a long way since I last conducted here!

The notion of the mad Bluebeard was disturbing. It dredged
up . . . other memories. He decided to concentrate on the
opera.

They had reached the seventh and last door. Amelia, as
Judith, had begun to question Bluebeard about his former
wives. Now she was accusing him of having killed them and
hidden them in the final locked room of the castle. The minor
seconds rang, spine chilling, through the orchestra. Resigned,
Bluebeard gave up the key. Judith looked up and saw Stephen
in the box; he waved. Misdirecting the audience's attention
with a flowing hand-gesture, like a classical statue, she blew
him a kiss and mouthed the words *später, später*, later, later.

He was hardly able to sit through the rest of the opera:
Judith learning that the wives were not dead at all, being
forced into the room herself to take her place among Bluebeard's eternal tragic memories. The production was rather
dull, the conducting uninspired, and Amelia a far more
wooden singer than he had remembered, with a repertoire of
about three gestures and three facial expressions: grimace
number one, grimace number two, grimace number three. The
voice was showing its age, too; he hadn't known that Amelia
had been reduced to taking mezzo roles, and even the upper
range seemed taxed here.

As soon as the final curtain fell, he left the box and found
his way backstage. In a moment Amelia Rothstein had rushed
into his arms and enveloped him in an overperfumed embrace.

"Schätzchen!" she squealed. "Oh, Stephen, I have missed
you! In thirty years I have perhaps bumped into you at a
cocktail party, but now you do me an unexpected honor! You
will stay at my house, no?"

"I hardly expected to revive our relationship—" Stephen
began, embarrassed, conscious now that a stage hand and the
prompter were eyeing the two curiously, but Amelia burst out
in a fit of giggles.

"Oh, you are so *komisch*, darling. After all these years! What I should have said was, Heinz and I and the children will be delighted to have you visit us. Heidi will be asleep, of course, but Hans and Toni and Kurt will be awake still, and my husband, they are naturally watching that amerikanische TV show, what's it called, *Die Engel des Charley*. . . ."

"*Charlie's Angels*," Stephen said, groaning at this sudden junction of the mundane and the exotic. Which was which?

"Come on. There's a new back way out."

Soon they arrived at a small house on the edge of town. In one room, several adolescent children and a dour man were watching television. Amelia introduced them, and then made coffee. Her domesticity amazed Stephen.

"You will spend the night?" she asked him as they sat in a kitchen hung with sausages. "We do have a guest room."

"Thank you."

"I heard your Mahler Two on the radio last week. *Westdeutsche Rundfunk*."

Stephen was grateful that neither of them had had the tactlessness to comment on the other's performance.

"Wolfgang, still here. I thought he was a hundred years old even then."

"Ach, he's indestructible. But you, you have a purpose here, no? I remember that driven look. How could I ever forget it?"

He reached into the pocket of his tweed jacket and pulled out the clipping from *TV Guide*.

She looked for a long time.

"Konrad Stolz!" she said at last. *"Aber er ist tot."*

"Yes, he's dead. And yes, I think it is him, too."

"He is quite dead. He is buried right here in Thauberg, I am sure of it, I was at the funeral."

"Have you ever visited the grave?"

"Of course not! You think I would not try to forget a little child of such . . . of such sexual perversity?"

He saw that she was trembling. "What do you mean?"

"Er hat mein Blut getrunken," she said in a whisper, to herself, so that Stephen could barely hear her.

"Did I hear that right?" he demanded. "Did you just say that the boy drank your blood?"

10

night-child

"OK, Timmy," Carla said, as Timmy eased onto the couch. "I'm going to try something new. Are you listening?"

"Yes."

"Hypnosis doesn't work. And we can't seem to tell if your dreams are really dreams, or whether your realities are simply concretizations of dreamstates, or whether your dreams are actually dreamifications of reality. . . ."

"My case is certainly going to create a lot of new jargon, isn't it?"

Carla laughed. "If my peers don't decide I've finally let go of reality myself." She sat down beside him. "So. Instead of sitting here and having you free-associate . . . I think we should play a game."

"Game?" He sat up now, regarding her emotionlessly.

"With the trains."

For a moment, she saw his eyes light up strangely.

"Have I ever told you about Vampire Junction?" he said.

"Not exactly."

"It's in Idaho. Maria bought it for me. It's going to be my secret castle, my hiding place."

"Yes?"

"There's a tiny railway station in the town of Junction. A night train passes once a week. There are some stores, a school, churches . . . forests."

117

She listened.

"Do you want to see it?" He got up and began to pace the room. He moved fluidly, almost blurring where the tall lamps made shadows against the couch and the armchair. "Come with me. Take my hand." She did. He led her from the room. Her heart began to pound when they reached the stairway that led to the attic. "No, it's OK, just stay close, and don't look too hard at anything. . . ."

The corridors now, forking and unforking. At first she saw only the hallways she had seen before. "Don't look too hard," he whispered urgently, "but remember every step, in case you have to find it yourself. Sometimes you'll seem to be walking backwards or sideways. The house will fool you with sudden vistas. Don't believe them. Feel. Know. This is the labyrinth of the unconscious, of many unconsciouses. . . ."

A window with a view of the sea . . . a scene from childhood? Suddenly, catacomb shelves with bodies that decomposed before her very eyes—

"Do not look!"

Four paces forward, three paces left, the third doorway—

Mirrors lurching into view, she saw herself being pulled by nothing at all, saw herself grow fangs and reach out to devour herself, and—

"Stop. This is the center. The heart."

A room. Mirrors. How big was the room? It seemed almost a closet. Wherever she looked the mirror walls loomed close, but she felt that wherever she didn't look the room might stretch forever. . . .

"Here. A secret chamber of the soul."

And the boy smiled at her. And now he was sinking into the psychiatrist's couch, the one from the room downstairs from her New York office, and yet she knew that it had always been *here*, too. "Magic," she whispered.

"No. Magic is illusion, Carla. Not magic, but truth. That is what you want from me, isn't it?"

"No! It's what you need me for, to draw it from you, to understand your own aloneness!"

A model railway track was snaking out from under the couch.

"We will play," said Timmy, settling back and smiling a disarming smile.

Go with the flow, Carla thought, desperately trying to cling to some illusion of control. "What first?"

"Look behind you."

She did. "Boxes, piled up."

"The top box. We'll open the top box together."

Pieces of track. "We'll build it together," he said.

"What about plugging it in? And the transformer?"

He opened another box. An engine lay in the wrapping paper, and he took it out and rubbed it on his T-shirt until it shone, then set it down on the track. "Here's the cord. I'll plug it in. And the transformer." They were on the wooden floor now, and he opened up a little trapdoor of some kind that disclosed some electrical outlets. "Here we go. Hurry up, join it all up."

She hesitated. "What sort of shape do you want?"

"Oh, any shape. I'll do this side. Here's a tunnel. And here—" almost an afterthought, she thought, admiring the subtlety with which he'd worked the therapy into the play, "is the first piece of the puzzle."

"Oh, the train shop in the Village," she said. "By the undertaker on Sullivan and Bleecker." She had walked past it on occasion. He tossed it casually to her. It was a handmade model.

"The owner made it for me. He's my friend," said Timmy.

"I get it!" she said at last. "And the next thing we're going to set up is the summer camp, right?"

"Pick a box."

She did. It contained trees, firs, mostly. "The forest," she said.

"We'll add to it later."

She began to arrange the forest on one side of the track, next to the couch. I'm actually enjoying this, she thought, an aging woman playing with toys. "Do you have the cabin?"

"Sure." He handed it to her.

"Now, Timmy," she said, as he touched a knob and sent the engine whizzing through the forest, "where shall we go next?"

A brief pause.

My God! she thought. Maybe I wasn't casual enough. He knows that I know that we're playing this game as a means to unlock his past, but maybe he's not ready, maybe I should have played along for a few more minutes, or even a few more sessions.

"We will go," said Timmy, and his voice became very faint, monotonous, almost as if he had fallen into a trance, "to Germany. To the town of Thauberg, which boasts a modest opera house. To the year 1947, when a youngish conductor named Stephen Miles—"

The illusion of control shattered.

"Stephen! What do you mean, Stephen?" She felt as if she was drowning. And then, grasping at straws, "You knew Stephen before, didn't you? Those visions he had—"

The boy vampire waited, idly hefting a plastic mountain from hand to hand.

"He wasn't having visions at all!" said Carla. "You weren't just seeking out a Jungian analyst! You had . . . other plans, sinister plans! You've always known that Stephen was my ex-husband, and—"

The boy put a finger to his lips.

"Is he in danger?"

He scrunched down and began to arrange inch-tall boys in summer camp T-shirts beside the log cabin beside the forest under the mountain. . . .

"I've got to know, Timmy. Is he in danger?"

"You still care for him, then?"

"I'm the fucking analyst, not you! It's none of your business!"

"Why do you persist in thinking that I am somehow manipulating you?" Timmy said sweetly, pulling an opera house out of a box and setting it down on the other side of the mountain. "We are both at the mercy of the unconscious, aren't we? You and I, dead and undead, shadow and self. Yes. Are we each other's shadow, perhaps? Or is it even more complex?"

"I have to call him."

"Of course. You know . . . " he looked at her, all innocence. "You know, in this story the word 'junction' seems to mean a thousand things."

memory: 1947

Thauberg is not like the big cities; it seems almost like a picture postcard of the past. He has prowled them all. He has witnessed the rubble of cathedrals. If he did not know it before, he knows it now: the power of the cross over him is broken.

He has found a childless war widow to take care of him, one Frau Stolz. She works at the Konditorei on the Wolfgasse, only a few doors down from the Opernhaus, and she lives in a small flat over the shop that she has rented from its owner.

On Sunday Frau Stolz makes her little Konrad go to mass twice. The church is farther down the narrow street, over a little bridge; it was built in the eighteenth century, and has for its altarpiece an unremarkable *Deposition from the Cross* by an unknown painter. The boy vampire does not like the name Konrad, but the widow is adamant as she introduces him to the priest. "You must forget your past," she whispers to him, bobbing a smile at someone in the congregation as they kneel in a front pew. "You are my son now."

He wants to ask her: *And what about your past, woman? If you are so keen on forgetting, why do you insist on this name?* He decides not to ask her who this Konrad was; he knows that he will hear some melancholy tale of a boy lost to some disease or to the war or to the corruption of the Hitler Youth, perhaps.

Her hair is bunned; she wears black, and a tasteful veil covers her face. She is not very old, perhaps in her early forties, but she has adopted her profound melancholy as a defense; even her taking in a street orphan is part of her new persona. She wears a muted, musky perfume. He can smell her blood through it; it seems sluggish, unappetizing. That is good; he does not like to feed on surrogate parents; it seems somehow ungracious.

He sees the choir through an incense-haze. The singers are elaborately cassocked and surpliced, but they do not sing well. They are struggling through a Palestrina motet: *Sicut cervus desiderat ad fontes; as the hart panteth for the waterbrooks, so longeth my soul for thee, O God.* . . . The boy remembers the music. He even, perhaps, remembers the first time it was ever sung.

He seems possessed. Quietly he begins to hum the soprano line of the motet. Frau Stolz turns to shush him, but he does not hear her. Instead his voice swells up. Startled, the kapellmeister looks up from his conducting. The choir stops dead in midphrase, and he is alone. He does not sing in the rather stilted style considered proper for church music; instead the music soars impassioned from his lips, and he seems to be reliving its very moment of creation.

The kapellmeister shakes his head, whether in wonder or disapproval the boy cannot tell, and then turns to urge the choir to cover the embarrassing silence, and now the motet picks up from the unbroken arc of the soprano line.

"Du singst aber so schön," Frau Stolz whispers, awed.

"I know," says the boy who is called Konrad Stolz.

"There is something strange about you. Are you . . . a changeling?"

"What do you mean?" Konrad says, afraid that he has revealed too much. "No. But . . . somehow I remember the music from my dead parents' house."

"You are not an ordinary street orphan."

"I don't know what I am," says Konrad. The two rise together for the taking of communion. When the line thins they kneel side by side at the communion rail. The boy sees that his new mother is staring strangely at him, when she thinks he is not looking.

"I thought you might be evil," she says afterwards. "But then you did not shrink from the Body of Christ."

"Evil?" He allows her to tuck him in, and dutifully kisses her cheek, trying to make the contact as brief as possible to spare her the burning cold of it. He knows that as soon as he hears the sound of her snoring he must coil into the shadows and slip out into the street.

"But how could you be evil, *mein Schatz*? You are only a small boy with an angel's voice."

As he lies there, unable to sleep, he is thinking: Perhaps she has a need for me to be evil. Perhaps this too is part of her persona of melancholia. She yearns to be what I am, though she is both more and less than I can ever be.

The next day he goes over to the Opernhaus. There is a visiting conductor, an American, one Stephen Miles. It is quite something, to have an American conductor on tour here.

At the facade the old usher, a man named Wolfgang, sees a young boy, neatly dressed in gray flannel shorts, a dark tie, and a matching jacket; his complexion is strangely pale. His hair is dark and zealously combed, with a perfect part on the left side. He smiles and sings out a cheerful "Grüss Gott."

The usher blinks; the boy is gone.

A rehearsal is in progress as the black cat slinks into the auditorium. They are running through Mozart's *The Magic Flute* for tonight's performance. The orchestra is working in shirtsleeves; the conductor is wearing clothes decidedly American in their loudness, and is speaking German rather poorly. To one side of the orchestra pit are some steps, shadowshrouded by the velvet drapes. He leaps up, his claws sinking into the soft fabric—

"Get that damn cat out of here," the conductor says in English. Something about the voice—

He is startled; for a moment his shape-control slithers from him. Has he been seen? No. He is behind some flats now: painted castle walls.

The conductor stops to say something to the orchestra. It is an adult's voice, but in it he hears a child's . . . he hears a softness, the edge of an old beauty . . . and he remembers Stephen Miles—

The boy facing him before the altar in the church with the bleeding woman and the smell of burning childflesh and bitter incense, the flailing sacrificial knife, the eyes of the child—

He yearns to make himself known to Miles. Miles, whose childish treble has haunted his memories for thirty years—

—but he does not know how Miles will react. The last time they had met in fear. Yet they had been kin. How else had the little boy seen him in his true shape, when all that the others saw was some private terror plucked from their own minds? He seizes control of his shape once more. He funnels it back into the cat. Avoiding the stage hand that Miles has despatched to shoo away the cat, he insinuates himself between two pieces of scenery, disliking the pungent smell of paint and canvas.

Miles says, "Amelia! Are you ready for the suicide sequence now?"

"Yes." A voice from the other side of the auditorium. And, through a crack in the canvas castle, Konrad Stolz sees Amelia Rothstein for the first time, walking down the side aisle towards the stage.

She is wearing a red dress, daringly short, and her long black hair has not been brushed. Her thin nose is in strange contrast with her ample breasts. She is in her twenties. As Miles waves for her cue, she is already singing. She flings herself onto the stage and carries on. In the story she, the ravishingly beautiful Pamina, will commit suicide because she has heard nothing of her dear Tamino and fears him dead. Her voice is good—nothing spectacular for one who has heard many great performers over the centuries, but acceptable—and she has a habit of compensating for her technical shortcomings by heaving her bosom distractingly at the orchestra stalls. The cat gazes upward at the flies.

Extraordinary! There are three little boys up there, frockcoated and powder-wigged, and each is perched on a little cloud! Why are they in costume? This does not seem to be a dress rehearsal. Perhaps they have just been trying them on. One of them has his wig on lopsided. They are peering down anxiously at the conductor. Konrad recalls the opera's plot: at this point, the three mystical boys will appear in order to tell Pamina that Tamino is all right, and she is to go and join him for the trial through fire and water. So this production has clouds dropping down from the flies, he thinks. Quite precious.

He watches Amelia Rothstein, and, in the strange way of his kind, he desires her.

He looks at Stephen Miles and knows that their fates are linked, and that somehow he must make himself known to him once more, he must understand why Stephen's gaze penetrated his disguise and his secret self. . . .

The three boys are giggling now. One is telling a dirty joke about the sexual performance of Americans; only the boy vampire's acute ear has picked it up.

He sweeps up the darkness around him. He leaps now, he transforms in the midst of soaring. He is a bat, flying from canvas cloud to canvas cloud. He is a crow, a raven, black hawk, tearing at the ropes with his talons, and—

A cloud snaps loose. A boy tumbles to the stage floor. The canvas castle shivers and collapses. Amelia screams.

A black cat runs across the stage, leaping over the boy, and in that moment ascertaining that he has died.

The screaming is general now. Old Wolfgang has arrived. A stage manager is protesting that the ropes were sound. The orchestra has gone mad.

The cat springs into the pit, toward the conductor's podium. Stephen Miles turns.

He sees a pale boy standing beside him, a compact boy with compelling eyes. They stare at each other, Stephen's mouth open in astonishment.

"Do I know you?" he says, too surprised to speak German.

The boy called Konrad Stolz is careful. He does not answer

in English; does not betray that he has understood Miles. He only says, very quietly, *"Darf ich für Sie singen? May I sing for you?"*

cemetery

She woke Stephen up with a kiss, her hair tickling his neck. "Where am I?"

"Thauberg, you silly old conductor," Amelia said, laughing. He rubbed his eyes; he had fallen asleep in an overstuffed armchair in the living room. "Don't you have a performance in Munich this evening?"

"What time is it?"

"Seven in the morning."

"But—"

She pulled him up. She was already dressed, in a well-worn calf-length floral dress. She had loosened her hair. "I thought you wanted to visit the cemetery before you left?"

"The cemetery. . . ."

Thauberg in the morning mist. They walked hand in hand toward the center of town, pausing for pastries at the bakery beside the Opernhaus.

A child's voice: *"Grüss Gott, Frau Eckert!"* and he remembered suddenly that her name wasn't Rothstein anymore, though he had hardly noticed the husband and the children the night before.

An alley overshadowed by gables that admitted only a thin line of light between them; the bridge; the stream; the little church. Ah yes. He remembered now. They went inside; he felt an urge to remind himself of the bombastic *Deposition* altarpiece. A priest was mumbling; two devotees knelt in the front pew. Selfconsciously Stephen genuflected and walked out.

Amelia took his hand now. "Now you will see," she said, and it was as if she knew, somehow, how he had been troubled all these years, "that you have nothing more to worry about. For a long time I too felt . . . yes, guilt, yes? Because of that strange boy."

Stephen lifted a gate-latch still wet with dew. Gravestones now. "It was at the far end, wasn't it?" he said.

"Yes. You know, Stephen, the day after that . . . accident, when the child fell and broke his neck . . . do you know, I met that Frau Stolz in the Konditorei, and she ordered me to beware, she lifted that veil of hers and said, '*Er ist übel, mein Kind, übel!*' And I said, 'What do you mean, evil? He is only a poor orphan whom you are rearing, and that is quite admirable, of course, but what is this *evil*?' And I said also, 'You should be proud of him, he has a beautiful voice, and Herr Miles has selected him to replace the child who died in that unfortunate accident, broke his neck.' "

Stephen clutched her hand tighter. He wanted her to stop talking, but he knew that he could bear the silence even less. They walked by mossveined gravestones that leaned against a white fence where a horse was tethered. Ahead was a line of mistveiled oaks. "Behind those trees," he said. And he added, "I think." He didn't want her to realize how clearly he remembered the funeral. The two mourners, the unweeping mother, stalking away into the rain. . . .

"And you know what she said?" Amelia went on. "She said, '*Das war kein Unfall.*' And I said, 'Of course it was an accident, my dear Frau Stolz. Why, my dear, you have become quite morbid since your husband and child were killed. But the war is over and we must begin again. Perhaps you think that because the conductor is an American, that some sinister force is involved, but my most respected Frau Stolz, we cannot help what we are, *nicht wahr*? I have heard the boy sing. He's an angel! Why, if his adult voice is anywhere near as good as this, he should have a formidable career.' And Frau Stolz said, 'I wish he were dead.' "

"He did die."

"Yes."

They reached the oak trees. Stephen knew what he would find there: two or three immaculate graves, among them that of Konrad Stolz, adorned with a statuette of a singing angel. He himself had given a little money for that.

"I'm glad he died," Amelia said. "He was quite mad."

"Mad?"

"And you know, if Frau Stolz had not spoken such words to me, if she had not tried so hard to sound like an oracle or one of those prophetic gypsy women in operas . . . " She laughed a little. "If she hadn't made me so *angry* at her macabre superstitions, I would never have taken such an interest in the boy, you know."

Idly he began to read the inscriptions. Yes, it was much as

he remembered it. He read them off. *Stefan Koenig, Joachim Hassler, Christa Stockhausen. . . .*

"And of course, if I had not taken it upon myself to look after the boy, I would not have discovered his . . . perversion."

There was no grave of Konrad Stolz.

"It's not there," he whispered.

"Why, of course it's there! It's probably somewhere else in the graveyard."

"It's not there!" he shouted, hysterical.

"Come now, Stephan, you're acting as lunatic as that Frau Stolz."

On his way back to Munich, just before reaching the Autobahn, Stephen Miles pulled off the country road and set a small haystack on fire.

11

witch

Muriel Hykes-Bailey's arrival at Prince Prathna's leafy palace was a quiet one; one evening, as Francis Locke and the prince reclined on silken cushions in the pavilion, being fanned by tireless attendants, Prathna looked up from his rice and fiery condiments to see a wheelchair propelling itself down the garden path. A white-haired woman wrapped in a blanket lifted a hand in greetng.

"I say, Prathna, you old rascal! And you, too, eh, Francis!" Prathna snapped his fingers for one of the servants to attend to her.

The wheelchair clattered on the priceless wood of the antique pavilion.

"But my dear Prathna—the eighteenth-century wood—the score marks of the wheelchair—heavens, aren't you going to stop her?" Sir Francis exclaimed.

"Oh, rubbish, Francis," cried Muriel. "Prathna doesn't care about anything anymore. Certainly not about a few million pounds' worth of damage. We've bigger fish to fry, haven't we, Prathna?"

She has not aged gracefully, Locke thought, trying to associate the ravishing woman of 1918 with this rodential creature. He got up to plant a wet and feelingless kiss on her forehead.

"Ah, quite the aging beau," Muriel said scathingly. "But

Prathna, I've brought my things."

"Oh?" said the Prince, scratching his domed head. "You mean, your instruments of magic, and all that nonsense of yours?"

"Oh, the dead newts and things, you mean? Well, I had a devil of a time with customs over those. I'm glad you had someone meet me at Don Muang. But I thought we might need this, too." She pulled a package from the blanket, and when Locke took it from her she seemed even tinier than before.

"Come into the house, my dear Muriel," said Prathna, "and we'll examine it. Shall I push your wheelchair?"

"I prefer to propel myself, thank you, Prathna."

"Ah, one of those . . . liberated women. How charming."

The three of them, with their retinue, followed the path. The prince unlocked a room Sir Francis had never seen before, and they went inside.

On the walls were murals, painted in the two-dimensional Siamese fashion; Locke had seen such things in the tour of temples and other sights that Prathna had insisted he take. But these were not scenes from the *Ramakien*, the Siamese epic poem; they depicted the torments of hell. Here were people being boiled alive, burned, baked, castrated, gutted, flogged, and sliced; demons such as Locke had seen guarding the temples presided over them. Nine tiers of fire encircled the mural; above the door was painted a pavilion, much like the one in which they had lately been ensconced, in which sat various deities, gesticulating at the spectacle of torture and despair like Roman nobles at the arena.

"Do you like it?" said the prince, grinning proudly. "I used to use it for flagellations, in the days when I . . . ah . . . indulged in such pleasures. A rather popular subject for murals during the Ayuthaya period. I had the whole thing peeled off a monastery outside Chiengmai, you know, in the north of Thailand. Heavens, though, how dusty it's become!"

Locke noticed, then, the manacles attached to the walls. The prince flicked on a few more lights, and pressed a button; Locke heard the whoosh of air conditioning. "We wouldn't want to be without our creature comforts, eh, Muriel, Francis?" He indicated some chairs that had been placed within a mosaic-stone pentagram. There were five identical rattan chairs, one at each point of the pentagram.

"Oh, I say," said Francis, floundering once more.

"For the Gods of Chaos," Muriel whispered. "Why Prathna, this is marvelous!"

"There aren't five of us," Sir Francis protested. But he already suspected the answer to that.

"My dear fellow," said the prince, "though it is true that there are six or seven survivors of our youthful escapades, it is also almost certain that some of us will die before this is all through! Eh, what?"

"I think perhaps I'd better go home," said Sir Francis.

"Coward!" said the prince.

"Come now, Francis old thing," Muriel croaked. "You love the appurtenances of evil."

He looked around him at the walls. Here a man was being flayed alive by a demon; several already skinned people lay in a heap, where a demon prodded them; another, having squeezed himself into an ill-fitting human skin, was dancing as he clawed at his writhing captives with long, curved finger-nails.

"It's very atmospheric," he said weakly.

"Of course it is!" said Muriel. "And now, open the package."

Locke did so. Then he set its contents down on the floor, in the exact center of the pentagram.

It was half an idol, sheared by a jagged line. The face of an angel. One radiant eye; a blue gem of some kind. Half of a serene smile. It was bronze, greenish with age.

"I bought it at an antique shop in London," said Muriel. "I was told that it came from hereabouts."

"Well," said Prathna, peering at it with beady eyes, "I don't recognize it as an artifact of the Siamese historical periods, but of course I shall have it looked at. Why did you bring it?"

"I rather thought, Prathna, I might be able to find the other half. I think it would be quite something then. An object of great psychic energy."

"What makes you think so?" said Locke huffily. "None of your other mumbo-jumbo has ever worked."

"None of it, eh? What about the apparition in College Chapel, sixty years ago, my dear Francis? That's what this reunion is really about, isn't it? Let me tell you, my friend. I buy many antiquities; I have them around the flat in order to strike dead the minds of my clients—not that I really believe in the psychic auras and things, mind you. But when I bought this, Prathna and Francis, I seemed to hear a voice—a child's voice, singing."

"The febrile imaginings of a self-deluded old woman," said Locke uneasily.

"Let her finish," Prathna said calmly.

"That night I dreamt of you. I dreamt of all the Gods of Chaos. The contents of my dream were . . . intimate. I was young again, and naked. I was in a jungle. You were all there: you and Prathna and the others . . . also young, also naked. And all of you had sexual intercourse with me."

"Heavens!" Locke exclaimed, remembering briefly the one night Muriel had spent in his Cambridge rooms, drinking port on the sheepskins in front of the fire. Sweat broke out on his forehead. "What then?" Prathna was clearly enjoying his discomfiture.

"At the moment of climax, I seemed to be sandwiched between the two halves of statue. And then, as it crushed me, I looked into the eyes of the apparition, and it was a wolf and a panther and sometimes a child, and it wept."

"You have gone mad, my dear," said Locke.

"I've had the dream constantly now for several years. And then I saw Stephen in London last week, and he showed me some pictures."

"Of what?"

She produced two xeroxed pages from beneath her blanket and handed them to Francis.

"The creature in my dream bore a certain resemblance to this."

Sir Francis Locke took the proffered sheets. One was a page from the American *TV Guide*; the other, a scene from some opera in which three little boys on clouds dangled from the flies. Looking from one to the other, he gazed at the image of Timmy Valentine for the first time. "I don't understand," he lied.

"You will," the prince said.

Muriel Hykes-Bailey shrieked, theatrical witch's laughter.

And around them, garish in the flourescent lighting, danced the flames of hell.

analyst's notebook

Putting together the model trains is quite helpful. It gives him something to concentrate on. But there's a certain point beyond which I think things will get harder.

I asked him about Blade Kendall, the man from the studio. He told me that the body had been disposed of, and that, since he's well known to be a flake, they won't even miss him for a while.

"And after a while?" I asked him.

He said, "I am beginning to suspect, Carla, that the end of my rock and roll career may be drawing near."

Well, where the fuck does that leave me, I wonder?

He always says, "You will be taken care of."

The room upstairs, the one with the mirrors and the trains . . . it seems to grow a little bigger every time we go there.

Does it represent his . . . his self? As he reveals more and more of it to me?

I said to him, "What about mirrors? Garlic and crosses don't work, but you're still not 'real' enough to fool a mirror?"

He said, "I *am* a mirror. When people look at me they see themselves. It is not necessarily a part of themselves that they want to recognize, but it is there." He quoted Shakespeare to me, *The Tempest*: "This thing of darkness I acknowledge mine." Then he said, "Prospero says this of Caliban. You see, he must face the monster in himself before he can leave the island, which is as much a creation of himself, of his own need to flee reality, as it is of nature."

I remarked that this was an extremely classical Jungian interpretation of Shakespeare, and he only beamed at me, like a pupil when his favorite teacher praises him.

Then I asked him: "What do *you* see in mirrors?"

"I see myself."

"Do you see *me*?"

He thought for a long time about it. Then he said, "I don't know."

I thought: We are one another's shadow, then. If I, as his analyst, make him face, acknowledge, and absorb his shadow, that process will inevitably happen to me, too, won't it?

Are there other people in our lives that have these links to us? What about Stephen? It was Stephen who started all this.

Timmy has told me about Stephen the choirboy in 1918. I heard something about it from Stephen, but I thought it a dream. Timmy tells me that he thinks Stephen may have seen his true shape.

That means he wasn't a mirror, doesn't it? I seem to be toying with the pivotal concept of all these events. But I am too afraid to probe. Instead. . . .

Instead, tonight, I'll ask him to finish telling me the story of Thauberg. I'll put off the moment of truth for a while, whatever that may be.

memory: 1947

After the opera Konrad Stolz comes to Amelia's dressing room; for a week now he has been coming to her. A low-budget repertory opera company must be very versatile, and so is Thauberg's; Amelia has appeared not only as Pamina in *The Magic Flute*, but in *Tosca* and as understudy in Cherubini's *Medea*. Konrad has managed to find roles in all three of these. In the Mozart he is one of the three little boys popping down from the clouds; in the Puccini he plays a shepherd boy, who sings a charming rustic melody in the last act, before the carnage of the finale; in *Medea* he does not sing, but has wangled an extra's role as one of Medea's children, in which he is alternately caressed and thrown about the set and finally gruesomely butchered by his own mother. He enjoys playing dead, and indeed, Herr Miles finds time to praise him for being able to keep still for half an hour without even seeming to breathe. ("It seems to come naturally," young Konrad told the conductor, and smiled one of his inconstruable smiles.)

Now he waits once more. He is hungry; before the opera he has fed on the blood of a stray cat. It has no taste.

He has never fed on Amelia Rothstein, but he is drawn to her. Perhaps by the way she smiles at him, her lips half-parted and moist from her favorite lipstick, scarlet as hot arterial blood.

"Come in."

He turns the doorknob. She is sitting in front of a mirror in an ornate gilt frame of cupids. The lights are off; the room is half-lit by candles set in a silver swirl of dolphins and putti.

She does not see the door open; this is good, because he has a chance to slip quietly over to a corner of the room away from the mirror, where a purple velvet drape conceals the peeling wallpaper's repetitious larks and peacocks and twist-twined vines.

She says, "Who is it?"

"Konrad."

"Oh. You are so silent, dear boy. Like a cat." She turns. The Egyptian gown that she wore to play the role of Pamina is half-off; one breast is exposed. "Oh, I am sorry, I should not let you see . . . " In mock shame she covers herself, but he has seen her hesitation, her embarrassment mingled with desire.

"Do you have any errands for me, Fräulein Rothstein? I . . . came to ask."

"Oh, you are so charming. Come sit by me." He waits until she has completely turned away from the mirror before he complies, and he sits down on the bench. She is wiping the last remnants of makeup from her face; her left eyebrow is still swathed in deep blue eye shadow, and a line of mascara runs from the corner of her eye halfway down her cheek. "I have no errands," she says. "But tell me, Konrad, why do you wait for me every night? Are you afraid a young man will come snatch me away?"

"Du bist hübsch," he says. It is daring of him to use the informal *du*, for she is a lady, a *prima donna* at that, and he is only a child.

"Really? You think I am pretty?" she says. She seems concerned. "You're an orphan, aren't you?"

"Yes . . . Amelia."

She blushes. "How strange. Sometimes I think you're so much older. Almost like . . . a grown man. I wonder why that is." She lets her robe drop a little again, so that he can see the outline of her breasts. Her uneven breathing makes them shiver. They seem warm. Beneath them he hears her heart. She says, "It's because you have grown up unloved, alone, isn't it?"

"You do not know how true that is."

His lips twitch into a half-smile. They are silent, but he cannot avoid hearing her heartbeat. In his own way, he loves her; but he has the shape of a child, and the power to procreate was shorn from him even before he became undead. He knows that he can never know her sexually. And yet she flirts with him, a child.

Tenderly she begins to stroke his cheek. She is whispering, "Why, Konrad? Why do I feel this attraction?" He labors to retract the caul of cold that clings to him, and still she feels it and her fingers stiffen for a moment. "Have you been outside, dear Konrad? Surely it is not so cold. It is summer."

"Summer."

The hunger hones itself to the beat of that heart. "Why does Frau Stolz say you are evil, Konrad?"

"Evil? What is evil?"

She smothers his face with her hair. She loves me, he thinks, she has compassion for me. Love and hunger play tug-of-war in his mind. "Evil is what we are doing now, isn't it?" says Amelia. "I mean, a voluptuous young woman and an immature child. Do you know the facts of life? But of course you do. I am sorry. You came from the streets."

He begins to understand her. She is curious about him because he has been a wild child, a piece of rubble thrown up by the war. She disdains his origins, but this disdain only heightens the piquancy of her feelings for him.

"I know what sex is," he says firmly. And he unlaces the bodice of her opera costume. "But I am not capable of it." He does not tell her why.

But there are other things we can do," she says. She takes his cold hand and slips it down the dress, past her cushiony abdomen. Wonderingly he traces the wrinkled lips of her vagina . . . there is blood there and his hand shakes as pleasure and terror shudder through her body. . . .

"Can I lap it up? Like a cat?"

"I don't know, I had no idea you were so . . . experienced . . . " But she does not resist the touch of his tongue, silver-cold at first, but quickly warmed by the dark blood. "You little vampire," she says fondly.

"Yes. That is what I am." She does not, of course, believe him. He lets his agile tongue dart deeper, probing for more menstrual blood, and the special warmth of the moonblood floods his senses like a bath of fire . . . he clasps her tighter, he has scratched her just below one armpit, and the smell entices him, draws his head higher, so that now he moves against her navel, now he brushes her breasts with his nose, and she feels the moving prick of cold, and his mouth finds the wound and he sucks at it, considerate always that he must not let his fangs out, must not hurt her too much, that he must protect her from the final cold. And she looks down demurely at him, child clasped to her bosom, an obscene madonna and child, and he knows that she has seen the red rims of satisfaction around his eyes, but she says nothing, she is awed and shamed and in the throes of orgasm all at once . . . he is glad that she, perhaps unwilling to admit to herself the fully sexual nature of her desires, has not tried to touch his penis. He does not want her to find out about his mutilation. No. He wants only this . . . love he must call it, this fragile momentary junction in the lives of two alien creatures.

She sleeps now, lulled by the rhythm of his lapping, drowsy from the loss of blood. I must not kill her, he thinks, I must not.

Sadly he pulls away. He looks in the mirror and sees a shadow's shadow over the long dark hair and pale body of Amelia Rothstein. He covers her loosely with the costume, and licks clean the wound in her side.

Then he opens the door and slips out through a network of passageways to the stage door, on the Zuckerbrotgasse, and alleyway behind the Wolfgasse.

It is dark. Frau Stolz is standing there, still wearing her veil and her black dress. "Where have you been, child?" she scolds. "I should never have adopted you. What have you been doing, you causer of accidents, you witch-child?"

He says nothing; he merely smiles.

She says, "And there is blood on your mouth, Konrad! You terrible child, what have you been doing?"

12

little lost girl

Rudy, it's five in the morning! Almost dawn! Why do you insist on driving out of town to this beach?

You have to see this.

What?

You will see, master Timothy.

Slow down, then. We don't come here very often, do we?

No.

I see. There's a pavilion, stretching over the sea on concrete stilts. It's windy. Will he have to get out?

No, master Timothy. You will see what you have to see. It is better that you don't get out.

But you're driving right onto the sand!

There now. Do you see it?

Just a row of poles or pikes, sticking out of the wet sand. The tide has almost reached them. They've got some kind of rubber masks dangling from them. Some kids' prank, probably.

Look again. I'm driving over to them now.

They're not masks!

Human heads.

They're all pale and puckered, as if someone had drained their . . . I see blood dripping, beading on the sand beneath . . . the stumps are staunched with seaweed that trails the stakes like the ribbons of a maypole . . . what horror is this? Rudy, you know I didn't do this! I would never do this!

I know. Nevertheless, someone has done it. And this is not the first time.

You have seen others?

No. But I have heard reports. When I agreed to serve you . . . I didn't realize there would be others, Timmy.

When you call me Timmy and not master, Rudy, I know you're not playing games with me anymore. But who *has* done this?

You know.

Seaweed crams their mouths, a salty bouquet . . . some have no eyes, but seashells modestly conceal their sockets . . . a crab is scurrying about in the matted hair of one . . . a paste of blood and sand smears another's face like macabre stage makeup . . . five heads in all . . . they seem to be young people, those who crowd the beaches all summer long with nothing to do . . . where are the torsos?

Buried, I think. Mangled beyond recognition. One was found in Venice last week. Another yesterday, in Redondo Beach. She loves the sea; she fancies, I think, that she died in the sea; and so she haunts the seasides and kills there. Hideously warped her mind is, even in death; but in her own way she is a poet, and these grisly memorials are samples of her art.

Lisa!

Even in her coffin the sea clings to her.

We've got to stop her.

It can easily be arranged. She is at the stage when the stake in the heart is still a viable solution.

You think I should command the death of one of my own kind?

But she jeopardizes *you*, Timmy! Everything we've worked to create, this rock star persona, this mansion, this career Maria and I have struggled for . . . she's jeopardizing us, too, you know. Look at those heads in the sand. How long do you think it will be before some clue is found that will link the murders to a certain mansion in the San Fernando Valley, master Timothy?

At least she's cutting off the heads. She's not giving birth to dozens more of our kind.

Still—!

Containment. That's what we must have. When she comes back, cover her corpse with garlic. Stick crucifixes on all the exits. She won't die, but she'll have to stay put. You or Maria can feed her out of my own kills, or we can find bottled blood or something. It's not the same thing, but it'll stop this for a while.

For how long? Until she begins to learn to conquer her fear of garlic and crosses?

That will be many years. It took me hundreds of years.

But when you had to cope with them, Timothy, there was far more faith in those things. She's only fighting her own misconceptions and superstitions now, not the combined beliefs of millions of people. You don't know that it'll still take hundreds of years to get over the fear of garlic.

Kitty is still afraid.

But you yourself have told her not to fear, and Maria must now actually bring the cross up to her face to control her. These are all only temporary measures.

You're advocating murder!

And this . . . this isn't murder?

Don't mock me. It is not murder to kill an alien species.

Alien? I thought that psychiatrist of yours had proved that you're not alien; that you're an integral part of us . . . our shadow!

Don't force such conflicts on me! Do you think you're immune to my attack?

. . .

I'm sorry, Rudy.

. . .

I shouldn't have said that. You are my friend.

Shall we go now, master Timothy?

Yes, but—oh, Rudy, I must ask you this, because a terrible time is coming, I can feel it deep inside . . . dozens of lifelines and deathlines hurtling towards the same junction . . . oh, Rudy, do you love me?

. . .

Do you love me?

Since when have you needed love, master Timothy? Are you turning into one of *them*?

I am afraid of that. Compassion, Rudy, is a terrible thing for a vampire to feel.

fire

Stephen had four hours; he decided to go for a stroll on the Bayreuth grounds. There were certain advantages in the Bayreuth tradition of having very long breaks between the acts of the Wagner operas; the audience, of course, could take meals or simply recover from the opera house's hard wooden seats (for Bayreuth was a shrine, and comfort had not been particularly high on the list of priorities for its construction); and it was good not to have to take the final act with your arms feeling like solid lead.

He felt grateful, too, for Bayreuth's covered orchestra pit. Ordinarily he'd have been peeved at not being able to exert full control over the singers, and especially irritated that the audience might not see him and lionize him properly. But now he preferred anonymity. His face was not too familiar to German audiences (or indeed, he reflected, to any audiences), and he was in any case replacing someone else, so nobody paid any attention to the wiry old man as he came down the wide side steps of the red brick monstrosity that was Bayreuth, down to the lawns, where people were already milling about. Stephen Miles was not recognized. Or was he? Occasionally, as he passed a small group of people, they would fall silent for a moment. Was it disappointment, that the ersatz Wagnerian conductor they had brought in at the last moment was not up to snuff?

A pretty little student tugged his arm. An autograph. He obliged offhandedly, then stalked off in the direction of the fewest people.

An old woman now. Wearing black. With a veil over her face. "Herr Miles—"

"I'm busy. I have to meditate before the last act. Sorry."

That was what he should be doing. After all, the final act of Wagner's *Götterdämmerung* encompassed nothing less than the destruction, by fire, of the entire universe. It was seeing Valhalla burst into flames at the Met, in his late teens, that had first drawn him to Wagner.

"Herr Miles, do you not remember me?" She lifted her veil and threw it back over her black, feathered hat.

So old, though . . . she had seemed ancient even then . . . "Frau Stolz!"

"Forgive me for continuing in German," she said, and went on in that language. "I heard you were in this country, and I could hardly miss one of your performances, after all these years." She did not smile. He knew that she wanted to talk about Konrad, but she did not mention his name. He decided to get it over with.

"I visited your son's grave, Frau Stolz, in Thauberg. You are no longer living there?" he asked her in German.

"No, in Munich." She led him away from a crowd of matrons in flamboyant attire, all screeching their appreciation of the opera and belting out the *Redemption by Love* theme from the third act. She took his hand now. They passed a thicket of rosebushes, set off by a marble sundial. "I heard your Mahler on the radio, and found out the date of your Bayreuth appearance. You say you saw the grave?" she added, eyeing him suspiciously.

"No. It was not there."

"I knew it!"

"You've not been back to Thauberg, then, in thirty years?"

"No!" she said, a trifle quickly. "I have been . . . sick."

"Yes?" he said, trying to show concern, although in truth all he wanted was to escape from this maddening woman. Even thirty years ago she had made herself a thorough nuisance, with her doom-laden pronouncements about young Konrad's satanic origins.

"More than sick, Herr Miles. I was in a mental home."

He pitied her then. He too had known what those places were like. He remembered it . . . the place they'd sent him to, to treat his pyromania . . . only Carla Rubens had seemed to understand him. And now she didn't understand anymore.

"You seem sad?" said Frau Stolz. Still no emotion.

"I too have been . . . mentally ill."

"I am well now. I had to see you. I wanted to tell you something—"

"Where is your son's grave, Frau Stolz?"

"He has no grave. He is not dead."

"But I saw him . . . the chest-wound . . . didn't someone try to stab him with a sharpened chairleg? Most bizarre," Stephen said uncomfortably.

"I did it! *I!*"

He backed away.

"I did everything I could. I first tried garlic and crosses, but he did not fear them," she said, relentlessly backing him against the rosebush.

"What superstitious twaddle! This is the twentieth century. . . ." he said, trying to fight off his own terrors.

"I had to do it. I sharpened the chairleg. I crept up to him in his sleep. Do you not understand? He had blood on his mouth every night, when he came home from the Opernhaus. Do you think I didn't know what he was doing to that Fräulein Rothstein?"

He tried to dodge her now. The squealing matrons were on the other side of the bush, and Frau Stolz clutched his arm and said, "I took to following him. He was a devil child! I wanted only to help someone after my own was shot in the war, but no . . . I received no decent child for my pains, but a vampire!"

"A vampire. . . ."

"I it was who killed him . . . afterwards I claimed to have done it, they took me away, they confined me to a mental hospital, and the psychoanalysts said it was a delusion, an accident, a senseless murder by a madman, there had been other cases in the town, severed necks and stakes through hearts, and I said it was Konrad who had done them and they gently persuaded me it was not so . . . they traced my childhood and found traumas I never knew existed, and they convinced me and released me from the asylum. . . ."

"I must go."

"He is alive and you must kill him! You are the only one who might believe me. I implore you. Kill him, Herr Miles, kill him!"

"Frau Stolz—"

But she was walking away from him, across the immaculately-mown lawn with its benches and cul-de-sacs of sculpted hedges. The sunlight streamed down. Her stern demeanor and severe clothing made her seem out of place. It was as if they had somehow met in an intersection between past and present.

A distant blare of trumpets and Wagner tubas . . . he must hurry back. At Bayreuth they sounded no bell at the end of the intermission; instead, the scattered hordes were summoned to worship with selected *leitmotifs* from the opera itself, thundering out over the lawns and courtyards. God, it was like living in the middle of one of those Cecil B. de Mille spectacles. Time to hurry back. Time to burn down the universe!

He turned back towards the opera house, remembering
what Amelia had said only the week before: *He drank my
blood.*

labyrinth

Carla and Timmy were at the breakfast table when Maria
announced that someone from Stupendous Sounds Systems
was here. Carla looked up and saw a slender black woman.
Her hair was long and fell in ringlets over her chic suede suit.
She sat down with them, and Maria poured coffee.

"I wanted to meet you at home before we go to Stupendous,
Timmy," she said. "Oh, what a neat house."

"It's in poor taste," he said. Carla saw that he was apprais-
ing her very carefully. "Where's Blade?"

"I don't know. He just walked out on us, I think. He's done
that before, you know. What a flake!"

Timmy looked at Carla, an I-told-you-so look. Her hands
had started to shake.

"Oh, Carla," Timmy said, "I want you to meet Blade's
temporary replacement, Melissa Pavlat."

"Missy."

"Of course," Carla said, smiling nervously. "Hi."

"Carla is my analyst."

"Cosmic," said Missy. "You know, I think I've gotten to
the stage in my career when I oughta get a shrink myself.
Good for the image, you know? You expensive?"

"She works for me full time," Timmy said possessively.

"Oh, ex-*cuse* me!"

"So, Missy," said Carla, trying to make conversation,
"Things are pretty messy over there with Blade's disappearance, I suppose."

"Shit, no. Never more mellow. I got it all under control,
baby. You know what we got in store for you, Timmy?"

"No."

"First, the tour you know about. Couple of weeks from
now it starts. But then there's the video game—"

"Video game?"

"Ain't it just cosmic? *Bloodsucker*, it's called. You're a
vampire and you have to jump these trains that are rushing
around these mazes, see, and once you hop them you gotta attack the passengers, and they all have all different scores for

killing kids and businessmen and little old ladies, and then they have these Van Helsing-type characters chasing you, and if you pass through—get this—a *Vampire Junction* you go ZAP and get these superpowers and you can give the old stake-in-the-heart treatment to the Van Helsings for a while and—get this—the machine plays your song, kid, all the time the vampire's got the superpowers. It's more than a Pac-Man clone . . . it's got something for everyone! Get it?''

"Cool," said Timmy.

"And with every machine they produce, kid, royalties! Fat fucking royalties! Plus your song sounding in every arcade in America, insinuating its way into the unconscious mind of every trigger-happy kid in the country!"

"I'll take it."

"Take it? The company already signed!"

"What about my contract?"

"Kid, you gotta get that chauffeur, or butler, or adopted father or whatever he is of yours to read all the fine print. We make the deal, Timmy-boy, and we split the take sixty-forty. Our favor."

"Well, who cares. I've got plenty of money. But a video game based on me . . . I guess every kid dreams of that."

"Well, I wanted to wait till next week and surprise you with the finished product, but I thought you might be sad about Blade leaving us in the lurch like this. You liked him, didn't you?"

"He was . . . very nice."

"Aw, you poor kid. Want to come to the studio now? We've got a version of the whole album on the 16-track, and we're gonna mix it down today."

"Sure," he said. He got up, indicating to Missy that they should leave; and then they were gone.

For a while Carla sat finishing her breakfast. She was thinking over all that Timmy had told her last night in session, the bizarre goings-on at the Opernhaus Thauberg.

Perhaps she should warn Stephen. But where would he be now? In Germany? She could call his agent. . . .

She finished her coffee and started up to her room, wondering what she would do until Timmy came home. She could swim, or play tennis with one of the staff; she could get Maria to drive her somewhere, to a mall or to some touristy thing.

She could make more notes. None of these alternatives seemed appetizing.

As she was about to turn the knob into her bedroom, she realized what it was she wanted to do.

No! I don't want to go upstairs again. I'd be like those airhead young women in horror movies who simply have to go into the one dark spot where they know something terrifying lurks. Or like Bluebeard's wife, insisting and insisting until he yields up the keys to the darkest chambers of his castle. No.

But she did want to go back to the attic.

It's broad daylight, she thought. If that girl vampire is there, she won't wake up . . . isn't that what Timmy said?

Again she knew how deep she had fallen into his fantasy. She was accepting all his statements, outlandish as they were, as facts.

I am not the darkness, she thought. It is day. They can't get me.

She tied her robe a little tighter, and turned away from the door, and found the hidden staircase that led to the attic . . . paused a moment. She went back to her room, and plucked one of the crucifixes that Maria had provided off the wall—a little one, about a hand's-breadth high, a longfaced pouting Jesus in gold strapped to a silver cross. Then she found the stairs again and ascended.

Must remember not to look too close—

Two paces left, three backwards—

Corridor walls bursting into hellflames, oriental demons tormenting the damned, and. . . .

Four paces sideways—

A skullface, peering from the window of a train rushing at her, veering at the last moment, with a clatter that turned into the sound of skeletons colliding and a whistle that became a screaming child. . . .

The room with the trains, still set up as they had been left at the last session: the couch. More piles of boxes, and beyond the mirrors, mist . . . she looked down at the little Opernhaus model . . . beside it Timmy had set up a tiny cemetery, each tombstone no taller than a fingernail . . . just marble chips with the names scratched on them with a needle.

Timmy didn't have to be there, then. He wasn't somehow dreaming this room into existence, having it blink out whenever they weren't there. That was something for her notebook.

Though the attic was fluid as a funhouse, there were certain rooms in it with an objective reality.

Was that comforting?

Comforting to know that she might actually be going mad?

Carla left the room. As soon as she had gone a few paces, she realized that she had lost her way.

She had known all along she would lose her way.

Now she reached the Rapunzel room, as she thought of it. An open coffin. She knew what she would find there. Stone walls; outside, the medieval castle walls overlooking lush terrain . . . but not the Valley, not even California . . . maybe . . . France? In the field, two knights jousted.

She tried to glance past the coffin, but she couldn't resist getting closer. For some reason she felt no fear at all.

There it was . . . the corpse of Kitty Burns . . . her eyes stained with hastily applied mascara, her cheeks anemic, her hands crossed lightly over the crotch of her jeans. Carla was uneasy now. What if I can't get back, she thought. She held out her cross and backed out slowly.

And stepped into another stone room. Another coffin: a middle-aged man in a business suit. Handkerchief and gold Parker pen neatly tucked into the coat pocket. This one's skin was gray, rubbery.

Another room. Two corpses, two coffins; young men. Another room: this one looked like a transvestite in high heels and a taffeta dress.

I've got to find a way out of here!

She stepped back again. How many paces to the right was it, damn it? How many?

And she whirled round and she was in another room and there was a glass coffin full of seawater and seaweed trailed from it and left green stains on the tiled floor, and she saw the young girl that lay there with the bite marks all over her body, and the wall was all TV sets stacked all the way up to the ceiling and side by side and there were no windows, only the TV sets, and they all showed a windy seascape and a sharkfin slicing the water and coming nearer and nearer and now the jaws and the icecold eyes bursting from the water, a hundred sharks coming at her, bursting free of the screen, and she was in the dark green water and couldn't scream, and the corpse's face contorted into a fanged smile, and she gasped and swallowed only salt water, drenching her nostrils, pouring down her lungs, and—

"Quickly," a child's voice: flutelike, innocent. "Come with me."

She opened her eyes. She was in the piano room that she'd once found before. She was still in the attic then, she still hadn't found a way out of here—

"Timmy!"

"It's all right."

"The sharks—"

"You had to find out. I hide nothing from you, Carla."

"This room—"

"—is all rooms, Carla. There are no single rooms here in this attic, but all flow into each other. They are dreamrooms, but here the dream is the only reality we can know."

"There are more of them! This place is becoming—"

"A vampire junction? Surely not. But there are more of us now. We have put Kitty under restraint, but she still grows bolder and bolder. She won't listen to reason."

"Can't you kill them?" Carla was hysterical.

"My own kind. . . ."

"No, no, are you weeping?" Carla put her arms around him. Like embracing marble: the softness an illusion. Cold. Had he been weeping? He was only a child and cosmic dilemmas racked his mind. . . .

"Do not pity me. I do not weep," he said. "We do not have tears."

"You're hiding something," Carla said. And truly believed, for the first time, that she could heal him.

fire

The underworld of Bayreuth: passageways. Somewhere, a soprano sang over and over from a practice room the words *Weialeia, weialeia . . .* the siren song of the Rhinemaidens who were about, unsuccessfully, to try to seduce Siegfried into giving up the ring and averting the curse. From another room sounded a quartet of Wagner tubas, rich and watery, as if out of a marble bathroom . . . perhaps they *had* retired there to try something out away from the rest of the orchestra.

Stephen opened a little door and stepped into the orchestra pit, which was completely concealed from the audience by an awning. Most of the orchestra was there already, engaged in tuning or chatting softly; he found the podium and glanced overhead at the monitors which would be his only way of knowing what the singers were actually doing. Part of the set, an enormous canvas Valhalla that would be concealed from the audience until the last moment, when a scrim would be pulled back and Valhalla would burst into flames, was descending from the flies.

"How much time do we have?"

"Five minutes," someone whispered.

The score was already open to the right page. There was a note there; it must have come during the intermission.

Herr Miles: a telephone call. You could not be found. From California. From Carla Rubens. She said that you must be told that you are in very grave danger. You must come to her as soon as you can. You are in danger.

What on earth was this all about? He'd called the woman twice, three times, and she had just brushed him off. She'd been no help at all, and now . . . a bizarre warning.

But she was with the boy! And the boy was evil! So Frau Stolz said. So all the evidence said. After all, wasn't it an evil presence they had been summoning up, that day in Stephen's childhood?

No. I'm not going to trust her.

He lifted his baton.

Is this the last time?

The thought had crossed his mind before. But the step he now must take, the final step of the journey that had begun when he fled the burning house into the arms of Francis Locke and then stood swinging a censer in the college chapel of Saint Cecilia's face to face with a supernatural entity . . . this step must be away from music.

He would no longer flee.

He would walk through fire into the arms of darkness.

At his downbeat, music surged around him. Music of the primeval forest and of the dark river that flowed through it, out of which the temptress Rhinemaidens were about to appear.

As he started to conduct, he became aware of . . . a new fire in him. Had he suddenly grown young again? He delved into the forest music, finding new nuances, new shadings. The players began looking up from their music stands in surprise, following his new tempi only by the skin of their teeth. A new joy took hold of him. So he'd always dreamed conducting would be, when he was a small boy asleep by the fire in a townhouse on Warkworth Street in Cambridge. . . . He didn't look up. He didn't want to see the startled looks on the singers' faces. . . .

Then came the hunt scene, now Siegfried's death, now the funeral march, the double death-chords interrupting the melodies with anguished abruptness. No singing here, so he pulled out all the stops, he protracted the poignant arcs of the heroic themes and brought the death-knells crashing down as if he himself were strangling someone . . . he didn't feel tired at all, as he always had by this part of the opera. They were playing like telepaths now, divining his every thought even as his gestures became wilder and more cryptic. . . .

And now the immolation scene. He glanced up at the monitor. The pyre was burning. Fire! Brünnhilde singing of heroism, of the universe's impending fall, and of redemption by love . . . leaping now into the flames . . . giant fans now billowing through the cellophane fire . . . and now the scrim whisked away, and heaven itself aflame, the gods on their thrones as Valhalla crumbed around them—

Fire! he thought. Fire, the most beautiful thing in the world, the bonfire of his parents' house that burned down his childhood, fire that could destroy cities and even universes . . . he conducted in a frenzy now.

And then, almost too fast, the theme of *Redemption by Love* swept over the strings like a mountain wind, the final chord now, and he held it long, long, not wanting to let it go, he let it diminuendo on and on, he knew the audience was poised on the verge of applause and still he would not let go, he clung to the traces of the D flat major chord until it was just an echo, and. . . .

His baton fell from his hand.

He was conscious of the clapping, very far away.

He did not come down from the podium.

The concertmaster got up and whispered in his ear, "I never dreamed you are understanding Wagner like this, Herr Miles. They are overwhelmed. You know what the critics will say? They will say you have broken through to greatness.

Finally. They are shouting for *you* Herr Miles! Not for Siegfried or the Brünnhilde, but for you! This is unprecedented—"

He didn't answer. He just stood there. Perhaps he had a madman's look about him, because the concertmaster scratched his beard and looked uncomfortable. Stephen picked up Carla's phone message and deliberately began to tear it into little pieces.

"Do you realize, Herr Miles?" said an oboist, coming up to congratulate him, "that you can probably come here next year . . . and not as someone's replacement, either?"

"I will not come back."

The applause continued, deafening now.

"I am going to Thailand," he said, "and what I have helped create, I will conquer and destroy."

They did not know what he was talking about. They shrugged and left him alone.

I suppose I should go and acknowledge the applause, he thought.

He closed his eyes and saw fire.

memory: 1947

Dark. Dark.

His eyes open.

He is under the earth; through the walls of the coffin he can hear the soft slithering of worms; overhead, as from an infinite distance, rain pattering. It is dark, so dark. He has known this dark so many times, and still he has never grown used to it.

He listens.

The rain: he imagines the gravestones slick with it, the moist tall grass sticking to the marble, and the droplets beading the cassocks of the angel statuettes.

I'm dead again.

Layers and layers of earth above him; he imagines their weight, crushing down on him, squeezing the life from him. Dark. Dark. But darkness is not a frightening thing for him; it is a fact of existence; it sustains him. In his long unlife he has found a hundred surrogate mothers, but it is the darkness that is his true mother. And the huge darkness hugs him, heavy, stifling. It is an impersonal mother. It has no love for him; the sustenance he draws from it is not polluted by emotion. But he grows stronger.

A slow throbbing in his chest, where the woman's stake went through. But no pain, never any pain.

There is fragrance in the earth. The cedar of the coffin; beyond the odor of pulp-pounded leaves, the smell of corpses fresh and stale, the other denizens of the graveyard. He is reviving now.

And he feels the hunger.

At first only the memory of that hunger: the taste of Amelia Rothstein's menstrual blood, the blood of a cat, of a mouse, of an old dying dog. Memory piles on memory, feeds on memory, until remembered hunger becomes real hunger, raging, irresistible—

He fights to shift position now. The wood confines him. He must break out. The hunger inflames him. He is strong, and the darkness gives him more strength. He smashes his fists against the polished cedarwood. His hand finds earth now, a thick mush from the rain. For a moment earthworms twine about his fingers, and a lone maggot crawls up his heavily starched sleeve, a refugee from some other grave. His arm is loose now, thrashing about in the mud, grasping only slimy roots and tickling insects. He is incensed now. He beats against the coffin lid with his whole body. The wood cracks now, and mud drips inside. It is unbearable. He tries to sit up; his head batters the wood and smashes it. Mud floods his nostrils and beetles crawl across his eyelashes, and now his hands encounter hard metal, the steel bands which Frau Stolz has ordered to be welded around the cedarwood, because she had divined his secret, but insensate rage has gripped him now, his hands rip steel apart, the sharp shorn metal gashes his hand but he feels no pain, he cannot feel it. . . .

Now the mud comes pouring in, and he reaches up, flailing for the surface, his fingers find the roots of an oak tree, slick with rain, and he grasps them tight and pulls himself up, sliding through the sludge. . . .

Now his head is free. The rain soaks his hair. He pulls himself up through the hole he has made. He stands up. The rain drenches his clothes and strips the mud from his face, so that patches of pale skin show through. He stands before his own tombstone in the sartorial splendor of death: the dinner jacket, the little bowtie, the striped trousers, all starched to cardboard stiffness by the embalmers.

And the wound in his chest has been sewn shut, for the dead must not, in the last moments that their loved ones see them, shatter the illusions of the living; they must be beautiful.

And Konrad is beautiful, in the first moments of his resurrection, when the rain has washed him clean. He is a perfect little gentleman in his attire; and his face is suffused with the soft luminescence peculiar to his kind.

Where to now? he thinks. Another country, perhaps? Another language, another identity? Or perhaps he should return to the dark forest, as he once did? He misses the forest. There were no words in the forest; things had no names, not even he; so he had had a kind of freedom. But he knows the forest is not to be found easily; it must find him.

Perhaps, he thinks, I should have remained in the earth. If I stayed long enough, perhaps this nightmare of unlife would have gone away, and I would never waken. . . .

But he knows these things cannot be. He has always thought these thoughts whenever he has had to come forth from the tomb; but he has always come to the realization that he must go on as he is. We do not choose what we are, he tells himself.

For a long time he stares at his grave. It is as he has imagined it. The little statue is a maudlin touch, but he longs to possess it, he who cannot see himself in a mirror. Rain bounces from its face and from the many folds of the cassock and the finely sculpted feathers of its wings; rain streams from the outstretched hands, runs in two rivulets down the open pages of the music book to meet in a miniature waterfall at the spine and spill onto the statuette's base, the tombstone proper. Water collects in the chiseled letters of the name Konrad Stolz. In the eyes of the statuette, the raindrops seem like tears. He is moved, for he himself cannot weep; weeping is one of the things that immortality has taken away from him. He loves the statue. One day, he decides, he will come back for it.

13

labyrinth

Crowds . . . crowds everywhere as Francis Locke surveyed the Bangkok cityscape from Prince Prathna's air-conditioned minibus. The chauffeur was painstakingly zigzagging through the traffic, which appeared to follow no humanly recognizable patterns, now and then frenziedly pounding on the horn for no apparent reason. The Prince, seated next to him, merely laughed at Locke's discomfiture; while Muriel Hykes-Bailey, whose wheelchair had had to be loaded from behind, merely closed her eyes. She throve on cacophony, it seemed. Others had joined them; the skeletal Lionel Terrence and the enormously corpulent Archibald Strathon had arrived only that morning from London, and had already found suitable mates, twins, in Prathna's labyrinth of lust. Only with some difficulty had they been persuaded to leave them behind at the palace.

"The Gods of Chaos," Prathna had reminded them, "do not invite guests."

As they drove past the bizarrely modern Siam Intercontinental hotel and its nearby shopping mall and rounded a corner to find themselves amongst tenements, Sir Francis asked the two newcomers for news of the others Prathna had invited.

"It seems," said Terrence, giggling unpleasantly, "that Lord White has died of a stroke brought upon him by his exertions in the lavatory."

155

"Heavens!" said Locke, who, of all the little horrors of old age, dreaded incontinence the most.

"And dear old Richard Cooperthwaite has also, alas, ah . . . passed on," said Strathon in that same squeaky voice that had led his peers to nickname him "the eunuch" when they were up at Cambridge.

"What happened to him?" Muriel said.

"He'd become increasingly involved, you know, with those parapsychology people . . . he was funding some investigation on poltergeists out of his own pocket. One day, at the scene of one of these happenings, a chandelier fell from the ceiling and killed him."

"Heavens!" said Locke. "Was the investigation fruitful?"

"No," said Terrence. "Unfortunately, it was all a hoax. Later they found all the machines that made the whole phenomenon possible: wall-shaking devices and what have you. It was a malfunction of the equipment, in fact, that killed him; the chandelier was only supposed to wobble, not actually drop on his head!"

"Remarkable," said Sir Francis, observing that they were now driving along a *klong* or canal.

"There are only five of us, then," said Muriel, opening her eyes.

"Six," said Prathna. "Miles is due, you know."

"What if he doesn't come?" said Locke. "After all, he wasn't really a proper member of the Gods, was he now? I mean, he didn't join voluntarily, exactly. And since he's no longer ten years old, our little bluff about revealing his crimes is hardly likely to have any power over him."

"We will never lose our power over him," Prathna said.

"And why not?"

"Because he too has seen . . . what we saw."

For a while they drove in silence, interrupted only occasionally as Prathna pointed out the sights. Here a park where dirty children knocked about a rattan ball or *takraw*; here a convoy of yellow-robed bald monks crossing a street, bringing traffic to a screeching halt; and now, as they neared the city's ancient heart, the baroquely twisted spires and golden pointed eaves of the Temple of the Emerald Buddha, the weekend throngs on the ground watching teams of kite-fighters tugging away at their five-pointed kites . . . the kitestrings, Prathna explained, were coated with ground glass so that they could be used to saw down their rivals. And always the sun beating down; the crowds with their sweat-drenched faces; clothes, ancient and modern, plastered to perspiring bodies. They made slow progress around the grand circle bordered by temples and government offices, but as they managed to get all the way round and to begin threading their way down a narrow side street, Prathna ordered the chauffeur to put a cassette on the car stereo, and one of those silly modern songs began to tinkle away.

"Heavens, Prathna! Have you actually started listening to pop music?" said Strathon.

Then came the voice, and they all said nothing.

"Do you like it?" said Prathna at last. "My niece sent it to me from America. It is . . . the boy I told you of."

"A remarkable voice," said Locke. "But what can it possibly have to do with us?"

"We shall see."

"Might I inquire," said Muriel imperiously, "where we are going?"

"To see my cousin Durianga. He's about ten years older even than us, if you can imagine such a thing. Oxford man. Read archaeology, you know, was head of the archaeology department at our Chulalongkorn University for a while, and had some important position at the National Museum. At least, he thought it was important. Not that I keep up much with the family, but Durianga is almost as much a renegade as I am myself. He knows everything about antiquities, real, forged, or even just rumored. Thought he might tell us about your little *objet d'art*, Muriel dear."

"Why this trip?" said Muriel. "You know how I loathe motorcars. In view of my condition, you might have invited the fellow to dinner."

"That's impossible, Muriel. You see, my cousin has taken up the yellow robe. His notion of the contemplative life, my dear, did not include your convenience; that's why we've to cross the river, in Dhonburi, to see him in some beastly little monastery of his."

The beastly little monastery turned out to be a vast compound. A mango orchard hit its walls from the dirt road onto which they had turned after leaving the wealthier side of the twin cities. A narrow path, which they had to negotiate single file, led to the gates. Within the compound, half hidden amid luxuriant clusters of banana trees, were temple buildings, including the *vihara* that housed the main Budda image. Stone *yakshas* or demons stood everywhere; all seemed in disrepair, and the flagstones of the courtyard were cracked and lined with tufts of grass.

"It's terribly hot," Muriel said, fanning herself as her wheelchair squeaked over the uneven flagstones.

"Well, where is he? Your cousin, that is," said Francis.

"This way," said the prince. He beckoned to the chauffeur, who had followed them with an offering-tray laden with food. "Is it noon yet? Oh, bugger, it's one o'clock. This food will be wasted. And I ordered all his favorites from the kitchen!"

"What's the matter?" asked Francis.

"It's their bloody two hundred vows," said the prince peevishly, like a child not getting his own way. "They can't eat after bloody twelve o'clock."

"Such language!" Muriel said.

"Bloody right," said the prince, furiously scratching his bald head. He called to a little boy who had come dashing down some steps. After a brief interchange, the boy took the tray full of food and wandered off, munching.

"Princely food," said Prathna, "and now I have to waste it on a temple attendant. Riffraff! You have your idol, Muriel?"

"Yes, it's in my purse, and I must say, old thing, that you're acting very ill-tempered suddenly."

"You may have gathered, friends, that I am not overly fond of my cousin."

"Nevertheless," Muriel said, "none of us is overly fond of this heat, and I think we should get it all over with."

The procession of ancients rounded the *vihara* and reached the steps of a palatial building.

"What's this? Another *vihara*?" said Locke.

"No. This happens to be cousin Durianga's *kuti*; the humble dwelling place wherein he is supposed to live simply and frugally, thinking only of the Lord Buddha's teachings—"

A voice from the top of the stairs: "I say, Prathna! What a pleasant surprise! And visitors, what!"

Prathna groaned. "Don't forget to remove your shoes," he said. "And step *completely* over the threshold, or you'll anger some spirit or other."

"Someone will have to carry me," said Muriel; and Terrence and Strathon hastened to succor her. They removed their shoes and washed their feet in the trough provided at the bottom of the steps, and then went up.

The air conditioning was on full blast in the room. Simple mats were spread out on the floor; it seemed that they were to sit on them, which they all did, with various complaints about arthritic legs and aching backs. Sir Francis looked around and noted that the walls were covered with a mural similar in style to the one in Prathna's secret chamber; but this one depicted angels, *devas*, and mythical beings floating on clouds, playing musical instruments, and generally enjoying the nine levels of paradise. Other scenes showed previous incarnations of the Buddha, who could be distinguished from the others by the size and radiance of his halo.

Sitting on the only chair in the room—a Louis Quinze, Locke noted, pricing it mentally and realizing that even he · could not have afforded it—was a man in a saffron robe, so shriveled as to resemble a cricket. He stretched out his arms in a posture of benediction. When he spoke it was in the same aristocratic Old Etonian accent that Prathna had, but it was so soft that it was almost drowned in the whirring of the three electric fans and the air conditioning.

"Stop scratching your head, Prathna old chap," he said. "I at least am bald by choice."

"If you're expecting me to *wait* on you—" Prathna began, as though picking up the thread of some ancient quarrel.

"I am indeed," said Durianga, as Prathna suddenly made a prostrate obeisance. "I only joined the monkhood so as to enjoy the spectacle of having my relatives abase themselves to me and crawl around like monkeys. Of course, since becoming a monk, I have learned compassion, and no longer take pleasure in ridiculing you. Eh, what, old chap? And what brings you here?"

"This," said Muriel Hykes-Bailey, and inched forward on the mat to hand him the idol.

"Don't touch him," Prathna said. "Not even by accident. They can't touch women."

"The two hundred commandments?" said Muriel.

"Yes, the two hundred commandments!" Durianga said, laughing. "You could never stick to it, could you, Prathna?"

"I tried," said Prathna, and Sir Francis learned for the first time that the prince had spent some time in the monkhood. He took the idol from Muriel—it was cold to the touch—and handed it to the prince, who handed it, with ceremonial gestures, up to the ancient monk. "I found," the prince went on, "that evil was a much more enjoyable practice than good."

"You always were one for pat answers," said the monk. "Good and evil, indeed! What is this, a Western film, cowboys and Indians? Tush! I expected better of you. Evil, my foot! You are a phony, my dear boy. Don't think I don't know you're up to some mischief. Well, let's see what this is . . . hello! What have we indeed?" He turned the half-statuette over several times in his hands. "Well, it's certainly not Thai. Nor is it Khmer, Mon, Dvaravati, Srivijaya . . . my dear Miss . . . Hykes-Bailey, is it? . . . I fear you have been hoaxed. This thing is of quite modern manufacture."

"Modern?" said Muriel. "What do you mean?"

"I mean, my dear woman, that it's no more than a few thousand years old. Barely an antique, let alone an antiquity." He laughed heartily at his own joke.

"But it's of no interest, I suppose," said Terrence, who seemed utterly bored with the situation. Locke knew that he and Stathon were anxious to return to their dusky pleasure-girls.

"I didn't say it was of no interest," said the monk. "It is of vast interest . . . but not to you. Nevertheless, someone has been trying to obtain this statuette of yours for the past thirty or forty years."

Locke felt a sudden frisson of fear. He stared wildly about him. Had the others felt it too? He wished they would leave. Prathna's mumbo-jumbo about karmic nexi . . . and now the enigmatic and oracular pronouncements of a tiny withered man in a pop-guru costume . . . why were they so frightening? He forced himself to sit still. I killed someone once, he thought, deliberately remembering that sixty-year-old act to hide his present terror.

"I knew it!" Prathna cried delightedly. "A few seconds of groveling, cousin dearest, and you reveal all."

"I'm afraid not," Durianga said. "I sense. . . ."

"Oh, get on with it," said Prathna irritably.

"But one of you has not yet arrived," said the monk. "And a little discomfort now will be in good practice, I'm sure, for the grueling odyssey that lies ahead."

"We're to be off again, then!" said Sir Francis. "I say, I'm not sure these bones can take much more of this travel, what."

Strathon shifted his bloated torso and swabbed at his sweat-drenched shirt.

"The choice will be yours," the monk said mildly, "but if I know my brother, he will not hesitate to forge ahead. He will do anything to avoid facing the specter of his impotence." A noise from outside, footfalls on the steps. "Heavens, I see there's no holding you fellows back! Your friend has arrived." All eyes were on the entrance, where Stephen's shadow suddenly blocked the afternoon glare.

"Don't—" said Francis.

It was too late. Stephen's foot had come down inauspiciously on the threshold.

"Oh, bugger!" said Durianga.

fire

"This is the twentieth century, after all," the monk went on. "We no longer bury pregnant women under thresholds so as to have fine, vengeful spirits to guard the house. Oh, come in, come."

Stephen had been burning up in the sun only a moment before. Now the air conditioning blasted him in the face. He was more unnerved by this than by the fact that he was once more face to face with those with whom, for sixty years, he had shared a nightmare. "Your driver brought me straight from the airport," he said to Prathna. It was just like the excuses he'd made as a child, when he was late for one of their occult rituals. The others waited, allowing him to flounder in his own confusion.

"All right," Sir Francis said at last. "Let him speak. What is this Timmy Valentine, and why is he so important?"

"He is a vampire."

Muriel shrieked in glee. No one else spoke. Stephen saw the flicker of disbelief in the faces of the others, so he said quickly, "I have proof."

"Fascinating," the old monk said.

Stephen told the whole story, looking long and piercingly at the others as he spoke. Look at Francis Locke, he thought. He's probably wondering how this madman can really be the little boy who fell so easily into his clutches once. Terrence and Strathon . . . Laurel and Hardy, he thought. Muriel . . . desiccated, her beauty shriveled. And Prathna, supreme manipulator as always.

"Your story is patently absurd," Francis said. But Stephen saw that he wanted to believe so badly that he was shaking.

"Children, children," Durianga said calmly, "you have a great need to believe. Why don't you go ahead and pretend it's true? Sit down together. Plan the destruction of the vampire. Perhaps you will all come to some mutual catharsis, and I can get on with my afternoon nap."

"Garlic and crosses," Muriel screeched.

"They don't work," said Stephen, and told them more about Konrad Stolz; reminded them, moreover, that the first confrontation had been in front of the altar at Saint Cecilia's.

"He goes about in daylight?" Strathon said.

"Seems to," said Terrence, mulling over the details of Stephen's tale.

"If garlic and crosses will not work," Prathna said irritably, "what is the point of this bloody exercise?"

"Ha!" said Durianga. "You have forgotten something very important. You have forgotten the original purpose of your visit to my humble *kuti*."

The monk began a long tale. He was ten years older than any of them, and very conscious of his seniority; Stephen knew he was not to be hurried. He shrugged and settled down to listen. It was only a mention of fire that made him pay attention.

"Fire . . . yes! The Persians worshipped fire, did they not? They had their Ahura-Mazda, the principle of light, and their Ahriman of evil. Rather quaint and simplistic, if you ask me, but. . . ."

"Back to the idol!" Muriel said impatiently.

"Ah, yes. But fire is interesting, is it not?" He stared directly into Stephen's eyes. What did the Gods of Chaos know about Stephen, what had they told this madman? He had paranoid visions of dossiers and hidden tape recorders. "I mention fire," the monk said, "not only because it has a vague bearing on our case here, but because I wanted to give your Miles a bit of a jolt, eh?"

"Sorry," said Stephen. "I'll pay attention." But his mind began to wander again.

"Be that as it may . . . you have heard no doubt of the

Golden Triangle, a tract of territory at the corner of Thailand, Laos and Burma, completely in the hands of various hilltribes, uncontrolled by the three governments, who run the opium and heroin trade?" The others mumbled. "Well, I'm sure you've all heard of the major tribes—frightful people, you understand, aborigines really—not at all civilized, I mean the Mhong, the Meo, the Karen and so on. But there's one particularly secretive tribe called the Isao. Their leader is one Ai Tong. He's become quite a powerful warlord, ever since our border police broke up the last alliance in a big raid last year, and he's embarked on a plan of conquest. Sort of a backwater Alexander the Great, if you get my meaning. Actually, what's involved is only a hillock or two to the north, a few more poppy fields—"

"What possible use is this poppycock?" Prathna said. "I expected better of you, cousin."

"Well," Durianga said, "the Lord Buddha sat under the bo tree for forty years before attaining enlightenment. Five minutes is scarcely a great deal to expect, from that perspective. But religious instruction, I see, is not my wastrel cousin's cup of tea. Well then. The Isao speak a language quite unrelated to any other, unless it be distantly related to Greek. From time immemorial, it is said, they have possessed a certain idol—"

A shriek from Muriel, quickly stifled.

"—split down the middle with a thunderbolt. One side evil, the other good. Simplistic. Very like the Persians, you might say, this primitive dualism. About thirty years ago, they lost half their idol in an opium war with the tribe on the other side of the hill. The beneficent side. The side that some called lord of . . . *fire!* Ha. I knew that Miles would start at that word. You youngsters are positively Pavlovian in your conditioning! Since then: plague, famine, constant pushings-back, till now they're virtually confined to the summit of that single hill. But now comes this Ai Tong fellow and a final bid for power, you see. And you, somehow, have come into possession of this very object. And the Isao believe with utter certainty that when the two halves of the statuette are joined again, they will possess psychic power of such magnitude that they will eventually ride the wind, sweep down on the plains, even, heaven forfend, on Bangkok . . . a place so distant and alien that they

can barely imagine its existence save as a mythic locale. Now
I'm sure they're dying to have their fire lord thing back."

"I haven't come sll this way to give away one of my favorite
antiquities," Muriel said.

Stephen said: "This idol . . . it came from far away, to the
west? Perhaps it dates from Alexander's invasion of Paki-
stan?"

"For a child of seventy," Durianga, "you're no fool."

"This is all very interesting," Sir Francis said. "But what
can it possibly have to do with us?"

"You want a last fling, don't you?" the monk said. "Would
an opium war among barbarians be your idea of going out in
style, I wonder?"

"Not what we had in mind," Prathna said.

"Then why did you come to me with that thing?" said
Durianga, and fell back on his Louis Quinze chair, apparently
asleep.

"Not so much as a dismissal!" Prathna said. "He's always
popping on and off. Like a bloody toaster."

"Wait a minute," Locke said. "I think he's dead."

"Don't I wish! What a sodding nuisance that would be. Do
you realize how much the funeral would cost?"

The monk was absolutely still for an impossibly long time.
Then, abruptly, he opened his eyes and said, "I know what
you're thinking. That you came to see me in vain. Use your
heads, fellows! And you, madam. After all, you did all go to
Cambridge." Then he dozed off again, and the Gods of Chaos
filed out into the heat-haze.

labyrinth

In the next few days Stephen sought out the company of
Strathon and Terrence. They had always seemed more
moderate than Locke, Prathna, and Muriel, and Stephen was
grateful that they did not constantly exhort and rave at him as
did the others. Their very dullness was refreshing.

Each day brought more spectacle. Prathna had declared,
"If we can't figure the old boy out, we might as well see the
sights before we die." They took canal trips and saw the
Temple of Dawn, glittery and bulbous against the setting sun.
They saw snake farms and crocodile farms; they visited
massage parlors as a change from what Prathna called his

"homely comforts" of the garden of pleasures.

And at night they went to their separate suites in Prathna's palace. Even the air conditioning could not mask the pervasive scent of jasmine. As they lay in their soft beds, sometimes in the arms of soft young women, the Gods of Chaos dreamed.

In Locke's nightmares, the wolf leaped and slavered. He wanted to kill it forever. To have one peaceful night before he died.

Stephen Miles saw fire, and behind the fire the dark eyes of a child. He woke up, put on his dressing gown, and went outside for a walk in the garden.

Jasmine, stronger than ever: crickets screeching, mosquitoes buzzing, frogs croaking in Prathna's pavilioned pond. The breeze hot, damp. Stephen crossed the ornate wooden bridge into the pavilion. The other Gods were already there. Somehow he knew they would be.

"We are waiting, Miles, for one of your insights," Prathna said. Candlelight flickering in his face; incense. Stephen's eyes smarted.

Stephen said, "We're just not equipped to deal with Timmy Valentine. Garlic and crosses indeed! This isn't one of your superstitious concoctions. Amelia told me that little Konrad had taken communion, for God's sake!"

"Perhaps," Muriel said, "it is simply that all those priests and preachers have it all wrong. They're not on the winning team after all! I've always suspected that."

Stephen felt intimidated. He turned to the less threatening Strathon, but Strathon and Terrence had withdrawn to a corner of the pavilion and were tossing pebbles into the water. What is this? he thought. I'm not a ten-year-old boy. They can't order me around anymore. But he only said—and it seemed that his ten-year-old self spoke, the child in front of the flaming building gripped by the arms of a young man in a tweed jacket—"What do we do now?"

"If you're sure," said the prince, "that the garlic and crosses thing is obsolete—"

"The lord of fire!" Stephen blurted out. They all stared at him. He felt like a child with a guilty secret. He had to speak now. "Nobody seriously believes in crosses nowadays. But something truly animated by faith . . . such as the faith of the Isao in their idol. . . ."

"What! You think we should—" said Locke.

"Steal it. The evil half of the idol." There. It had slipped out.

"Go north," Prathna said, "overpower a few aboriginal savages, and make off with the dark side of this fire lord?"

"It's worth a try," Terrence ventured.

"It's outlandish," said Prathna.

"But it makes perfect sense!" Muriel said. "Why else were we brought together here? Why else did I bring my idol? And it is just as your cousin said, Prathna. These savages have a faith in this object that we, in our civilized enlightenment, could not possibly equal. Enough faith, I think, to endow it with absolute power—when it is brought together again. It is destiny." She began to cackle.

"Destiny!" Prathna said. "Harnessing superstitions. Vampire meets primitive tribal fetish. East meets west. How deliciously primal! It's too good an idea to waste."

"But will it work?" Strathon said faintly. The others ignored him. Except for Stephen, who had learned in his childhood that he had to observe every tiny thing the Gods of Chaos did, if he was to stay out of trouble.

14

seeker

Brian couldn't sleep. He didn't think he'd ever sleep again.

A hotel near the Boulevard: pretentious Spanish decor. Seedy. What time was it? Midnight, later? He got up, made sure the blinds were drawn tight shut. This hotel didn't have a swimming pool. He'd made sure.

He flicked on the TV, a black and white with only one channel working. He sat on the bed, chin in hand, thinking. Hadn't shaved in days.

Was it a dream?

Quick image on the TV screen: a decapitated head on a pole stuck in the sand by the beach, a tongue of seaweed protruding from his mouth. Voice-over: "... *one found at Venice two weeks ago ... mystery madman ... police baffled....*"

He glanced at the head; the camera didn't linger. Gruesome. And the seaweed in its eyes—

I'm dreaming.

It was gone now, but the newscaster's voice continued, a drone of weather figures and sports results.

Seaweed....

He touched himself all over. He'd just awoken from a nightmare like that, but ... had he really awoken, or was it still going on? He slammed the switch on the bedside control, put on a pair of jeans, T-shirt, sneakers, decided to go out.

167

Down there, in the street, there'd be people, thousands of
people, and maybe he wouldn't see Lisa whenever he closed
his eyes. . . .

Outside the hotel, heat: even at midnight he felt stifled. It
was a heat that oozed up from the sidewalks, emanated from
the people that jammed the streets . . . the night mixed musics
from blaring ghetto-blasters like a blender. By a shop window
two transvestites postured. A blinking neon sign across the
street, a dancing pig, made green and red pigs on the sidewalk.
Smells: beer, french fries, exhaust, cheap perfume, marijuana.

Brian bought some fries at a sidewalk counter, didn't eat
them; he just held them in his hand, their heat gushing into his
palm.

"Honey, show you a good time?" The voice pitched so low
that only he could have heard it. He didn't turn, but saw a
vague glimmer in a furniture store window, maybe a face,
flashing red-green-red-green from the dancing pig overhead.

"Get lost," he said.

"Aw, come on, gimme a break." He turned to look at her.
A smile. Mousy hair, a feral face, a teenager it looked like. A
strange shine to her skin . . . must be those garish lights, their
colors clashing . . . that lurid red tint to her mouth . . . he
looked away.

"Please leave me alone." And then, on the other hand, if
Lisa happened to be on the street too, this one might know
her.

But Lisa was dead!

No. That thing last week . . . I'm just cracking up, I didn't
see a shark-bitten corpse rise out of a swimming pool, I didn't
see a woman gutted on my bed . . . movie stuff.

"You seen this girl?" He took the photo from his wallet and
held it up.

The girl laughed. Were those fangs? Surely no. He didn't
like the look of her.

"You a cop?" she said.

"No, I'm her uncle."

She shrieked with laughter. "Have you tried Castle Valentine? You like being eaten, mister? I'll blow you till you die of
pleasure, fifty bucks. Just ask for Kitty, on the street, any
time."

"The girl?"

"Go home, Van Helsing!" she said, grinning wide, and suddenly he saw that there were fangs indeed, fangs striped green and scarlet from the neon lights, and he knew that if it was a dream then he was trapped in the dream, he couldn't get out, so it might as well be real . . . and he turned to the store window and he saw himself reflected but he couldn't see her at all, just the vague shadowy thing, he looked at the window exhibit, deluxe bedroom with brass bedstead and fake Chinese celadon lamps and a goldframed wall-mirror and his own face in the mirror but no one else's . . . and he looked at her closely and saw that when he wasn't watching her face became immobile, she wasn't even breathing, she was like something from an embalmer's workshop . . . he started to inch away.

"Get away from me. Fuck, get away from me. . . ."

Slow laughter.

A voice, a bearded man wearing a Dr. Demento T-shirt calling from the wheel of a beat-up Camaro: "Hey, sister, you fool around?"

Slowly, slowly, the girl corpse turned away . . . swiveling, like a mannequin on a pedestal, not the way a human would turn . . .. the john said, "How much for half and half? I ain't got much time."

"Fifty."

"Who do you think you are, Marilyn Chambers?"

"All right, thirty . . . but only fifteen minutes, honey, I'm a working girl."

"Get in, bitch."

Brian watched the Camaro pull away for a moment.

If this were all true now, hypothetically . . . no. I've got to think of it as a dream, or I'll go mad. But if it were true . . . what's Castle Valentine? Lisa mentioned it too. I'll need stakes, I guess, and maybe crosses and . . . garlic. God, I hate garlic, always forced Mom to make one portion of roast lamb without it, and my rah-rah brother would always jump me in bed and breathe it on my face . . . garlic, fucking garlic.

He threw the french fries in a trash can and walked further, down to where the street intersected with the Boulevard.

Gotta find something to do, forget this craziness. . . .

A sign: *VIDEO FUNHOUSE!* A glass door: beyond it, beeps and explosions and bursts of electronic music over a driving rock background. He checked his pockets for quarters

. . . yeah, a couple. He pushed the door, quickly taking in the sign taped to it: *Exclusive to Video Funhouse—an advance model of BLOODSUCKER, the latest, greatest video game! High score this pre-release week gets two free tickets to a Timmy Valentine concert!*

He entered. It was a two-level arcade; in the front a couple of souped-up Pac-Mans, a Stargate, two Tempests . . . all old hat. Only a few seedy-looking characters clustered around these, kids, hustlers maybe. A fat man, belly jutting from his leather jacket, sat at a desk.

In the back, up some steps, there was a crowd; aficionados here. He elbowed his way in. They were all hunkered around a new game. The facade around the screen was a big plastic Dracula cape, and the word BLOODSUCKER was scrawled over it in fluorescent scarlet. There was black light around the controls. He tried to push closer to see.

"This screen's a bitch," someone remarked.

The guy playing was using a joystick to manipulate a train through a bewildering maze of tracks. A vampire, his head sticking out from the caboose, was endlessly flashing his fangs. About six little Peter Cushing figures wielding stakes were running around the maze. Other creatures—victims: little old ladies and children, businessmen, even a punk who carried a bonus of 500 points—were running hither and thither along the tracks, now and then ducking into train stations where they couldn't be attacked. Now the train crossed a junction, and the screen started to flash the words VAMPIRE JUNC-TION VAMPIRE JUNCTION and the music changed abruptly to a wailing tune over vibrato horror-movie chords, and the train started to charge the Van Helsing clones.

I need this like I need a hole in the head, he thought. But he went on watching, fascinated. That tune that played whenever the roles were reversed and you could attack the attackers . . : he couldn't place it yet, but . . . what was it, damn it? He'd heard it . . . on the radio, maybe. *Dah, dah, da-da-da dah* . . . yes, of course, *Vampire Junction* . . . who was that by now? Some kid singer. He was on the cover of *Idol Magazine*, Lisa used to buy it sometimes.

He watched. "Shit! He got me!" the player shouted.

The screen showed a vampire splayed out on a railway track, like in those old movies, now it cut to a stake being hammered into his heart and an explosion of blood-droplets, finally to a single drop of blood and the legend: *Congratulations! You are among the twenty highest scores and may enter your names in the BLOODSUCKER Hall of Fame!*

Brian turned away. What a morbid game, he thought. But he couldn't get the tune out of his mind. And those high-resolution graphics of the stake ripping into the vampire's chest, so cartoonlike and yet so imbued with the violence of contemporary life.

I should be writing a book about this, he thought, thinking of missed deadlines. He clutched his unspent quarters in his pocket and went to the door.

He stood in a daze for a moment, reading the sign over and over.

Vampire Junction . . . Timmy Valentine . . . Vampire Junction . . . Timmy Valentine . . .

They'd both said something about Castle Valentine, hadn't they? What if this whole rock star thing, with all its exploitation merchandise, its arcade games . . . was a front for—

He started walking back to the hotel. He was running as he entered the lobby and went through to the parking lot. He started up the station wagon, cursing. Then he drove out and began to cruise the street, slowly, up and down and round the block. Dozens of other people were doing it; he wasn't conspicuous.

Then he saw the girl again, that Kitty. At first he wanted to pick her up, tell her he'd changed his mind . . . but he lost his nerve. He remembered Rita's corpse on the bed, and Lisa bleeding in the mist.

And then, as he waited at a red light, he saw Kitty turn into a black cat.

The cat was slipping in and out between people's legs. He could see it heading toward the Boulevard. Driving as slowly as he could, he followed.

A few more streets, and the cat was running down the side of the highway entry ramp. He didn't stop to think. He just turned into the ramp and got onto the freeway. The cat was running steadily, not fast, along the shoulder. A dozen cars hooted furiously as they whipped past him. All he saw was the cat. It was moving faster now, leaping like a miniature mountain lion. He sped up. Now he was doing maybe thirty, and nobody else on the road was liking it. But the cat was sprinting now, and he got up to the speed limit and still it was just ahead, a silvery thing in the street lights, a streak now, and then . . . it took off! It was a bat now, for a second he saw it firmly silhouetted against a street lamp, and then it melted into the night air. . . .

Whatever you are, fucker, he thought, I'm going to follow you till I find out where you live. I'm going to cruise the streets until I find your Castle Valentine.

I don't care if it's a dream.

labyrinth

After a few more days of thrashing the problem around, the Gods of Chaos began to trek north. At first it was the prince's luxurious minibus, zooming through the countryside of paddyfields and the small towns with a few temples and markets and fleets of pedicabs. A night in a modestly comfortable hotel with air conditioning and Bangkok tourists. A monsoon squall came that night, shorting out the air conditioning, and Stephen lay sweating in the humidity, listening to the strident cries of geckos and strange amphibians and insects. Then off the highway onto dirt roads that degenerated into slush, leaking from flooded paddies; overnight in a village under mosquito nets, in a thatched house that rose up on stilts. No more shopping malls or traffic jams, though the village's one television set showed *Charlie's Angels* that night, dubbed in Thai; the headman's house was packed. Children stood on the backs of water buffaloes and peered through the open windows.

Farther now, farther and farther from the Chao Phya River, into the wilderness. Now there was a fort, where scruffy vigilantes squatted on a cement floor and played cards and quaffed the abominable Mekong whiskey. They traded the minibus for two Land Rovers and obtained, through the intervention and bribery of the prince, an armed escort of two, one facing behind, the other forward.

In the back seat of the second Land Rover, Stephen sat next to the soldier; Strathon and Terrence were in the front seat along with a driver. It was hard to speak as they bounced northward; Stephen said nothing, while the other two Gods of Chaos, like a closed-loop Laurel and Hardy routine, chattered unceasingly and inanely.

"Look! Mountains, old thing," said Terrence, pointing. "Up ahead."

"Mountains? Barely hills."

"What's on them, jungle?"

"How should I know?"

"It's pretty sodding hot around here."

"I suppose you want one of those monsoon rains to come tumbling on us, eh, what?"

"Oh, bugger it. Prathna's gone quite daft, I think. Leading us out here. And believing all that about a vampire, for heaven's sake. If you'll excuse our skepticism, Stephen old chap."

"Just a wild goose chase," Strathon said, barely admitting Stephen into the conversation. "Eh, Miles, what?"

"Bloody hot," said Terrence.

"Worse in India, you know, what," said Strathon. "Nothing but wogs."

"Wogs here too, if you ask me."

"But colonial wogs in India, you know—abject, miserable, groveling things. At least the ones here seem like self-respecting chaps."

"Aren't you a little prejudiced?" Stephen said at last. "And what about Prathna?"

"*He's* not a wog," said Terrence. "Cambridge man. As you well know. I suppose your years in America have addled your brains, Miles, but—"

Stephen stopped listening. Never had he felt more alien to these jaded, desiccated relics who had once preyed on his innocence. But he needed them. They had listened to him when no one else had. And he had to use them to get through to that boy. To Timmy Valentine.

Now they were at the outskirts of a jungle; there was a mud road, winding, canopied with dense, dripping foliage, lined with banana trees. They were between two hillocks; the road seemed to twist uphill, to the left. Large patches of the hill were treeless, dandruffed with opium poppies.

Turning to the soldier, he said, "What is this hill?"

"This hill Isao stronghold. Very dangerous," said the man,

pointing upward with his M-16.

"What are they going to do, attack us?" said Terrence scornfully.

"Savages," said Strathon, turning to look behind; at which point a shot rang out and his head split in two.

A glob of brain tissue hit Stephen in the face and ran down his neck.

"Good God!" said Terrence. The two jeeps accelerated, skidding, wheels churning up mud.

"Duck, you blithering idiot!" came Prathna's scream from the other car, as Stephen swabbed frantically at the brainstain on his face.

He crouched down. Staccato gunfire now. They were jumping down from the trees, they were swarming over the jeeps, the soldier slumped forward on top of Stephen. He peered out and saw the tribesmen in their black tunics and their embroidered sashes, brandishing rifles and knives, whooping, they were on top of him now, he saw silver ornaments piercing their ears, their noses, circling their necks and arms, and then—

A weird ululating, and—

A pounding, a rhythmic chanting from all sides, and Stephen knew somehow that the danger had passed . . . he forced himself to sit up now, almost retching as he pushed away the dead soldier . . . the Isao seemed to burst from every cranny of the jungle, their legs swinging from branches, their faces thrust through fronds and foliage, their heavy silver bracelets clinking ceaselessly as they chanted. . . .

He looked ahead. Muriel Hykes-Bailey, supported on one side by Prathna and on the other by Locke, was holding up the beneficent half of the thunder-idol.

The jeeps started up. This time it would be a triumphant procession into the warlord's lair, and Stephen knew that the idol would soon meet its other half. Its evil half.

seeker

Must have dozed off, Brian thought, slumped over the wheel. Must be almost dawn.

He was parked down the road a little way from the Valentine house. He had finally been able to follow the girl Kitty after trying for three or four days. He'd tracked her here. This was it, Castle Valentine, with its wrought-iron gates. The house of Timmy Valentine, the rock and roll teen idol.

He forced himself awake. The car was just off the road, wedged between two trees. Through the bushes he could see the gates and the brick wall, and through gaps in the gates, a shadowy house.

Wait . . . someone was moving across the lawn. Who? Brian opened the car door and slipped out closer to the gate. He had a plastic souvenir rosary in his clenched hand; he could feel the point of the crucifix dig into his palm.

Damn, it was dark. He peered out from the wall through the gate, and he saw—

Starlight on the lawn. A grove over a gravestone. And now a howling, very far away . . . from the house, did they keep wolves in the fucking house? Now the clouds shifted. A wan half-moon glimmered in the foliage. Then the wolf. Springing from the headstone into the garden path, silver in moonlight. Prowling, pawing the grass . . . a very old woman in black came out of the house. She had a flashlight. The wolf ran to her. The woman knelt, embraced the wolf. The dress looked like it had come off the rack of an antique costume store; she dropped the flashlight, the lightbeam swung up to illumine her face, deeplined, the rouge and the carmine lipstick standing out against the white foundation . . . she bared her breast to the wolf . . . silently the wolf suckled . . . or did it draw blood? Yes . . . the milk was dark . . . in the moonlight the crimson seemed almost black. The old woman opened her mouth in a silent moan—pain or ecstasy? He couldn't tell. He had to get away. This was just too kinky, too weird.

He started back toward his car, when he saw a figure walking up the road toward the gate.

Shambling, as though unaccustomed yet to motion. The figure came close—Brian could almost have touched it. A bearded man in a Dr. Demento T-shirt. With bloodstains. And a black fluid dripping from his mouth.

Where had he seen him before? Yeah, in the Camaro, picking up that girl Kitty . . . he was one of them now. It was just like in those movies. And Lisa was in there. Somewhere in there. Going through something so awful that she had begged him to end it for her with a stake in the heart—

The vampire paused. Had he seen Brian? Didn't they have extra-keen smell? Could he already know he was there?

Brian didn't wait. He made a dash for his station wagon and peeled out down the hill.

As he hit the highway, he thought: And where do you buy stakes, anyway? Do you just walk into a stake store and say, Look here, I need a couple two foot stakes to rub out these vampires with? Make 'em sharp?

Have to make them myself.

mother-image

Carla found Maria in the kitchen. "Where's Timmy?"

"Rehearsal. He took Rudy." Maria looked up from a table piled high with papers. "Coffee? Care to help me?"

"Yes, sure." Carla sat down. "What are you doing?" She poured herself coffee.

"Is fan mail answering day. Day of answering of fan mail," Maria said in one of her accents.

"What shall I do?"

"Please to stuff envelopes."

Carla saw there was a pile of brown 5x7 envelopes and a stack of glossy photographs. Maria was unpeeling a boxful of computer-generated mailing labels and addressing more envelopes and adding them to the pile. "If the labels have a little 'p' in one corner," Maria said in her normal voice, "they get signed photograph A; if they don't they get photograph B." Carla began stuffing.

Photograph A: Timmy serious, borderline preppy, staring soulfully at the looker; photo B, a more humorous pose, Timmy sitting on a coffin lid in a Dracula cape with jokeshop fangs in his mouth. . . .

"Those fangs," Carla said. "Are they. . . ."

Maria laughed. "You think they're real? Or maybe Valentine Brand, with Timmy's picture on the box, available at novelty stores everywhere, free if you send in the coupon from his latest album?"

Carla went on stuffing envelopes. "Tell me," she said, "how do you find your way around? Upstairs, I mean."

"I have worked for him for many years. I am like a mother to him. You think I wouldn't be able to read his mind?"

"His mind?"

"I'll tell you a secret, Miss Rubens. Don't go up there unless you know exactly what you want. Because *it* knows what you want, even if you don't. It can hear your heart. You will always find what you are looking for, Miss Rubens. It is that simple."

"But I didn't *want* to find those vampires!"

"Are you sure? Would you have become what you are if you were not drawn to dark things, to the shadow side of man?"

"But—"

"Stuff the envelopes. Since the first concert of the summer they haven't stopped coming."

She thought: Available at novelty stores everywhere. It's come at last. Not the grand demoniacal figures of mythology, but the five-and-dime shadows. . . .

"Have you ever tried analysis, Maria?"

"I not need! I good housekeeper!" The accent, thicker than ever.

That was it, then: a defense machine, a wall against prying.

She went on stuffing envelopes all morning, until a paper cut sent her back to her room to work on her notes.

15

dissolve

Maria . . . where are they? I mean, Lisa and Kitty. And
the others. The coffins are empty. I thought I had given
orders. . . .

Garlic over the coffins, Master Timothy. Yes. Crucifixes.
Yes, you gave orders.

Why are they empty?

Could you stand to listen to their piteous wailing, master?
Their cries of hunger? Oh, they are like babies, newborn into
your cruel universe, where the bloodthirst is the only driving
emotion . . . how could I not let them go, master Timothy?

But Maria . . . must you play mother to a whole brood of
vampires? Am I not enough for you?

Of course you are, my baby, of course you are. . . .

Quiet. I sense . . . someone is watching us. I hear his breath
across the lawn, beyond the gates, through the thick walls.

He will only see a wolf and an old woman.

I smell his blood, Maria, heating up. I fear for him.

Master—

Keep them down, Maria, keep them under control.

But they are blood of your blood, bitten by you, awakened
into the cold eternity by your own whim. . . .

Then they must know me for their master.

Do you love them?

I am trying to remember what love is like.

Poor baby.

Of course. Mother, mother.

You're beautiful as a wolf.

I bay the moon.

You need not remember love, my master, my child, my lover. You're a pure thing, a force. Love would only sully what you are. I have enough love for us both. For a whole generation of vampires.

I bay the moon as it peers between the spruces—

—as long as I live—

—trembling in the wind of night.

huntress

"They won't be back now. Your parents. You're sure."

"For sure! Throw me a beer. Hey, Helen, you got that hot tub running yet?"

Helen was on the deck overlooking the patio of her best friend Lulu's house. She was about to dip her hand in to test the water when she saw something scurry across the planks . . . "Here now, here now." Was it a cat? It was dark. It just lay there staring at her, a ball of black fur and two eyes. "Go on in there, kitty. Here, kitty, kitty."

The steam was rising. She tiptoed over to the whirlpool switch and turned it on. "I didn't know you had a cat, Lulu!" she shouted down.

No answer. Lulu must be too busy making out. Scattered chatter from inside the house now . . . a little scream. Overhead, a clear night, a half-moon.

The cat or whatever stretched its paws and darted into the house.

She crept over to the sunken Jacuzzi and stuck in her hand. Perfect! "Like *totally awesome*!" she shouted at the people below.

She splashed at the water idly with her hand, and then she felt something soft and squishy . . . what? She tugged at it. It felt like . . . seaweed or something. Or human hair. Probably one of Lulu's parents' marital aids, something slimy that you'd rub against yourselves while you were screwing, she thought.

She pulled it, dripping out of the water, like one of those plastic bathtoys maybe, only this one had sort of a black gooey liquid all over, oozing onto her fingers, and it was covered all over with kelp.

"A practical joke," she said to herself as she stared at the half-boiled head of her best friend. . . .

Then she started screaming.

She didn't stop when another figure, draped in mist, rose out of the bubbling water. A girl's corpse with fire-opal eyes, with bloody punctures all over her body, swathed in seaweed, smiling now, her braces swimming in dark blood, her fangs—

And Lulu's head falling into the water, the whirlpool buffeting it against the redwood, a long swirl of blood marbling into the churning water, and now the kelp-gloved hands on her hands pulling her into the water, her body welcoming the warmth and the pounding massage of the whirlpool as the corpse embraced her and the sea smell rose suffocating and the corpse's mouth now, open, no breath coming out but a stench of compost and old meat, the dead head on her shoulder, the jaws cracking her collarbone, her own blood welling, spurting, and—

Dimly now, the patter of tiny paws, and far away another scream, another terror, and—

seeker

At the Safeway he bought a dozen brooms and two pounds of garlic. At a dingy religious bookstore he picked up a handful of plastic crucifixes that had been marked down for quick sale. It was late after noon by the time he pulled into the first Catholic church he saw, a garish orange building with a Disneycastle steeple. He went inside and furtively filled two Tupperware containers with holy water from a basin beneath a doe-eyed Jesus surrounded by plaster lambs.

What else? Wolfsbane, maybe? Brian didn't even know what that looked like. He'd heard of it in vampire movies, but he didn't know whether it was a real plant or some screenwriter's fabrication.

This stuff would have to do.

Back at the hotel, he put on a turquoise Hawaiian shirt with a pattern of tikis and palm trees. He'd always hated it but it had a lot of pockets. He started to stuff them with garlic.

He sat down on the bed, hacked the handle off one of the brooms, and began sharpening it.

After a couple of hours the stakes were ready. He stuck a few crosses in each pocket. He tried to stuff the Tupperware thing with the holy water in his pocket too, but it wouldn't fit, and he spilled some on the floor. Shit! Need something smaller.

He looked in the bathroom. There were a couple of those little plastic shampoo bottles that you got in hotels. He emptied them into the toilet, then came back to the bedroom and refilled them with holy water. Then he crammed them into his pockets beside the crosses and the garlic, put the makeshift stakes under his arm, and started out of the room—

What had he forgotten?

Stakes, garlic, crosses, holy water . . . silver, maybe? His watch had a silver wristband, but was it real? He dropped the stakes and took off his watch. Peered at the legend on the metal links . . . *stainless steel* . . . no, no. Wait a minute. The back of the watch, though, what about that? . . . it was shinier, more silver-looking, though Brian hadn't really thought about it before, it had been a gift from long ago . . . yes! *sterling silver* . . . in a pinch it would do, maybe. What about—

What was he going to use to bang the stakes with, didn't he need some kind of mallet or something?

He went downstairs with his hunter's tools, found his car, started driving around. A mallet. . . .

Found the freeway. Took an exit at random. Maybe a 7-Eleven? No mallets. A shopping mall . . . he was getting desperate. He wandered into a Toys 'R' Us . . . paced up and down the aisles, past endless hand-held arcade games and racks of sale-priced Smurfs and rows of gleaming Jedi Knight action figures, till he finally came upon, in a section devoted to less popular toys, a croquet set.

He bought the set with his VISA card, silently praying that their computer wouldn't discover he didn't have enough credit left.

When he got back in the car he hurriedly unpacked it, took out two mallets, and threw the rest in the back seat.

Then he got back on the freeway—

A few minutes later—

Rope! How am I going to climb in there without rope?

A fifteen-minute detour back to the hardware store in the mall, and then back to the freeway.

Maybe I won't remember the way, he thought wildly. Maybe I only imagined it before. But there was the exit, there was the winding, uphill road.

It's too late, he thought.

Lisa had said that in a few days she might have changed completely, that her new self would have devoured her old . . . perhaps she wouldn't even recognize him.

He reached the spot where he had hidden his car before, behind a clump of trees. As he put his station wagon into park, the iron gates of the Valentine mansion were flung open, and a black limousine emerged. Brian tried to get a glimpse of the passengers, but the windows were polarized; he could only see the chauffeur, the peaked cap perched over a skull-like face, white gloves resting on the wheel. Was he one of *them*? Probably not. Sunlight was bad for them, wasn't it? That's why the windows—

The gate was still open. Maybe he could make a dash for it, slip into the garden, then improvise from there. He gathered his tools under both arms and made for the gate. He got in easily enough. There was that old woman, standing on the lawn, staring after the car. He wondered if he could bluff his way past her, or whether he should tie her up or something.

"I've come to . . . er . . . fix the . . . " he started to mumble.

"Go on in," the woman said abstractedly, as if to someone else. It was almost as if his coming had been expected.

It was about an hour before sundown. Ahead was the house, a weird jumble of Spanish, Elizabethan, and functional modern. I'll go in, he thought and just look around.

The old woman had turned now and was eyeing him curiously. He tried to think up another excuse, but he couldn't speak.

Finally she said, in a parody of a Bela Lugosi voice, "Dinner will be at sundown. That is why you have come, is it not?"

Shit, he thought, *I'm* going to be dinner—

And he dashed into the house, fishing in his pocket for a cross. When he reached the front door, he saw that she was still watching him, a tiny figure in the expanse of grass. Her voice barely carried, though she seemed to be shouting. "You're going to die, young man! But you might as well take as many of them with you as you can. They are so much sloppier than the master . . . it is such a nuisance to clean up after them. . . ."

He went inside.

witch

"Listen!" Muriel Hykes-Bailey was whispering urgently in the candlelit halfdark of the Isao shack. Francis Locke blinked; he had been dozing. A soft, slow drumbeat had begun outside the hut. Then an old man's quavery voice; other voices, younger, chimed in. Soon it seemed to be coming from all around them. Periodically came the women's voices, ululating, shrieking.

"Heavens." Stephen, looking round the room, saw that it was Locke who had answered her. They were seated in a half circle; Muriel had been given back her wheelchair. They were facing an altar on which Muriel's artifact had been enthroned; beside it was its missing half. They had not yet been joined.

An opium mist clouded the hut and infiltrated his senses. The candles cast looming shadows. There were no windows; a side door, covered with a black drape stitched with silver coins, afforded the only exit. Stephen did not move but saw Sir Francis get up from the wooden chair. The other Gods of Chaos were the only ones in the room. In front of the altar, forced into a sitting position and tied to a chair, was the waxy corpse of Archibald Strathon, whose head wound still exuded dark blood and brains. Beneath the idol were several buckets of . . . water? Blood?

Stephen stared at the idol's dark side: where the right half's lips were parted in a beneficent half-smile, the left half sported a supercilious leer; its eye glared wildly, its body was covered with reptilian scales, and its arm held aloft a flaming trident. The lord of fire. . . .

The chanting outside continued. Now women wailed, and their cries were punctuated by the pounding of flesh on flesh.

"Disgusting creatures," Prathna said. "They are beating their fists on the corpses of their slain. My cousin tells me they eat their enemies' livers raw."

"What a charming people," Muriel said.

"What ı don't understand," said Lionel Terrence in his militant whine, "is why they feel obliged to put old Strathon's corpse in here with us. Fine chap he used to be! Nothing much upstairs, but a fine fellow. What a stench, though!"

"I believe," said Prathna, "that the natives have put his

corpse here with us by way of apology. They didn't realize we were bringing back their precious idol."

"What now?" Stephen said. But he knew what they would do. He felt the tug of the fire lord's power. Didn't the Gods of Chaos understand his special relationship with that ancient fire? No. It was all a game to them.

"They will chant the night away. And in the morning, they will begin a new wave of attacks on some rival warlords," Prathna said. "Few of them speak Thai, but I've been getting some idea at least."

"And we're prisoners?" said Locke.

"Prisoners!" Prathna grunted. "Hardly. Honored guests, actually. We're here to observe Ai Tong's final and crushing victory. When the chanting reaches its climax, something dramatic is supposed to happen—"

"We've the run of the place, then," said Muriel.

"Very much so. And the Land Rover is parked right here in the middle of the village. We have but to snatch this thunderbolt idol of yours and make good our escape."

"Oh, I say, what!" said Terrence, squirming as his gaze encountered the propped-up corpse of his corpulent friend.

"Listen! Listen!" Muriel whispered.

Locke stood up and began pacing. Let him pace! Stephen thought. Candlelight danced eerily over the two halves of the idol; wisps of yellow light tendriled through the smoky gloom. The chanting grew in intensity.

Louder now, louder—

Stephen got up and pulled the curtain back just a little bit. A sea of backs . . . the men prostrate. Torchlight. The thatched huts in the mud, not a single right angle among them . . . on the steps of one, incongruous, playing to no audience, a miniature battery-powered television set was broadcasting an episode of *Star Trek*. And there was the Land Rover, less than twenty yards away, and the soldier-driver standing guard; they had even let him keep his rifle.

"Look!" Muriel shouted. He turned around.

The surviving Gods of Chaos had all risen from their seats now, stood in a semicircle around the altar with the surrendered idol. As the chanting crescendoed, a blue glow seemed to emanate from the idol . . . was it his imagination? Was it simply the madness of their mission that enabled them to see such things as realities? Was it senility, was it the guilt of that moment sixty years ago, grown huge, topping them into insanity?

The two halves—

A jagged streak of light shot from one to the other . . . a bolt of blue lightning . . . more of them now, cross-stitching the space between them . . . the idol-halves were shaking, they seemed to be inching toward one another . . . Muriel gave a scream of wicked pleasure, the others cried out at once, in astonishment and fear and glee . . . Stephen felt the fire of his boyhood tugging at him, animating him.

"Quick! Before the idol comes together!" he rasped, reaching to grasp the idol. But Terrence was quicker than he. He was already staggering towards the altar. In his haste he tripped over the chair containing Strathon's corpse, which sprawled onto the floor. He grabbed the left half, screamed in pain and dropped it—

"Use a cloth or something, you fool!" said Muriel, propelling her wheelchair forward and throwing a fold of her dress over it. The cloth caught fire at once. "Those buckets—" she screamed, pointing at the pails at the foot of the altar. Francis hobbled over and kicked them at the flaming mass of cloth, and a bubbling, seething fluid spilled out. Reddish steam hissed, swirling into the clouds of opium smoke. Muriel bent down to scoop up the nauseating goo in which the idol lay, and cradled it in her blood-stained dress. Sir Francis seized the right half, the beneficent half . . . "It's ice-cold!" he shouted. The shock made his hands shake.

"Now," Prathna said, "while they're still occupied—"

He yanked the door-drape down.

The stepped out into the steaming night. Terrence was last, Francis in front, Prathna motioning to the driver, who scrambled to open the doors.

The chanting rose, a wall of sound—

For Stephen it seemed to happen in slow motion. He moved in rhythm with the drumbeats. He ran behind Francis, who clutched half the idol in a fold of his shirt as they both clambered into the back seat. The drums, beating, beating, beating—

Then stopping. The chanting garbled, dying to nothing; far away, crickets, frogs, the chattering of distant monkeys.

The accelerator roared. Prathna seized the soldier's M-16 and began to fire randomly as the Land Rover hurtled down the dirt path that ran steep and sheer into the jungle. The tribesmen were shaking off their trance-state; many were glassy-eyed from opium. They flung themselves at the Land Rover, dashing themselves against the doors, throwing themselves down to be crushed under the tires. Hands reached in and seized Terrence's arm; he jerked, strained, was pulled out, and Stephen heard a bloodcurdling yell and the sound of flesh being ripped apart. "Don't look back!" came Prathna's voice faintly over the tumult. Louder and more horrible was a collective slurping, a hundred mouths slavering in unison, wolves worrying at a carcass. It couldn't be what he thought it was, but . . . "Yes," came Prathna's response to his unspoken surmise, "it is their custom to eat the livers of the slain. . . ."

The roar grew fainter. Beside him, Frances drew out the idol. "Magic," he murmured. "Genuine magic. Not the mumbo-jumbo Muriel practices, eh, Miles? But magic such as brought the shadow-thing into our world."

"Which you will now destroy," Stephen said.

"*We* will destroy!" Francis screamed. "Don't you share our exultation, acolyte?"

"Strathon . . . Terrence. . . ."

"Nothing at all," Francis said. "I feel only elation." The Land Rover continued to grind its way downhill.

Stephen saw that Francis felt warm and secure in the presence of the Gods of Chaos. As the moonlight, occasionally breaking through the leafy canopy, fell on the others' faces, he studied them. He understood them all. Muriel, in the grip of her crazy joy; Prathna, who loved most of all to orchestrate the lives of those around him, smiling a secret and contented smile, like a child sleeping with his favorite teddy bear. And Francis, who had been the first to hold Stephen in his power. . . .

I will break free now, Stephen thought. Now the others are playing with fire, but the fire will forsake them, because it belongs to me alone.

He searched the faces of the Gods of Chaos. Surely they must feel some twinge of guilt, Stephen thought. But no—they were wallowing in their childish elation. He alone felt the burden of all their guilt.

But we will all burn soon. This guilt will be purged from us. For now I will give in to the joy. . . .

He closed his eyes and shut out the dark forest.

labyrinth

Brian stepped into velvet darkness. There was a staircase with an ornate balustrade of carved mahogany. And music from far away; a record player, perhaps . . . the voice of a child against the tinkle of keyboards and light percussion. He listened for a moment.

I know the sun's going to set soon. If it's like in the movies, I'm doomed. It's suicide.

But he didn't try to escape.

The voice, upstairs somewhere—

Clutching one of the cheap crucifixes and holding it out in front of him, he started up the steps; they were pile carpeted, and he made no sound. On the landing he stopped to look at a curiously carved oriental bookcase inlaid with mother-of-pearl . . . he recognized it. He'd heard the voice once, for a few seconds, playing roulette with the TV channels. It was Timmy Valentine. He remembered the face, too: his pallid complexion, the billowing dark hair, the huge clear eyes, the half-smile, surly and seductive. . . .

Where was the music coming from? He tried a few doors; locked. Here was an open one . . . a closet stocked with linens. Then another door, a steep walled stairway. He didn't stop to think. He went up.

Pattering of tiny paws—

He turned quickly. A cat prowling in the shadows of the floor below? He gripped the cross tighter. The plastic was clammy, the emaciated stainless steel Jesus slithering in the sweat of his fist.

He reached the top of the stairs and saw corridor after corridor. Room after room. He opened one and saw—

The sea, the smell of fresh kelp, a salt wind tousling his hair—

He slammed the door shut. The wuthering stopped. Memories, he thought. Plucked from my mind, trapped somehow, time-frozen.

He opened another door. An old room with see-through people . . . his brother, unshaven, lurching drunkenly over Lisa, the girl about to scream—

He retreated and kicked the memory shut. He'd never have known if he hadn't stumbled upon them that night. . . .

He turned into another passageway. Darker now. He knew

that he was beyond his own memories. Human arms with flaming hands stuck out of a wall. Here were funhouse mirrors. He saw himself fat and thin . . . then as an ancient man, rotting alive, in a rocking chair, his skin peeling away. . . .

Left. Left again. "Lisa!" He called out the name and was answered by faint echoes. He walked faster now. He didn't want to look. More staircases, draped in cobwebs. An army of cockroaches trickled down a wall.

Where?

Something brushed his shoulder. He turned to see a skeleton on a string, leering, aping his every gesture. He began running upstairs, his feet slipping on cobwebs. The skeleton followed. He turned and waved the cross. It copied the gesture. He lashed it across the breastbone with his fist. His hand felt as if it were slicing living flesh, the skeleton shimmered, lap-dissolved into darkness . . . "Illusion!" he cried. "You're only an illusion!" He ran faster now, his steps creaking in rhythm with the pounding of his heart. . . .

A room, an open coffin . . . inside, the man in the Dr. Demento T-shirt, his face almost phosphorescent, and Brian grabbed one of the broomstick stakes and aimed it at the heart and took the mallet and began to pound savagely at it, and the corpse's eyes came open at once, the mouth flared wide and the fangs glistened and there came a growl of terror, not human at all, and the blood gushing out, freezing cold, making him scream as it drenched his shirt, and then the unlife left its eyes and greenness seeped into its face—

More doors now . . . more coffins. He had maybe seven, eight stakes left. He despatched a transvestite who lay demurely in a pink coffin, who whimpered like a puppy as reddish rheum oozed sluggishly from his chest and mouth, over the painted face. He stuck a garlic bulb and a cross in its mouth.

"Lisa! I'm coming for you, Lisa!" he cried, feverish. He'd staked a half a dozen vampires now. His arms were lead-heavy from swinging the croquet mallet, and still there was no sign of Lisa—

Through a window he caught a glimpse of the night. He realized that his grace period was over—

He staggered down the corridors yelling her name, his throat raw. There was blood all over him, so much blood . . . old, oozing blood.

A corpse fell across his path. Started twitching. An old woman, a shopping bag lady maybe. Beer smell mingling with the odor of putrid flesh. It was struggling to rise. Perhaps it was its first night, it didn't quite know what it had to do. Brian didn't wait to find out. He stabbed the old woman's face over and over with the cross he was holding, and the dead flesh sizzled where it touched the cross, and he emptied a shampoo bottle full of holy water on its face and it began to howl, and its voice was the voice of a pitiful old woman, and it croaked out, "Help . . . help . . . don't mug me . . . I ain't got no money, mister . . . " over and over, but he had seen the glint of fangs and he knew what she was, and he held her prostrate with the cross until he found another stake and started to pound again, this time the vampire struggled and rasped out its cries for help, but he managed to impale its heart and the blood welled up like a fountain, splashing his face, caking on his hair, streaming down his Hawaiian shirt and pants . . . then it lay still and he knew it was gone beyond, forever . . . and he stared at the bag lady's face for a long time, a wrinkled old face with wisps of white hair, a tattered dress spattered with blood, and he remembered that only a week ago he'd been a rational man, a writer, a peaceful guy, not someone who could club old women to death, and he couldn't stop himself, he started crying right there in the musty corridor in the attic that was real and wasn't real . . . I've gone mad, he thought, mad, mad, mad—

Footsteps behind him?

Cautiously he stood and turned. Nothing. He could hardly see through his tears but began to make his way onward. He didn't know where he was going. He only had one stake left.

He looked ahead and saw Lisa.

Sliding from shadow to shadow. Lisa alive skipping on the flagstones in front of the house with a ray of Sunday sunshine on her, turning to watch him solemnly now, a toothy smile . . . no braces . . . just a memory leaking from his mind . . . everything was real here: dreams, desires, dark fantasies . . . "Lisa!" he called after her as she drained into shadow . . . he started after her, the floorboards blood-slippery, the rope on one shoulder, the stake and mallet in one hand, he followed her, and now came the music of Timmy Valentine again, welling up around them. He walked into a room with shiny audio equipment and a tape whirring, spooling continuously onto the floor in the bright lights for a second and then he stepped into darkness again, another room where the walls were lined with video monitors and he was choking on the sea smell and the screens showed sharkfins circling in the ocean and there was a glass coffin there, open, with strands of seaweed trailing onto the damp tile floor, and the coffin was empty—

"Lisa—"

An open window: through it he could see the hills hulking, spangled with suburban lights. Through a crack between spruces, the moon. Outside, the trees didn't stir, but in the room the sea wind gusted, churning up the water in the coffin, making the seaweed flap and flutter like kitestrings.

"Lisa, Lisa. I've come. Like you told me to. I've brought the stake. Lisa, come to me, come to me. It's Uncle Brian."

The wind roared, soaked his face. More seaweed flying in through the window. Brian went to the coffin and dropped a crucifix into the water. Then he emptied the other bottle of holy water into it. Slowly the wind fell still. He could sense her now, but he didn't dare look behind.

"Uncle Brian," came Lisa's voice. "Oh, Uncle Brian, you've come to me, take me away, I don't want to do the daddy thing again, I don't, I don't. . . ."

The death-stench steeping the still air. Brian said, not looking, "I've come to kill you, Lisa."

"No, Uncle Brian, no—"

"You asked me to—"

"You don't have to now. I like it here. They're nice to me, I'm always close to the screen and the sea and I never have to do the daddy thing anymore . . . oh please Uncle Brian take the cross away from my bed oh please please. . . ."

"I can't."

He turned and saw her.

She was standing against the window. Though he felt no wind, he saw wind twist her hair, hair twined with kelp. She wore a white summer dress to hide her wounds, flecked with red where she had bled. It wasn't like that night at the hotel. She looked almost human this time. He wanted to hug her and take her home.

Instead he took another cross from his pocket.

"Put it away, Uncle Brian, that's not nice." She smiled; her braces showed. "Don't kill me. I love you, Uncle Brian. I love you."

He advanced toward her.

"Get into the coffin," he said, almost choking.

"No. . . ."

He thrust the cross into her face. Tears spurted from her eyes. Tears that were drops of blood. "You're not really crying," he said. "You're not really Lisa. Lisa begged me to kill you."

She moaned in a little-girl voice.

"Please, Lisa. Don't make it hard for me."

She moved to the coffin.

"I love you, Uncle Brian." But it rang false. It was the thing that wore Lisa's shape, trying to beguile him into sparing it. He must be hard. He must!

"I love you too, Lisa," he said softly.

With the cross he drove her into the watery casket.

As she touched the water she began to scream . . . like a child, an abused child, and he remembered stumbling into the dark room and discovering his brother's hideous secret and the girl screaming for him to stop and he hated himself for making her scream and it made him feel like his brother *stop hurting the girl you asshole stop it stop it* and she didn't stop screaming even when he pulled Mark off her and punched him in the face and saw the blood spurt from his nose and now the same scream again and again and he was his brother and holding up the stake and pounding and pounding and his brother thrusting and thrusting and the stake riving the girl-flesh and the blood bursting out and his brother coming and blood spurting from his nose and his brother thrusting and the stake driving down and the same scream again and the blood bursting and his brother coming bursting coming bursting—

And now, in his arms, in the red sea water—

The corpse of a little girl. And Brian crying again because he'd killed her, he'd driven in the stake again and again while she screamed and cried out "I love you, Uncle Brian." And he kissed the carrion lips and cradled the slight body in his arms and tried to warm it up with his body heat. But he could not. And got up to look for a way out. . . .

He couldn't remember how he had come upon this room. And he didn't dare brave the labyrinth again. What other route was there? The window? He could use the rope. He tied one end around his waist and another to a railing over the window. As he tightened it he kept glancing at the girl's body.

Already the phosphorescence was leaving her face, and the gaping wounds on her torso were closing up, and peace seemed to have fallen over her.

"I do love you," he whispered.

"Very touching," said a woman's voice, mocking him.

He saw a young woman standing over the corpse. He'd seen her before. Kitty.

"You won't escape," she said. He held out a cross. He thought: I'm too tired, too tired . . . he brandished the cross menacingly. She squirmed a little but did not step back.

"It's still a long time to sunrise," she said, "and I can worry at you for hours yet."

"Let him go, Kitty." Another voice now: musical, sweet.

Another figure beside Kitty. Brian recognized him at once.

"Let him go, Kitty. I'm sorry, Brian," said Timmy Valentine.

"Sorry!" Brian's rage and grief exploded all at once. "I could have saved her. She had a chance, finally. Her own father raped her, did you know that?"

"Yes."

"And you come along and turn her into a monster—"

"She might have found redemption. We are not without compassion, you know."

"Let me kill him!" Kitty hissed.

"Brian—"

Timmy came forward. They studied each other. The boy seemed so earnest, so innocent. Uncertainly, Brian held out the cross. It had no effect.

"Maybe you're right," Timmy said seriously. "Maybe I shouldn't have awoken her to the cold eternity. But it was the only chance *I* could give her! Don't you understand, mortal?"

"Why," Brian said, "you're weeping!"

For a moment he thought he saw real tears on the boy's cheeks. But Timmy shrugged and the tears were gone.

"A vampire does not weep," he said coldly.

"But you're not like the others!" said Brian. "You seem to . . . understand a little more . . . you seem to be more like a human being. . . ."

"No!" Timmy said, clenching his eyes tight shut. And now Brian sensed that he was truly alien.

I probably just imagined the tears, he thought. A trick of the light.

"I'm going to kill him!" Kitty screeched, and he saw a blur in the air, a wolf, a vulture, a shimmer of fangs—

"Go, you fool!" Timmy said. He tugged at Brian's arm and pushed him through the window. The boy was strong, so strong, with the strength of darkness. Brian fell. The rope jerked taut. His body slammed against prickly foliage. He let himself down and ran for the open gate. His arm burned where the boy vampire had gripped it, searing cold.

labyrinth

They were in the secret room of Prathna's palace, the remaining members of the Gods of Chaos: Prathna and Locke and Muriel and Stephen, who was watching the prince put down the morning edition of the *Bangkok Post*.

"Well, the Isao attacked anyway, it seems, and in the resultant confusion the Thai border police moved in and mopped up the lot of them. There are no Isao left at all now, bless their barbarous little hearts!"

"Isn't that a little drastic?" said Locke.

"Well, I daresay a handful of them are still around, and they'll be farmed out to some reservation, and become permanent employees of some Ford Foundation grant anthropologist," Prathna said callously. "But there is a bright side to this dour business."

"Yes?" Locke said.

"This idol," said Muriel, "was this people's life and death. It drew power from their worship. You might think that the people's collective death has eradicated that power; but I think that, in the moment of their dying, all their psychic energy was absorbed by the idol. Our search for a weapon is therefore complete."

"But *our* plans are much more important, eh? I mean, the final spectacle which we will engineer before we die," Prathna said.

"The vampire," Muriel wheezed.

"There are only four of us left. We leave for America tomorrow; you Muriel, are guardian of the idol. I'm sure the thing will work. Won't it, Muriel dear? I mean fire fights fire, doesn't it? And death fights death. What can defeat us now? I can almost hear someone thinking"—he glanced at Stephen—

" 'Ah, but *love* can defeat death.' But I don't think we need fear that. After all, a vampire is intrinsically evil; it has no truck with love and compassion and other such silly emotions. It should be a simple matter to track down this demonic presence, in whatever guise he may have assumed, and to stage a suitably pyrotechnic demise. I shall take care of the *mise-en-scène* myself."

"The great director," Muriel said. The prince grinned, pointedly ignoring her sarcasm.

"Before we leave, let us have a little moment of truth," the prince went on. "We share so few truths, we Gods. I think we should each make a declaration of what we are hoping to achieve in this, our grandest adventure."

"Simple enough," Muriel said. "All my life I have puttered around with false magic. Only one thing I did ever worked . . . the ceremony at Saint Cecilia's, sixty years ago. Before I die, I want vindication. I want to make magic. I want to be a true witch." Stephen winced.

"I," said Sir Francis Locke, "am interested purely in killing. I'm too old to deny it any longer. I want to annihilate once and for all this thing that has haunted my life."

"My purpose is as simple as yours," Prathna said. "My garden of delight has failed me. I'm jaded, Francis, so jaded! Nothing arouses me anymore. But when I think of a vampire . . . a thing simultaneously dead and capable of movement and thought, a simulacrum of life, a creature of violence and darkest sensuality—"

"What a filthy mind you have!" said Muriel, chuckling delightedly.

"And you, Miles?" Prathna said at last. "What about you?"

The three turned on him like vultures.

He knew what he had to say.

labyrinth

The last song in the concert: *Vampire Junction*. And Carla was in the audience for the first time.

The band enveloped in darkness; a lone spot on Timmy as he began the song.

All at once a murmur broke loose from the crowd. Like the

sea at night. She watched him. The crowd fell silent. It was a miraculous thing, this silence of thousands of souls. Into the hush came the song's strange words, each image unlocking the next, like a Chinese puzzle.

She watched him. For a moment she saw a puma leaping from crag to crag in slow motion. She wondered if anyone else had seen it. For a moment, just standing there, poised in the pause before the next soaring phrase of the song, he was the most beautiful thing she had ever seen. This was his magic. Only an archetype made flesh could possess this magic. She believed in him utterly now.

It seemed that their eyes met.

"But . . . he is weeping!" she whispered to Maria, who was sitting beside her.

"He cannot weep. He is a dead boy. Don't you understand?"

But Carla thought: In time, could he not achieve humanity once more? He has been on the road to individuation for almost two thousand years. . . .

And she remembered what he had asked her on that first visit in the spring: *But can an archetype itself be susceptible to analysis?*

The answer should have been no.

But if an archetype could be analyzed, then maybe a vampire could weep. And if an archetype could grow more human, then maybe a human could—

Suddenly she saw where all this was leading. She couldn't bear to think of it. She had to run away. Before it was too late. Get out of this whole thing.

"Maria, I have to resign," she said impulsively. "You understand, don't you? I've just realized what's going to happen if I go on. . . ."

"As you wish," said Maria. But Carla knew that she didn't believe her.

labyrinth

And Stephen said, "I want to burn down the whole world."

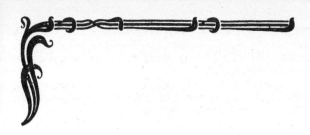

AUTUMN

Bluebeard's Castle

A freight car crossed the bridge
It turned into a hearse
Don't look out at the countryside
You can't escape the curse.
—Timmy Valentine

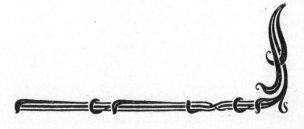

16

I said: "What about the massacre in your attic?"
He said: "Soon we will go to Junction."
"Will it make any difference?"
"I don't know."
"When you try to remember things, what do you see?"
"Fire."
"And behind the fire?"
"A forest."
"And in the forest?"
"A dark castle."
"And behind the forest?"
"Fire."

The room with the mirrors has grown to accommodate a lot more train track. Behind a hill he has put up a barbed-wire fence and a factory.

I dream of the forest every night. It is becoming more and more vivid.

I told Maria I was resigning, but we both know better.

I dream of the forest every night. In the morning I awaken and I have lost the power of speech.

I searched the attic for Lisa's old room with the salt wind and the TV monitors; it has gone.

This is what I asked him: "Timmy," I said, "there is a theory popular with Bible-thumpers about the creation of the world . . . that the geological record does not disprove God's creation of the world in six days at all; that, in fact, the geological record exists to tempt us. If Adam, the first man, was perfect, he must have had a navel, mustn't he? Yet he had no biological need of one. Do you see what I mean? Thus . . . the earth, the bones in the rocks. And so you, with your past . . . couldn't you have sprung into being only this year, and be endowed with a past only for the sake of being a perfect vampire? Could your past be an illusion?"

"You believe this theory?"

"No, I think it's just a theological casuistry."

"Well then."

I had a waking dream. I felt the forest. Felt the damp earth pounding my paws, mush against my snout, a sweet wild smell.

"You feel its reality," he said. "You do feel it! We are kin."

"How can you say that?" But I remembered that I had seen him weep, although vampires do not weep.

. . . leaves, stirred by a lugubrious mountain breeze, fluttering a little . . . each one has its own particular acridness . . . dry, they drain from the branches as I batter them into the wet mud with my leaping . . . and then I woke.

He pressed a control on the black box, and a model engine —one of those German trains—buzzed through a tunnel. He said: "If you think you are dreaming, why do you dream within your dream?"

I struggled with myself and him; with myself to banish my forest reverie to some more remote corner of my mind, with him to gain control of the session. "I'm the analyst," I said, only half believing it. "Tell me what fire you see now, Timmy."

He said: "They are burning the bodies. That was when I first met Rudy, you know." He pointed to the barbed wire. He had built a guard tower over the fence, and, in the distance, a cabin. It was one of the summer camp cabins; he'd just picked it up from one side of the mountain and plonked it down on the other. "Do you know what this is?"

I knew then how far we still had to go.

memory: 1942

At first he is only conscious of the darkness and the over-powering smell. Two smells: a clinical, chemical odor, and a stench of putrefying corpses. The air is heavy, so heavy. And he cannot move. He has died again.

Dead people, all around him, in the darkness. He moves his hand a little; he hears the thud of one corpse tumbling onto another. He tries to sit up; he is caught in a dead man's rigid embrace. The corpse's arms and legs have locked into the semblance of a stiffened spider.

Darkness is not kind to the boy, as it is to the living. It cannot cast over the world's uglinesses a warm soft blanket of unseeing; it cannot be drawn over the faces of the dead. The boy is cursed with too much seeing.

He sees the corpses: skeletal, gray-skinned, naked, the faces the papery leather of starved skin. Interlocking, corpse hugging corpse, limb clasping limb, like a box of jigsaw pieces. They are hundreds in number, piled up almost to the ceiling, where the boy sees a metal glint of showerheads.

As always, the boy reaches his memory for his name; he is Emilio, a gypsy. He and his adopted family have been rounded up barely a week ago and sent here by cattletrain. He is not sure where this place is; but it is surrounded by barbed wire and ringed with observation towers, and in the distance stand factories from whose chimneys gush a constant stream of black smoke.

For a year he has lived with the caravan. They have juggled in villages full of small children and housewives and old men, their performances bringing brief smiles to wan faces, de-flecting for a moment or two the constant terror of war.

Sometimes they have seen panzers. They did not even always know what country they were in; usually it was Poland. The night before they were captured a villager told them strange rumors: in a distant city, someone has conceived a plan to exterminate all the Jews and all the gypsies and all the lower orders of humanity. His parents laughed, he remembers.

Now he lies among the exterminated. He jerks himself upright; bodies sift. How can he get out? Must he gnaw out a path? Amid this plenty, he cannot even feed. The blood is tainted. He smells it; it is thick, foul, devoid of that life-force from which he must replenish his own. It is the gas, he thinks.

He feels the thirst, unquenchable, raging.

They are crowding him! He turns and collides with an old man's head. The eyes are bulging, and trails of pus are drying on the edges of the sockets and around the scabs of old wounds.

He is shocked; abruptly he shifts shape.

He is a rodent now. He blends perfectly with the dark. He scurries through the fissures between the corpses. He runs along the pipestem limbs, over bony buttocks. His paws stumble over the chasms of frozen screams. The smell of the deathgas fades as the night passes; it is swallowed up in the fetor of decomposition. Somewhere else in the gas chamber there is another pattering. Another of his kind? He squeals an anguished search-call in the night-language that all his kind know; but there is no answer. It is a true rodent then. The rats of this place have learned when to come out and feed.

He thinks: how can they do this? It is beyond reason.

He hates them then, the world of men! The weight of the dead oppresses him. There is no more space to run . . . he shrinks once more . . . he is some carnivorous insect, a crawling cockroach. Now there is more space, for the corpses are as mountains.

He longs to have truly died. But for him death is only a sleep, and does not hold the darkness he has craved so long. All night he explores the landscape of the dead. The crags of heads topped by forests of stiff hair. The plains of flaking skin. The crevasses of cupped limbs. Lakes of foul water and urine. The cavernous mouths with their floors of caking saliva. He skitters over a tongue bitten off in the frenzy of dying, and he remembers their collective death-throes: the writhing, the convulsing, the screaming, stilled now.

He thirsts.

The night goes by. At last he reaches the peak of the grisly mountain. His compound eyes perceive the fountainhead above. Like a moon it glimmers over the surface of his world.

He thirsts. Befouled as it is, this blood must suffice. Still he clings to his tiny form, for with his insect eyes he cannot count the dead.

A quick, percussive sound . . . the fleshland quakes. A monster has squirmed from the abyss of the corpse's armpit.

It is the rat he heard earlier. He hears the rat's blood racing; in the deathchamber it is the only noise, and it thunders like a waterfall. He circles the rat. His hunger quickens, for this blood is living, untainted, full of the power he needs. The landscape resounds with the sound of rat's teeth tearing flesh. The rat does not see the insect; it is too busy gorging itself on poisoned meat.

He leaps.

His mandibles rend the rat's flesh now. The blood is thin but warm. It showers him. His tiny body shudders as the red rain hits him. Greedily he laps at it . . . his hunger is everything now . . . he cannot even control his shape . . . abruptly he is human, lying at the top of the corpse-heap; he has bitten the rat in two and is spitting the pieces from his mouth, and the trickle of blood on his lips has sent the warmth shooting into his dead veins. It is only a ghost of that intense pleasure that comes from feeding on a human, that wild joy that comes like orgasm to his kind; but he is as tired as any mountaineer who has attained some difficult peak, and those few drops of blood, after such travail, are sweet to him. And so he becomes drowsy, and he sleeps, in fetal position, on his bed of the dead.

Time passes.

He feels a wind on his face. Overhead, someone is barking commands. When he opens his eyes he sees he is outside now. The corpses are being piled onto wheelbarrows; a gaunt man in a prison uniform is inspecting each one, occasionally knocking a few teeth from the mouths with a little hammer and putting them into a bag. He realizes that the man is collecting gold teeth. There are two men standing guard; they are wearing the same uniforms as the ones who arrested the caravan of gypsies.

The prisoner draws near; he is on his hands and knees among the dead. Emilio the gypsy boy reaches out to clutch his hand. The prisoner starts and looks at him.

"You are not dead," he says in Polish.

"No."

Emilio studies the man for traces of emotion. But he sees none. It is as if all feeling has been siphoned from him. "What is this place?" Emilio asks in faulty Polish.

"Oswiecim."

The prisoner bends over to extract another gold tooth.

"Why do you do this? Are you, too, destined for this place?"

The prisoner betrays nothing.

"Do you understand why I have survived?" says Emilio.

"No."

"Do you know what I am?"

"I cannot tell."

"My name is Emilio. I am a vampire."

"My name is Rudy Lydick. I am a stripper of corpses."

"Why am I here, Rudy?"

"Are you a Jew?"

"No."

"A gypsy?"

The boy nods.

"I'm dreaming."

"No."

"They will kill you again."

In the distance, a burst of gunfire. Dawnlight, blighted by the factory smoke, is beginning to invade the steel-gray sky.

"I cannot die."

Screams. They are beating someone.

"Where am I?"

"Oswiecim."

"What is Oswiecim?"

"Hell."

arcade

One boy came whizzing out of the woods on his bike; another came down Main Street from the direction of the mountain, doing a wheelie over the railway tracks.

"David!" the first one yelled.

Laughing, they pretended to ram one another. Then they leaped off their bikes and began walking them downhill, away from the sign that read *Junction, Idaho: population 573*.

"You skipped school, Terry Gish," said David Gish. They looked exactly alike: slim, jeans, lumberjack shirts, freckles, red hair. "You skipped school, you asshole."

"I had to," Terry said. "I was too excited."

"It's dumb to miss the first day of school. I had to pretend to be both of us again."

"I'll make it up to you," said Terry. But his mind was far

away. He'd been up the trail, all the way to that spooky abandoned house. "It was a good idea for us not to take the same classes, wasn't it? I'll cover for you tomorrow."

"Asshole!"

"But I gotta tell you what I saw!"

"Eat shit! I take a bus for thirty miles and run in and out of a million classes and forget what name to answer to, and nothing you saw's worth that."

"Someone's moving into the Spook House."

"Shit!" But Terry could see that his twin brother was getting excited.

They walked down the street a ways, stopping to throw a pebble into the parking lot by the general store, darting into the drugstore for a Coke and a Snickers bar, hugging their shirts hard to themselves against the brisk wind from the mountain. Red leaves were raining down on them, piling up against the fire hydrant and the mailbox. Terry had to shout above the wind: "I saw this convoy of trucks all heading uphill to the Spook House. I saw them unloading piles and piles of shit, I mean sofas and cupboards and big wooden boxes—"

"Yeah! Coffins, I'll bet."

"Coffins! All right!" Terry giggled, half nervous, half thrilled at the idea.

"Well," David said, "wait till I tell you what *I* saw!"

"Come on. Nothing could be more exciting than someone moving into the Spook House." He looked up at the mountain, gold and bloody with the colors of autumn, peppered at the peak with snow. You couldn't really make out the Spook House from the middle of Main Street, but you always knew it was there. Nobody had lived there for longer than anyone could remember. "Nothing could possibly be weirder," he said, with all the authority of being two minutes older than his brother.

"Oh, yeah? There's a new game at the arcade."

"You're shitting me!"

"It's called *Bloodsucker*."

"What are we waiting for? Got a quarter?"

"Yeah, I ripped it off Alex Evans' lunchbox."

"Come fucking on, brother!"

They leaped back on their bikes and pedaled like maniacs, ignoring the town's only stop sign at the bottom of the hill.

●　　●　　●

night-child

She took a wrong turn on her way to the therapy room. She found a corridor lined with doors: heavy doors, oak braced with steel, locked.

She reached for the cross she always carried with her now and held it before her.

Somehow, standing before the first of the doors, she felt Timmy behind them. She beat on the door with her fists, calling his name.

The door swung open; a cold wind whipped through a patch of darkness; dry leaves whirled, blood-colored . . . she saw that she was in the room of mirrors, the heartroom, where she and Timmy always met, and that Timmy was already taking shape in the couch beneath the antique lamp with its shade of silk and lace . . . the train tracks ran under the couch, disappearing beneath its decorously skirted legs . . . beside the footstool, a miniature concentration camp . . . next to her plaid armchair, a guard tower.

Carla said: "I didn't know if you'd make it tonight. Aren't you giving a concert in . . . Arizona, or Texas, or somewhere?"

For a moment she thought of Stephen and his Wagner stand-ins.

"As you know," Timmy said, "I occasionally avail myself of rather unorthodox travel methods."

She dreaded the talk to come; for Timmy was still reliving his time in Auschwitz and his strange relationship with the prisoner Rudy Lydick. "I'm angry," she said.

"Why?"

"What's this new corridor up here with the locked medieval doors? I thought we were here to open doors, not to shut them in my face."

"You want the keys?" All innocence.

"You're like . . . like a Bluebeard!"

"You do not know," Timmy said slowly, "how much you hurt me." He closed his eyes. She waited. He was still in costume from the concert, in black superhero tights, with a velvet black cape spangled with stars and moons. Rouge tinged his anemic face, and his already dark large eyes were touched up with a deep purple eye shadow. He seemed completely androgynous.

"What do you mean, hurt you?" Carla said at last.

"Don't you know who the real Bluebeard was?"

"I've read the case history. A mass murderer of children."

"Don't call me Bluebeard," said Timmy.

Carla felt on the verge of some key discovery. She dared not press her advantage. At a certain point in his past, they reached the dark forest; and beyond that forest he would or could reveal nothing. Had he known Gilles de Rais, the mad killer whom Joan of Arc had once befriended, and who had died at the stake? "What does Bluebeard mean to you?" she said, unable to keep a twinge of excitement from her voice.

"You provoke me, Carla Rubens!"

He seemed to be in pain. Not some brief anxiety, but a millenial anguish. Though he is dead, she thought, I can touch something living, deep within. Beyond the dark forest. Even if it is only pain, smoldering like magma beneath the rocky crust of his undeadness.

Her gaze wandered from mirror to mirror. In the mirrors the trains collided and the tracks kaleidoscoped, and she saw herself endlessly reflected, but she could not see Timmy.

She said: "I am your anima, Timmy. And you are my animus. I see that clearly now."

"But who is our shadow?"

She said nothing, but she thought: Stephen. Stephen.

labyrinth

Stephen stepped from a phone booth at Narita airport, Tokyo, where they had an hour to wait in the transit lounge for the connection to Los Angeles.

Three Gods of Chaos on two plastic armchairs and a wheelchair, against the huge expanse of glass and the arc of the Narita monorail. Old, old. Like the three Fates, waiting to snip the thread of Stephen's life.

He said: "I've called L.A. I don't have many contacts in the pop music industry, but my contacts do have contacts, and those contacts have tracked down the name of an executive at Stupendous Sounds Systems: Melissa Pavlat. She's been newly promoted after the mysterious disappearance of her superior, Blade Kendall."

The three Fates nodded in unison.

"Have we still got a little time?" said Prathna.

"Forty-five minutes before the plane leaves."

"Arrange an appointment," said Sir Francis Locke, for all the world as if the clock had been turned back sixty years, and Stephen was still a little boy swinging a censer and watching a virgin being carved up on the altar of College Chapel.

He turned to obey, understanding completely their hypocrisy, their emptiness. They would never touch what burned in his heart. Never, never.

seeker

In a phone booth in a motel in Hollywood, Brian Zottoli was saying to the publicity woman at Stupendous Sounds Systems: "I'm a very avid fan, and I'd really like to know every city he's going to play on the last leg of this tour, and all the dates, and who to get tickets from."

To his agent in New York, he said, stalling, "Look, I just got this idea for a novel. See, there's this twelve-year-old rock and roll star, only he happens to be a vampire. . . ."

"Are you trying to borrow money?" his agent said.

To his brother in Phoenix, he said, "Mark, I've found her. She's dead. And it's your fucking fault, your motherfucking fault, you asshole, you asshole."

He heard his brother crying and he hung up. Hypocrite, he thought, fucking hypocrite.

Then he drove to the Safeway to buy more brooms.

17

analyst's notebook

Now we are two as we run swiftly into the forest . . . his dreamworld invades mine. Or mine his. I don't know.

I'm becoming increasingly suspicious of this Auschwitz business, despite its grisly grandeur. The theory that he may be manufacturing his past has once more become attractive to me . . . once more, the vampire in the concentration camp business is a juxtaposition so pat, so clearly directed at self-mythologizing, that—

Can a vampire be a megalomaniac?

Can an archetype be insane?

The forest is all there is. He runs beside me. We sense the prey, far off, through the scent-veil of decaying autumn leaves. We are joyful. We are the wind and the darkness. We need nothing but each other.

Every morning I wake with the scent of the forest in my nostrils. But I'm no longer afraid. I am not alone there. He runs beside me. My dream is his waking.

Sometimes, as we run, I feel the shadow of a third entity. I am afraid to acknowledge its existence; but I am drawn to it. One day I must embrace it. I know, I know, it is a part of me that I dare not face yet.

Who is it?

And then, when the shadow comes, swooping overhead,

there is music: overwhelming, Wagnerian. I almost recognize
it.

Look, in the distance—is the forest on fire?

arcade

Sunrise on the sea; the huge open-air stage, overhung with
scaffolding, in shadow; the empty stadium, facing the ocean,
striated with red-ripple shadows. Stephen Miles looked down
and saw a woman on stage, a tiny figure in an afro and stylish,
executive-looking suit. As he watched, she clapped her hands,
and the back of the stage exploded with quick videogame
images: a hurtling train, an exploding coffin, a maze of tracks
and junctions . . . through the laser projections, the sun like a
crimson pinball about to be shot into the game.

Stephen went down towards the proscenium, and the
woman saw him as he reached the stage.

"Oh. Hi. You're that conductor, aren't you?" she said.
Then, shouting toward somewhere backstage: "The blood effect! Give 'em the blood effect."

As Stephen watched, a bloodstain bubbled out of the sea
and started to spread. He would have cried out, but the effect
shimmered and vanished . . . now a snake of fire along the
seashore . . . his heart leapt in response to the fire's cruel joy.

But he must remember why he'd come here. The Gods of
Chaos had tracked the boy vampire for almost a month now,
shadowing his concert tour from city to city; this was to be the
final appearance of the year, in the Marina Stadium of Boca
Blanca in Florida. Prathna's spectacle would have to be
tonight or they would have to seek out a new strategy.

"Hey—famous conductor guy—"

He almost didn't hear her when she started to make conversation: "So what's a longhair like you doing among the
punks?"

"Well now, Beethoven and Wagner were punks themselves,
you know," Stephen said, using one of his stock answers.

"And you've got some kind of message from a Siamese
prince? Far fucking out! 'Scuse my French."

"I have him right here. May we talk?"

Stephen turned away from the sunrise. There was a special
aisle for the handicapped that ran down the side of the bowl
towards the proscenium rather like a kabuki ramp. Down it

came the three Fates: Muriel, in the center, clutching two velvet bags that contained the two halves of the thunder idol; her wheelchair was flanked by Prince Prathna in a crimson Thai silk Nehru jacket and Sir Francis Locke, cadaverous in a dark suit, as incongruous in the Florida dawn as an undertaker at a cocktail party.

The two stood silent for a long moment, watching the processional, at once grotesque and grand. "Jesus!" Missy said, pulling a pair of New Wave glasses from her pocket and donning them abstractedly. Stephen noticed that the frames were in the shape of a muscle-flexing nude man. "Weird friends you have, Mr. Longhaired Conductor!"

Stephen looked her over, raising an eyebrow.

The prince approached. "Miss Pavlat!"

"Like wow! Are you related to the King in *The King and I*?"

"Very distantly," Prathna said, charming to the hilt. "You are, I am told, an executive of the ... ah ... Stupendous Corporation, I understand, and in charge of this ... Timmy Valentine's career?"

"Well, yes. But why are you folks interested?"

"Our tastes may diverge," said Prathna, "but there is one lust we share. Money."

"Money?"

"Do you realize, my dear Miss Pavlat, what a vast vein the Asian tour circuit is to be mined?

"Just who are you from, Your Majesty? Is that what I'm supposed to call you, Your Majesty?"

"Your Highness will do very nicely," Prathna said in that commanding tone, at once disdainful and gracious, that only those bred from birth to walk all over people seemed capable of. "But as to your question, I don't think we're quite ready to reveal just who we are yet, but we do have a fascinating proposition to make to you. ..."

"Why don't you people hang around backstage, then, tonight? Here,"—she reached into the same pocket from which she had produced the dark glasses— "backstage VIP passes." Stephen sighed in relief; their purpose had been accomplished.

For the next half hour or so they stayed on, for the sake of propriety, while Missy Pavlat showed off some of the special effects that were to ensue that night.

"Oh, and we've got this *awesome* funhouse sequence where

all sorts of ghosts and ghouls are going to pop out while he's singing, and then we've got him actually riding a toy train onto the stage, and then we're hoisting him and his piano skyward with like a million helium balloons, and—"

"I wish," Stephen said, thinking of the fire that was made to burn on the sea, "that we could afford such a thing in the opera house. Imagine the end of Wagner's *Ring* like that now...."

"Laser-holography," said Missy in reverent, mantra-like tones.

The sun had risen; stagehands were hammering on scaffolds; from beyond the tiers of seats came the sounds of traffic, blending uneasily with the whisper of the sea wind. On a command from Missy, another sequence of video images billowed out from the sea: a train rushing at the audience, Timmy riding the engine, laughing. "That's *Bloodsucker,* the video game they've put out; we've incorporated its imagery into the six videos Timmy's doing for Stupendous Cable, and—"

"Arcade games, eh what?" the prince mused. "Have a few hundred of them sent over to my palace in Thailand, won't you? My harem could use a mild amusement."

"But Your Highness—the expense—"

"Ah, but—" Prince Prathna flashed his wallet. "I have an American Express Card, isn't it?" Stephen realized that he was really laying on the oriental potentate routine. "But I impose, my dear Miss Pavlat. I hope you'll tack on ten or twenty thousand dollars for yourself, as a little token of my esteem."

"Prince—" said Missy. "Aren't you being a little hasty?"

"It is nothing," the Prince said expansively, pocketing the backstage passes with which Missy had occasionally been gesticulating. "We will have breakfast together?"

"Why, ah—" Stephen could see that Prathna's peculiar charms were working rather well on this somewhat pretentious creature. "I'd be—" she said. "Why, I—I feel like I'm in the middle of *The King and I*!"

"So you are, my dear, so you are." Prathna turned Muriel's chair around and began to wheel her uphill; Locke followed, gaunt and impassive; then came the young woman.

Halfway up the ramp, Prathna turned to Stephen: "Aren't you going to join us, old chap?"

"No," Stephen said. "I think I'll . . . stay and watch the special effects a bit longer."

Fire danced on the water.

memory: 1942

Dusk, a black cat leaping from the rooftop of a wooden cabin—

Against the setting sun, silhouettes: hanged men. They are swinging a little in the wind. The cat that is the gypsy Emilio hears in the distance the sound of a string quartet; it comes from behind a stone wall that surrounds the garden of the Kommandant. He has seen the garden, flying ravenlike over its crown of barbed wire, pausing to preen his night-black feathers in the birdbath. From far above, the garden gleams in the wasteland of black smoke and piled corpses like the emerald-decked navel of a dark-skinned belly dancer.

He is drawn to the garden. It is the music that draws him, the slow movement of Mozart's *Eine kleine Nachtmusik*. He hears the first violin spin out the long lines of the haunting melody, and beyond them—for he is cursed with the gift of hearing—a dissonant cluster of deathscreams from the gas chambers, so softened by distance and the intervention of walls of stone and steel as to seem almost an afterecho of the Mozart, almost another layer of implicit resonance. And he knows too that the players are doomed to die.

There is a gate. A guard stands stiffly to attention; Emilio miaows and curls his tail about his boots. The guard kneels to pet him. He paws at the gate; presently a solemn child comes. "A cat?" he says. "Here, puss, puss . . ." To the guard he says, "Don't tell father; he'll only tell me I have to send it to Dr. Schweiss to have its filthy Jewish diseases burned out of it." Then he cradles the cat in his arms and they go into the garden.

He smells the child's blood: sweet, racing. A pang of hunger shakes him. He must not feed. He must stay calm. The even stateliness of the slow movement dissolves now into a more impassioned, minor melody, darting, trilling. As if startled by the music's abrupt change of tempo, Emilio contrives to spring from the child's arms and to bolt into the bushes that ring the garden, where he blends easily into blackness.

German voices over the music now. Among the gypsies,

wandering from country to country, he has picked up a smattering of many tongues, among them this one, but his understanding is still imperfect.

The voices: "Yes, Kommandant, I do believe it very firmly. Their threshold of pain *is* different from ours. To this end I have conceived a series of experiments. . . ." A woman's voice. He sees her now: prim, blonde, sharp-nosed, in a laboratory gown.

The other he cannot make out; an apple tree conceals him. But the voice is gentlemanly, deep and cultured: "By all means, Schweiss. What did you have in mind?"

"A little device similar to the *question extraordinary* once beloved of the Spanish Inquisition. . . ."

"How charming, Dr. Schweiss. And this Mozart . . . exquisite, isn't it?"

"The players are prisoners, I take it, Herr Kommandant?"

"Naturally. But how they play. Life was never this elegant back in Ulm! Amazing how well they play, for all that they are Jews."

"Perhaps it is their proximity to death that charges their playing with such emotion. Or perhaps their very nearness to the animal side of human nature enables them to portray so convincingly the dark, dionysian aspects of—"

"Well said, Doctor. Perhaps you ought to perform some kind of experiment along those lines."

"A wondrous thought, Kommandant!"

"Well, my dear Doctor, you have but to submit an official request for . . . ah . . . subjects. I'm not an unreasonable man, when science needs to be served." Emilio senses the man's unease; he radiates an aura of domesticity that seems somehow alien to this Dantean landscape.

"Science is a cruel mistress," says the doctor, compounding her commander's discomfiture.

It is then that Emilio notices the string quartet. They sit in a gazebo ringed with shrubbery. Candlelight plays over their music, their skull-like, impassive faces. Their skin is like bark; their arms are like bent twigs on which their camp garments hang as if to dry; their wooden instruments seem to grow out of their very bodies, their bows extensions of their sticklike limbs. And, playing first violin in the quartet, his eyes listless, lifeless, is Rudy Lydick, the man who pulled Emilio from the pile of corpses. Not once, but several times now. For every few days Emilio would be spotted and consigned to the death chamber, and again he would waken to the crush of corpses, to the fetor of unpalatable blood.

The boy vampire's shape sieves into darkness. Windlike, he gusts towards the gazebo. They are playing other music now, sentimental German popular songs with repetitive hurdy-gurdy accompaniments.

He is standing behind Rudy now, a whirlwind darkness, boy-tall. He whispers for Rudy alone: "Rudy, Rudy. We are more kin than I once thought. You too have music."

Rudy trembles. "How have you come here?" he says under his breath. "What are you?"

"I told you. A vampire."

"Some private vision; some angel of death." Rudy does not look behind.

Across the garden come inmates bearing trays laden with fine victuals; beneath their baggy garments they resemble animated skeletons. The Kommandant sips champagne.

An officer enters, walking softly so as not to disturb the music. He whispers in the Kommandant's ear.

"Stop the music!" the commander says harshly. The violin falls from Rudy's hand. Emilio feels fear, a palpable thing; then he is a cat once more, crouching between two rosebushes.

Two guards drag Rudy from the gazebo. They trample his violin; it snaps.

The Kommandant says: "What is this report, prisoner, about resurrecting the dead?"

"I don't understand," Rudy says faintly.

"You were seen by the ovens . . . actually pulling a boy out of the heap of corpses . . . a boy still moving . . . what does it mean? Are you some kind of necrophile?"

"I—"

The cat darts between his legs. Gnaws at the neckpiece of the crushed violin as it lies on the grass. He hears the commander shout gruffly to the remaining players: "Continue! You may be missing a man, but you can surely come up with some trios."

Tentatively the music begins again; it is a Boccherini trio, repetitious and harmonically unexciting. To one of the guards, the commander says: "Hang him. Now."

Dr. Schweiss says: "Why not make him the subject of one of my experiments?"

"Oh, very well." He beckons to the musicians. "Louder, please, louder."

Dr. Schweiss gets up and crooks her finger. White-robed men come from the house wheeling a chair to whose arm is attached a wooden contraption linked to a control panel with dials and flashing buttons. They force Rudy into the chair and strap his hand into a tight wooden box. A guard sticks wooden wedges between his fingers, and at a signal from Dr. Schweiss, who has pulled out a leatherbound notebook and begun to scribble in it, he begins to hammer in the wedges with a mallet.

Rudy opens his mouth in a soundless scream. The Boccherini wells up, trivial and metrical. The guard picks up more wedges and begins to beat them in. Emilio sees that the hand will be squeezed so tight that the bones will be pulverized, the flesh jellied. The doctor continues to take notes; her face is impassive, like that of a plumber or carpenter at work. Blood shoots up into the guard's face, but he continues to hammer. Still Rudy does not scream; he seems to have fallen into a trance.

"I see you are right, my dear Dr. Schweiss, about the pain threshold of these Jews," said the Kommandant. "More champagne?"

"I do not drink while I work."

The boy vampire smells Rudy's blood; but the sight of the shrunken man, defenseless, having his hand pounded into ribbons, sickens him. And he understands why Rudy does not scream; it is because he will now lose music, and music is all that has sustained him in this hell. He has played all the songs he will ever play; he is already dead. Why can't they understand this?

He hisses; he scratches at the roots of the apple tree; then he springs up, transforms in mid-leap into a bird of night, and he takes to the air, circling the tortured man. The Boccherini swells and subsides; it is over. Still Rudy makes no sound, though Emilio can see the tears stream from his twisted eyes. High above the garden he wheels; beyond the wall, beyond the circle of candlelit green, the lines of cabins radiate outward to the barbed-wire fences. Searchlights scan the sky, smoky from burning corpses. He hears the banal chatter below, and the clink of champagne glasses, and the zombie pacing of attendants.

I will scream for him, he thinks.

And, wings spread wide, he begins to sing the melody line of the Mozart, the last thing Rudy played. But as the song comes whistling through the syrinx of the crow-creature, it is transformed into raucous cawing . . . the Germans look up, disturbed for a moment . . . but a smile steals across Rudy's face, although the pain must now be unbearable.

And Emilio knows that he has heard what the others have not: the sweet voice of a young boy, a pure sound, beyond joy and terror. For a moment they have touched souls, aliens though they are.

I cannot feel heartbreak, Emilio thinks, as he forces the melody through his tiny borrowed lungs, through his beak. He feels a twinge of envy for Rudy. Even for this pain, which he can no longer feel himself. . . .

Later comes dawn. An assembly is called, and they hang Rudy in the sunrise. But as the rope snaps taut a wolf-creature jumps from the crowd and gnaws the rope apart and drags the prisoner away, snarling, his jaws foaming, his eyes bloodshot. The guards shoot at the wolf, but he does not even seem to notice.

Several guards run after him with rifles. But at times he appears to throw a gauze of darkness about himself, a haze shrouds him. He reaches the first of the fences and chews easily through the barbed wire. Then the second fence. Bursts of gunfire now as the bewildered guards shoot randomly, confusedly. Then, assuming human form for only a second to lift Rudy into his arms—malnutrition has rendered him light as a rag doll—he cloaks himself with darkness and begins to sprint swiftly, sometimes a wolf, sometimes a tiger, sometimes a black cheetah—

A forest springs up around them, so thick as to admit no sunlight, and fragrant with rotting autumn leaves. Night has fallen when they reach a clearing; a full moon silvers Emilio's fur as they come to rest.

Rudy stirs.

When he opens his eyes he first sees a small black cat lapping the blood from his shattered hand. The tongue is cold. The cat's form shimmers. At first, Emilio knows, he will think it is merely a play of the moonlight; only gradually he will see that it is a young boy condensing out of the shadows, a boy whose face luminesces with the pallor of death, and whose long hair billows behind him like stormtossed seaweed.

The boy vampire who has been a gypsy allows a wan smile to cross his face.

Rudy says: "There should not be a forest here."

"This forest is not where you think it is. It is a forest of the soul. It is not to be found easily."

"What do you come from?"

"I have crossed over the line between life and death."

"Why did you save me?"

"I owed it to you."

"I have no life now."

"No, Rudy, that is not true." He wipes a trickle of blood from the corner of his mouth. "They have broken your hand and stolen the music from your soul, but I will be your music now. I will sing, and you will heal."

He sings now, his voice clear and infinitely cold.

night-child and huntress

Twilight streaks the Atlantic Ocean. In a soundproofed dressing room whose double-glassed walls look out at the sea, Timmy waits to come on stage. He has come alone; for though the buses with his soundcrews and his backup players and his makeup artists and his props have crossed the continent in convoy, he does not share their journey. Sometimes he arrives by night flight, sometimes he is carried on the wind itself.

There are many mirrors in the room, though Timmy cannot use them. It is an inconvenience as he applies a deep blue eye shadow that echoes the midnight of his hair. One wall is taken up by a bank of monitors; swiveling cameras are trained on the stage, on the audience, on the aisles, on the ticket booths, on the crowds that are already milling around, even though the warmup band, the Vultures, is nowhere in sight.

He turns his back on the monitors and stares at the sea.

Even the soundproofing cannot block his hearing. The ocean is calm and crystal-black. Almost at the limit of his vision, a porpoise leaps. A sharkfin churns the water in a deadly circle. Timmy remembers Lisa, lost forever now. He wonders whether there is any truth to the afterlife, or whether there are only the two realities, man and vampire, shadows of one another.

"What's wrong with you, Timmy?" Kitty has come, whirlpooling through the keyhole of the dressing room, for the sun has set now, and freed her from her coffin. "The force has gone from you. It's that psychiatrist woman, Timmy! She's bleeding you of something. Are you dying, Timmy, dying? You're older than all of us, and you're becoming invulnerable. But the killing lust doesn't seem to excite you anymore, and compassion taints your bloodjoy. I'm afraid for you. That man killed all the new friends that I made, and I don't want to be alone."

"I don't know. Perhaps I must get worse before I can heal, Kitty."

"There was nothing wrong with you before, except the curse of compassion! Do you want to sink to their level, the level of our prey? Oh, you should be pitiless, you should consume your victims like wind and fire."

"If you think that the act of analysis has lessened my power, you may be right. I may no longer be an archetype."

"I have heard that you wept, Timmy."

"No." But he thinks it may be true.

"And Timmy, I've seen something terrible."

"What?"

"Look at the monitors. Follow them. The crowds. There's a man sitting near the front. He's straight, not punked out or anything. He has a black bag under his arm. Doesn't he look familiar?"

She points to the bank of screens. One shows the lowest tiers of seats, and the camera pans slowly from face to face: young girls chewing gum, a boy diligently combing his purple mohawk, another in a Timmy Valentine T-shirt, two girls yapping feverishly, another intent, her eyes closed, holding the hand of a bearded man . . . "The next row up," she says. "Coming up—"

He recognizes him now. When last he saw him, he was driving an ersatz stake into a young girl's heart. . . .

"Brian Zottoli," he whispers.

"You should have let me kill him!" says Kitty.

He is stung by her disdain. But, to his own surprise, he can no longer sympathize with her. It is true that something has begun to change in him.

Another emotion now, one that he has not felt for so long that it takes him a moment to recognize it. It is dread. It is not the presence of Brian; he knows that it is love, and love's dark companion vengeance, that have brought him here, and these are emotions he can easily deal with. Nor is it the crowd itself, the chained beast of a thousand heads, whom he will tame with cathartic spectacle. Something else is present too.

Quickly he glances from monitor to monitor. There now . . . the Vultures, strapping themselves into costumes with elaborate waldo circuitry. One of them is complaining about a blown synthesizer chip . . . in another monitor, Melissa Pavlat is deep in conversation backstage with . . . whom? The faces are strangely familiar, but he cannot place them . . . they are three, sitting together on a sofa, a witchlike woman in the center, a bald, fat Asian on the right, a gaunt, fleshy-nosed one on the left . . . all three so aged as to appear sexless . . . who can they be?

The camera moves slightly. Another man is there; not quite as old as the others, still spry. Timmy can only see his back, but this one is very familiar.

A snatch of *The Magic Flute* runs through his thoughts . . . a kaleidoscope of images, stained-glass windows, frightened eyes of a little boy, fire, the old Opernhaus. . . .

"What are you staring at?" Kitty says.

Once more the dread. Its newness stirs him, like the smell of fresh blood. "Don't you recognize them?" he says, pointing.

They gaze for a long time at that screen. Finally Timmy says, "You are touched. You remember what you once were."

She says, angry, "I don't want to know."

He says: "Can't you see that it's you who have become like them, not I? It was not hunger that made them kill you, but whim, lust!"

"And I will feed on them now, and take my vengeance."

"Our lifelines cross once more at the vampire junction."

He turns away to watch the sea. A wind has swooped down on the palm trees, and they sway in melancholy rhythm. Kitty has gone to seek new prey, for she loves the crowds, vibrant, bursting with the life force she craves. He has an hour or more to be alone with himself.

He watches the sea that, twenty years before, he crossed with Rudy. . . .

memory: 1961

There is a museum here now, he has spent all day looking at the blown-up photographs of shriveled corpses, the Nazi documents, the memorabilia. But he does not yet see the man he seeks, although he has found out that he frequents this place.

He has left behind the Opernhaus in Thauberg; he has found another name, and another, and another. He has returned to Poland. He has not been stopped at the border; he has come as a raven, on the wings of night.

The museum has wide bay windows; as if in defiance of its grim subject matter, it is full of light and air, and there is a strange feeling of peace over the frayed framed documents and the grainy black and white enlargements.

At last he sees the man he has been searching for standing in front of a photograph that covers half a wall. He stares intently at the picture; soundlessly the boy vampire has come up behind him, and looks himself. He sees the corpses piled high, a jigsaw of stick men, and in the background an emaciated man in an inmate's uniform, with a satchel in one hand and a small hammer in the other, bent down over the corpses—

"The incriminating photograph," Rudy whispers to himself. "The one that got me hanged."

The boy vampire pulls at his sleeve. When Rudy turns he seems not to be shocked. There is a sense of inevitability about this meeting. Perhaps, in the back of his mind, Rudy Lydick has fantasized such a meeting over and over; perhaps that is why he comes here, to the scene of his ancient anguish.

"Emilio," Rudy whispers.

"Your hand. . . ."

"It no longer pains me. I can do most things with it, but nothing too precise."

"Once I promised I would be your music."

"It's been so long . . . you haven't changed at all . . . it must be true then. You are eternal. The dark angel from beyond the grave. I hardly remember what happened . . . sometimes I think that I dreamed it all. What are you, Emilio?"

"My name is no longer Emilio," the boy says, playing with a sleeve of his conservative white shirt. "I am . . . Krzysztof. Krzysztof Lydick."

"Lydick?"

"I am your son."

"But . . . my emigration papers have almost come through now. I am to go to America."

"Do you think I haven't found this out?" For a moment they both stare at the photograph. Krzysztof can barely make himself out in it; there is the barest outline of a boy; perhaps it is a play of shadows. He says, not yet meeting Rudy's eyes, "I have come to collect the life you owe me."

"You will drink my blood?" Rudy says, unsurprised. "It means nothing to me. Nothing does anymore."

"You're lying. Why, otherwise, would you apply to go to America?"

"I had a feeling. . . ."

"And I too. That is why I will become your son, Rudy. But only for a short time, because after a year or two people will become suspicious. I can never grow up. I will leave you. But, because you know what I truly am, and because we are linked by life and death, I may have need of you again."

"I am yours."

"I believe that, Rudy."

"Come to my house. There may be documents to be forged."

"Yes." He has been there already today; the squalor has dismayed him. He must free this man who pulled him out of the dead, again and again, until it cost him his life, his music.

There is nothing else to say; in silence they express their deepest thoughts, their common memories. The boy who now calls himself Krzysztof Lydick reflects for a time on human transience; this man has aged twenty years while he has never changed. He longs to change, but he changes only his name, his clothes, the languages he speaks. Only men can change from within.

Finally he says, "Before we leave Europe, can we go to Germany for a few days? There is a gravestone there that I have grown rather attached to. I want to take it with me. You will keep it always, even after we go our separate ways in America, and you will sometimes think of me."

"I will think of how you might have been dead."

"Dead, in the soft warm earth." For a second there is a trace of longing in his voice, but he dismisses it quickly.

And now the boy Krzysztof Lydick walks slowly away from the photograph, the open evidence of his true nature, to get his coat and scarf from the garderobe, to walk out into the quiet streets of Oswiecim.

arcade and labyrinth

In another room backstage, this one without a window on the sea but with the same array of video monitors, Missy Pavlat was taking leave of Stephen Miles and the three Fates.

"I'll call you when it's time to come and meet Timmy," she said as she closed the door behind her. "Meanwhile you can watch on these screens. The group that's on now is called the Vultures, like they're really weird, you know, gets the audience really weirded out for Timmy's act. 'Bye now."

They were alone, waiting.

Stephen watched the screens for a bit. He didn't really want to watch Muriel, Francis and Prathna, who were themselves like vultures.

Before long he noticed the camera overhead, craning from side to side like an admonishing professor. He took off the jacket of his safari suit and threw it over the camera. A petty gesture, perhaps, but it made him feel more comfortable.

The air conditioning wasn't working properly, he realized. The Florida heat in the unventilated room was oppressive, stifling. He had to say something, if only to relieve the tension.

"How can we be sure, Muriel that your theories will work?"

"Silly man," the old witch croaked. "You saw how the chanting of the crowd made the statue come together. It needs . . . a large crowd sharing a common consciousness, inflamed to fever pitch . . . when we were in Los Angeles, we drove past a demonstration, teachers striking or some such thing or some such nonsense, and I felt the two halves shake. It as palpable, I tell you."

"Shall we unveil them now?" said Prathna, more excited than Stephen had seen him since the Cambridge days.

"Might as well," Muriel said.

The prince and Sir Francis each produced half the thunderbolt idol from a paper bag.

On the monitor, four men dressed as vultures were leaping up and down on the stage. They had robot necks and vulture heads attached to their shoulders, which craned and slavered hideously in time to the music. The music itself, which they could hear faintly on remote speakers, consisted of repetitive, dirgelike percussion, over which guitars glissandoed; they shouted the surreal lyrics, now and then embellishing them with screeching, quasi-avian melismas and the distorted, amplified sounds of snapping jaws and rending flesh. Suddenly huge wings unfurled behind them and they rose into the air on wires, the black canvas flapping and adding a rhythmic electronic wheeze to the cacophony.

"Charming music, isn't it? Like a sort of Walpurgisnacht. I can well imagine myself whizzing through the air on a broomstick and mixing vile potions," said Muriel, delighted at the bizarre noises.

"My God," Sir Francis exclaimed suddenly.

"What?" Stephen said.

"I felt a tremor in the idol."

"Perhaps you're just nervous, old chap," said Prathna. Then he seemed to feel something too, for he grew suddenly silent.

Try as he might, Stephen could not quite feel the others' excitement. Something was not quite right about this operation. This was not the day when he, Stephen Miles, would burn down the world in a private *Götterdämmerung*.

Reaching into his pockets, Sir Francis next produced four revolvers. "I think we'd better arm ourselves with these, eh?" he said, passing them around. Stephen pocketed his without a comment.

He watched the camera panning across the front rows . . . they were leaping, dancing in the aisles, clapping their hands. Once or twice he saw someone who looked strangely incongruous . . . like that man clutching his black bag, his eyes closed, his expression one of concentrated hatred. Was this someone who knew Timmy's true identity, perhaps? Were there dozens out there, clutching their stakes and their garlic bulbs and their crucifixes, waiting for the moment to rush upon the stage and attack the prince of darkness?

He laughed to himself. Impossible, of course, impossible.

After all, who knew?

Only Stephen and the Gods of Chaos, and, by now, Carla.

Would Carla try to stop him?

Those wolf-eyes sixty years ago . . . had they really gazed at him with malice? What had the boy vampire really said to him? He tried to squeeze the memory into consciousness, but nothing came, nothing at all.

Too late for doubts! he told himself, fingering the revolver in his pocket, ignoring the three Fates as they cackled over their fiendish plans.

18

On the evening of the last concert of Timmy's tour, I found myself irresistibly drawn to the hall of mirrors. I walked by the corridors of specters and hauntings, feeling somehow superior to them; they no longer frightened me, because I had run wild with Timmy in my dreams, in the dark forest of the soul.

Here and there were rooms laid waste. Some seemed to have been set to the torch, and shards of an artificial sky shone through the sundered walls. Vampires had lived here once. But now the man Brian had come and pounded the stake into them and extinguished the cold flicker of their lives and shattered the bubble of deathdreaming that surrounded and nurtured them.

They were dust now, and their chambers, furnished with the half-remembered fantasies of their old lives, were dying too.

Lisa's room: the hundred TV monitors black, screens broken, melting into one another like Dali clocks. Other rooms: I walked right through walls and coffins, through stone, through scentless cedarwood and pine.

A wind of sadness wuthered through the passageways, a haunted castle in an old black-and-white movie.

Somewhere a phone was ringing.

How absurd, I thought. How can the phone ring here?

I climbed up more steps. The hallways became almost organic, fleshlike. The guts of a monster. The phone rang

227

louder. When I reached the analysis room its noise was deafening.

I stood, glancing from mirror to mirror, stopping my ears. I saw the phone on a little antique table by the couch, which had never been there before. I grabbed it, annoyed.

"Yes?" For some reason I half-expected Stephen, although he couldn't possibly have known the number, or even where I was.

Laughter. A coil of shadow on the nearest mirror that was suddenly Timmy. The phone went dead in my hand, faded out, a remembrance of cold plastic in my hand. I watched, fascinated, as Timmy drifted into being. I turned around automatically to see the real form that was casting the reflection, but there was no one.

"You're not supposed to be able to be seen in mirrors!" I said angrily, thinking it was another trick.

Again the wind gusted. I recognized this wind now. It was the wind of his infinite aloneness.

"You're not even here," I said. "You're in Florida."

"That's why I called."

I waited.

"I'm just about to go onstage."

"God damn it, you don't cast reflections!"

"Aren't you interested in what I'm doing? I guess not." The smile left his lips. "But I thought that we'd established in analysis, Carla, that you and I are each other's soul, our anima. Is it me you see in the mirror, which is mythologically untenable, or is it just yourself? Not my reflection but yours? Have you ever wanted to know what *I* see in mirrors?"

"I'm sure you didn't call me for a philosophical discussion on the nature of the soul," I said.

"Right. Well, I'm standing in my dressing room, putting on my Dracula cape. Beneath it I'm wearing these oh-so-cutesy eighteenth century ruffles. Little Mozart probably looked like this."

Suddenly the mirror exuded a bleak smell. I knew it: the odor of a blighted forest, of diseased foliage, of animals dying of starvation, of poisoned brooks. I looked away but he was in all the mirrors, and the stench wafted from them all, and behind it was a whiff of burning sulphur. A thousand Timmy Valentines, and they all showed me a new face, a face of dread. "What's going on?" I said.

"It says a great deal for the progress in our relationship, Carla," said Timmy, "that you can reach me through this mirror, across the void itself. But then, death is a far deeper abyss, and you and I have touched souls even across that."

"Why are you afraid?"

"Afraid? Me? Impossible!" he screamed at me from a thousand mirrors. "Am I not fear itself, the substance of all men's terrors?" But he sounded like a little boy.

"You *are* afraid then."

"And why shouldn't I be?" He waved about him wildly. "Look, woman, see what I'm seeing."

Behind him more mirrors seemed to open up. Or were they television monitors? I saw Brian clutching his bag. I saw old men sitting in a room. A witch in a wheelchair, shaking with palsy or sexual excitement. Drumbeats, distorted guitar shrieks, a raucous melody whose range encompassed the deepest roaring and the shrillest birdcry.

Smoke poured from the mirrors behind the mirrors, sulphur smoke. This room was the center of his mind so I saw what he saw, that the mirrors were hellmouths, entrances to ultimate darkness.

"They're all waiting for me, don't you see?" he shouted.

. . . men dressed like vultures swooping from a tinsel sky. . . .

"What will you do?"

"I don't know!" He was whimpering like a lost child. "Stay here with me. Watch the concert. Do what you can."

"Do?" I screamed into the wind. "I'm three thousand miles away!"

Behind the wall of hellflame I saw the silhouette of Stephen, clutching something, a baton, a firebrand, a revolver.

"You're invulnerable," I protested. "They're fools with their garlic and their crosses."

"They've got something else now! I haven't felt this power in almost a thousand years."

"What else?" I was panicking, almost unable to control myself.

"I don't know!"

I felt this unknowing in the pit of my stomach, small, hard, knotted. I seemed to understand this dread completely. Perhaps it was another of his illusions—Timmy was nothing if not a seducer of minds—but it impelled me to stay in this room and watch the concert to the end. A battle was about to be fought.

"We have seen the forest together," I told him by way of commitment. It was the first time I had dared, other than obliquely, to mention our night journeys in the forest of dreams.

He nodded abstractedly; his mind was elsewhere now. The tumult was overwhelming as the monitor-mirrors swept over the audience and the shrieking man-vultures. I closed my eyes and was at once transported, without the intermediary of sleep, to the dark forest.

Side by side we ran, but the flames were encroaching; we hungered for blood, our jaws were parched, we were as emaciated as the inmates of a concentration camp.

seeker

They were dancing in every aisle now. Brian edged toward the gangway, pushing away elbows and legs, his bag in his hand. On the stage, the vultures started to breathe flame, and the audience began screaming anew as the flares went swirling up.

They were singing a refrain over and over as they craned their necks and snapped their beaks: *I like corpses, rotted corpses.* People in the front row began pelting the rock group with pieces of raw meat. Their wings spread wide, the vulture men darted down and began devouring it.

"How *rad*, oh, it's just so *rad*," squealed a young girl beside Brian, who seemed to be with her father.

Brian reached the aisle and started to jostle his way down to the stage. I have to be near when Timmy Valentine comes on, he thought, so I can have a chance to kill him.

A dead dog landed on the stage. The four vultures dropped onstage with a thud and began to tear the creature limb from limb.

"Like, what a spectacle," said an older man in dark glasses who was standing beside him. "I can really get into post-minimalistic neo-expressionism, you know?" He blew a cloud of some aromatic smoke in Brian's face.

"So motherfucking *rad*," the girl continued to shriek, while her father appeared to be berating her for her foul language.

The crowd was seething now, shocked, angry, ecstatic. The vultures continued their maenad dance. Blood was all over their costumes.

"Kill the fuckers!" someone was chanting. Suddenly they were all yelling it. Then, as the wires yanked the vultures back into the air, the lead vulture held the dog's head aloft, and a mass of wires was trailing from the bloody neck down to the stage, and they were singing the chorus of the song.

> *It's a dog's life.*
> *It's a dog's death.*
> *Death is an illusion.*
> *The mirror is blood.*

Above the roar of the crowd, Brian heard the same girl screaming out the song's lyrics. One by one they were taking up the chant. Even the anachonistic hippie who'd been making the pretentious remarks, even the squealing nymphet's father; the words swept like a tempest over the throng, headily rhythmic: *death . . . illusion . . . death . . . illusion. . . .*

Now he edged forward again, a lonely vampire killer with his black bag. Squeezed past girls with jiggling breasts who chewed gum and snapped their fingers. Past men with rampant mohawks . . . was that one really masturbating into a paper bag? He couldn't tell.

The words came, again and again, his thoughts were surfing on the swell of their screaming—

Death . . . illusion . . . death . . . illusion. . . .

He was in the front row now. At that moment, the four vultures, dangling overhead, threw the remains of the robot dog far out into the audience, and he heard the distant rumble of scrambling souvenir hunters, and then they spread their wings wide, so that four black batlike shadows swept over the audience, and a wave of terror and ecstasy burst from the viewers.

Then they were swallowed up in a swirl of brimstone, and the stage was empty, and the tiniest split second of a hush fell over the audience, and then began the slow chanting:

Timmy! Timmy! We want Timmy!

Brian took his stake out of his bag and waited.

arcade and fire

"Heavens," Sir Francis Locke said, looking away from the television monitors at last. "They call this music."

"There seems to be a lull," said the prince. "It must be almost time for the main event."

"Yes, indeed," Muriel said. "I've prepared everything. Hand me those paper bags, Stephen."

They had taken to ordering him around again, as if he'd reverted to the ten-year-old boy of long ago. He fetched the parcels for Muriel to open.

There were paper crowns for the three Fates. Robes of crêpe paper with glued-on magazine cutouts of moons, suns, comets, and stars. "Awfully cheap looking, what," said Sir Francis disdainfully.

"In magic, as in everything else," Muriel said, "it's the thought that counts."

"Perhaps a human sacrifice or two?" the prince said.

"Ha! We will be sacrificing the monster itself!"

"So what is the strategy then?" said Locke.

"Do you not feel it?" said the old woman. "The roar of the crowd, exciting the thunder idol. I can hardly keep the halves apart. What power! A whole nation died that we might play the endgame of our lives. How wicked! And now to reverse the ceremony we perpetrated sixty years ago."

"Then I suppose," said Prince Prathna, "that instead of sacrificing a young virgin, we'll use an old whore?"

"Not appreciated!" Muriel said in a simulated huff as she placed the paper crown on her head. "Help me on with this robe, acolyte."

Wordlessly Stephen assisted her. The crêpe paper draped completely over the wheelchair, giving the impression that she and the chair were a single object, grotesquely welded together.

"You look lovely, my dear," said Prince Prathna, robing himself.

"I suggest, Miles, that you watch the monitors," Locke said. "The time approaches." He took a censer from his shopping bag, filled it with an ash from a silk pouch, and lit it. "Your Fumigator of Power, O Acolyte," he said.

Stephen took it and began swinging it to and fro. It stank of brimstone and burning meat. He dared not ask what it contained.

Coughing, he watched the televsion screens; they were taking down the tinsel sky now, and the real sky showed, starstrewn, lovely. There was a full moon over the water. Soft tinkly music began to play, wafting away the bitter taste of what had gone before. The audience, at first chanting Timmy's name over and over, was still now, waiting.

"Shall we begin now?" the prince said impatiently.

"No. Let's wait till our friend has had a chance to sing a few songs," said Muriel, cackling.

night-child and funhouse

As he is lowered towards the stage on his flying white piano, Timmy does not so much play as toy with the keys, adding an embellishment here, an extra chord there. His cloak is partly draped over his face; partly it flutters behind him on an artifical breeze, giving him a strangely Byronic appearance.

He has not yet sung a note, but the accompaniment to his first song has already begun, deceptively quiet. It will repeat itself until he gives the cue, until he has composed himself. He is waiting for the audience to settle down after the violent blandishments of the warm-up band. Another storm is to come, and he relishes this moment: the piano sailing over thousands of souls, its smooth surface reflecting a thousand random colors from the light show, soaring on the tide of their emotions, on the night wind, under the full moon.

The music swells a little. It hardly sounds like music yet, but like the whine of distant whalesongs, elemental. The audience murmurs. They're getting restless, Timmy thinks. Still he is not quite ready. He is thinking of his dread, though he knows it must now show; to show fear is to admit defeat.

He presses a button on the control panel concealed in the piano lid, signaling to the stage manager that he is not quite ready.

Once more the piano arcs out over the stage; although its passage takes but a few minutes, Timmy seizes the fabric of this time and spins it out, now wanting it to end. One by one he studies his audience, although his gaze rests on each perhaps only a microsecond. He scrutinizes their faces; they know his eye is on them, for their blood begins to race. So much blood, so much, and their communal emotion so overpowering! He hears it as the joyful rush of a thousand little rivers, clear, clean, vibrant.

Then the dread touches him once more.

Why?

Once, Timmy remembers, I felt neither guilt nor compassion. I killed because I am what I am. I have to regain what I've lost, my elemental quality.

He thinks of the old people in the waiting room. He is not afraid of them. But they possess something whose power they themselves cannot know. Timmy alone feels it.

Let them try to kill me! he thinks. And that poor grief-maddened Brian Zottoli too. Even if I die, I will seize the split second of my dying and stretch it to eternity, so that the moment of my dying will come ever nearer but will never be reached, like the speed of light. Within that tiny moment I will live forever, and perhaps discover eternity's meaning.

The piano settles onto the stage. He starts to sing. The words and harmonies are trite—indeed, he has concocted the song simply by running all the most popular love songs of the previous year into a Cuisinart, thus ensuring its success—but his voice breathes a life into them that they could not have had without him. Each tone, whispery and bittersweet, is flagrantly erotic. As he sings, the offstage fans thrum into action, and his cloak billows, its scarlet lining showing for the first time.

The music is slow, coiled, a cat preparing to pounce; at times, when he lets loose enough to feed upon the audience's emotions, he is like a black cat, pacing back and forth on the keyboard, and the audience gasps at the transformation, the magic of the special effects artists.

And now the music leaps, quickens. Behind him the holography comes into play. He is inside his own video game, a coffin rider, zinging through the twisty maze, belting out the lyrics of the second song in a barely comprehensible catlike yowling:

> *Come into my coffin*
> *I hate to sleep alone*

and twenty Timmy coffin riders tall as buildings are converging at the superjunction of video traintracks, and Timmy zooms earthward on the rollercoaster of the audience's thoughts, the surfsounds twine into the twang of screaming guitars, the bass drum pounds like a deathknell, the wind from the sea wars with the manmade wind for possession of Timmy's cloak, which swirls and flaps and roars and soars; a lone spot on Timmy center stage now as he shrieks, the backup vocals imitating the howling of wolves and winds, and he dances, a tiny figure in the maelstrom, elegant and at peace at the eye of the raging lightstorm.

As the song draws to an end, dissolves into the murmuring of the crowd, the boy vampire sees that Brian Zottoli has crept up to the front. He is holding one of his sharpened broomstick handles in one hand and is extracting something from his black bag with the other.

The dread touches him lightly, toying with him. But it does not emanate from this crazed man. It is a feeling far more ancient, as though thousands of souls had been sacrificed to secure his death . . . he has not felt it since the days when he feared the sun and crosses and garlic and wolfsbane and silver.

He continues to sing. One song becomes another. By the magic of holography the dark sea is dyed crimson. He sings a dark song, laden with images of violence, accompanied by surging ostinato drums and repetitious guitar phrases and wails of an out-of-tune electric violin; this song has no melody, but is a mélange of half-familiar fragments, disquieting, nerve-wracking. He feels the disturbance in his audience, the hidden fear. They do not know how they are being manipulated. They mutter among themselves uneasily, like an ocean made choppy by a distant storm.

And now comes the funhouse sequence, which the fans have been talking about all summer. Distorting mirrors pop up all around him. As the song segues into an instrumental free-for-all, and the drummer, freed from monotony, goes into a frenzy of improvisation, Timmy moves from mirror to mirror. The audience gasps at the special effect, for Timmy cannot be seen in any of them; only faces from the crowd, distended, bloated, hideously contorted and garishly lit. Timmy moves along the edge of the stage with his cloak held high, as stately as a kabuki player. Hands are reaching for him. The smell of human sweat rises up to his nostrils, but it is masked by the intoxicating scent of blood and adrenaline and sexual pheromones. Slowly he moves, floating almost.

Suddenly Brian Zottoli leaps onto the stage with a stake in one hand and a mallet in the other. Two bodyguards jump up after him and are about to wrestle him to the ground, but Timmy only smiles, and they release him.

The audience, seeing a new piece of stage business, stirs. Timmy transfixes Brian with his eyes.

"You are not the one," he says, "who will kill me. Go, you poor fool." Only Brian has heard him.

Brian fishes in his pocket for a crucifix, now he advances, bearing it aloft. The audience is shocked at first; then, realizing it's merely an act, the crowd begins to laugh. Timmy feels the despair in Brian, but cannot fear him. He begins to sing again, and Brian stalks him, a ludicrous figure staggering across the stage, a shambling echo of Timmy's feline grace.

Brian stabs with his stake; but Timmy waves his cloak like a matador, and then he disappears, pops into being on the other side of the stage.

Timmy sings, all the while eluding the crazed man with his broomstick and his croquet mallet.

And now the funhouse effects begin in earnest. Pianos and coffins pop open to reveal demons and Frankenstein monsters and leering vampires. The air is rent by a cacophony of amplified chuckles, farts, screams, whispers. In the background the video game, magnified and holographic, is still running its course, with a dozen Timmy Valentines and Van Helsings pursuing each other across the high-resolution landscape.

And Timmy bursts into the song *Vampire Junction*; the crowd joins in, screaming the words so as to render Timmy almost inaudible.

It is only now that the dread becomes really palpable.

A gunshot has rung out somewhere backstage, sparking off more hysterical laughter in the audience. Timmy looks around in surprise; the audience takes it as mock alarm, and laughs louder. He goes on singing, but his voice is charged with an unfamiliar terror. The crowd loves it, thinks it a new and masterful artifice. He beckons to the backup musicians, who are standing behind the rank of funhouse mirrors, and they turn up the sound so that the speakers are groaning and shrieking from the distortion, and he screams out the lyrics of the song, transforming its surreal elegance into primal terror. Catching his mood, the lead guitarist begins to improvise a neurotic countermelody, and the drummer smashes wildly at the cymbals and flagellates the snare drum, and the other players forsake their prepared parts and burst out in a contrapuntal frenzy.

A bizarre procession emerges from the wings now. A gaunt old man—it is Stephen Miles—in a choirboy's cassock and surplice leads it; he is swinging a censer from which issue the perfumes of hell itself, sulphur and methane and rotting corpses and old shit. Behind him an ancient, white-haired woman in a wheelchair, in a crimson robe and paper crown, both spangled with suns and moons and cabalistic sigils; flanking her a bald and portly Asian and another old man, puffy faced, phlegmatic. Both carry platters on which rest the two halves of some idol.

Now the dread strikes Timmy with millennial force, and he struggles not to panic, to keep singing . . . the crowd, wild now, applauds frantically, but cannot drown out the hysterical music.

The dread . . . the dread. . . .

Blue lightning now, forking and unforking, flying from one half of the idol to the other, as the three aged figures begin to recite strings of nonsense syllables, and the old woman raises her arms histrionically as she propels her wheelchair forward.

And now he sees Missy Pavlat, her arm bleeding from a gunshot wound, crawling behind them, trying desperately to hold back the wheelchair, and the audience, delighted by the ever-changing theatrics, is convulsed with laughter and excitement now, applauding, cheering, moaning, and now from behind Missy comes Kitty Burns, fresh from her coffin, her shroud still clinging to her, and Brian has run forward now and has pushed her back into a funhouse mirror with his crucifix and is impaling her heart and she is screaming, screaming, and the music swells up even more; and the jags of blue lightning are pulling the statue into a single entity, the pieces are flying together, the old woman is holding the united idol aloft, and all he can see is her twisted smile as the lightning coalesces into a single ray of laser brilliance and shoots toward him—

I must have time! he thinks, and he seizes the moment and pulls it out wide, wide, wide, and now he stands alone in a tiny fragment of eternity and despairs and does not know whom to turn to, until he cries out *Carla, Carla*, into the funhouse mirror—

analyst's notebook

—and I saw him in the mirror and knew his anguish and knew then that I loved him utterly and could redeem him with my love if I could only reach him across the barrier of time and mind and space and I saw Stephen and the witch woman and the old men surrounding him and I felt their hate their mindless hate and the beam of killing light fly from the idol and I knew that my love could save him, I knew I had to run to him somehow, through the mirror like Alice in the looking-glass, reach across the Red King's dream, and I smashed the mirror with my fists and felt blood run down my arms and there was another hall of mirrors and I smashed it too and another and another and smashed and smashed till my arms were raw and bleeding and scored with glass-shards and still I smashed, until I saw a great oaken door with iron bolts and I pounded on it and I shouted for the key and I cried *Give me the key Bluebeard because I love you* and pounded and pounded out my love—

night-child and funhouse

—and sees her face form, contorted by the funhouse mirror, shimmer for a split second, and then he sees Kitty crumble to dust and the wind whip up the putrefying ashes and Brian still stabbing madly at the vacant mirror, and the hidden terror wells up, he cannot cling to the moment any longer, the blue light rushes at him and he knows that he must die—

—and then Carla's face appears crystal clear between him and the lightbeam for a microsecond, and he feels the touch of her love, and her face deflects the beam, it bounces back into the united thunder idol, and then—

The old woman explodes! Her skull shatters, splattering brains across the entire stage and front rows. An eyeball lands in the mush and slides to a staring halt. Her arms and legs fly apart in a cloud of cogs and spokes from the wheelchair. As shreds of flesh spray the audience, souvenir hunters begin clambering over seats, knocking each other over in their haste. Fragments of bone riddle the stage flats with holes, through which the sea wind comes whistling.

A shard of the statue decapitates the prone Melissa Pavlat and turns her head into a grisly projectile as the crowd screams in shuddering delight. It crashes into an open grand piano and rolls about on the strings, sizzling, sending up an eerie jangling as it begins to char. The sound of snapping piano strings reverberates through the loudspeakers in the house. Missy's torso rolls slowly off the stage onto the laps of some startled New Wavers, who attempt a panic-stricken escape but cannot penetrate the congested aisles.

The remains of Muriel Hykes-Bailey are now smeared across every funhouse mirror on the stage. The distended faces of the crowd seem to be gashed and bleeding. A pool of thickening blood boils to stage left.

Timmy sees Brian Zottoli running out through the back. He does not try to stop him. He sees Stephen Miles still swinging his censer, and his mind is suddenly cast back sixty years, he sees only a frightened little boy; they exchange the same glance, they see each other as they truly are, but only for a moment.

Then the old men flee, following Brian.

Only a few of the audience have guessed that this is not make-believe. The others, as thrill after thrill convulses the stage, continue to yell enthusiastically and to clap and stamp their feet in time to the music, which continues without pause, for the band is used to weird new special effects and, professionals that they are, will play through anything.

For a while Timmy stands transfixed amid this pandemonium. He is back in Saint Cecilia's Chapel watching young Francis Locke carve up Kitty Burns with a knife. Now she is dead again, irrevocably dead. The two moments are one, time-frozen, eternal.

He screams for Carla with his mind again and again, for he knows she can assuage his grief, but he sees only one image, mist-shrouded, indistinct: a huge bolted oaken door, and from the other side, as though from an immeasurable distance, a pounding. . . .

Something snaps.

It is the ancient bloodlust, chained for so long, visiting him with all the precipitous force of the old times, before the long journey through the dark forest. He changes form. Proteus-like, he runs through a hundred shapes in as many seconds, he becomes a panther and a wolf and a lion and a dog and a serpent and then on to hybrid animals so monstrous that they have no names, while the audience eggs him on, cheering each transformation, and at last he soars up on wings of night, an avian chimaera of hawk and vulture. He flies squawking across the full moon's face and swoops down on the front rows, he tears at a man's face and pecks out an eye and sips the blood that froths up to the socket, and the taste maddens him more and he cannot hold his shape, before he is through he has become a slavering wolf, ripping open a girl's throat, dragging her along the aisles, he is a bat clawing at a leather boy's cheeks, a dog chewing on a woman's amputated hand—

Finally he is on stage again. Only a few people in the front rows seem aware that something truly terrible has taken place, and even they make no move to leave, for they are stunned, hypnotized, by the emotional vehemence of what has gone before. Almost casually the boy vampire drifts back into the shape of a small boy.

Maria and Rudy are here now, dragging away the bodies; and now only a handful of viewers remain who think that what they just saw was anything other than sleight-of-hand, and even these are being mocked by others for their credulity.

The band plays a slow music; the intro to one of his love songs.

Timmy stands before the funhouse mirror.

His own face flickers there for a minute. How can that be? Then it is gone. He thinks: It is hopeless to become as they are. Even as I approach them, the gulf widens. I am not human, not human. I am only an echo cast off randomly by their great unconscious. He is bitter, drained; for even Kitty is gone now.

"I am so alone," he sings, fitting the words awkwardly to the old melody. "They have all vanished. I am the only one who has learned to endure the day."

He knows he is weeping openly, shamelessly, that he is throwing his vampire nature aside even as he realizes he cannot reject it without destroying himself. Not for a millennium has he felt more burdened by eternity.

And now applause comes, like an earthquake, deafening.

labyrinth

Her emotions spent, Carla fell asleep on a heap of broken glass.

19

dissolve: forest

Have we crossed the state line, Rudy?

An hour ago, master Timothy. Soon we will leave the highway and find the mountain road that leads to Junction.

How beautiful it is! I thought all those funny states, you know, the ones with *O*s in them, were flat and drab and boring. But look at the mountains, the thick pine forests that climb the sky, the gold-red streaks of deciduous trees touched by autumn . . . and the air is fragrant, bracing. Is Carla still asleep?

Still asleep, master Timothy. Hunched in the front seat. She must be exhausted from what happened.

Is she angry with me, Rudy?

I cannot tell. In fact, she has hardly stirred since we found her in the upstairs room—

I forbid you to speak of that room!

—since we found her, although she did make a most enterprising and inventive statement to the press yesterday.

It's just you and me again, Rudy.

And Carla and Maria.

Yes. Maria will be pleased. You know how she hated cleaning up after the others. The two of you did very well with the Boca Blanca police.

Of course. But they were also somewhat awestruck by your fame, master Timothy, by your mask of innocence, and by your physical beauty. As are all mortals. But you mustn't think of any of this anymore. Miss Rubens says you are to rest.

Yes. Renew myself. Regain all that I've been losing. Oh, I am orphaned by eternity. I will wrap myself in the dark, in the forests, I will immure myself behind great mountains . . . and in the quiet, find my lost secret self. Look, Rudy, a waterfall!

Beautiful, master Timothy.

Look at the mist that clings to the treetops. I will love this place. And what is that, to our left, that billboard, that fence?

It is the entrance to a Shoshone reservation, master Timothy. We are not far from our goal now.

Is Carla still dreaming?

Yes.

I wonder what of.

Perhaps of what happened. . . .

It was so terrible, Rudy! I was afraid.

You are never afraid.

Oh, don't sound so disappointed in me. I was extremely fightened. Even now I can hardly bear to think of it.

Be at peace.

I will never sing again!

Come. Time will weather your grief. Even these mountains will become soft hills with time. You have time if nothing else.

Where did you learn such wisdom, Rudy?

From you, master Timothy.

dissolve

STAGE TRAGEDY
TRAUMATIZES TEEN STAR
Must Rest, Says Analyst

A freak accident claimed several lives during a concert at the Marina Stadium in Boca Blanca, Fla., yesterday. Popular child star Timmy Valentine was giving the final performance in a national tour, involving several stage effects hitherto unseen at live concerts, when an explosion, apparently caused by a backfiring of an improperly-tested laser holography device, resulted in the deaths of Melissa Pavlat, an executive of Stupendous Sounds Systems, the Los Angeles-based recording empire, and a number of members of the audience. The situation was complicated by the apparent escape of some wild animals who appear to have attacked and killed three people; police have not determined as yet whether these came from the local zoo or from a visiting circus, also in town and due to set up in that very stadium the following week.

Timmy Valentine, whose latest album, *Funhouse*, has just been released, was unavailable for comment, although a statement was issued today by his agent and guardian, Mary Karney: "He's terribly upset by all this. He's even said that he may never sing in public again. Our lawyers have settled out of court with the families of the deceased for a total of $1 million."

Reporters have been turned away from Timmy Valentine's San Fernando Valley mansion all day. The *Herald* was able to speak briefly with Carla Rubens, exclusive New York psychiatrist now working full time at the Valentine residence. "He's been severely traumatized by all this," she says. "Of course, you can well imagine this, because, for all that he has become one of the country's most popular teen idols, and he's still a little kid. Children are so shielded from death these days, it's hard for them to understand it. I've decided that Timmy should have a period of complete rest. He's going away somewhere far away. I'm not allowed to reveal where. He will be under therapy until he snaps out of this shock. It may take quite a while, I'm afraid."

Asked what Timmy would do with himself in his secret hideout, Miss Rubens replied: "He has the largest collection of model trains in the world."

Interestingly enough, sales of all Timmy Valentine's albums went up 117 percent today, as compared to last month.

seeker and labyrinth

Brian was fleeing down a corridor when he saw the three old men. They turned; in the dingy light they stared at him, their faces creased with shadows.

"Who are you?" Brian cried out.

He heard his own voice re-echo; in the far distance Timmy was still singing, his voice floating on an ocean of murmuring. The three old men said nothing yet; their tattered vestments clung to their business suits and had lost their magic, were nothing but shreds of paper.

"We are the Gods of Chaos." The one who spoke was Asian, bald, portly, but spoke in a flawless British accent. It was impossible, dreamlike.

Brian said: "Are we pursuing the same thing?"

"I think so. I am Prince Prathna of Siam. These are old friends. There are so few of us now. We are hunting him down, but we have lost our primary weapon."

"What will you do now?"

"I don't know." The three turned away, as if to end the interview. Then the prince said, "Wait. Who are you? And what is it that you know?"

"I killed one of them tonight. He is the last."

Another spoke up, the gaunt one with the mottled face. "You killed one, you say! How did it feel? Was it a great thrill, to watch millennial life crumble to dust in your hands?"

Brian was uneasy. "I don't know if I should tell you." Lisa and Brian's brother Mark seemed so far away now, as if they'd never existed. Why was he still thirsting for revenge? Was it that he had acquired a taste for zonking vampires back to hell, was it that simple? That was what the old man seemed to be asking. Brian searched for an inner motive in his obsessive stalking of Timmy Valentine, in his rushing up to the stage and stabbing the vampire girl again and again until she shattered on the funhouse mirror. He didn't like what he found. He didn't like himself at all anymore. Anguished, he cried out: "Are you good or evil, that you should ask me these things?"

"We are the Gods of Chaos," the prince answered implacably.

"Will you join us?" said the second man, who now introduced himself as Sir Francis Locke. The third man, spryer than the other two, still dressed, distressingly, as a choirboy, had said nothing.

"If it's the vampires you're after," Brian said slowly, "I guess we're in this thing together."

"Come then. Stephen, lead the way," said Locke. Thus Brian found out the name of the third old man.

They turned a corner. They slipped down another passageway of the unpaneled brick . . . how strange, that no one pursued them . . . out into the steaming Florida night, the VIP parking lot, where a limousine waited.

Prince Prathna said, "We will, of course, pay handsomely

for any information you may have about . . . our little friend."

"I don't want any fucking money."

They climbed in; before he knew it Brian was sliding into the back seat. He panicked suddenly. "You know, I have my own car, you could just drop me off there," he said.

The prince smiled, an eerie, half mocking smile. "Come now, Mr. . . . ah. . . ."

"Zottoli."

"Come, come. You know this is much more than a chance meeting. We did not both happen to stumble onto that stage in search of the same vampire, my dear fellow, without being fated to meet! What a delicious, mystic feeling it was, running down those corridors, what? I felt as though I were in the Cretan Labyrinth itself. Sometimes you must let me explain to you my theory of karmic nexuses, of junctions within the lifelines of individuals which—"

"Enough of this philosophical claptrap, Prathna, old thing!" Locke said. "We're all exhausted. We've just seen one woman blown to smithereens and another decapitated by an exploding statue. Frankly, I'm done for the day."

"Well, what do you suggest, old chap?" Prathna said, laughing coarsely. "A visit to the fleshpots of Boca Blanca?"

"I think we should all go and get ourselves sodding, buggering drunk."

dissolve: arcade

. . . wind stirring the dead leaves, brown-red leaves clustering at the foot of the peeling mailbox, an old man sipping a soda . . . from the front of the drugstore you could just about see the amusement arcade at the bottom of the hill. Naomi Gish didn't like it much, but then in Junction they only had three TV channels. Her boys now, they'd been raving about the new game, Bloodsucker, all week.

"Ah, but have *you* played it?" said Kyle Gallagher, opening the till with one hand and putting his soda down on the counter with the other.

"Oh, you startled me." The man had always had a strange knack of reading your mind. "How did you know—"

"My own son's becoming something of an addict himself. He just lives and breathes it, Naomi. They tell me kids ride their bikes all the way from Highwater to play."

"What the world's coming to."

"Sell you something?"

"Well, not really. I just dropped in because of Alice, you know." Her eleven-year-old daughter was in the back, leafing through the new magazines. "Though I wouldn't say no to a candy bar."

"Well, Nay, it's like you never growed up."

She smiled. "You wicked man. You knew my husband was away."

"When'll he be coming back?"

"I don't know. Sometimes I think we should move the family to Boise, be with him all the time, but then I'd never get to hear your wisecracks again."

"Thirty-two cents," said Kyle, handing her her favorite kind.

"Alice, Alice. . . ."

The front door opened. For a moment she breathed in the fragrance of the mountains, of autumn. "This is a perfect little town."

"Yeah," Kyle answered, although she had not really been talking to him.

"When Terry and David come in later, don't give them any more quarters, you hear? You spoil them rotten."

"Not a dime." He winked. "Oh, did you hear about the Spook House?"

"What about it?" Suddenly an image came to her from years back . . . her and Jeff Gish, daring each other to go on in . . . spending the night once. She shivered; it was half fear, half pleasure. That night had had the same smell. But headier, more intense. The woods immensely still. The dew seeping onto the porch of the dark house. Yes, the same fragrance. It was autumn too, then . . . how long ago? She was only sixteen when she'd gotten pregnant with the twins. "The Spook House, yes," she whispered.

"Did you know someone's moving in to it, someone's bought it?"

"Didn't know you could *buy* that place. Thought it was just . . . part of the landscape. A place lovers go sometimes."

"I ain't kidding. My son PJ saw it, and he's got eyes like a hawk. His mother's a full Shoshone, you know," he added unnecessarily; who didn't know that? But Naomi knew how proud he was of his young wife, so she only smiled. "But what was I saying? Oh, trucks and vans swarming all over the place."

"Lord. I guess I'll bake them a pie."

"My son said they didn't look too friendly. Truth is, they scared the shit out of him, Nay. He bolted home like a rabbit down a hole."

"Now ain't that the weirdest thing."

dissolve: arcade

"I dare you, PJ!" Terry shouted over the whoosh of laser-blasts.

"Leave me the fuck alone, I'm nearly on the seventh screen, stupid."

Intermission now. A coffin exploding in technicolor over the screen, a blaring, triumphant, trumpeting melody, half a dozen little vampires marching across the monitor as the sign flashes EXTRA VAMPIRE, BONUS, EXTRA VAMPIRE, electric pink and electric blue. Then PJ was off again, wiggling the joystick with the lightest wristflick, tapping casually at the garlic control button and the crucifix shield button and the coffin lid control.

"PJ, you gotta come," said Terry Gish.

"I been there already, Terry."

"I'm David," Terry said.

"Think I can't tell? I can smell the difference between you two guys, 'cause I'm—"

"Part Shoshone," David piped up from the battered Ms. Pac-Man across the aisle.

"Aw, fuck," PJ said as the stake came tearing into the innards of the high-resolution vampire, "I almost made it through that bitch of a screen. Look what you made me do."

'You're still the best in town," Terry said, knowing that flattery was a far more effective tool for manipulating PJ Gallagher than insults.

"Guess so," PJ said, smirking contentedly, fishing in his pocket. He turned to Terry; the smaller boy saw a mane of sleek dark hair on an incongruously Irish-looking face. He was tall for a fourteen-year-old, and sometimes handsome, when he wasn't too grubby. "Got a quarter?"

"Only if you come up to the Spook House with us tonight."

Terry was rather pleased at having tricked PJ into this predicament.

"Man, you don't know what you're asking!" PJ said.

"Chicken! Don't tell me they got coffins and shit there."

"Well, actually, I did see coffins today," said PJ. "And this weird guy all in black, tall, kind of like a skeleton."

Terry and David shivered deliciously, anticipating the horror to come. "Then I saw this old lady," PJ said, "she was in black too. You could of sworn they were undertakers or something."

"We just gotta go there," David said. "Why can't you, anyways? I know you used to sneak up there with that Charlotte Woods girl."

"Yeah, well, there wasn't no one living there then. What if they came after us or even shot us?"

Terry thought about that for a while. It had never occurred to him that there might be real danger. He said, "Well, I'll give you a quarter now and I'll give you a dollar tonight."

"You got a dollar?"

"I'll steal it from Mom."

"Terry—!" said David, who was the more cowardly of the two.

PJ said, "You just want me with you 'cause you're scared to go up by yourselves. You're hiring me like a bodyguard or something."

"Yeah," Terry said, realizing a little more flattery would do no harm, "yeah, a bodyguard, like." He pulled a quarter from somewhere in his pants and held it up. "Well?"

"Oh, don't torture a guy," PJ said, grabbing it and thrusting it into the machine. "This time," he whispered fervently, "I'm going to get through that eighth level, damn it!"

dissolve: arcade

Disappointed, Naomi Gish looked at the empty wrapper of her candy bar. I'm getting fat, she thought, although she had actually kept her figure rather trim, for a mother of three.

"Guess I'd best get going, Kyle."

"Sure."

"Alice, are you done looking at those magazines?"

"Mommy, can I buy one, huh?" a girlish voice from somewhere out back.

"I suppose."

Her daughter came out with Shannah Gallagher, Kyle's wife. An enigmatic woman; Kyle had met her one day when his station wagon broke down somewhere near the reservation. That was how Naomi had heard the story, anyway. She was a tiny woman, delicate-featured, with very long, braided black hair. Although she was wearing one of her husband's lumberjack shirts, she still looked irritatingly sexy. Naomi wondered idly whether Jeff was being unfaithful over in Boise, if that was why he hardly came home anymore.

Alice, red-haired and freckled like her twin brothers, ran up to her clutching a copy of *Idol Magazine*. "Can I get this, Mommy, please?"

"Sure."

"See this pinup? It's Timmy Valentine, Mommy!"

"Yes, dear." Naomi wondered what her daughter was talking about, but decided it would be too complicated to inquire. "It's getting dark now. Run down to the arcade and tell the boys to get on home, honey. I'll hang on to this magazine for you."

She took it from her and watched the girl run down Main Street. The sun was setting behind the mountain. The peak glinted with orange snow. For a second she remembered Jeff and her and the moist floor of the Spook House, fourteen years before, vivid, like it was yesterday. Then suddenly, with even more startling clarity, she saw an image of Jeff with Shannah Gallagher. The Shoshone woman stood in the doorway, her black hair caught the sunset just so, it shone a brilliant gold . . . Lord, she was just too beautiful, and that Kyle Gallagher was old, and the woman had to be getting it somewhere else . . . what was she thinking?

"Got to get dinner started," she mumbled as she edged past the woman into the chilled evening, fumbling through the pages of her daughter's magazine in order to avoid Shannah's clear brown eyes.

dissolve

WILL YOUR FAVE IDOL EVER SING AGAIN?

We all know he's just the cutest teen hunk in the whole world, but adorable, sexy Timmy Valentine isn't feeling that great these days! You've probably heard of the awful accident at his last concert a couple of weeks ago, and it really seems to have gotten him down. He's really a sad boy right now. Don't you think *you* ought to try and cheer him up?

Write him a note care of Stupendous Sounds Systems, 8865 San Agapito Boulevard, Hollywood, California. Who knows? You may get a personally autographed picture from your fave idol, or even a note! "When I'm down," says this foxy hunk, "I just love to read my fan mail over and over again."

And remember, his latest album, *Funhouse*, is just out. You're going to love it—I do!

Keep sexy Timmy Valentine happy now!

dissolve: night-child: labyrinth

Carla dreamed she was on a long train ride. The scenery rolled by: great plains, foothills, finally great mountains girt with rainbows. She did not know the name of the country but somehow she thought it was Transylvania, because they all spoke in frightened whispers. There was a castle towering from the tallest crag.

Now she was going up the stone steps that dripped blood and moaned as her feet touched them, as if they were flesh and blood. There was an audience and a heavy velvet curtain, maroon, and an orchestra playing creepy music, so she knew she was in the opera. Stephen, in dark robes, came down to greet her. He was like in the old days, back at the rest home, when she had healed him; his eyes sparkled. They were singing in some strange language; somehow she thought it must be Hungarian, for the words did not resemble any others she could think of, and they tripped awkwardly on her lips: *várad, kekszakállu, ájtot*.

She turned to the prompter's box for guidance but it was empty, and the orchestra had no conductor, the violinists were living trees in tuxedos playing their own branches, the winds were hollow bones of skeletons, animated by a chill wind.

In the dream she knew she dreamt, and was not afraid. She called out lightly, "*Kekszakállu, kekszakállu . . .*" and knew that it meant Bluebeard, Bluebeard, and that her name was Judith, and the opera was Béla Bartók's *Bluebeard's Castle*, which she'd seen Stephen conduct once in New York, soon after his release from the home, substituting for the indisposed

Isztvan Takacś. That was why it was all in Hungarian. But she knew the gist of the plot, so she didn't have to understand too much of what she was singing. What a fine mezzo voice I have, she thought, wondering why with a voice like this she'd taken up a career as a Jungian analyst.

It was all going according to the score, as far as she could tell. There were the seven secret doors; one by one Stephen was handing her the keys to them as she cajoled, demanded, implored . . . she opened the first few and saw the torture chamber, the armory, the treasury, the inner garden. The doors grew more ponderous, their bolts harder to pull, their hinges unoiled, the oak richer and heavier to push open.

Now she saw the vast kingdom of Bluebeard, which was mountainous and verdant, somehow like tourist photographs of Idaho, with Indian reservations, with potato fields, with solemn grand ranges of time-twisted mountains . . . and now the lake of tears . . . and now Stephen was refusing to hear the final key, and she was growing strident, pounding on the iron-barred oak, shouting that he had other lovers before her, that he had killed them and hidden their decapitated bodies in the room—

And finally there rose a great sighing and the portal flung wide of its own accord and she stood in a hall of infinite mirrors and at its center was Timmy Valentine. He stood in flames, fire pouring from his eyes and lips. The flames were spreading out of the door now, engulfing the castle, and it was Valhalla and the gods were dying, and he stood there, on fire, unscathed, and Stephen was screaming over the hiss of spurting flames, "This is the one I loved before you, the one that pierces the eternal flame—"

The fire became a sea. She stood with her arms outspread, like Moses, willing the flaming ocean to part so she could reach the two of them, but the fire still came, and she began to scream as it touched her, as it ate into her limbs—

Carla woke up. But she might still have been dreaming, for she was still in a medieval-looking room, with stone walls and a door of heavy oak.

Then Timmy was beside her with a tray, and he wasn't on fire any more. He was looking solicitously at her as she lay there, still cold from the dream. "I brought you some warmed red wine."

"I never drink w—" said Carla, smiling weakly.

Timmy laughed his little-boy laugh. "It's all right," he said. "Welcome to my secret castle. If you look out the window, carefully, through the thickest of trees, you can just make out the train station. A train passes through every couple of days, around midnight. It almost never stops. I watch for it all the time."

Carla smelled the perfume of an autumn forest.

"You've been asleep for days," Timmy said.

"I had a dream."

"Wait a minute. I thought *I* was supposed to be the patient around here."

"Yes."

"Speaking of which, I think we're going to have a break-through soon. I'm beginning to remember . . . oh, so much. It's the nearness of the forest. The forest is like a womb. All forests are one, you know."

"What does Stephen have to do with us, Timmy?"

"I believe that, as you are my anima, he is my shadow."

"And you are his?"

"Scissors, paper, stone."

Carla laughed. "You're a psychological genius."

"Let's just say I've been observing the human race for a pretty long time," he said, casually tucking his pale blue Tokyu T-shirt into his jeans.

"I'm really sorry about the concert," Carla said. For a sec-ond she saw an image of Missy Pavlat's severed head bouncing in slow motion on the strings of the grand piano.

"Come on, half a dozen people died."

"No, I mean it," Carla said, suddenly knowing with crys-talline certainty where her loyalties lay now.

"And they will come again, Carla."

"I thought I had saved you, though I don't exactly know how."

"They will come again. You were the stone that broke the scissors, but Stephen has the paper that will wrap the stone."

"You don't seem too upset."

"I intend to be ready for them. I intend to be strong from now on, Carla, not to flinch from the truth any more."

"The truth?"

"That I am the junction of love and death."

20

As I suspected . . . although we have physically moved a couple of thousand miles from the San Fernando Valley, psychically speaking we have gone nowhere at all. I knew this for a fact a few days after my dream of Bluebeard's castle, when I noticed for the first time, at the back of the walk-in closet into which Maria had unpacked all my clothes, a door. When I unlatched it, I saw familiar wooden steps. I knew that if I went upstairs, if I ignored the hauntings and followed the path, I would reach the room of the model trains and the infinite mirrors.

At first I was in no hurry to resume the sessions with Timmy. Although I felt more and more committed to him—in some way I didn't quite yet understand, I seem to have saved his life—I was actually afraid of the new breakthrough he had promised me.

I contented myself with the view, and, once or twice, driving into the town with Rudy.

It's a lovely town, like one of those old faded postcards. It has a couple of little shops and a drugstore run by an older man, a Mr. Gallagher, and his Indian wife; they have a strikingly handsome—if grimy—teenage son. Other people go in and out, and I've met a few families: the Woodses, the Gishes, the Trees, the Turningbrooks, and Cherry Cola, the obliga-

253

tory village idiot, who is a woman. Liberated town! There's a
general store which has, for some reason, a large display of
wigs in the window. There's a library, the only one for several
towns, and an arcade for the youngsters, ditto. Actually there
seem to be many more than the 573 advertised on the signpost,
but I guess it's because these are the only shops in miles. Come
winter, though, Mr. Gallagher says, the population really does
shrink to nothing. They often have twenty, twenty-five feet of
snow during the season, he says, probably trying to scare off a
New Yorker like me.

You get a whiff of the town, though, with the half-pulped
leaf-piles almost ground into the corners of the flagstones, and
that biting wind from the mountain . . . I've never smelled
anything like it. I think it's the smell that makes people not
want to go live in cities.

There is an oval mirror, in a mother-of-pearl frame, hanging on the door in back of the closet; usually I pay it no heed
when I go in to change my clothes, but today I happened to
glance at it and I didn't see my face. I saw Timmy's, or rather
an outline of his face superimposed on my own. I found
myself either gliding through the door that had become a veil
of mirror mist, or opening it and going through, I'm not sure
which. I followed the well-trod route and found the hall of
mirrors.

He was on his hands and knees on the floor, wiring up a new
control box and connecting more tracks. He had two full
trains now, one a model steam engine with antique boxcars
and a caboose, the other very sleek, streamlined, one of the
Japanese bullet trains by the looks of it. "One for you," he
said without looking up, "and one for me."

"What makes you think I'll play? As the doctor, I'm supposed to let *you* play, and sit back taking notes."

"So pretend to be objective, if it makes you feel better. But
you know different."

I said, "What shall we talk about today?"

He said, planting more and more trees on a hill that he had
made from an upturned armchair, "The forest is behind us as
well as before us."

"Forest?"

"You know."

I pulled out a notebook.

"It opens in both directions. To the here and now, and to the forgotten and forgettable past." He sat up, smugly content with the academic nicety of his turn of phrase.

memory: perhaps 1716, but maybe A.D. 119

He sees her, smells her, calls out to her. They come together, rejoicing that they are no longer alone. She is in heat. As she pants, she exudes an earthly stench that drives him mad with a desire that is not the old bloodlust.

They wallow in the thick warm moist mud of the forest floor. "I see a way out," he cries out suddenly. He is in human form now. It confuses him.

Suddenly he realizes that he can talk. He remembers what speech is now. A sentence in a language he does not recognize comes to his lips: "*Das Ewig-weibliche zieht uns hinan.*" He does not know the meaning of the words, but perhaps it has something to do with the bitch that lies beneath his feet, pawing the dirt, yammering with sexual passion.

"Will you lead me out of the forest?" he says, still marvelling at how the sounds spring to his lips unbidden.

The boy and the dog walk slowly towards the light.

There is a shadow overhead; a bird of prey perhaps, or the edge of a dragon's wing.

The strain toward the light.

memory: 1440

The man stands in flames. It is dusk.

memory: A.D. 79; 1440

. . . *spatter* . . .

analyst's notebook

"It is true," he said, setting up a medieval castle upon a great plain he had fashioned from a green blanket, "that I have known Gilles de Rais, murderer of perhaps 800 children, known as Bluebeard, also Marshal of France, friend and devoted fighter in the cause of Joan of Arc. And that through him I learned the true meaning of evil, and that I could not bear the truth I uncovered, and that I was driven by it, for many centuries, into the dark forest.''

I said, "Will you tell me about it?"

I waited.

He said, half-mocking, "Your fifty-five minutes, Miss Rubens, are up. Send in the next patient as you leave, won't you?"

I bit my tongue. "Tomorrow, then."

In his winsome, baby-boy voice, he said, "Please Miss Rubens, do you know the way out of the forest?"

memory: 1440

A half-perceived rustle of voices in the darkness. The boy vampire stirs. Has he been asleep then? How long? Vague images spring to his consciousness: a tiny wiry body leaping in darkness, claws digging in soil redolent with freshly killed blood, speech striving to penetrate bestial vocal cords, time that is not time. He touches himself and knows he has assumed human form again; perhaps the proximity of humans has brought it about. It is time to return to their world.

"Tiffauges. Tiffauges."

He hears the word over and over. It is whispered, and it carries unspeakable terror. He wonders what it refers to.

Now he springs up the trunk of the nearest oak, blending catlike with its shadows. Now he is crouched in a crook of a bough that extends over a clearing, and he can see two men in the half-light . . . no, a man and a boy, poachers, speaking softly but animatedly to each other.

"The forest ends here."

"We should have been more careful: we are too near Tiffauges. Don't you know what that means, Jeannot?"

"No."

"The Baron will come for us. Aren't you afraid?"

"Should I be?"

"They'll only hang me. But you, Jeannot . . . but you are still a child, and. . . ."

"What, father?"

"Tiffauges . . . Tiffauges . . . the castle of Gilles de Rais."

The conversation is a blur, and the boy vampire cannot follow it all; they speak some Celtic dialect . . . the folk language of Brittany. The forest has brought him far this time, he thinks.

The hunger burns.

These are not important, he thinks. Poachers. They might be hanged anyway. No one will miss them.

He no longer hesitates, but leaps down from the bough, baring his fangs. The boy Jeannot does not have time to scream. He dies at once, showering the cat-boy with hot blood. It is a sweet blood, prepubescent and, because the attack came so abruptly, free of adrenalin. Shuffling off the cat shape, the boy vampire feasts. The blood rushes into his veins. He is drunk on it. He does not see the father, who has been cowering behind the same oak tree, who has now crept out; only when the man has come quite near does the boy notice him.

There is a deadness in the peasant's eyes. His long hair and beard are crawling with lice. He wears a shapeless, dirty woollen cloak. The boy vampire is astonished; the man shows no fear. Only the glazed eyes, the dull expression. He says to the boy vampire in broken French: "You are from Tif-fauges."

"No," says the boy vampire, perplexed.

"Why do you not devour me? Has the Baron corrupted you so much, then, that only other children will sate your lusts?"

"I don't understand—"

"Don't trick me with your innocent smile. I have ammunition." The man pulls out a cross from under his cloak; it is wooden, and crudely engraved with a relief of roses.

The boy vampire cringes.

"I knew it. You are from Bluebeard's castle."

"Who is Bluebeard?"

The father laughs bitterly. "Don't mock me. Let me do to my son what must be done." As the vampire stares curiously, the father kneels down and tenderly hugs the body of his son. There is little blood, for the vampire has been without sustenance for a long time. The man seizes the boy's head and snaps the neck with the practiced hand of a forestman. He does not weep. It seems to the vampire that the man has done this many times before.

"He was my last child," the father says softly.

Although the boy feels little regret that he has killed, for his hunger must always be assuaged, he now feels, in his repleteness, pity. He says, "What kind of an age is this, when fathers no longer weep for their sons?"

The father listens. It seems that the French the boy has

spoken must be archaic; and it is not the man's native tongue, so he appears to be translating what the boy has said to himself. Then he answers: "Go back where you belong, demon! Go back to your Lord of Tiffauges. Go fuck the darkness with him. You see what I had to do to the boy, so that he wouldn't become like you—" And now, overcome, the man weeps at last, although he cannot be more than middle-aged he seems a thousand years old. Once more he holds out the cross. Once more the vampire cringes. And flees into deeper darkness, drawing the shadows around him like a cloak, until the tiredness of satiation overwhelms him and he rests. The forest is thinner here.

Night has fallen, thick and starry. There is a meadow just beyond this clearing. Gingerly the boy vampire steps beyond the forest's edge. Almost at the horizon there is a castle; flecks of light dance on the turrets, on the crenellations of its walls. This might be Tiffauges. It is little more than a smudge of deeper black against the purple of night. Bolder now, the boy vampire walks to meet it. There is no moon. Dew tingles on his bare feet as they tramp the uneven grass. He wonders if his clothes—woollen tunic, woollen cloak—will seem antiquated.

As the night deepens, giving him strength, he begins to sing a Provençal song that once was popular, wondering if they still speak the language . . . "*Kalenda maya ni fuelhs de faya, ni chaunz.* . . ." The words have slipped from his memory. Again he begins to sing it, hoping it will come back to him. His voice swells in the chill darkness, haunting, bittersweet.

Out of nowhere, something tightens around his shoulders. A lariat! Horses' hooves, shrill neighing, as he is roughly pulled to the ground. Three or four horses pawing the earth around him. Men are pulling on him in all directions now, tightening the ropes. He struggles, but the ropes have been treated with something supernatural, perhaps wolfsbane.

Other men now, in armor, holding torches aloft. Finally, riding a white stallion from the castle gates, a young man, about seventeen, effete, blond, his cloak sparkling with golden thread; he dismounts and comes right up to the boy and stares him in the eye.

The vampire looks at his captors. They are underlings, and all have that bewitched, glazed expression that he has seen on the peasant and his dead son. Only the youth does not have it.

"What is this?" he says, his eyes sparkling. The boy vampire smells a fine wine on his breath, and garlic, which makes him feel faint.

"An addition to His Grace's choir, I think," says one of the soldiers gruffly.

"His *heavenly* choir!" the youth says. He laughs wholeheartedly; the others snicker a little, as though it is expected of them, but their hearts are not in it.

"Bring him to dinner," the youth says. "His Grace the Lieutenant-General of Brittany, Marshal of France, etcetera, will be delighted at this opportunity for an unexpected . . . entertainment."

They begin to tug the boy forward. The stench of garlic, the unguents with which the rope has been anointed, combine to make the boy vampire ill. He vomits up a sludge of human blood in which a finger of the boy Jeannot, swallowed in the feeding frenzy but not digested, floats.

The soldiers gasp and cross themselves. But the young man merely laughs again, a pleasant, resonant laugh. "I am Etienne," he says, "though they call me Poitou. I am a special procurer of . . . entertainments . . . for His Grace. A pimp of the macabre, if you will." He comes close, fearless, and pats the boy amiably on the shoulder. "And, for what it's worth, you impertinent little boy, don't worry too much. Life is but an illusion, is it not? You have reached your journey's end. Just think! By tonight you will be warbling way *up there*, and meanwhile you will have assuaged the inner torment of a very great man. Not to mention your liege lord. Tell me your name, boy."

"Jeannot," he says, thinking: I have already robbed that boy of his life; I may as well steal his name too.

"Bah. He will not like a name so close to Jeanne. Have you no other name?"

"Jeannot," the boy repeats weakly through the poison-haze of garlic and wolfsbane.

He is almost losing consciousness as they drag him forward. They pass the portcullis and traverse a stone courtyard. A stablehand stares curiously and averts his eyes. Jeannot's mind drifts. Always there are stone walls, always damp, sometimes dripping blood. A scullery maid sees them approach and begins to scrub fiercely at an imaginary stain on the floor.

Dogs bark. There are worn steps, archways, and once he sees tonsured men, whose garb is not quite that of priests, cackling at obscene jokes as they play at dice. He faints.

When he comes to he has been strapped to a table. He is naked. Leather binds his feet, his arms, his wrists, his neck. He struggles but cannot move. It is the proximity of silver that is sapping his strength. As he looks from right to left, he sees that this is a dinner table, for everywhere there are silver platters piled with food: mountains of white and red grapes, a boar's head, slabs of bread, a stuffed goose whose head has been inserted into its anus, carafes of wine, half a venison draped over one end of the huge table. He hears laughter. Trying to crane his neck so he can see ahead of him is difficult, but he does succeed in lifting it a little, and he sees an enormous jar of greenish glass full of tiny dried penises. Farther down, in other containers whose bizarre shapes are more reminiscent of an alchemist's laboratory than a dinner table, are little hands floating in variously colored fluids, hearts preserved in brine, a platter of more diminutive genitals, bleeding and putrefying.

Men in dark robes, holding torches, stand guard. The corners and walls are shadowed; in his weakened state he cannot tell how large the chamber is.

And now comes Poitou, and another man who bends down to peer excitedly at him. At first all that Jeannot notices is the silver crucifix that dangles from his neck, for when the man bends over him it grazes his chest and he screams in pain.

"Fascinating," the man says. Then he carefully unclasps the crucifix and hands it to some attendant Jeannot cannot see, and the boy vampire observes his face more clearly. He wishes the man would order the silverware removed; it is the only obstacle to his escape.

The man is in his thirties; he is handsome. He has tinted his beard blue with some dye, and it lends him a menacing appearance. But he does not seem unkind. "He is so beautiful, Poitou. You have done well." He reaches out to touch the boy, then snatches away his hand. "But he is cold!" He turns to scold an attendant. "Why have you let the poor child freeze so? It is not your place to inflict suffering on him . . . but mine, when we celebrate the mysteries." Again he starts stroking the boy's chest. The man is agitated. Even through the silver daze Jeannot can sense the racing of his blood. "And who dared to mutilate your little genitals?" asks the man, caressing the cold penis and the scars of castration. "Did you escape from some choir? Did they mistreat you?" He rubs the boy all over with his hands. "Did they beat you?" he says conspiratorially. "Molest you?"

"Leave me . . . alone," the boy vampire gasps. "You don't know what . . . you're dealing with. . . ."

"Leave you alone, alone!" says Gilles de Rais feverishly. "Are you mad? Oh, I'm burning up with love for you, my little death-angel, my Cupid, my pretty gelding."

The boy vampire struggles in the grip of the silver's drugging effect, to fend off the madman. "The mysteries of evil," Bluebeard whispers, impassioned. "Yes, evil, evil, evil. Am I a bad man? Tell me, tell me. Is it so wrong to wring beauty out of even death? Oh, how your coldness warms me. Before I kill you, you will tell me your name. . . ."

"Jeannot."

Gilles de Rais recoils, pauses for a moment. "Ah, child of my heart, you gave me a turn," he says, as a momentary frown crosses his face. "Do you not see, on the wall, behind us?" He beckons for one of the torchbearers to step back and hold up his flame so that Jeannot can see a painting that hangs on the wall.

It is a man in armor . . . no, a woman, her hair cropped short like a man's. Her gaze seems to fall upon them both. Bluebeard shrieks, an animal cry of insufferable grief. "Jeanne, Jeanne, do not torment me," he shouts. He rages theatrically about the chamber, distracted for a while; then, almost as an afterthought, he notices the boy strapped to the dinner table and returns to continue his odious caresses. "Are you surprised that I celebrate only the mysteries of evil now? They burned her at the stake, did you know that? They called her a witch! The savior of France, a witch! Am I an evil man? Am I evil, evil?" He begins to kiss the boy on the mouth now, his tongue never flinching from the icy lips. "Your breath is already cold, as if it knew already what was in store for it . . . you do not breathe at all . . . are you already dead? Oh, you are beautiful with your wild deep blue hair and your snow-pale face and those huge dark eyes." The boy is hardly able to flinch from the thrusting, winestained tongue. Now men in robes and paper crowns have entered and have begun chanting nonsensical words and a smell of unholy incense wafts into the

room from somewhere in the castle, and Bluebeard has torn
off his cloak and has climbed up on the table on top of Jeannot, and in his frenzy he has kicked the boar's head onto the
floor and upset the jar of dried penises onto the boy's legs, he
feels them skitter down his flesh like cockroaches, he sees the
man's rampant erection, now he feels a dagger plunge into his
guts, bore into his intestines, pound again and again into his
belly, he feels the old jellied blood quiver and liquefy at the
unwonted touch of body heat, he feels the spurt of semen on
his ravaged stomach, and all the time the silver chains him
down and he cannot move, and he is thinking, How can this
man wear a crucifix and how can this crucifix wield power
over me when its wearer has become so possessed by evil? and
still the madman thrusts into him until, in the grip of uncontrollable passion, he hugs the boy to him, the weight of
him crushes against the wounds and forces the intestines to
ooze out against Bluebeard's own flesh, and now he buries his
face and his hands in the pit of the abdomen and screams and
screams in intolerable ecstasy, and his mouth is bloodied from
kissing the boy's internal organs, and he collapses, spent,
upon the pile of extruded guts, weeping and moaning, murmuring over and over, "Am I not evil? Answer me, am I not
evil, evil, Jeanne d'Arc whom they burned alive, am I not
truly evil?"

The boy thinks: Surely I will die this time, I will truly die for
the last time.

The blood of his namesake, which has so recently brought
him back to life, seeps into the table, drips onto the floor.
They lift up the unconscious Bluebeard and carry him gently
out of the room. Then they cut Jeannot free and drag him
away. He is too dazed and weak to fight back. They are joking
as they push his body down a back staircase. They think that
he is dead, and in truth he has lost so much blood, and been so
tormented by the silver and the wolfsbane and the crucifixes
that he is barely clinging to his undeadness. But they cannot
know that by taking him out of that room, with its oppressive
silver, they have unwittingly begun the process of self-healing.

He feels earth being thrown into his face. They are burying
him. Good, he thinks. Earth will revive him. The slithering of
worms as they writhe through the topsoil will lull his ears like
the nightsong of a mother. Night will heal him.

And when he has been renewed he must go back. He must exact a fearful vengeance..That this mortal has dared to touch him, to violate him!

Vengeance! he thinks, as he sinks into the soil's softness and succumbs to its subtle embrace.

arcade: labyrinth

"We shouldn't have left those bikes so far back," Terry whispered as they crouched behind a partly denuded bush.

"Shut up," said PJ. "Just don't forget you owe me a dollar."

"I shouldn't even pay you. That was last week we made that deal, and you never came. I waited up till midnight."

"I was grounded. How could I? Doesn't count."

"Does."

"Shut up," David said, behind them.

Their bikes were about 250 yards away, where the mountain path forked and the right trail led up to the grounds of the Spook House. There were no gates anymore, just the brick archway and one or two railings buried in the thick grass. Terry saw the house now, a hodgepode of Gothic elements, gables, gargoyles, an earnest and tackily affecting pastiche. The front walls were blanketed with ivy, shivering in the midnight breeze. Where autumn had not yet touched them the leaves were individually silvered by the moonlight; elsewhere the walls were freckled with red-gold, like patinaed copper.

"That's where the coffins were," said PJ, pointing at the driveway, where a limousine and two vans were parked. "They were being unloaded, carried into the house, I think."

"Right, uh-huh, sure," Terry said scornfully.

"Christ, man, it's true." PJ shook the hair out of his eyes. "Look now. Someone's coming out of the house."

Terry looked. He could see part of the front door in the space between the two vans. It opened now with a wheeze. Far away, a wolf or something howled, making him jump.

"Chicken," said PJ.

"Just a little surprised is all."

Something was coming out of the house. A blur; sequins maybe, or some kind of evening gown. It belonged to an old woman—to Terry she looked about a hundred years old—

whose face and arms were completely plastered with heavy white makeup, as if she was acting in one of those silent movies you sometimes saw on TV. She squeezed between the parked vans and came out into the lawn. There was a statue over a gravestone that hadn't been there the last time Terry'd sneaked over to the Spook House. She walked slowly up to it and started to embrace and kiss it.

"Holy shit," PJ whispered.

She stopped, seemed to prick up her ears. Howling, closer now.

"Shut the fuck up! She heard you."

"Did not."

They went on watching in silence. Now and then the old woman froze in listening posture. Finally she must have heard whatever it was she was waiting for, because she slowly started to peel off her clothes and, humming languidly to herself, to toss them randomly around the statue. Terry could see two small, wrinkly breasts, and a puckered, balding vulva. "Sh-i-i-it!" he exclaimed.

The other two gagged him with their fists.

At that moment a wolf came bounding in from the forest beyond: sleek, sable-furred, with silver ears and ruby eyes. "I'm getting out of here," David said abruptly.

"Oh, shut up, asshole," Terry said. "Nothing's gonna happen. They can't even see us."

"I don't like it," David said.

As the woman continued to hum, a weird melody, half dirge, half lullaby, the wolf trotted up to her. He must have been tame. Now, to Terry's utter disgust, he began suckling at her breasts while she crooned and stroked his head, and he could see blood oozing from her nipples, mud-colored in the moonlight—

"Gross," he whispered, shuddering deliciously at the risk they were taking and how gratifyingly kinky the inhabitants of the Spook House had proved. "Gross, gross, gross, *gross*."

David screamed.

"Shut the fuck up!" Terry and PJ both yelled. Jesus, why couldn't he ever leave his fucking brother at home?

It was too late. The old witch scooped up a sequined skirt from the grass to conceal her privates, and then began to berate the three in a grotesque fake Bela Lugosi accent: "You horrible horrible children, I come after, I kill, I use in experiments, run home you dirty smelly children!''

It was ludicrous. The next thing Terry knew he was screeching with laughter. It was too absurd. Then he saw that the wolf was attacking David, had his neck in his jaws, was dragging him from the house. David was struggling weakly; Terry's mind couldn't quite catch up with the flipflop from funny to dangerous—

"Come back, fucker, I knew I shouldn't have let you come," he was yelling after them, and then: "David, oh, Jesus, David—"

"He's bit, he's really bit," PJ was yelling. "Help me, help me." Terry sprinted after them and they grabbed hold of his brother's hand and pulled as hard as they could, they yanked him free and started running awkwardly down the path, supporting the wounded kid between them . . . Terry couldn't think, it was like running in place, he was so shocked, he ran blindly, and David was so limp, his neck and chest and ripped-up parka were all bloody, so much blood, and the howling rose up behind them, savage, bloodcurdling, and the old woman was still cursing at them in that eerie voice—

They stumbled, reached out for the bikes. Terry saw David's lips move, like he was trying to say something, but he was so heavy, he gurgled, he threw up blood, and Terry said, "For Chrissakes, go on ahead, tell Mom," to PJ, and PJ said, "What the fuck am I going to tell your mom, I'm not even supposed to be with you, I'm supposed to be asleep—"

"I don't care, he's bit, don't you goddamn see?"

He held his twin brother close now. God, was he breathing? Yes. A little. Why did I ever bring him, why did he ever get born, the little fucker, at least I edged him out by two minutes, he was thinking, as he tried leading both bikes with one hand and holding up his brother against his left shoulder with his left arm around him, but he kept dropping one of the bikes, he realized he'd have to abandon them, he'd be in for it now especially if Dad ever fucking came home.

He was supporting David with both arms now. He heard the bikes drop, plopping against the mud. "Come on, little brother, just hold on a few minutes, we'll be home soon, soon. . . ." He slipped in squishy mud, sprawled a few feet, tasted dirt in his mouth. Where was the wolf, did it go back in the house, did they keep a wolf there just to bite kids? Oughta be a law against it. Goddamn it, my own brother! He pulled

David from where he lay face down in the mush and staggered downhill with him, one painful step at a time. "Come on, Dave, Dave," he whispered urgently as they reached the edge of the woods and he could see the train tracks and the general store with its wig display through the thinning trees. A few more steps, then screeching tires as his mother's station wagon pulled to a halt just in front of the traces.

Mom and PJ were dashing towards them now. They lifted David and the three of them put him in the back seat, and then Terry squeezed in beside his brother and they went screeching down Main Street, lurching at the stop sign as they turned towards the house—

"What happened, what happened?" Mom was shrieking, incoherent.

Terry clutched his brother's hand hard to his chest. "He's bit, Mom. There's wolves out there." He was trying not to cry. Dad used to say he'd be ashamed of him if he cried. As they turned onto the dark street near the driveway he noticed something odd about David. "Mom . . . Mom . . . I think it's serious. I . . . I think David's _dead_, Mom." He felt an awful burning cold inside.

"Oh, fuck," PJ said softly, "fuck, oh, fuck, oh, fuck."

It was appalling. The worst of it was that Mom didn't even tell PJ to watch his language. That was it, the most appalling thing.

He dropped his brother's lifeless hand. It dangled over the edge of the seat. Small pools of blood had collected in the places where they had slashed the vinyl with their Swiss army knives.

His mother didn't even seem to be there anymore, didn't even seem to notice him. She just kept saying, "I'm going to have to call Jeff in Boise, and what if he's out screwing some city bitch, what if I'm not good enough for him anymore?"

21

scissors, stone, paper

Stephen sat alone in his room at the Plaza in New York. The television was on, although it showed nothing but a pattern of gray dots. He took another swig of vodka. Life was good, almost as exciting as an opera.

And what if it really were an opera—a Wagner opera? Imagine if, wherever one went, one were surrounded by the monumental outpourings of a symphony orchestra—as if everybody one met were wearing the same invisible Walkman! Life would have a libretto with all the words written down, and translations. If it were Wagner, there would be leitmotifs for every major character and event in the opera. He could imagine them now, their names printed between asterisks, popping up here and there as glosses in the libretto of his life. Perhaps *fire* would be the most important one in my case, he thought, hearing in his head the magic fire music from *Die Walkure* and remembering that in Wagner *fire* also meant the trickster-god, and illusion, and transformation. . . .

A knock on the door disturbed this rather arcane reverie. It was Brian Zottoli. "Have some vodka!" Stephen said expansively. Where are all the others?"

"In Prince Prathna's suite, plotting more mischief," Brian said. "I slipped away; I wanted to see you. You're the only one of these people who seems even remotely sane, Stephen."

Stephen laughed. "And to think that I'm the only one ac-

267

tually to have once been committed to a lunatic asylum! Sit down." He beckoned to a heavily padded, fake-nineteenth-century armchair. "You regret that you've joined us?"

"No. I want vengeance."

"Ah, vengeance, lust, the stuff of grand opera," said Stephen, hearing only the *fire* music in his head.

"But why New York, to hunt down an Angeleno vampire?"

"Ah, but you're naive. You think this is a problem of a few deaths, of a lost niece, of one possessed mansion. You don't know this boy as I do." He started to tell Brian one of the stories of his former encounters with Timmy Valentine or Konrad Stolz or whoever it was, but became confused in mid-narration, sank down on the sofa, and took another slug. "Do you see these?" He emptied the contents of an attaché case onto the coffee table. "Telegrams inviting me to conduct anywhere I want. A letter from Therese Benzineau, telling me they're ready to renegotiate my contract at four times the money. Now look."

He started ripping the letters into shreds. Then he piled them up on the ashtray and set fire to them with his lighter. "Behold, an old man's career down the drain. Now you think I'm the only sane one?"

"In a way."

"But as to New York . . . we're here to pursue some musical contacts of mine who might tell us where Timmy Valentine is. Well, it's better than hanging around the gates of a mansion all day. You haven't figured out anything more from those newspaper clippings?"

"No."

Stephen said: "Once I loved a woman. But she is possessed now. By that vampire. Once I had a vision—at least, I thought it was a vision, but when I last saw it I knew it was in the flesh—"

"You're not really one of them, are you?"

"What do *you* think?"

"That you're after something else."

"Of course I am! Do you think I care a fig for Prathna's grand celebration of the mysteries of evil? I only want to regain possession of myself, don't you see? Sixty years ago I gazed into a phantom's eyes and my soul was stolen from me. Since then I have existed only in the shadows of reality, becoming flesh only when I see fire. Fire! Fire is life itself

That's what the ancient Persians believed, you know. Their philosophy conceived of a never-ending battle between life and unlife, good and evil, creation and destruction. And fire to them was life itself."

"They worshipped fire?"

"Yes. They believed in a universal spirit called Ahura-Mazda and a dark force called Ahriman. . . ." Stephen paused, thinking that he must be boring Brian. After all, to most people, fire was just fire.

"I wish," Brian said, "that those two upstairs would give up this obsession with grandeur and spectacle. You understand, don't you? We're not like them. We're driven by love, by desperation."

"No!" I am as obsessed as they." The fire was going out. So is the light from my eyes, Stephen thought.

arcade: labyrinth: dissolve

Jeff Gish stepped off the train alone. He stood nervously for a moment, wondering if Nay would come, but it was past midnight. He would have time to think things over before he had to face his wife and her little jealousies. And David's death.

There was no awning over the platform, just a couple of signposts, a locked ticket booth, and a stairway down to the parking lot.

As he hesitated, he saw David at the top of the stairs. Only it wasn't David, David was dead, it must be Terry. "Terry," he said.

"Hi, Dad." The boy seemed unusually pale; it must have been the moonlight.

"Why are you dressed like this? Why are you even here? It's midnight. Don't you have school?"

"Dressed?" The boy smiled. Jeff moved closer. "Oh, it's for the funeral." He frowned as he straightened the bow tie and the tuxedo jacket. "I just felt like wearing it."

"Terry, I—"

"I know, Dad. These things shouldn't happen to no one. Don't worry about me or nothing. I'm fine. It's OK, Dad."

"No it ain't. I should have been home."

"Don't blame yourself, Dad. We gotta get going. Mom doesn't know I'm out here, she thinks I'm asleep."

Jeff resisted an impulse to hug the kid. What if Terry rebuffed him? They'd never been close, they'd never been physical at all.

"Your beard's longer, Dad."

"Huh? Oh, yeah."

They walked down the steps together. At least we're sharing something now, Jeff through. Grief. Once their hands almost touched, and Jeff recoiled from the intense coldness. He thought: This must be what grief does to you.

They reached the old Malibu he'd left in the lot a couple of weeks before. It was the only car in the parking lot. Jeff got in, threw his overnight bag in the back seat, and started up. As he looked to the right, he saw the boy frantically knocking at the window.

"What's the matter, forgotten how to get into a car?" He laughed, over-loud at his own feeble joke.

"You have to *ask* me," said the boy with a twinge of impatience.

Sighing, Jeff opened the door and let him in. As the boy closed the door behind him, Jeff became conscious of an unpleasant stench in the car, like rotting meat. "Jesus," he said. "Some raccoon's gone and died in the trunk or something."

The boy snuggled up to him, a curiously unfamiliar gesture. "Oh, Daddy, Daddy," he said, "when are you going to stay home forever?"

"Come on now, you know I can't."

"I could make you." The kid started laughing, an eerie, high-pitched laugh that he'd never heard before.

"Stop that, it's creepy."

"I can't get over it. You think I'm Terry, don't you?"

"What kind of game is this? Of course you're Terry. You have to be, because—"

"Dad, look at me." He seemed so pale, so pale; you could hardly see the freckles at all, and the red hair seemed stiff, lifeless, and there was another smell now, some chemical, formaldehyde maybe.

"Terry, cut this crap. I know you've had a terrible time, and so have I—"

"Screwing some bitch in Boise?"

Jeff slapped the boy's face. But the boy didn't flinch and his

hand had encountered something hard, like solid ice, his hand
was burning up from the coldness of the face—

"You didn't even recognize me," the boy said resentfully.
"My own fucking father. You flunk, Daddy."

He bared his fangs.

memory: 1440

He is not alone in the darkness. All around him clamor the
voices of other children, all violated in the moment of their
violent deaths . . . they twitter like bats, like little mice. They
cannot move; they do not have the true unlife, as he has. Their
whispered keening is indistinguishable from the insect noises
of the night; but the boy vampire senses that it is the ghost of
an outrage so profound that it still clings to old bones, to
putrefying, shredded flesh. To human ears, even to the most
sensitive, the sounds might seem undisturbing. But to the boy
vampire who is now called Jeannot, whose ears cannot
perceive the subtexts of reality, the inner music, it is insensate
discord. He cannot bear it. As the nights pass (he can feel the
invisible moon wax to a crescent) he grows impatient. He must
rise. He must avenge not only himself but those myriad others,
these childcorpses that cannot even walk the night as he has
learnt to.

He funnels out of the earth. Dirt still clings to him. He is
still naked; they have not allowed him so much as a shroud.
He stands in the starlight before the walls of Tiffauges.

They are tall, these walls. He cannot scale them in his present shape, so he shifts, he leaps up batlike on the night wind.
He soars over the arched gateway and the outer courtyards,
and the stables, rank with the sluggish blood of sleeping
horses. He circles a parapet, dark save for a square of yellow
light from a narrow window. The light wavers, is ghosted with
shadows; it is firelight. The bat-thing swoops on the window
with the moon on his back; as he hits the ledge he shifts into a
small black cat and peers inside.

First he sees only fire; at the far end of the room is a
fireplace, whose mantel is untidily stacked with some of Gilles
de Rais's grisly souvenirs: a bell jar full of hearts, a child-sized
skull. The stone floor is covered with the skins of wild
animals: boar, bear, deer, and fox. There is a bed, too, near

the fire. Presently he sees that it is occupied by Bluebeard and by Poitou, who are whispering to each other. The whispers echo along the moist stone walls.

"Did you see that one . . . what was his name, Poitou?"

"Jeannot."

"Did you see his eyes? Daunting, unfathomable, eh? Like a doe in a trap. But, so beautiful. I wish I had him to play with all over again."

"But His Grace jests. Let me kiss his lips. Let me soothe his sorrow. Let me bugger His Grace's lubricious anus."

"Come, you know I don't like such sordid activities."

"Do you know what I heard in the village today?"

"I cannot wait."

"That you are a vampire, My Lord, and that your victims have the ability to become revenants, and to prey on the living. . . ."

"Ha, ha, ha! My appetite is aroused, Poitou. Let's visit the dungeons at once."

"No, My Lord. They are almost barren. One must shore up one's resources against a possible dearth, you know. Perhaps the villages and towns of your demesne will cease to allow their children to wander alone. . . ."

"But I am their lord!" Gilles de Rais is genuinely amazed at the idea that he might be forbidden his games.

"Come. You killed four last week, including that ravishing Jeannot. Enough, enough. You must atone."

"Atone?"

"Yes, you wicked man! Out of bed at once! On all fours!"

They leap nude from the bed. Bluebeard is on his hands and knees. Poitou rides him, belaboring the buttocks with a short quirt. "Atone, you evil, evil man!" Poitou shouts as he forces Gilles de Rais to gallop about the room. The furs muffle the thudding of Bluebeard's limbs. The madman cries out in pain and rapture, he whinnies, he barks. The black cat in the window is astonished at this display. It takes him a few moments to register his emotion as revulsion, for he has seen many horrors before, yet they have never touched him. As the feeling rises to the surface of his consciousness, he shifts shape, and now he is a naked, dirty little boy sitting in the window, his legs swinging against the stone, silently watching.

Bluebeard sees him and stops. "Oh, God," he says. "At

last, it's happened. One of them has come back. Are you real? Do I suddenly discover that I have a conscience that has decided of its own accord to torment me?"

Poitou gets off the Baron's back and tries to regain his composure.

"You must invite me down," Jeannot says, already knowing that he is welcome. Soon, he thinks, I will take my revenge. I'll send this creature of darkness down to where he belongs! And the clamoring in the earth beyond the castle walls will grow silent.

He lets himself drift down; he stands now on the skins of the wild beasts. Bluebeard is calmer now. They look at each other. Jeannot sees a man who might yet be called handsome, but for his haunted, hunted look, his hollow cheeks, his musculature beginning to run to fat from too much debauchery, and that indigo-tinted beard. He knows what Bluebeard sees: a small boy streaked with mud, bloodlessly pale, his dark eyes charged with a primal innocence.

"Do you know what I am?" Jeannot says.

"I think you are from hell. You have assumed a beautiful shape, but you are not what you seem."

"You are wrong. I am not like you humans. I do not deceive, although I can twist your self-deceptions to my own use. I am a vampire."

He sees a greedy glint in Bluebeard's eyes. "I've always dreamed of you," he says. "Of the beautiful creature I can kill again and again, who will come back to me. Oh, child, I love you. You fulfill my most cherished desires. Oh, I'm in love, Poitou, Poitou, I am faint with love—have pity, child of my heart, have pity!"

The boy recoils at this grotesque mimickry of the chivalric vocabulary.

"Oh, Poitou, Poitou," Gilles de Rais continues relentlessly, as Poitou comes to succor him and to hold him upright, "I have gone mad with love, I must have him again, now, now—"

"You cannot," Jeannot says. "I am no longer in your power." For there are no crucifixes in the bedroom, and the only silver object is a chalice on the mantel, far out of range, though he has no intention of alerting Bluebeard to its existence.

"But we are kin. We are both utterly evil, are we not? We belong to Satan. And to each other. Can you not make me what you are?"

"That was my intention," says the boy vampire, "but now—"

Suddenly things do not seem nearly so clear. What kind of vengeance would it be, to give the man what he pleads for?

"Isn't that why you came, why you are so felicitously named after the heroine I worship, the saintly one whom they burned at the stake? It's a perfect junction of events! Tonight you shall drink my blood. We will become one blood, you and I, and wreak evil together. We will make love in lakes of fresh-spilled blood. Oh, this is perfect, perfect, my love, my love."

But suddenly Jeannot no longer feels the desire to attack this man. He fears this man, despises him . . . knows he will be twice the terror he is now if he is admitted to the undead. He thinks: I thought *I* was supposed to be evil. How is it that I demur from perpetrating evil so hideous as this? The paradox is profoundly disturbing, for it is the first time, in almost fourteen hundred years, that he has doubted the purpose of his existence.

"You hesitate, my angel of death? You think I am not evil enough for you? Come with me now! No, I insist! Poitou, my cloak!"

He robes himself. He yells for assistance; outside, weapons clang, footsteps clatter. "I'll show you my little chamber of horrors. I realize it is a big step, my beloved demon, to admit me into your ranks, and I will prove to you my utter depravity —I will demonstrate the epic and monumental nature of my personal evil!" He flings open the door of the bedchamber, and guards with torches are already rushing to him.

Now he half swaggers, half capers, down flights of stone steps. Finally they reach the dungeons of Tiffauges, and Gilles de Rais proudly explains the magnitude of his crimes.

Jeannot and the others step down. The floor is slippery. It is dark and the room seems silent at first; but then he hears a faint whimpering from every side.

Children, chained, half-dead, hang from the walls like trophies. Many are so contorted that they seem more like dolls than humans. The moaning wells up now, the cries of "Let me go, I'll be good now, let me go." Their eyes are crusted with dried mucus. Some have been mutilated. Some are suspended from the ceiling by their feet. One has been crucified, and blood is clotted on his palms. A few have no tongues, and their plaint is a piteous gurgling.

"See, see, my pretty demon . . . am I not evil, evil, evil?" Bluebeard cries. "They burn you at the stake for being good, you know. Did you know that Jeanne d'Arc actually conversed with Saint Catherine? Have you ever seen a woman in flames? The flesh bubbles up and pops apart, like an enormous pimple, you know. I shall not burn. You will set me free, my boy vampire. I will be one with the night."

They pass more cells, each more repellant than the last. Jeannot thinks: How can men do this? They do not need blood to sustain them. They do it because they enjoy it! Again his thoughts are disturbing. What is this evil of which Bluebeard rants so glowingly? Am *I* evil? Am *I* as he is? I have killed as many people. Children? I have killed children. Often they have died as painfully as these. . . .

The final room. A pile of children's heads heaped up in a pyramid on the straw-covered floor. At the apex they are fresh, still beautiful. Deeper down they are rotting. Flesh drying on the skulls. The tongues protrude. The eyes exceed their sockets. Brains drip from their nostrils. Blood trickles down matted hair and cheeks overgrown with mold.

Bluebeard screams: "Evil! Evil! Evil!"

A continuous cacophony of wailing and shrieking from the other dungeon cells. Why can he not shut it out? Why can he not simply close his mind to them, as any human is capable of doing? "Evil! Evil! Is this not proof enough that we are alike, you and I that ours will be a magnificent union that will bring hell on earth to pass? Evil!"

Jeannot stands, speechless with outrage. He cannot answer. Bluebeard takes his silence for a taunt. "Not evil enough?" he raves. "I'll show you how much we are akin! I'll fuck these rotting remnants of childhood." He tears off his cloak and throws himself on the mountain of heads, thrusting at them randomly, the riven brain of one, the mouth of another . . . he froths at the mouth and cries "Evil, evil, evil," again and again in time with the harsh rhythm. "Ha! You don't even dare look! I *am* evil enough for you—" His semen spurts wildly over blood, brains, mucus, vomit.

The boy vampire cannot shut out the vision of this madman who claims to be like him. For the first time in his long life he feels helpless. He cries out with his mind for the forest to swallow him up and heal him, but he knows there will be no rescue. There is a truth here that he must learn. Can it be that they are two sides of the same evil?

Has the boy vampire at last seen the mirror image of himself? It cannot be! He turns his back on Bluebeard.

"What have I done wrong?" Bluebeard screams after him. "Do you envy me? Is that what it is? Am I too black for hell itself? Please, don't torture me. Don't reproach me. I have longed for you all my life." He throws himself down and clasps the boy's feet with his bloodstained hands. Feverishly he kisses the vampire's feet, heedless that they blister his lips. "Oh, take me now," he says, "into your death-embrace, breathe into me the kiss that sucks my soul away, I beg you—"

When the boy vampire finds his voice, it is to scream "No!" at this absurd monster, to panic, to flee toward the darkness along the walls' edges . . . until, night-winged, he soars toward the crescent moon.

Something is wrong. Always, before, there has been the forest. But now the forest will not receive him. Has he become so tainted by his contact with what humans call evil that the mother darkness knows him no longer?

Unless he has never left the forest.

Could it be that the forest, the salver of wounds, the place of warmth and rest, contains at its heart a more terrible darkness than the world outside?

He feels, behind the horror he has just experienced, despair. A human emotion, dimly recalled. Like a little child whose village has been sacked and who wanders among the wretched ruins . . . it is, he realizes suddenly, a true memory from before his changing. He has not thought about it for more than a thousand years. But he knows now that no matter how many millennia go by that child will still exist, and will still be crying, somewhere, somewhere.

dissolve: labyrinth

Terry didn't want his dad to know he was waiting up for him, so he hid in the big closet that linked the twins' bedroom with Mom and Dad's. Nestled between a pile of shoeboxes and an imitation fur overcoat, he could see quite well through the slits in the closet door.

He waited, hardly daring to breathe. He needed his dad. He needed someone to tell him it was okay, that it wasn't all his fault . . . Mom had told him that, but it had not sounded convincing somehow, because her mind seemed to be on something else.

Now there was a noise from downstairs. A gust of chill air. Terry shivered in his T-shirt and shorts. He should have gotten out a sweater or a blanket. Too late now. Voices.

"Let me in, honey, let me in."

"Here." The door slams. "Don't rush to kiss me hello now."

"Let's make love."

"So you can forget whoever you left behind in Boise? Our son is dead, Jeff."

"Please, let's go upstairs. I can't talk. I need you, I need you, darling."

"Let me turn the light on or you won't see your way up. Are you drunk or something? Is that wine on your jacket?"

"Don't turn on the light. I can see fine."

"But it's pitch black!"

"Shush, my love. You'll spoil the surprise."

Footsteps now, strangely uneven. His father must be drunk after all. He never walked like that. The bedroom door opened. In the dim glow of the bedside light, Terry saw his father for the first time in almost a month.

He came into the middle of the room, and then he stood stock still, unearthly quiet. Jesus, he didn't even look like he was breathing. There was red stuff oozing down his neck from two little holes, like . . . like. . . .

"I'm coming, Jeff," his mother's voice called out from downstairs. Jeff Gish sat down on the bed and loosened his jacket. What was wrong with him? He would lurch into a position and then he would freeze like a statue. It wasn't natural. He must be really upset about Dave, Terry decided. Abruptly his dad got up and flung the windows wide. Dry leaves rained onto the bed, brown patches on the silk white sheets, and the wind came, spine-tinglingly cold, but Jeff didn't even react to it. Jesus God, Terry thought, as he scrunched up close to the closet door, he really isn't breathing. Or I'm just spooked because of David. But Jesus, look at his eyes. Like bits of crystal, no fire in them or nothing. What's he staring at? Please, don't let him see me hidden here, I know he's going to do something awful. . . .

As his mom entered, Jeff got up and walked to the door.

"It's so cold, Jeff."

"I need the cold. I need the night."

"Jeff, the funeral's at eight in the morning. We've got to think of—"

"Come here." He seized her hands roughly.

"God, Jeff, you're freezing! What's the matter with you? We can't have sex now, not while you're so drunk, and—"

"Got a surprise for you," Jeff said, slurring his words as if he was just learning to talk or something.

"Come on, let's sleep."

"Kiss me. Got a surprise for you, hon. I'm a vampire. Ain't that the weirdest thing? A vampire, hee, hee, a vampire."

Terry started shaking like he had epilepsy. It felt like a nightmare, but it felt so true, too. He trembled so hard he knocked a shoebox off the pile.

"What was that?" said Mom. "Terry, go to bed."

"I'll deal with him later. Right now, I'm going to drink you dry, woman . . . you remember that day at the Spook House, when we were just kids, and you sucked me dry, you bitch, you were so hot to get hitched, you sucked my youth away from me . . . now it's my turn."

"Don't talk that way. Terry's awake."

"Fuck him!" He clasped her waist, pulled her close, kissed her hard, Terry saw that it was hurting her, he sat crunched up in his corner and didn't know what to do, and then Dad bit her neck and he saw the dark red spurting over her nightdress and his jacket, and he was lapping it up while the icy wind churned up her hair and her flimsy gown and spattered the blood on the leafstrewn bedsheets, and Terry was so scared he couldn't even force out a scream, and then he dropped her on the rug like an old puppet and she was limp and drained and dead and bleeding from her neck her eyes her nostrils her mouth and Jeff stared about now, his head swiveling like a robot's, and he started to shamble toward the closet and Terry knew his dad could smell him, could feel the boiling racing blood of his child, and he jerked himself out of the corner and Dad was banging at the closet door now and Terry felt the coats and the jackets all around him pressing against him and stifling his breath and he battered his fists wildly at them and then he stepped out to the other side into his own bedroom and there was the big blowup of him and David in summer camp hanging on the wall and Dad was breaking the door and now he was coming after him with fur and feathers and taffeta and wool clinging to him, sticking to the bloodstains and Terry found the bedroom door and he was running down the stairs and he was shitting himself and it was running out of his shorts down his leg but he had to get out and he made it out of the front door with his dad a few feet behind him and he took off down the street toward the Gallaghers' house, the dirt road clammy with mud and moist leaves, he was drenched with sweat and the T-shirt was plastered to his chest and his hair was in his eyes but he ran blindly while his father strode behind, his clockwork footfalls pounding the pavement, there was PJ's house now maybe fifty yards away and through the hole in the bush thorns tearing his arms and around to the back, and now he was banging at the kitchen door and screaming PJ's name and banging and screaming and the door jerked open and he fell on the linoleum floor bawling his guts out, and his dad was still there in the shadows by the doorway behind the garbage cans and PJ had a hold of him and he was puking now, puking right on his best friend's robe, and he didn't care anymore.

"Terry, Terry—"

"Don't let him in, he can't come in if he's not invited," Terry gasped.

"It's OK Terry, OK, you're safe, I won't let him in . . . Jesus fucking Christ, it's Mr. Gish! Sir—"

"Don't invite him in!"

Through his tears he saw a watery vision of his dad, and the blood everywhere, dripping from his mouth, the holes in his neck, matting his hair, clogging against the zipper teeth of his corduroy jacket, coagulating in pools on the welcome mat. . . . mat. . . .

"Please, PJ. Please, Terry," Dad said now. His voice was so seductive, so persuasive, it sounded like Dad in the old days when they'd been a happy family. "Let me in, I won't come after you anymore, I'm OK now. . . ."

"Got a crucifix?" Terry whispered to his friend.

"With a name like Gallagher? What do you think?" PJ said

with a strange bitterness, and Terry sensed, far in the back of
his mind, how uncomfortable it must be to be an Irish
Shoshone. "Look, stay here a moment. I'm going to get my
mom and dad. It's OK. Just hold the fort, don't let him in, for
Chrissakes."

PJ was only gone for a moment. He returned with the big
metal crucifix they had hanging over their living room
fireplace, which Terry always used to make fun of. Mr. and
Mrs. Gallagher were coming through the bead curtain that led
to the rec room. PJ went up to the back door and held it up.
Terry saw the emaciated Jesus, saw that the artist had stylized
his suffering with three deep furrows on the brow, and the
crown of thorns looked just like barbed wire.

"No . . . please . . . let me in, please, I'll be good," said the
thing that had once been Jeff Gish.

Terry couldn't see much of what was going on now. Everything was blurry. He knew that Shannah Gallagher was kneel-
ing beside him, and that she was wiping his leg with a warm
sponge. He could hear old Kyle Gallagher from somewhere
above his head muttering to himself, "If I hadn't seen it with
my own eyes. . . ."

And PJ, standing in the doorway, brandishing the bronze
crucifix; and finally an animal wail of terror outside, almost
one with the wind's incessant howling.

PJ was saying: "If this is true, we gotta get crosses. And
garlic. And silver maybe."

"I've got a silver necklace," Shannah said in her voice that
barely went above a whisper.

"I'll take Terry to my room, Mom."

Terry felt hot towels swabbing at his face, and then he felt
PJ's arms on his shoulders, lifting him easily. Suddenly he
remembered something, and he gasped: "Alice, what about
Alice?"

"Oh, my God," said Kyle Gallagher.

"Take the car, darling," said PJ's mom. "Take one of the
crucifixes from the bedroom. I think we've got garlic in the
refrigerator."

"God, oh my God," Kyle said. Terry heard him stomping
about the house gathering things together.

"If this is true," Shannah said (and Terry felt how intense it
was, the way this woman whispered, he felt her strength),

"we'll have to get supplies. We'll have to be ready for a siege, Kyle."

"The daytimes'll be OK," PJ said.

The voices were beginning to sound muffled. Terry was tired, so tired. He was being carried upstairs. He heard Mr. Gallagher leave and the car start up. It was so unreal. PJ was laying him down in his own bed, more like a bunk, really. He opened his eyes and quickly took in the room where he and PJ had so often spent the night . . . a cowhide shield, painted in bright colors . . . the glass terrarium where Ernie the rattlesnake lay coiled, he'd been defanged but they would use him to pretend to be going through that manhood ceremony, where you get bitten and you see a vision . . . this room where he had fled so many times to escape having to be a twin brother and he could fantasize about being in a real family and PJ was really his brother and now it was for real, kind of. But the twin brother was dead. Undead.

"Hey, scoot up. You want me to sleep on the floor?" PJ said. Terry turned on his side and faced the wooden wall, where a crayon picture of some Indian ceremony that PJ had drawn when he was six years old was thumbtacked up, and one corner was torn . . . and the blue paint on the walls was peeling. PJ got in beside him. "Don't snore," PJ said.

"I can't sleep until your dad brings Alice back."

"Sleep, asshole."

"I—"

"Don't shake so much. It's going to be all right. And you owe me a dollar, you creep."

dissolve

Phil Preis was just shutting down his store when the old men came by and gesticulated at the window. They seemed well off, so he hobbled over to the door and let them in. They didn't say anything at first, just shuffled around, snooping, fingering the engines on the open shelves. All the trains had been turned off; in the yellow light from outside you could see dustmotes everywhere, like tiny insects; the presence of four strangers, three of them old and richly if conservatively dressed, seemed to exacerbate the dinginess of the surroundings.

"May I help you?" Phil said, a trifle overawed.

Their leader was a bald, somewhat corpulent Asian. When he talked he had one of those stiff-upper-lip accents you hear in old movies. He said, "I say, isn't that a poster of Timmy Valentine on your window?"

"My best customer," Phil said. "But what can I show you? It's really past closing time."

"We've been to twenty hobby shops in New York alone," said another, very haggard, very pinched, very hawklike. "All because of that blasted newspaper article you clipped, Brian, which happened to mention that he has one of the largest model train collections in the world. I don't see the bloody use of it."

The youngest of the four, perhaps only in his mid-thirties, said, "Where is he?"

"Who are you fellows?" Phil said suspiciously. "Do you have a warrant?"

"If you don't talk," the fourth man said, and he looked vaguely familiar, maybe from a classical record jacket, maybe from TV, Phil couldn't remember, "I'm going to burn down your store." He pulled out a gold Dunhill lighter and flicked it in Phil's face.

"All up in smoke," said the fat Asian. "Every pine tree in your miniature forest. Every box of track. Every engine."

"I've got no idea where he is! I just know—"

"What do you know?" the second one rasped, pulling out a revolver from his London Fog overcoat.

"A—a town called Junction. Somewhere. He talked about it once."

The man with the gun shot him three times. He was not a very good shot, and Phil did not die instantly. He fell back against the counter; blood began to collect in the crannies of an antique boxcar. He could hardly feel the pain, it seemed so distant; and all he could see was a thin red gauze drifting dreamily over everything.

The voices still rang clear through. He heard them as he slowly fell into darkness.

"Why did you have to shoot him, Francis?" the younger man's voice.

"I don't know. I think I'm going mad."

"What will we do?"

"Oh, don't be so panicky, young man," said the fat one.

"By the time they find him we'll be gone. And besides, I am a prince, and we are not subject, as you know, to the ordinary rules of human conduct. I think in this case I had better extend my parasol of protection over old Francis here, eh, what?"

"Where shall we go?" The man who spoke most rarely, the one whose face Phil almost recognized.

"To a town named Junction," the one who called himself a prince said. "Surely there cannot be that many. We will return to the Plaza and consult an atlas. You, Brian, will be in charge of renting a suitable vehicle. We leave tonight."

Phil Preis, whose death at the hands of Kitty Burns Timmy had once prevented out of friendship, fell lifeless to the floor of his dark shop.

His death, undiscovered for some days, was attributed to a robbery attempt. A halfhearted effort was made to solve the murder but it soon petered out.

Meanwhile, the Gods of Chaos, with Brian Zottoli as their new chauffeur and acolyte, were well on their way to Junction, Kansas, the first of many Junctions on the circuitous route that Prince Prathna had drawn up.

labyrinth: arcade

Terry rubbed his eyes. The room was much too bright. Light streamed in through the window, where PJ's *Return of the Jedi* drapes had been pulled back. "What about school?" he murmured.

"It's Saturday," PJ said. He was up and pulling on his jeans and a gray sweater. "Anyways, it's past three."

Terry said, "What happened last night?"

PJ didn't answer. Terry remembered it all at once. His throat went dry and he couldn't talk. PJ said, "Dad couldn't find Alice, Terry."

"Jesus. I'm alone." It was unthinkable.

"You got us." He was very matter-of-fact about it.

"Is David—"

"One of those things? Shit, Terry, I don't know, and there's only one way to find out."

"We have to go back to the Spook House."

Terry digested that for a moment. Then he heard Shannah Gallagher's voice calling them down to eat, so he jumped out of bed. He had no clothes except the soiled shorts and T-shirt, which he could see out the window on a clothesline. "Got anything to wear?"

"You can wear Ernie," PJ said, taking his pet rattlesnake out of his terrarium and draping him decorously around his crotch.

"What if he wasn't defanged?" It always made Terry uneasy the way the boy handled his snake.

"Then I'd"—his voice went up an octave—"be talking like this, wouldn't I?" They both laughed, then stifled themselves, embarrassed, because of the terrible thing that had happened last night.

Downstairs, Shannah Gallagher was frying hamburgers in the kitchen. She turned as they trooped through the bead curtain. "After you eat," she said, "I want you to take your bikes down to the store and pick up as much garlic as you can. Your dad's driven over to Highwater, PJ, to pick up crosses."

"I'll have to dig up my silver dollar collection from the back yard," PJ said sheepishly, revealing its existence to his friend for the first time. And I thought we had no secrets from each other, Terry wondered, as he hugged PJ's sizes-too-big sweatshirt to his chest and stuck his arms inside.

It's for real, he thought, never really believing until this casual discussion of anti-vampire tactics that it could be anything other than a terrible dream.

Later they biked up and down Main Street. The sun was painfully bright, but the wind was fierce. "I'm freezing my balls off!" PJ yelled, doing a spectacular wheelie over the train tracks. They studiously avoided David's name.

They went into the market. It wasn't locked. But there was no one in the store at all. They walked up and down the three narrow aisles, munching on stolen Twinkies.

"Hey, don't swipe so many, they'll notice!" Terry whispered. "Maybe Mrs. Brent's just in the back somewhere."

"Nuh-uh. You'd hear that clickety knitting. Or her cackling on the phone. She's out to lunch or something."

"It ain't lunchtime."

"Oh. Yeah."

Terry was a little disturbed, he didn't quite know why. "Did you pick up the garlic yet? Might as well get a bag from the back room and fill it up. We can always leave her a note."

"OK. I'll take a leak while you get it together," PJ said, scrupulously crunching up his candy wrapper and tossing it into a trash can by the cash register. "I wonder if she's got any money."

"Oh, fuck off," Terry said. He never could be sure if PJ was joking when he talked about ripping stuff off. (Big stuff, like money, that is; everybody snuck out of Mrs. Brent's store with candy bars, because the woman was half blind.)

"All right then." PJ disappeared into the john, which was just beyond the freezer with the ice cream and the frozen puddings. Terry entered the back room, where Mrs. Brent kept a supply of paper bags.

He was alone there now. The heat was on full blast, but he felt cold, creepy almost. There was a narrow aisle with metal shelving on either side, piled with boxes and crates and tin cans. Dust everywhere. At the far end, a shuttered window. Where was the fucking light switch? His clammy hand felt along the wall behind him, but he couldn't figure out where it was. He didn't want to call out, because he didn't want PJ to think he was chicken.

He stood groping along the shelves for where the bags were kept. They'd been moved somewhere. It was so dark! Suddenly he remembered the closet. That was last night, wasn't it? The closet with all the coats closing in on him and his dead father battering down the door . . . no! He wasn't going to be chicken about it. He wasn't even going to try to imagine living alone . . . alone. There, he'd thought it, in spite of their efforts, all day, to avoid the subject. . . .

He inched forward.

His hands brushed cans of beans, flicked the cobwebs off a crate of vinegar bottles. When he was littler he'd been scared of this room, Mrs. Brent had said if he was naughty she'd lock him up there and Mom had smiled indulgently, but she hadn't smiled in years and anyway she was . . . she was dead. A narrow sheet of light from the top of the closed window; dust-motes dancing. Forward. Dad's eyes were all red and shiny, like a photograph of the Star of Burma in the Smithsonian he had seen once in a slide show at school, maybe like Christmas tree lights, it had been Christmas the first time Dad went away for more than a few days. Clammy hands skimming the beer cans, skidding on the plastic thingies they hold six-packs together with. God, I hope I find a bag soon, I'm getting pretty fucking scared.

Oh, there was one. It had something in it, but he could

dump it outside. He picked it up and—

"Jesus Christ, Jesus fucking Christ—" PJ's voice, muffled by the bathroom door.

Terry ran.

Sprinted past the vegetables, still clutching the brown paper bag, knocking over some juice bottles and he could hear them gurgling to the floor as he pulled open the bathroom door and he saw—

PJ backed against the far wall, stammering, "I only saw it when I flushed the toilet and then I turned and saw it on the door," and then Terry saw it too, hanging on the coathook of the bathroom door, an old woman's head with her hair neatly bunned and the coathook poking though the bun, no blood at all on the neckstump, just a protruding vertebra, the eyes like wrinkled prunes, a tiny smear of blood on one cheek, coagulating . . . and on the linoleum tiles beneath, splotches of red-brown, like autumn leaves, and Mrs. Brent's mouth forced into a leering rictus of a smile—

The bag slipped from Terry's hands, and its contents sloshed onto the floor, dark blood like melted fudge topping, fingers, bone pieces, a left foot with a corn on the sole and garish turquoise nail polish, and a childsized bowtie—"

"He always hated dressing up," Terry said slowly, understanding it all now.

"Who, god damn it, who?" He'd never seen PJ so scared. It was good to have someone to be scared with, like shivering under one blanket at summer camp with a ghost story by the fire but this wasn't just a story anymore, that was what was so confusing about it.

Terry said, "PJ, David did this."

PJ nodded, knowing it already.

"We have to get the garlic now."

He put out a hand to still his friend's trembling. He thought: So many times you've been strong for me, you've stuck by me while I bitched about my parents and my twin brother . . . I guess it's my turn now. "We'll have to get the garlic," he said again.

"Not in that fucking bag, Jesus Christ, not in that bag."

"All right. I'll go back into the storeroom."

"I'll wait . . . no, I'll come."

"We'll have to check every bag till we find an unused one . . . are you all right?"

"I feel like puking."

"I puked on you last night, but this is your sweater I'm wearing," Terry said. "Come on then. Be dark soon. And I want to go to the Spook House tonight. I want to see him."

"Are you out of your mind?"

"He's my brother. I guess that's important." He had never known that before. Somehow he didn't feel the same about his parents or his sister. Even though he and David had done nothing but fight since they popped out of Mom. "You don't have to come, I guess."

"I guess," said PJ. But Terry knew that he would, anyway. That was the way PJ was.

22

analyst's notebook

I said: "Was that the trauma, then? That confrontation with the ultimate human evil?"

He said: "Bluebeard was not altogether evil."

"How can you say that? You've seen so much of what we humans do to each other."

"You are a psychologist, Carla. Surely you do not believe in evil. That is too . . . *superstitious* a concept. You deal in shades of gray, you psychologists. Traumas, complexes, whatever. Be truthful . . . do you think it was pure evil that I faced that night in the dungeons of Tiffauges?"

"Today such a man would be in a hospital. He might even be cured," I said.

Timmy said, "There was a dungeon more horrible than that one, Carla. It was the one to which Bluebeard had condemned himself. The innermost prison where he never ceased to torment himself."

I said: "Why could you not find the forest that night?"

"Because I had turned away from a necessary confrontation. I was on the verge of perceiving a terrible truth, not only about the nature of man, but about my own nature, and the link between us."

"But you did find the healing forest at last. Or else it was all one forest. I don't understand. You told me that you lost the power of speech for a time—" We were approaching the

289

trauma. I had thought that just being violated by Gilles de Rais would have been terrible enough, but now I reminded myself I was not dealing with the neuroses of the short-lived. The dilemma that had forced Timmy Valentine into centuries of fugue could hardly be something I'd find in the medical histories. I was beginning to think I would never understand it.

"As I prowled the woods of Brittany, speech came less and less easily to me. I did not seek out a surrogate mother, but preyed on unwary peasants who had strayed from their villages. I was neither in the forest nor out of it. I was lost, Carla, lost."

memory: redemption by love: 1440

A half moon shines over Tiffauges. Hawklike he circles the castle. But he cannot hear the signs of Bluebeard's perverse pleasures, nor even the murmurous heartbeat of the madman. He listens for other sounds, snatches of conversation. Perhaps the Baron has gone hunting by night, as the boy vampire himself has just done?

No. He overhears that Bluebeard has been arrested for heresy and is being held captive in a place called La Tour Neuve. They whisper of it in the castle kitchens.

In the dungeons, children have been unchained; they are turning them out into the night. A line of fugitives trails from the main gate, which is being lowered behind them. They are frightened, no less frightened than when they were being tortured.

Why? He understands: for them death was at least a kind of security, and now death has rejected them. He swoops down to glimpse their troubled faces: starved, pinched, with deep-sunken eyes. Old shackles slither in the grass like rusty serpents. One of them looks up: he has seen a raven fly overhead. He has looked unknowing into the face of a fellow survivor of the Baron's entertainment.

La Tour Neuve? Where is it? Batlike, he casts the net of his perceptions over the nightland.

Far, far away, a voice . . . as one might feel a gust of chill wind on the sweat-moistened hairs of one's arm, a fleeting prickle, he soars now, arrowing the half-light. Below are villages, thatch-thickets creased with the moon's quicksilver.

The voice, nearer. The landscape blurs; perhaps there is another castle rearing from the mist, perhaps a dark tower . . .
faintly comes the clank of armor, the buzz of a theological
dispute, the ragged snoring of a drunkard, the clink of
weighted dice on stone. He closes in on the topmost turret,
from which issues the telltale ticking of Bluebeard's heart.

Wings at the window. Bluebeard looks up, calls softly: "So
you have come. I knew you would, dark angel of my ending,
little-boy ferryman who cannot die, my eternal love." He is
half delirious.

The boy vampire swirls swiftly into human shape, slipping
phantomlike through the iron bars and only becoming solid as
his feet touch the straw, filthy with blood and dried excre-
ment. Bluebeard strains against his manacles.

The boy says—the words come out with difficulty—"Forget
me. It's over. Your twisted dream is dead. No other verdict
was possible."

Giles de Rais says, "Forget? You have not forgotten me."
It is true. The boy tries to protest, but the dumbness has come
over him again. "I will be burned at the stake tomorrow,"
Bluebeard goes on. "First I'll be subjected to the question,
both ordinary and extraordinary . . . do you know what that
means? They put your legs in a sort of box, and they beat in
wedges until your limbs are a pulpy mass."

Still Jeannot cannot speak. But he sees, as in a dream, another man, another prison, girt with fences on which are
strung metal wires like an unraveled crown of thorns. It must
be a fantasy, for no such fences exist; nor do the castles whose
turrets belch forth a smoke of charring corpses. Occasionally
these transient visions visit him. Perhaps they are from the
future.

Bluebeard says: "They offered me a choice today. If I will
recant, I will be given the mercy of strangulation, and spared
the torture. Laughable! They would take away even the meaning of my death. But you have come here as an answer to my
dilemma, oh lovely child, to give me redemption. You can give
me the kiss of death and rebirth. Then I will be like you, completely like you . . . oh, you turned away from my excesses that
night, but you have returned . . . you understand me now,
don't you?"

Jeannot shakes his head.

"I have a theory of the world," Bluebeard says calmly, as if his impending execution were of no consequence. "Listen, angel of death. Greatness is leaving the world. Where is Jeanne d'Arc? Perished in the flames. She was the last of the great and the good. A new breed is taking over . . . you might call them the middle class. Nothing but money to their name. Not greatness, not quality, not honor. After the great individuals will come massive nations whose collective voice will drown out such as Jeanne and me. Yes, me! I am the last of these great men. After me, evil will no longer exist as such: not private, personal, grand evil. It is inevitable that I should ring out the end of an age.

"Do you think, my angel of darkness, that in a future controlled by this bourgeoisie, that I, who simply command the deaths of innocents, would be allowed to exist? Of course not. In the future the man who emulates me will be a petty criminal, furtively luring his victims off the streets, bribing them with sweets, indulging his lusts in shame. He will have no castle; he'll live in a hovel identical to thousands of other hovels. He will not hurl the headless corpses of his victims from his bedroom window. He will inter them in secret, in cavities in the walls of privies. He will have shame, a most middle-class virtue. He will be a pathetic creature, society's victim and his own—in short, a madman!

"Whereas I am not mad. My unorthodox pleasures are not the result of insanity. They are a logical consequence of my pursuit of the shadow side of things.

"And now I must take the final step, you see. Become like you. Embrace the cold eternity. Don't you understand?"

The boy listens, inarticulate.

"Now," whispers Gilles de Rais.

"You are mad," the boy says at last. Rage, pity, confusion . . . so many human emotions. It would be so simple to sate his hunger on this man. To disregard the consequences. But he sees now that he stands at a crucial junction in his destiny. Suddenly, with a cold ludicity, he knows what he must say. "You've had a grand vision. But you do not possess the greatness to encompass this vast evil. You are a small man, Gilles, a pitiful man. I reject you. You will not be burned alive tomorrow. You will recant and accept strangulation. They will greet it as a miracle; only you and I will know that your redemption stems from cowardice. I understand now. You have walled yourself in with your own boasts. Your 'great evil' is just graffiti on the prison walls . . . vain words to hide the smallness of your heart. You've debauched the innocent and murdered the defenseless, Bluebeard, but you are not the type to be dragged still living into hell."

"I love you!" Bluebeard cries.

"You don't have the heart for it. The emptiness, I mean. You're a poor crazed nobody after all. But it is true that you have loved me. And all I can offer is this sham redemption." He can say no more. But Bluebeard is weeping.

"You've taken it all away!" he screams. "The horror and beauty of my vision!" Tears roll down the cheeks of the monster. He is racked with sobs.

The boy vampire looks at him for a long time. Why does the madman weep? Has Jeannot's rejection driven him into sanity? And if so, has the boy taken the madness upon himself, as Christ did the sins of the world?

Jeannot reaches out and touches Bluebeard lightly. Then he snatches his hand away. He has felt . . . pity? Can it be pity? If the madness of a human manifests itself in insensate cruelty, could it be that for a vampire, man's dark mirror-image, madness could be compassion? He tries again to speak, but his tongue feels like lead.

And now Bluebeard, delirious, seems to be reliving moments from the past. "Once," he is saying, half to himself, "there was not this darkness all about me. I remember Jeanne d'Arc leading the charge: the siege of Orleans it was. Oh, you should have been there! You would know how armor flashes when a fighter leaps, silver-minnow-like, from a river of men and blood! I dashed in after her. The sun in my eyes. Oh, the burning . . . at the stake the light was blinding . . . Saint Catherine and Saint Margaret spoke to her, did you know that? . . . but no. The voices were her own. She was mad. Mad! Or they wouldn't have deserted her. Oh, the blinding blaze . . . and I followed her into madness. Blinded! Blinded! Oh, she dazzled. There was no more light left in the world. I had to choose the path of shadow. And now the madness is gone . . . gone! Did you come to rob me of my last illusions, angel of darkness? And you . . . the darkness is coiling away from your face . . . you are gray now."

Though he cannot weep, the boy vampire called Jeannot understands for the first time the pity and terror of being man. He sees into the dark heart of the human universe, and he knows it for his own. A millenium ago he relinquished his human nature, when his soul and he parted company in the flames of a dying city, but—

We *are* kin! he realizes at last. And I *do* long to be like him! I envy him! He is a human who has longed to become a monster, and I . . . am a monster who yearns to be a man.

For this madman—even this man, who has raped children to death and cut them in pieces for souvenirs—even this man can weep! While the boy vampire, who possesses eternity for reflection, can no more weep than can the mountains or the forests or the winds or the long dark nights.

And now, at last, in this moment of self-realization, he feels the trees of the eternal forest sprout up around him, and he falls into the arms of mother darkness.

dissolve; night-child: fire

"There it is," Timmy Valentine said. "The dark heart of our narrative."

Carla couldn't meet his eyes. She said, "Am I supposed to heal you of compassion, then?"

"I don't suppose the Hippocratic oath leaves much provision for monsters such as myself," Timmy said bitterly. "But wait. There's one more mystery. The one about you and Stephen Miles."

"At least," she said, trying to dissipate the tension with a light remark, "your story solves one of the great mysteries of psychopathological history. Nobody's ever been able to agree on why Bluebeard *did* recant. It seems so out of character in the light of more modern cases. . . ." She turned away from him, to the view from her bedroom window; she watched the wind of morning shake the mountain pines and tried to count the flecks of dry leaves as they swarmed the sky in a hundred hues of red, maroon, sienna, umber, ocher, crimson, bronze, gold, vermilion, scarlet. "It's the mystery of fire, isn't it?" she whispered. "Even the sky seems on fire this morning."

"Fire that the ancient Persians worshipped," Timmy mused. "And soon they will come with their crosses and perhaps even more potent weapons."

"Like that idol?" said Carla. "Why was that so important?"

"It has to do with fire. You will understand at the end. But first they will come and we will meet them here, in this house."

"And the town?"

"External reality will reflect psychic truth."

"So you'll let the population of Junction turn into vampires then—"

"But soon will come winter. A great change will come. Just as the true beginning of day is the darkest moment of night, so the fire will be born out of the cold and the dead."

"And what now?"

"There is a final door, Carla. I know you want the key, but if you choose to accept it there will be no more turning back . . . do you understand?"

"I dreamed of the door once. But it was Stephen who withheld the key, Stephen in the guise of the operatic Bluebeard."

"No matter. You want me to open the last door?"

"I don't know!"

"Turn away from the window now. Look at me, Carla Rubens. Don't reject me."

Slowly she turned, and saw Timmy dressed in white jeans and a white tennis shirt, like an angel of death; and he reached his hands out to her and when they clasped hers, she knew that she desired him; and they kissed, chastely, once, and she was no longer afraid.

memory: fire: 1671

The wild boy comes running out of the forest . . . the hunters have come for him again. Yesterday they pulled him, dumb, naked, from a bed of nettles. Ugly sounds issued from their mouths. He growled as they pulled him into the sunlight; he shied from its brilliance, broke away . . . laughing they followed, caught him, caged him, exhibited him in a village square. He closed his eyes all day, wondering why it did not burn him alive. At night he was stronger; he gnawed at the crude wooden bars and returned to the forest. But they have tracked him down.

Again they bind him. They drag him in the wicker cage back to the village. There are the ruins of a castle . . . Tiffauges, they call it. The villagers cross themselves as they go past. Something centuries old stirs in the memory of the feral boy. Beyond the tumbled walls, overgrown with moss, are the houses of the village, the market square. All day long they gawk at him. He sits with his eyes closed, not moving at all. But as evening comes the people lose interest. There is a hub-bub in the marketplace. Slowly their speech is becoming in-telligible to him again, and he can tell that there is to be a witch-burning. Again a memory surfaces . . . a man in flames . . . a town square.

In the memory they congregate around the tall pyre, heedless of its heat. A monk holds up a cross. They are all jeering. He is in a town, but the town is a forest. Balconies sur-round the square like theater boxes, but they are also bulging from the trunks of gigantic trees. Elegant women watch and pant exquisitely as they fan themselves, but in the memory they also seem to be forest animals: skunks, squirrels, a lemur in a pointed hat. Who are they burning? The name Bluebeard comes vaguely to mind.

In the village they are dragging some old hags up to the stakes. Children are throwing a ball and darting in and out of the drab procession. Others watch, their eyes dull.

But in the memory the crowd is angry at having been cheated of their victim's death-throes. He has recanted. He hears hoots and catcalls as the throng presses forward. The air is suffused with incense and the smoke of burning flesh. He is choking. The forest presses in. It seems almost alive . . . in the memory the boy stares, inarticulate. The night drags on. As dawn draws near he is the only one watching the pyre. The stake has been consumed; only a mound of ashes, still freckled with orange sparks, remains.

Now, in the present, the old women have not been afforded the mercy of strangulation. They are screaming horribly. . . .

He remembers the other burning. A priest on his way to morning mass; a procession of choristers follows him. One holds aloft a crucifix. The boy vampire stares fixedly at its many-jeweled Christ, its face contorted, each bead of sweat a baroque pearl, each thorn in its crown an emerald, and the eyes of polished sapphire glaring heavenward, defiant . . . so much pain. He is so hypnotized by the expression of this Christ that he does not realize for a moment that he has not recoiled from the cross's power . . . that he has not felt terror.

The sun, in his memory, rises, as in actuality it now sets. The first rays touch his pallid skin. They do not seem to burn him. What has happened? For a thousand years he has fled the sun's radiance and sought out earth's reviving darkness. He thinks: I am of the darkness, I cannot abide the day, this truth is unchangeable!

Still he has not taken his eyes off the face of the suffering Jesus.

The executioner, masked in black leather, comes to shovel the ashes and scatter them to the four winds. He ignores the small boy watching from a corner of the town square, as the villagers now ignore the wild boy in his filthy cage. There is no wind this morning, and the ashes do not scatter, but drizzle back onto the mound. It is unearthly still. The choirboys begin to chant a Kyrie as the crucifer leads them down the street. As they turn a corner, the boy vampire loses sight of the face of Jesus. . . .

Why does this memory visit me now? he thinks, as he watches the old women sizzle.

Then he remembers one more thing: the man in those ashes loved me. A butcher, a madman. It was I who made him capable of feeling love. That is how he found his redemption. And what has this twisted love given me? It has taken away my fear of darkness.

I must walk the day as well as the night. There is no day and night but one bleak gray. Gradually I will learn to form words again. They will free me. I will venture out and find a woman and call her mother.

In the darkest of dark, at its very heart, there grows a seedling called compassion. That is the truth he has learned, the truth in the ashes of the madman.

23

dissolve: arcade: labyrinth

Night was falling. Terry stuffed another cross into his pocket, pulled on PJ's old parka, and shoved garlic bulbs into each of the pockets; then he left the house by the kitchen door. PJ was already there, getting the bikes ready.

"Where are you going? Be careful!" Shannah's voice came from behind a mound of dirty dishes. But Terry ignored her.

As long as they held on to their crosses and their garlic, they should be safe. Everybody knew that.

They took the dirt path, found the deserted road, cycled toward Main Street. Already they could see the solitary stop sign. A single street lamp threw the stop sign's shadow over the window of PJ's father's drugstore. "Stop!" PJ hissed. "Listen!"

Footsteps. They braked at the corner. Paused. More footsteps. And then the whoosh of a video rocketship. "The arcade?" said Terry. "But that's closed Sunday nights."

"And who's that guy?" PJ said, pointing at a gaunt figure in a dark suit, window-shopping the wig display of the general store.

The man looked up . . . could he have heard them from the other end of the block? "That's Mr. Kavaldjian, the undertaker," said Terry. "I recognize him now. He came over from Highwater to. . . ."

"He's one of them. Look, the face, that shine to it, un-natural."

"Jesus Christ. Ain't none of these *things* even going to get buried, now!"

Terry looked ahead. He saw the railroad tracks, and the old-fashioned ornate pavilion of the little train station, and beyond them the dirt road uphill, all pale in the purple-gray twilight.

He said, "I don't think we're going to get as far as the Spook House tonight."

PJ said, "I think they've come to us."

They laughed, trying to exorcise their unease. "Scared?" PJ said.

"Nah. Well, yes." But somehow he wasn't as scared as he knew he should be. It had all come out the other night. Now he was drained, there was nothing left inside to *get* scared. "Arcade?"

"Got a quarter?"

"I owe you a dollar," Terry said, "but I only have fifty cents."

"We can play Bloodsucker, doubles."

They wheeled their bicycles to the entrance of the little arcade and leaned them against the brick wall.

"It's so frigging cold," PJ said.

Terry watched a snowflake drift past his nose. "All ready?" he said.

"Maybe we won't have school."

"School." Terry had forgotten that there was such a thing. They went inside.

"Keep ahold of your cross," PJ said in his ear.

"I'm not stupid, you creep."

Glimmers in the gloom: a purple lightning flash, a grid of darting phosphorlines, a blue spiral dissolving into darkness . . . the machines were running. But where were the players? Terry couldn't see anyone at first. Then he saw something move behind the Ms. Pac-Man. Who was it? "Alice!" A girl giggled. He saw her now. Her face, powderwhite, reflected the pink of the Ms. Pac-Man maze. She had blood on her mouth.

"Keep away from me," PJ said, holding out his cross.

Alice whimpered, ducked behind the arcade machine. More sounds now, slurping sounds. Terry went closer, his cross outstretched. There was a body slumped behind the machine, and several figures were bent over it. It was Mr. Schwabauer, the man who ran the arcade. There was a lot of blood.

"Jesus. Mom. Dad."

They didn't look up from their feeding. The thing that had once been Alice giggled hysterically; then she bent down and daintily lapped at a wound in Mr. Schwabauer's groin, her tongue slithering in and out like a snake's. Terry saw the fangs. They glittered electric blue in the glow of a Tempest game next to the Ms. Pac-Man.

"Play you Bloodsucker?" a familiar voice.

Terry whipped round to see, perched on the Bloodsucker, his legs dangling over the demo display—

"David!"

"Big brother. Wanna play?"

"PJ, hold up that cross!"

"Oh, don't bother, you two fags. I know when I'm not wanted." He blipped out of existence. "Tee hee!" The voice came from behind a battered pinball machine. Terry spun around and saw him, his pale face rainbowstrobe-lit from the rank of video games across the aisle. "Thought you could be my big brother forever, didn't you? Well, Terry, you sure fucked up. I'm gonna be immortal, and you're gonna be dead."

"You ain't real," Terry said. "Just a thing in the night. A phantom."

David flickered on and off, like a slow silent movie. "I'll tell you something. We're a happy family now. Dad is always home. And he can tell us apart now. You always used to be the lucky one, now you're screwed, you're on the outside looking in."

Alice—fangs shiny—piped up: "And you know who's in here with us, who owns the castle on the hill? You'll never guess!"

"Try me."

"Timmy Valentine," she said, and she uttered his name with that half-choked prepubescent longing she always used to have when she was leafing through interminable weeny-bopper magazines. . . .

"That's retarded," he said, kidding her from force of habit. But did she mean it? Didn't they play that hit song in the intermission of Bloodsucker? *Va-a-ampire Junction*. "You're not my sister," he said, trying to convince himself. "It's a trick."

"You don't know anything, you—you *mortal!*" Alice's voice was miaowlike as she glanced up from her repast. "Timmy's up there on the mountain, and he says the name of this town is Vampire Junction now, and there's gonna be a battle."

Mom and Dad looked at him now. Mom said: "It's so nice here. No girl in Boise anymore."

"Just a happy family," Dad said. "I promise I won't scare you again, I won't even hurt you, just a little pinch in the neck like a fleabite, then it'll be over."

"Fuck you, Dad." But he wanted—he wanted—

"Play you Bloodsucker!" David said. "For keeps." His family stretched out their arms in a parody of pleading. Their faces were so pale, so luminous, you could see every high-resolution line of the Ms. Pac-Man maze superimposed like a pink window's veil over their features.

"No! You're not getting me!" Terry threw the cross at his mother—

A howl wrenched from her lips, no human could have howled like that, like a train whistle in your ear, and Terry ran now, fishing another cross from his pocket, while PJ pelted them with garlic—

From the change machine Alex Evans said, "You stole a quarter from my lunchbox, turkey," and leered, fangs glinting with the blast of a dying starship—

At the door old Cherry Cola, the village idiot, smiled; she used to have no teeth but now her grin betrayed two knife-sharp canines dangling from rotting gums—

PJ hit her with a cross, Terry saw the scar blistering on her forehead, a sizzling meat stink and a sound like a steampipe bursting, and behind came Alice's maniacal cackling and David was there now, jumping from machine to machine and karate-chopping them like Fonzie in *Happy Days* and making streams of quarters fly like casino jackpots and spaceships were zapping each other and a banana bounced through a pink maze and blood running down the video monitors and tinting the lightstreams red—

The door. The bikes. Faster now.

There, by the general store, Mr. Kavaldjian the undertaker

was breaking the door down, an alarm sounded but nobody came, Mr. Kavaldjian was dragging a corpse behind him, there were others on the street now, staring but not seeing, they were all corpses. He smelled their fetor on the wind, he saw the pinpoint coalglow of their eyes speckling the utter darkness of the street—

The house! The kitchen door!

Terry saw it then—

A small boy battering at the door and shouting "Let me in, Mrs. Gallagher, I'm so scared, they're after me again, oh, please, Mrs. Gallagher," and it was a redhaired boy with freckles but it wasn't Terry, he knew it was David and he knew what he was up to, and he started to scream "Don't let him in, don't let him, he ain't me, he's pretending, he's faking—"

The door opened.

Terry's heart stopped dead for a second. It's over, he thought. The final sanctuary. They've invaded. It's the end of the world.

Then the howling started again—

Shannah Gallagher had come out of the house in her nightgown. She was shivering, and only then did Terry realize how cold it had become. Maybe even snow tomorrow, he thought. Mrs. Gallagher was holding up the crucifix from the mantel. A silhouette with streaming hair in the patch of yellow light in the kitchen door, and the small boy screaming, thinning into the wind itself, and now, overhead, a bat or a raven, blackness slingshotting through blackness.

Slowly they walked toward the house.

PJ said, hugging his mother, "I thought we were gone, all gone."

Shannah Gallagher said, "You think I can't tell the difference between Terry and David? I'm a full Shoshone." As far as she was concerned, that ended the matter. "The radio says that the snow's coming early. The TV's out. I made hot chocolate."

"Mom," PJ said.

Terry saw how much love they shared, and he felt terribly alone, and he remembered his family clustered around Mr. Schwabauer's corpse, and he thought, that's the first time they've had a meal together since I can remember. . . .

And he was tempted.

dissolve: fire

As the plains rolled by, Stephen imagined them a sheet of yellow fire.

dissolve: seeker

As he drove, Brian Zottoli tried to think of nothing but his vengeance.

dissolve: labyrinth: dissolve

"It's getting sodding cold out there," said Prathna, and Francis wondered if he longed for the sultry greenery of his garden of delights. . . .

fire: dissolve: labyrinth

Stephen dreamt he was conducting *Bluebeard's Castle*. The deep bass voice of Bluebeard issued incongruously from the throat of a little boy with dark gazelle eyes and hair that streamed like blue-black fire. Carla was Judith.

The last door swung open, creakily, and revealed—

analyst's notebook

. . . a man standing in flames. . . .

dissolve

In the dark he heard PJ tussling with a nightmare. "What's the matter?"

Dark. Dark. Outside, the wind, fluting, rattling the shutters, swooping down from the mountain. Inside, the air close, still, overheated, sticky with evaporated sweat.

"I'm scared to go to the bathroom," PJ whispered.

It had come to this. "We're home now. Safe."

"Remember Mrs. Brent, on the coathook? I used to imagine doing stuff like that to her, you know, and scalping her and stuff."

"I'll take you to the bathroom."

"Don't think I'm chicken or something."

"Yeah." They got up. As Terry left the bedroom he heard a knock on the window. I didn't hear that, he thought resolutely.

In the bathroom he leaned against the radiator and watched PJ piss. "Remember when you and me and David always had those pissing contests?" PJ said. "By the ditch in Mr. Winter's potato field?"

"Yeah."

That knocking again . . . more urgent . . . but it could have been anything. Maybe a cup falling over in the sink downstairs.

"Maybe we should stay here a while," Terry said.

"Yeah, I hear it too."

"Maybe it's just—"

"No, it's from the bedroom."

"David?"

"Dunno."

Knock. Knock. Knock.

"Who's there?" Terry said. They giggled uncontrollably for a moment. Then he said, "Let's stay here."

"There's a window here too."

"The landing."

Knock Knock.

"The landing."

"PJ—when I saw my parents back in the arcade, I—"

Knock.

"The landing. Yeah."

They crept out onto the landing.

"By the linen cupboard." PJ took out some big towels and a blanket they kept there. They settled down in the corner farthest from PJ's bedroom door.

"What was your nightmare about?" Terry said as he dozed off.

"Dunno. A door. A guy on fire."

"Funny."

"What?"

"Let's sleep." He didn't want to tell PJ that he'd had the same dream.

The knocking went on for a while. But the roar of the wind swallowed it up and lulled them to sleep.

bluebeard's wife

The night was almost over when Carla went back, through the mirror in the closet of her bedroom, to the hall of mirrors.

She knew the way so well now that she hardly thought of it. There were new phantoms, new chambers with coffins; she did not pause to look. At last, climbing the final staircase, she came to the room. The mirrors she had once shattered with her bare fists still lay in shards, here and there, but the room extended far beyond them, and there stood mirror upon mirror, interlocking, interleaved, here a mirror in an ivory frame hanging from another mirror, a mirror within a mirror within a mirror. . . .

And the rushing of many toy trains.

"Carla," Timmy said, materializing on the couch. "It is time now. The story will end soon, a timeless artifact plucked from the stream of time." He smiled a little.

She heard children shouting; at first she didn't see them, for only Timmy seemed to exist . . . but now she saw a little girl crouched on the carpet, carefully arranging miniature pine trees alongside a plastic mountain . . . a boy about thirteen, redhaired, freckly, was pushing the buttons on a black box, making an antique steam engine run over a bridge put together from leather-bound books. There were others in the room too, she saw now. A cadaverous man in a black suit, very proper, who looked like a stage undertaker. Another kid clutched a lunchbox. A woman with the mongoloid features of Down's syndrome quaffed a reddish liquid from a Coke bottle. These people seemed to partake of some quality of the mirrors, for sometimes they shifted in and out of focus, sometimes they weren't there at all, and none of them cast reflections . . . in the myriad mirrors hers was the only face.

"There are many with us now," Timmy said.

What could Carla say? "Am I still your analyst? Or am I now to be analyzed?"

Timmy said, "You have healed me well, Carla. Without you I could not have traced those memories, or learned to face my aloneness. But having faced it I must now conquer it."

"Yes." She saw it all too clearly. "The Red King wakes."

She sat down beside him. Their hands touched for the briefest moment. At the touch the children's gleeful cries faded into a middle distance, and their outlines wavered. Timmy said, "Do you love me, Carla?"

"Can you doubt it now?" But she was bitter.

"You will have to die."

"Death, rebirth," she said, as if reciting from a textbook of Jungian philosophy.

"Do you really love me?" She saw that it was more than a ritual now. Her heart went out to him. He said, "Will you cross the final bridge, go through the last tunnel, meet me at Vampire Junction?"

Carla thought of the long journey they had taken together. From a plush New York office to a crumbling mansion in Idaho . . . from today to a postwar German opera house to a concentration camp to Bluebeard's Castle . . . from terror to pity . . . from darkness to the bitterest darkness. She said, "How can I call it love, this chill, bleak thing?"

He said, "Come."

And they were alone in the million-mirrored room, at the heart of an infinite crystal. He took her hand. The cold seared her, quenched her trembling. She said, "And Stephen?"

He said, "Remember? Scissors, stone, paper."

"Oh, I'm afraid. I'm afraid."

"No. I've made the crossing a thousand times, and I am unscathed."

They rose from the couch. With a languid whisk of the hand Timmy shattered the nearest mirror and they stepped through. She stepped gingerly among the lattice of train tracks, dimly conscious that dead children played at her feet. More glass splinters trickling in slow motion to the floor, like stepping through a waterfall, a fall of cellophane and tinsel—

She gripped his hand tighter, more confident now. They ran wild in a forest of crystal trees. The wind churned up snowflakes large as spiders and as animated. A grayness settled over the landscape. The world seemed to sink, like slipping into hypnosis, sheets and sheets of gray being drawn across the sky, and the sunlight extinguished, buried in a hundred strata of cloud. And always the mirrors, twisting, walling the labyrinth, crowning the castle turrets, growing from the surfaces of lakes and the foothills of mountains.

And it seemed to Carla that they stood at the center of a featureless gray plain, though they had not left the hall of mirrors or the clamoring of vampire children. There was the door she had seen in countless visions, waking and dreaming, standing free on the crystalline grass.

"Do you dare?" said Timmy, passionate at last. "Oh, do

you dare, dare, dare? I have longed for and feared this moment for an age—"

"Hush, Timmy." They embraced . . . he in his maroon
jeans and black Dior T-shirt, she in her flannel Evan Picone
suit . . . she smiled at the incongruity, the mundane and the
transcendent . . . they kissed, no longer chastely.

"Woman, mother, soul," said Timmy Valentine, tearing
her conservative jacket with puma claws, shredding it, dropping it to the grass. Exposing her breasts. Cold. Cold, this
eternal twilight. He shivered himself free of his clothes; and
though she had heard him describe his own body countless
times, she now saw it for the first time, as the last of her own
clothing peeled away of its own accord, like a chrysalis. Cold.
Cold. I am old, too old, Carla thought, coyly covering her
breasts with her hands, old, cold, cold. And she remembered
Stephen in the madhouse, how they'd made love for the first
time, and he'd started to hum the Redemption by Love leitmotif from *Götterdämmerung* and they'd had to bribe the
janitor, she was younger then, why, hardly more than a kid,
and he was worn smooth like a hill in Virginia where she'd
gone camping once when she was really little, but now she was
the wrinkled one and Timmy was the child, like marble that
steals the body heat from you, and Timmy murmured "the
key, you take the key, you clasp it to the door," and she kissed
the tiny cold penis and it sucked away the warmth from her
lips, and she cried out from the smart, and the cold came
again, waves of cold, welling up from the heartland of the mirror hall, and she thought marble, marble, his slender fingers
traced a blue vein down to the mole on her left breast that her
friends used to make fun of long ago, she clasped the key and
he entered her now, drugged her with the perfume of embalm-
ing, his mouth found the tastiest vein, she felt the pinprick
teeth now, a cold and bitter joy swooped over her and she
could not tell joy from pain anymore and she screamed from
the pain and the joy, marble, marble, the gods themselves
were marble, the blood flowed like wine, dark and joyous, the
blood streamed between them, slippery, lubricious, time stops
and turns back on itself and she no longer cried but is crying,
she cannot stem the torrent of upturned time but screams in
joy in the eternal cold and gray, and now they leap in the
crystal forest and are charged with the bloodlust and the earth
beneath her has come alive, it screams with a million death-

haunted voices and she knows them all, the death of a falling leaf, of a deer in a mountain lion's jaws, of a mountain ground to dust by the million-year wind. . . .

And Timmy's voice over the tumult—

"The door! The door!"

She clasps the key to the lock. She sees fire and brimstone and temples crumbling and tottering towers and sulphur rivers in the streets. . . .

"Enter. It is safe. It is a memory, a dead memory, living only by our collective will—"

She stands in the fire and the snow, and she knows the desolate hunger for the first time.

She is the darkness.

memory: A.D. 119

She feels his darkness as her own. He is trapped beneath the wasteland, beneath the rock. She is within him as he batters helplessly against the wombwalls of the earth, and yet she is outside too, phantom like, seeing yet unseen. Olive trees sprout here and there among the basalt and the sulphur outcroppings. A flock of sheep grazes in the sparse pasture, and a boy in a woollen tunic watches them. He nods against the boulder and pulls his tunic tighter around his shoulders. It is night.

She shifts her viewpont swiftly, darting from tree to rock to the broken Ionic columns of an old temple.

Now she is deep beneath the earth. She feels his hunger as her own, she shares his bafflement. What is this place? Where is the master? As he lies within the rock, like a fly in amber, he conjures up images of flames and brimstone, and she sees them with him, though she is not even there, she is a mere ghost of a time that has not yet come to pass. *What am I?* he thinks, she thinks with him. *Why do I thirst so?*

Voices now. She twists away from the rocky confinement, funnels surfaceward through the soil's interstices.

She sees men digging at the rocks. They converse volubly, perhaps to disguise their own fear of this place; she feels that it is haunted. She does not recognize the language at first, though it has a vague resemblance to the Latin she learned in school a long time ago. Then, listening with *his* ears, she understands them.

"It's been forty years since the disaster. Any spirits have long since been exorcised," says one. Moonlight glints on his plumed helmet. He is a centurion. "My uncle had a wine shop in Herculaneum. Never got out in time."

"What about these people-shaped crevasses? Do you believe in them?"

"Oh, I've seen one. They filled it with wax and put it on exhibit outside the Flavian Amphitheater. We can get maybe ten aurei for one."

"Keep digging then. Hey, do you hear that?"

"Just a shepherd. Did you pay him off?"

"With a stoup of drugged Neapolitan wine. He'll sleep."

"Mithra! I hear something too. Knocking. Under here."

"That's solid rock!"

"What if . . . someone somehow survived? A gift of the gods?"

"Very funny. Here, let me have a go with the mallet, and you hold the wedge."

Pounding, more pounding. Far away the sheep bleat. The olive trees rustle. Rock chips skid down the slope. Behind the men is a mountain; she knows, from a postcard Stephen sent her once, that it is Vesuvius.

One of them has seen something. "Mithra!" he shouts.

"What is it?"

"An eyelid—"

"Bah! A bit of grass, black in the moonlight—"

And suddenly she is in there with him, his eyes open, the wind stirs his eyelashes, he smells the bloodrush through the rock and knows that the hungry dream is ended, he feels the mallet smashing the stone, pounding life into him, and she is there feeling it with him, feverish with his hunger—

"A boy," one of them is saying. "Untouched by . . . I'm afraid. . . ."

"Witchcraft. . . ."

She is in him as he springs on them, exultant in his freedom, in the first taste of blood.

scissors, stone, paper

In his mind the *fire* music faded. They pulled into a town. The winding road, uphill all the way, had been slippery, but

Brian Zottoli had pronounced it manageable. As the music
dimmed, Stephen saw fiery dawnlight burst over the mountain. It was a quaint town, with only one thoroughfare,
blandly named Main Street: a drugstore, a general store, and
oddly enough an amusement arcade.

Stephen heard Prathna's voice from the back of the car:
"This can't possibly be the right Junction," he said. "I don't
suppose our friend would pick such an out-of-the-way venue
for our final spectacle."

"You mean," said Sir Francis, "that *you* wouldn't. But I
fear the *mise-en-scène* has been taken out of your hands, my
dear fellow." This petty bickering had been going on for some
weeks now.

"The drugstore seems open," Brian said. "Shall we stop
and look around, anyway?"

"Strange. No one in the streets. Look at the door of the
store, too," said Sir Francis. "I say, isn't that a string of garlic
bulbs hanging over the—"

"Oh, I say," the prince said, seeming less bored at once.
"Perhaps an investigation is in order."

"I'll stop the car," Brian said, and they braked.

The two oldest men, supporting each other, tottered into the
store. Stephen and Brian came in behind. Stephen would leave
the talking to the others. Dust on the counter, on the shelves.
It looked as if no one had been inside for weeks. But a coffee
aroma wafted in from the back, and soon an old man and a
young Indian woman emerged. There were two boys, too, a
ginger-haired one and a black-haired one. They were cowering
in the rear, as if they were expecting something terrible to happen. Stephen knew then, with utter certainty, that they had
come to the end of their journey.

"They're OK, Dad," the taller boy said, "It's after sunrise."

Prathna and Francis exchanged a knowing look. The prince
said, "I am Prince Prathna of Thailand." They looked
blankly at him; they had probably never heard of the place.
Abandoning his customary charmlarded preamble, Prathna
said, "We are looking for. . . ."

"I—ah—" the old man said.

"Don't worry, Kyle," the woman—clearly, Stephen saw
now, his wife—said, "I see that we can tell the truth in front

of them. Whoever they are." To the visitors she said, "We've got crosses. I've got the boys working on stakes in our back yard. But Jesus, we need all the help we can get."

It was coming together so quickly. All four of them were speaking at once now. They must have had nobody to talk to for some time. The boy was saying how he'd lost his whole family, the other boy was jabbering about a haunted arcade, they were all talking about the Spook House on the hill. . . .

"How many people are left here?" Stephen asked.

They didn't know. At night, they said, the street was full of them. *They* went to the Spook House to sleep in the daytime, the woman thought.

"And their leader. . . ." For the last time Stephen pulled out the clipping of Konrad Stolz, a piece of paper that had now crossed half the world.

They passed it round. "Timmy Valentine," the redhaired boy said without hesitation. "Alice mentioned him."

The other boy, the grungy handsome one, said, "She said the name of this town is Vampire Junction now."

Stephen appraised the store in his mind. Wood, all wood. Shelving. Paneling. Outside, logs. A row of bottles of rubbing alcohol. How would it all look in flames? I could have been a great conductor, he thought, save for the fire. He imagined the two remaining Gods of Chaos burning alive, at the stake, perhaps, that had happened to the real Bluebeard, hadn't it? Ah yes, he could hear it clearly now, the *fire* music. The end of the opera was at hand. I could have been a great conductor. They were shouting for *me* at Bayreuth. . . .

"We'll need somewhere to stay," Sir Francis said.

"You'll have to stay at the house," said the woman. Her name was Shannah Gallagher, they learned. She was a Sho-shone. She said, "It'll be cramped, but you'll be safe."

He wanted to cry out at first: Don't you know anything, don't you know you're admitting vipers into your house?

It just showed how desperate they were. The two boys were staring now, not disguising their curiosity.

Vipers into their house. But it didn't matter anymore. Nothing did. And this would bring down the flames all the sooner. And then, above the magic *fire* music, you would hear the strains of *redemption by love* and all would be pure once more.

Brian said, "I'm going to go walk around, while it's still

morning. I think we're going to have a lot to do.''

Stephen followed him out, leaving the Gods of Chaos to finish working out the proper living arrangements. The door jangled as they stepped out. He pulled his scarf and overcoat tighter. Snow tickled his face.

He glanced past the railroad tracks. A thread of road wound up the mountain, into the forest. They were up there somewhere, Timmy and Carla. But it didn't matter anymore. Only the music mattered.

night child

"Wake," Timmy whispers, "oh, wake," to the woman in the coffin. They have spent the night in each other's arms, each tenderly sucking the blood from the other. "Wake, wake." But he knows he must wait now. For—

fire

—the sun had risen now. It hung low, grazing the snow-specked roofs . . . the cold seemed to bore into Stephen's bones . . . only the *fire* could drive it away . . . even as he followed Brian across the street the snow grew denser, piling against a rusty mailbox, the ledges of the store windows . . . a general store, he had noted it briefly as they drove into town, with a display of wigs mounted on mannequin heads . . . Brian stopped in front of that window now. He shouted something, but the snow-thick wind began to howl, and Stephen didn't catch what he said. He went to stand beside him, and saw—

—the store window. Not wicker heads anymore but human heads, wildly mismatched to the wigs they wore. An old man with a bouffant. A matronly head, half-rotted, with a pink pageboy wig. "God," Brian was saying.

"Their idea of a joke," Stephen said, and the *fire* music raged in his mind, and—

Maggots swarmed in the eye sockets of a third head. A fly had settled on the bluish, protruding tongue of another—

night-child

—and he strokes her forehead, trying to warm it, but his ardor runs cold, he too is dead—

arcade

—and Brian saw that one end of the window had been
broken into by whoever had set up this grisly display, and two
schoolmarmish faces stared stupidly from a miniature snow-
drift and a purée of blood and brains was congealing on the
Cleopatra wig of a pudgy, gaptoothed visage, and—

night-child

—and now he kisses her cold lips with his own cold lips and
his cold hands touch hers and he cries out for the fire of his
death and birth—

labyrinth

—and right next to the hole in the window, as if discarded in
haste, lay a frayed decaying human hand; its stump still
sported a Casio calculator watch which Prathna, coming up
behind Brian and Stephen, regarded with distaste, and—

arcade

—Stephen heard Brian's retching as the *fire* music died
away, quenched by the chill snow—

labyrinth

—and Prathna's voice came over the whining wind: "Oh, I
say, chaps, it looks like we've come to the right place after all,
eh, what?"

night-child

—and Timmy Valentine, despairing, cries, "Wake up!
Wake up!" and draws tight the curtains so that the dawnlight
will not fall on Carla Rubens, mother, healer, lover—

fire

"Wife," Stephen thought, remembering Carla as he had
first seen her in the sanitarium, full of concern and adoration.

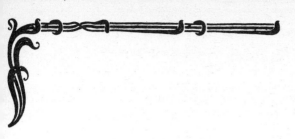

WINTER

I am the Darkness

Don't matter if you hitch a ride
Don't matter if you pay
I'll be waiting at the Vampire Junction
to suck your soul away.
—Timmy Valentine

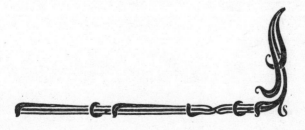

24

memory: night-child: A.D. 78

Once more she has become a phantom from the future,
haunting the memories of the boy vampire. She flits from
shadow to shadow. There is a cave here, and within the cave a
door; beyond the door, a glimmer of fire, a reddish puddle of
light in the dimness. On the walls are graffiti carved over other
graffiti; the rocky walls are like a crinkled New York subway
car, but she cannot understand the words: Greek mostly, some
Latin, other languages too.

Beyond the door, music. A plucked stringed instrument,
punctuating the breathy lilt of a young boy's voice. She is
drawn to it . . . of course, she has known—will know—this
voice so well. She is afraid of discovery; she knows it is a
sacred place, that others would fear to profane it. A priest
walks past with a lamb under his arm, destined no doubt for a
sacrificial altar. She tries to speak to him, though she doubts
he would know English . . . but he has walked right through
her. I am a ghost, Carla Rubens thinks. She grows confident.
The song, within, has broken off, and now she hears a creak-
creak-creaking, like a child's swing perhaps, and the boy
speaking softly. She does not know the language, yet his
words hover on the edge of meaning. She enters the room
beyond. At first she experiences some sort of forceshield, but
she is too insubstantial to be held back, and she knows by in-
stinct that its magic works only on people fettered to this time.

Within, she sees the boy. He is younger. From this she knows he is not yet a vampire. As she enters he looks up . . . has he seen something? He shrugs. Their eyes do not meet, although she tries to attract his attention. Perhaps he has seen a momentary apparition, but such things are so commonplace in this cave that he has not given it a second's thought. Now she hears a chittering sound, like that of a monkey in a jungle. It comes from an enormous glass bottle, slung from the ceiling in a net of stout cord. There is a creature inside, wrinkled, diminutive, monkeylike. The boy speaks to it some more; then he picks up his instrument, a kithara, from the rocky floor and continues his song.

The boy's voice, swelled by the cavern's resonance, has the clarity of fresh spring water; it seems to be born of the rocks themselves. Though Carla Rubens has lost, in her crossing of the bourne of life and death, the ability to weep, she still senses, with an unwonted detachment, the ethereal seduction of his song, the soaring curvature of its melody, the marble-cool purity of its timbre . . . the creature in the bottle is soothed . . . its chatter subsides, and it seems to sleep, but the song does not end, for it seems to possess the boy utterly.

She sits beside him now, breathes in his very breath, knows his thoughts. She cannot pronounce his name, the name they have given him, a lengthy Greek title, in archaic language, about his being dedicated to the mysteries of the Sibyl. But now she knows why she is here. This cave is Cumae, the place where the immortal Sibyl was kept in a bottle. Timmy spoke of this place once . . . the very first time they met . . . "Before I became a vampire," he had said, "I served the Sibyl of Cumae." So the thing in the bottle is human, she sees now. Shriveled, a tiny crone leaning against the green-tinged glass, rocking nervously back and forth, eyes closed . . . her face is so wrinkled that it resembles a wad of brown tissue paper; her chin is stubbled. Her parched mouth, bloated by the bottle's curvature, opens and closes to emit a series of flatulent wheezes.

The spirit-Carla flits toward the bottle, skimming its grainy surface. She tries to read the thoughts of the Sibyl of Cumae, but all she can hear is a stridulous sighing and the word "tired . . . tired . . . tired. . . ." The boy's thoughts are more active; they swarm in his mind like a school of fish, and only fragmentary images fall into the net of her consciousness: "Must shape the phrase more . . . must give with the diaphragm, so, so, to highlight the soaring tone . . . ouch, a false string on the kithara . . . will the old woman speak? I am . . . a thirst for unsulphureted water. . . ." His sense of the passing of time is not well developed; she sees that he has spent his whole life in this cave, serving the Sibyl, who is immortal and speaks of the future with as much confidence and obscurity as the past. His thoughts are fragile things, substanceless; if she tries to touch them they slither away; they are perhaps what flowers think.

And now she is conscious of another presence in the cave. It is a man in Persian dress, with a black, terraced beard. He wears bracelets of gold. His eyes are startlingly blue. When she tries to touch his thoughts she encounters an impenetrable barrier; he has girt his mind with fire.

He says, "I have waited till nightfall, Sibyl, to come to you. We share a problem."

She says, and her voice is like the wind among the olive branches, "But you are still so vigorous, Mage."

"The price was terrible." He smiles, and Carla sees that he is a vampire. Then he sees the boy for the first time. The boy has stopped playing; he cowers in the shadows, for no man may enter the sanctum unpurified, and it is not the Sibyl's wont to address intruders directly, but rather to afflict them with some curse. "What is this boy?" the Mage says. "I heard his voice in the cavern outside. It was that that drew me here. He sings like an Orpheus."

"He is my treasure," the Sibyl says. "Pirates sold him to me when he was a baby; he is from some barbarian country."

"Boy," the Mage says—his voice is rich as dark red wine, but to Carla it possesses an oddly familiar ring—"ask her the question, the question they all ask."

"Question?" says the boy.

"Bah! Have you not read Petronius?"

"No, *domine*."

"He died not long ago. In Nero's time, before the building of the Flavian Amphitheater."

The boy understands suddenly. In melodiously accented Greek he sings to the woman in the bottle: *"Sibyla, ti theleis?"* What is it, Sibyl, that you desire?

At this a monstrous cackling, muffled by the thick glass,

breaks out inside the bottle. "Do not mock me, old man!" she squawks. Then, almost inaudibly she replies, *"Apothanein thelo."*

"I want to die," says the boy, needlessly translating into Latin.

"And so do I," says the Mage. Carla realizes now that he and the Sibyl are ancient friends, millennial friends. Perhaps, when the world was young, they were even lovers. He is a priest of Ahura-Mazda, of the living fire. "But now," says the Mage, "I have a plan. For a thousand years I have studied the light and the darkness, and the fringe of gray between the two, that tiny no-man's land where all we can understand exists. I can end our curse, Sibyl of Cumae."

He draws a sword. The boy cries out. It is sacrilege. The Mage rasps, "Not a sound, boy! You are coming with us. A cart waits outside the temple. Now, help me cut down the bottle."

"You are profaning—" the boy says. They will beat me, he thinks, they will sell me to a latifundium and work me to death—

"Out of the way, boy!" the Mage cries, and with a slash he severs the ropes on which the Sibyl's bottle depends. It falls, shatters; she sits unharmed among the shards. And so he sees her for the first time without the magnifying effect of the curved glass. She seems frail, like a terra cotta doll. The Mage commands him: "Lift her up." He must obey. She is as light as his kithara. He expects her to smell rancid—all the aged suppliants who visit the cave have the smell, even the rich Romans who mask it with attar of roses—but she has a fragrance of cloves, and her parchment-thin skin feels soft against his tunic. He carries her from the inner cavern.

In the vestibule the guards lie dead or drugged. Horses neigh from somewhere outside. He does not remember ever seeing the world beyond the cavern. He follows the Mage as a slave must, never thinking for himself.

The cave-mouth is concealed behind an elaborate façade of Corinthian columns. When they go through he feels wind in his hair. He coughs. The Mage laughs.

"The cart," he says. The old man and the boy help the crone into it. It is canopied with some delicate material, and even in this dark he can see that it is painted in bright colors and highlighted with gilt . . . Sicilian workmanship.

Still cradling the Sibyl, the boy wedges himself into a corner of the cart. A goblet tumbles from a pile of treasure. The boy is afraid he may be whipped for this, but the Mage only laughs. Perhaps he will be a kind master.

The horses move.

The Mage says to the boy, who dares not look him in the face, "You do not speak, lad." He turns to the driver, a dour-looking Nubian who has no tongue, and gives him directions to the main road. The boy still does not speak. "You have no name, beautiful singer?"

"No, *domine*." For the name they have given him in the Sibyl's temple is sacred, and a title of the God.

"Don't be afraid, *kalé mou*, my pretty one," the Mage says, switching to Greek as is the custom amongst the educated. (Carla, who is part of the glint of gold on the treasure-chest, understands him easily now, though she still cannot penetrate his thoughts.) "I will not harm you . . . yet. And when I do it will be to reward you more richly than you could ever imagine."

The Sibyl scoffs.

"Don't laugh, old friend," he says to her. "The boy is necessary to our plan."

The Sibyl: "I believe in no plan. My contemplation of eternity has given me no such illuminations. Future, present, past, all is bitterness."

"No, Sibyl," says the Mage, as the cart begins to bump down the stony road. "I have found a way to cheat eternity. You and I will have what even this lowly boy possesses . . . the greatest gift of all . . . mortality."

The boys feels a terrible cold fear.

"We will go now," says the Mage, "to my new house in Pompeii."

"I have seen—" the Sibyl croaks.

"I know what you have seen," the Mage says, "and that too is part of the plan."

She laughs again, a birdlike twittering.

The Mage says, "Sing, boy."

"I haven't my kithara anymore."

The Mage rummages among the treasure . . . goblets crash, kylixes and unguent jars clatter, an amethyst big as a fist spills to the floor of the cart, but he seems not to care. At last he produces a kithara of ebony, inlaid with Neapolitan cameos, each tuning-peg carved from a different semiprecious stone.

"I suppose this will have to do," the Mage says as he tosses it to the boy, who catches it gingerly; in his eleven years he has never touched an object of such value. "Sing, sing," the Mage says. "Relieve my millennial anguish."

The boy pauses, afraid to displease his new master. Moonlight streams in through a hole in the canopy. The Mage's face, chalk-pale, glows eerily. The boy is terribly afraid. How can he disobey the man, though? He is only a slave. He sings, his voice wavery from the bouncing of the cart. The Sibyl, leaning against his shoulder, drawing warmth from his wool tunic, drifts in and out of sleep, febrile, dream-laden.

labyrinth: fire: funhouse

The boy—his name was PJ, and the redhaired companion was a friend, not a member of the family, it transpired— stoked the fireplace as Stephen sat back in an armchair. Kyle Gallagher hovered nervously over his important guests; Francis and Prathna were ensconced on a plaid sofa.

The woman—Shannah—said, "Let me go and check on the coffee." Brian Zottoli sprang up, eager to help. Stephen could tell, from the way he looked at her, that he was attracted to her.

Outside, the snow continued to fall, and the wind whined ceaselessly. As Brian and Shannah went into the kitchen, the others began to exchange stories about vampires.

"If this damn snow would only stop," Kyle said.

PJ said, "Need more wood, Dad." He didn't offer to go and get some.

His friend Terry said, "I'll come with you." They each took a cross off the mantelpiece and left the room. Kyle squatted close to the fire.

"Here we are, then," said Prathna. "Four old men with a mission."

"Becoming quite goody-goody in you old age, old chap," Sir Francis said.

"We gotta have a plan," Kyle said.

"The house on the mountain," Stephen said. "That's where it's all coming from, and that's where we're all going to have to go, in the end." He wondered whether Carla had already joined the undead, or whether they would have some tearfully maudlin reunion.

"I don't relish the thought of going out in this weather," said Prathna. "Really, and at my age! My bones, my bones . . . and I am, after all, a tropical flower, eh, what? Perhaps I should simply appear at the end to administer the *coup de grace*."

"It could snow for days," Kyle said. "I reckon we got a couple feet already. Can hardly see out the damn window. Come morning—"

"Better not to see out," said Sir Francis, "in view of the . . . ah . . . sanguinary habits of the natives, eh?"

Stephen watched the moisture collecting between the wall planks, felt the creeping cold. He moved the armchair nearer the fire.

Kyle turned to him. "I can't believe these guys!" he said. "Are they for real?"

"They're all we have," Stephen said.

Kyle said, "You think they're really taking this business seriously?"

Stephen said, "Several of their friends have already died." Kyle poked at the fire thoughtfully.

At last he said, "We got three spare beds in the back room. Kind of a storeroom really, I keep some of the extra stock for the drugstore there. One of you will have to take the couch, though, I reckon, here in the living room."

"Our driver will," said Prathna grandly. Stephen winced at his condescending reference to Brian. He wondered what Brian and Shannah were doing back in the kitchen.

"Yeah," Kyle said dubiously. "But they come knocking on the windows, and I'd hate to see a guy alone when they come."

"I can handle it," Brian said, coming in with a tray of coffee mugs. Shannah followed him.

"Amazing woman, your wife," said Sir Francis, intending it as mere polite flattery; but Stephen looked at her and knew that it was true. At that moment the kids came in with logs, interrupting his thoughts. He stared at the fire. Terry and PJ threw on more wood, and it flared up, dancing, delighting him, so that he almost forgot their predicament.

But then, when Kyle said, "We've gotta start making some

stakes now,'' his fear returned, worse than ever.

The snow continued to pile up at the window until there was only a watery porthole through which to see the night. The wind howled, relentless.

arcade

Three in the morning. They'd all gone upstairs now; Brian was alone on the sofa. He pulled the blanket closer. The fire glowed; the wind roared.

Presently he heard footsteps. When he looked up, Shannah Gallagher stood in front of him in a nightgown. She pressed a finger to his lips. ''Quiet.''

He said, ''You came.''

She said, ''I don't know why.''

He said, ''Because we're both so scared. Everything's coming to an end, there aren't any rules anymore.''

She sat down beside him. He kissed her, hard, but there was a remoteness in her he couldn't reach. He said, ''We're all going to die tomorrow.'' They kissed again. His erection stiffened. Abruptly he came. He said, ''I'm sorry, I—''

She said, ''I know. It's all right. Kyle's fast asleep. We can try again.''

''Aren't you afraid he'll—?''

''No.'' They huddled together under the blanket. ''He was my ticket out of the reservation, but for the past fifteen years I've done nothing but long to go back.''

''Do you hate him?''

''I am Shoshone.'' Carefully, teasingly, she started to unzip his fly, lightly swabbing at his come with a corner of the blanket. He'd been thinking about her all evening, about her fragrance, about her soft midnight hair. She babbled on about inconsequential things . . . and about her son, the only person she really loved: ''I've taught him to know what he is. I've taught him about our people. I hoped once I'd bring him back with me and he'd go through the snake vision, you know, and become a man in our people's way.'' Desire stirred again now. But when he remembered the hotel room on the outskirts of Los Angeles, and the woman he'd picked up lying bleeding and lifeless on the bed, and Lisa standing on the balcony with the seaweed strands trailing in the wet wind, he—

''Oh, I'm so confused, I don't know who I am anymore,''

Shannah was saying, "I don't know if I should stay or go back—" She was crying in his arms. He thought: But I'm a total stranger! and then realized that she truly had no one to turn to now. . . .

Almost casually, they began to make love. As they climaxed, she whimpered, "Who am I? Who am I?" and just wouldn't stop sobbing, and then they heard the front door rattling and she said, "The wind, the wind—" but he knew it was no wind.

And a voice at the door: "Mrs. Gallagher, please let me in, let me in . . . PJ and me went out hunting for David and Alice but they're after us now, oh, please open the door—"

She threw on her nightgown and unlatched the door, and—

A scream from the staircase. Terry and PJ appeared brandishing crosses. "It's David, Mom, for Chrissakes!" PJ shouted. The door flew open; at once the fire in the grate went out and they saw David in the door, Brian saw that he looked just like Terry except for the bluish pallor of his face and the bloody fangs, and David was on Shannah's neck now, Terry and PJ were hitting him with their crosses and blistering his face and he could see blood gushing from Shannah's neck, and David was dragging Shannah into the snow, plunging with unnatural swiftness into the mounds of white, and the snow was still falling, falling, the sky was thick with it, PJ and Terry rushed after David but they couldn't see where he went, and now Kyle, waked by the commotion, was at the head of the stairs with a cross and a shotgun; Brian was overcome with guilt, he couldn't speak, he just stood by the dead fire buttoning his shirt, and Kyle saw what had happened and he began to sob tearlessly, appallingly, while the two boys just stood gaping at the two men.

"Well shut the fucking door," Kyle said at last. Nobody moved.

Brian said, "I—"

Kyle said, "I'll kill you! I'll fucking kill you!"

PJ said, "Stop, Dad." To Brian he said, "She should have been able to smell the difference between them a mile off. Even I can, and I'm only half Shoshone. You made her forget who she was. That's why she let him in."

Brian started to stammer something, but PJ went on, "It's not your fault, Brian." Brian could see that he was desperately trying to be brave, like she'd taught him, while old Kyle had simply given up. What could you say to a kid when you've just been fucking his mother and it turned her into a vampire? Jesus God. He couldn't look the kid in the eye, couldn't face his anger, let alone his pity.

Finally he managed to say, "I'm sorry."

PJ said, "I'll never forget who *I* am."

For a long appalling moment they all stood around waiting for someone else to break the silence. The shutters rattled and the wind howled. No one closed the door, and snow swept over the floorboards.

Then Kyle said, abruptly, "Always knowed I was too old for her." He slammed the front door shut and shuffled upstairs.

Brian said to PJ, "It seemed so right . . . I mean, those others are all old, but she and I . . . it was like a last chance for us, a . . . God, why am I talking like this? . . . how can I ask you to forgive me? . . . I. . . ."

PJ said, "Used to want a Dad like you . . . younger . . . someone I could talk to, you know . . . but. . . ."

Brian said, "My niece is dead." Then he spread his arms wide to embrace them both, though they were the children of strangers . . . all the three had left were tatters of remembered affections. And so they remained, huddled on the sofa, clinging to each other, each one imprisoned in his private grief, for the rest of the night.

25

dissolve: fire: labyrinth

Morning now. The air was crisp and clear, the wind down to a distant wuthering. The two kids were struggling with the front door as Stephen came downstairs. It flew open, and snow flurried into the house.

"Three, maybe four feet," Kyle Gallagher said.

Stephen looked out. White, white. The roof of a station wagon poked through the snowy blanket . . . here and there firs . . . the mountain peaks electric orange from the dawnlight on the snow. "Can we get to the house on the mountain?"

"Might take all day, trudging. We got snow shoes in the store, if we can make it that far," Kyle said, "and maybe a couple pairs here."

"What about them two weird guys, the British-talking ones? Ain't they up yet?" PJ said. He was taking some perfunctory swipes at the snow with a shovel.

"They slept through the whole thing last night," Stephen said. "And they're still sleeping like babies." Predictably, he thought. "Brian?"

"He ain't said nothing since last night," PJ said, indicating the man still sitting on the sofa, staring into the fire.

They waited. Suddenly Stephen realized that he was now, for the moment at least, the leader. It was not a comforting thought.

At last, he said, "Can't we make a start, at least? Where's the nearest house?"

Terry said, "Mine, I guess."

"Kyle, stay here and see what the others do. I'm just going to the neighbors'. I suppose I'd better take stakes and things."

"I'll come," Terry said.

"What if you see your br—" Kyle said.

Terry said, "That's why."

"I'll go with them, Dad," said PJ. "Maybe Mom—"

"Yeah," Kyle said, "Yeah."

"You'd best borrow some of my dad's clothes, mister," PJ said, "or you'll get a heart attack or something."

"I'm not that old," Stephen said. But I am, he reminded himself, as the cold ate into his bones.

In an hour, after several cups of coffee and the ritual of putting on layers of clothing, the conductor and the two boys set off. "It'll be a good half hour to trudge to the house," PJ said.

"What about those tracks?" Stephen said, pointing.

There was a rough path beaten into the snow. Footprints of some animal, and beside them a furrow from someone being dragged. . . .

"If we walk in those tracks," Stephen said, "we'll get there faster, and you kids won't have to shovel."

Terry seemed to demur at this. "I know whose tracks they are. No way you're gonna get me to—"

PJ said, "It's OK. The sun's out, Terry. They can't do nothing to us."

They turned at the corner where the tracks turned onto the road. On either side the snow was piled almost waist-high.

"Where's the house?" Stephen said.

"Can't you see it?" Terry pointed. At first he saw nothing, except a haunching outline in the dazzling whiteness—then he made out the house, a small wooden structure painted white and blending almost perfectly with the snow.

"Camouflaged," he said.

"Not against vampires," Terry said sullenly.

"Look at the tracks!" PJ shouted.

Ahead . . . as they went toward the steps leading to the house . . . the prints seemed to be changing shape. Where the three stood they were still clawed, but a little further off the claws had retracted, and by the front steps they seemed like the bare feet of an adolescent. . . .

"Why did he come here?" Stephen wondered aloud.

"Maybe he couldn't make it back to the house on the mountain," PJ said. They were standing near the front door now, and the boys were shoveling to free the hinges. "Look, there's some other prints, there, leading off into the woods behind the house."

"He never was bright," Terry said.

"Could be a trap," PJ said.

Stephen took a look around. There were a few more houses, a lot of trees, and, at the bend in the road ahead, Main Street. "If it's a trap," he said, "it'll only work at night, I think. Let's go inside."

In the house the heat was off. Snow carpeted the floor. There were tracks in all directions; some were of beasts, some human, some hybrid. Against one wall were spatters of fresh blood.

"There's nothing here," Terry said hurriedly, nervously.

"What about upstairs?" Stephen said.

"Just bedrooms." Then, blurting out, "I wanna get out of here!"

"Shh. I want to look around upstairs. Help me." Stephen started up the stairs, which were deep in snow. The room was misty from the crisscross frosting of their breath. The boys crept past him to shovel off some of the snow. "Where's it all coming from?" said Stephen, noting that the windows downstairs were all closed. . . .

Upstairs, a little girl's room with Smurf wallpaper . . . the bedsheets ripped, bloodstained . . . dolls, some with their heads twisted off, littered the floor. Patches of snow, but the window was shuttered.

The parents' bedroom. A lot of blood here. The windows wide open; this was where the snow had come in. Blood smeared the bed, the walls, the shredded clothes. "I can't look," said Terry.

"He saw it happen," PJ said, and covered his friend's eyes.

Stephen saw a closet. Boxes in disarray; bloody clothes flung from their hangers, tatters flapping, a shoe sticking out of the snow. There was another room behind. "What's that?"

"Our—my room," Terry said.

Stephen pushed aside some coats and stepped through. Even more snow, now. On the wall a big blow-up of Terry and another kid who looked just like him, in summer camp T-shirts, smiling a gaptoothed, Polaroid-commercial sort of smile . . . bunk beds, the bottom one completely buried in the snow . . . a baseball bat protruding from snow banked against a desk with a model spaceship . . . a little morning light from the open window, a breeze stirring, a baseball card fluttering downward to the snow. . . .

On the bottom bunk, as the snow shifted, a pale hand. "Terry, PJ," Stephen said softly. The clothes rustled as they came through the closet. "Look. The bed."

He kicked his way across the room, the snow fluffing into the wind. "I think you'd better get out one of those stakes," he said to PJ, who pulled one out of his parka.

He was standing by the bunk now, brushing the snow off with his hands. . . .

A boy in the snow, arms folded, eyes closed.

Terry said, "Oh God, David, you always hated the lower bunk." He started shaking his brother's corpse. "Oh, God, David, David," he said, and the snow scattered from the lapel of the dead boy's tuxedo jacket . . . he wore no bowtie . . . onto the snow-piled floor. "Jesus, it looks like he's just sleeping, I can't do it to him, I can't."

"It's OK, kid," Stephen said, "I'll take care of it."

"Don't you touch my brother!"

The face so pale, bluish from cold . . . the red hair tousled, stiff . . . a cherry stain on one corner of his mouth. Stephen looked from one to the other. "Give me the stake," Terry said at last. "I guess I have to. I gotta do something for him." To the corpse he said, "I'm gonna set you free now, Dave." He took the stake from PJ and aimed it at his twin brother's heart. "Hold it, PJ, and I'll hit." PJ grasped the stake in both hands. Stephen felt strangely alienated from this scene, at once tender and horrific; he was thinking only of Timmy Valentine, of the haunting voice of Konrad Stolz, and of Carla, waiting for him on the mountain. But as Terry swung the mallet he saw the corpse's eyes snap open, and it spoke in a fluting, toneless voice: "Terry, Terry . . . it's not what you think . . . we're happy now, we're a family, don't take me away from them now, Terry, Terry—"

"Shut up, Jesus God, shut up!" Terry screamed, pounding again and again at the stake. Dark oily blood oozed from the wound. As the wood began to fracture the icehard corpse blood started to spurt up, spraying their faces . . . still the corpse of David Gish pleaded . . . then, as the stake ruptured the boy's heart, words came gushing from his lips, like a speeding record, "They're gonna get you for this—you're gonna die, you hear, die! die!—" and then came a protracted, high-pitched wail, the snow flurried, the photo of the two kids tumbled from the wall, blood spattered their clothes now, drenched their faces, two tears of blood squirmed from the lifeless eyes and clung to the snow-pale cheeks like garnets on white gold, and the scream went on, joined forces with the wind itself, and the body shuddered and fibrillated and was suddenly still, and Terry wrenched himself away from his dead brother, burying his face in his bloodsoaked hands, and Stephen saw him wracked with sobs yet dry-eyed, mask-faced, he knew how the boy was being torn apart inside and knew no way to comfort him, he tried to reach out but his mind seemed to encounter a barrier of impenetrable fire—

"Ain't never going back," Terry said. Without anger, without bitterness. He didn't sound like a kid anymore.

"Guess it's your house now," PJ said.

"Fuck that! You can burn it to the ground, I don't give a shit."

At that moment Stephen understood why he had come here. A higher purpose—the same purpose that had hounded him since that day, sixty years ago, when he had seen his parents flame and sizzle as they tumbled from the window of the house on Warkworth Street—had led him to Vampire Junction.

"We *will* burn it down!" he said fiercely. "All of it!"

"You crazy?" PJ said.

"Crazy! I spent two years in a nuthouse and he asks me if I'm crazy!" Stephen began to laugh maniacally. A sixty years' burden was dropping from his shoulders. "It's the way to the Spook House. To burn down the town. To smoke out the vampires. To melt the snow so we can climb to the final confrontation."

"Jesus, man, a fucking pyro!" PJ exclaimed. Then, admiringly, "You're cool for an old guy, real cool."

"Matches?" Stephen was hearing in his mind the opening pages of the great immolation scene from *Götterdämmerung*. *"So werf ich den Brand in Walhalls prangende Burg*—Thus I cast the firebrand into gloriously shining Valhalla!" He rummaged through the layers of borrowed clothes until he fished out his lighter. "A present from my ex-wife," he said, no longer. "Find stuff to heap on the corpse, kids."

"I'll go and tell the others about your plan," Terry said, eager to get out of the house.

"I'll stay," PJ said. Then "Wow, a fucking pyro conductor. Radical, man!"

Stephen was muttering to himself now, "Yes, the photograph, the shoeboxes. . . ." He started gathering up everything that looked like it might burn, even the plastic spaceship on the desk, and throwing them onto the body. Then, dissatisfied with the mess he was making, he began to array the objects around the body like funerary gifts. Terry had run off already, but PJ, catching Stephen's spirit, was sloshing through the kneehigh snow and digging up stuff from the floor beneath: a Monopoly set, some baseball cards, and—a gleeful shout now —a box of fireworks. "Sparklers, catherine wheels, a motherfucking Fourth of July here!" he said. "Terry never told me he'd stashed this stuff."

"Here. We'll crown David with them."

"I'll brush off more snow so the whole bunk'll catch fire." Then, suddenly, "Mister, you're mad."

"Yes, mad, mad, mad, mad, mad!"

"Whatcha singing?"

"Götterdämmerung," Stephen yelled at the top of his voice, knowing the kid would think it was a lunatic's gibberish. "Now stand back!"

He lit some old papers and threw them onto the bed.

For a few seconds, the fire sputtered, teasing him. Then it leapt up. His heart, too. It ran along the line of grubby science fiction paperbacks, it circled the Stonehenge of baseball cards that PJ had carefully arranged. Now it touched flesh, charring, sparking. Now it flared. Flames licking the boy's face, and then the catherine wheels spurting magnesium-white fire and the sparklers flickering. . . .

"Beautiful, God, beautiful," Stephen murmured.

"We ought to get out of here," PJ said, pulling him by the hand. They stood at the door now. The fire had reached the upper bunk and there was a teargas stink from the exploding plastic spaceship, and smoke enveloped David's face. For a few moments more Stephen stared at the fire, feeling its heady joy, and he yearned to *be* the fire, to be able to touch a human body with the most intimate of embraces, to love finally, ultimately, to consume utterly. There was a wall of fire in front of him now. "Come on, man, we gotta burn down more houses, we're gonna set the fucking town on fire, man!" PJ was shrieking . . . and Stephen knew that there was nothing for them now but this last joy, that they must give themselves to the joy, be swallowed in the fire, for ever and ever, and he closed his eyes and still saw the fire and behind the fire a dark door opening into more fire and behind the door a man in flames, like in the dream, and for a moment he seemed on the brink of a memory he could not possibly possess, a memory of an immortal in Persian dress with gilded eyes wielding a knife beneath a bursting volcano, and then the remembrance dissolved and PJ was tugging him down the stairs, opening the front door but there was another door into fire into a door into fire into a door into fire—

memory: A.D. 79

The Mage's house is wedged between a wineshop and a sculptor's studio. The boy (and Carla with him, in the gray fringe where his shadow meets the flickering torchlight) has been sent to the wineshop for a jar of Lesbian wine. The owner, rubbing his beard, says, "You're the Persian's new boy? Pretty little thing. Wish I could afford one. Brighten up the place."

"Yes, *domine*."

"Demure, too. Such a smile. Nights I hear you singing, since his atrium backs onto my shop. Tell me about him. Who is he?"

"I must hurry, *domine*." The boy does not like the wineshop, with its vinegary fragrance and suffocating smokiness; but he is afraid to risk the shopkeeper's anger.

"Yesterday he came in, just after sunset, to buy wine; I gave him a silver denarius in change, and he just stared and said, 'I've changed my mind; I'll send my boy in the morning,' and he had the most horrified look on his face, he was recoiling from my good silver! And me an honest tradesman, never touched forged money in my life.'' The boy secretly doubts this, but it is not his place to respond.

As quickly as he can get away, he takes the proffered wine-jar and slips into the alley, which is already filling up with whores, urchins, decadent young men on litters screeching to each other in heavily accented Greek, pickpockets, soldiers with their cloaks and plumed helmets . . . Pompeii's much overrated nightlife. He taps at the gate, and the watchslave, a tongueless Nubian who is nightly chained to the gatepost, admits him with a wheezy grunt.

The boy leaves the wine with the cook—the *dominus* does not drink wine, but keeps a supply for company—and is told that the Mage is waiting for him in his inner room. Afraid, confused, he goes to his master. As he enters the private chamber, he hears the Mage and the Sibyl quarreling, and he hides in the shadows, not wanting their wrath to fall on him by mistake. They argue in low voices, as if they do not want the staff to eavesdrop, and are speaking Greek as an added precaution.

"I did not know she would be so weak!'' the Mage is protesting. "I didn't mean to drain her—'' He stops. He has seen the boy. "Come, boy. Are you a virgin?''

"Of course he is,'' the crone says, cackling at some innuendo.

"All right then. I need a virgin. Go to the table. By the window. There is a bowl there.''

He walks past them. The bowl is solid silver, and full of water. "Shall I bring it to you, master?''

"No, fool! It's silver! No, keep it away from me.'' Suddenly the boy notices the young girl who has previously been the Mage's bodyslave crumpled lifeless against one of the walls. In the halfdark he had thought her pale body one of the erotic nudes painted on the plaster. Trembling, the boy glances into the bowl.''

"Tell me,'' the Mage says, "exactly what you see, and don't embroider, do you hear?''

"I see Vesuvius.''

"Good, good,'' the Mage says, excited. "What else?''

"I see fire. I see a man fall from a building.'' It is not a type of building with which the boy is familiar—certainly there is nothing like it in Pompeii—and the man's clothes are bizarre;

but the boy does not want to be accused of lying, so he says nothing.

"Good, good," the Mage says. To the crone: "You see, it will all be as planned. The moment is there to be seized. The three fates spin millions upon millions of life-threads; at times, I think, the threads become tangled, hopelessly tangled, and in frustration one of them snips wildly at the knot, and so unleashes some catastrophe. But that is to our advantage. Twenty thousand deaths . . . and ours will pass unnoticed! In that tiny moment of confusion, my magic will reach in and switch the lifelines as they pass through the treacherous junction . . . do you not see, Sibyl? And we will trade this boy's mortality for our cold eternity. . . ."

"Master—" the boy cries out. He has seen shapes wavering in the water . . . he has seen the three Fates, or something like them, all in that peculiar supernatural garb: but two of them seem like very old men, and the middle one sits in a chair with monstrous wheels, and they converse in a guttural, Germanic-sounding tongue.

"What is it child?" the Mage says.

"I am frightened, *domine*."

"And well you should be!" He claps his hands. Two of his attendants enter. They have been told what they must do in advance, for they immediately seize the boy and strap him to the table and gag him.

A knife glints in the torchlight.

"Do not think," the Mage says, sighing, "that I want to hurt you, child. Think of it as a gift; one less troublesome impediment to your endless future . . . and your voice, that glorious blend of innocence and pain, of rapture and profound melancholy . . . you must take the song with you in your journey . . . to melt the hearts of kings, to move men to tears, so that they do not suspect the terrible thing that you will have to become . . . besides, the testicles of a virgin boy are of vital importance to the magic. . . ."

The boy ceases to hear him as the attendant, who has lifted his tunic, slices deftly at his genitals. He cannot scream because of the gag. He cannot see through the hot spurting tears.

"I am sorry for your pain, boy," the Mage says sadly, though the boy is no longer listening, he feels only the searing knife. "If there were another way I would spare you. I am not without compassion. But your pain, too, is part of the essential ritual. And I, alas, cannot even weep for you. I can imagine your pain as an intellectual exercise, of course, but how will that avail you? I must harden my heart."

The pain is everything. But Carla, a shard of moonlight, continues to hear the Mage: "From pain, boy, beauty is born, as the hyacinth-flower sprang from the blood of wounded Hyacinthos, whom the god loved." And again: "In my limited fashion, boy, I do feel a kind of love for you. Try to understand that."

In her human life Carla might have felt rage at these words; now she is possessed only by a millennial melancholy. She feels what the wind feels, what the fire feels. Though the boy's pain lances her, too, though she strives to share it, she has lost the faculty of mortal anguish.

So the boy suffers alone, isolated by time and by mortality.

fire: seeker

Brian Zottoli sloshed past several burning houses and reached the stop sign where Main Street began. Sir Francis, Kyle Gallagher, and the prince had come up behind.

"Capital idea of Miles's," Prathna was saying, "to burn these houses down. Now I shan't freeze to death as I stake vampires; besides, I shan't be deprived of my grand spectacle. . . ."

"Find me a vampire quickly," Sir Francis said. They all carried sacks stuffed with stakes, crosses, garlic, and mallets. The two oldest men supported each other by the shoulders as they staggered uphill through the slush. Brian, still overwhelmed by last night's commotion, said nothing.

"Where are the others?"

Terry was standing at the entrance to the drugstore, waving madly. Main Street was still impassable; the car they had rented was barely visible at the curb by Kyle Gallagher's store. "What's the kid shouting?" Kyle grunted.

"Kerosene, Mr. Gallagher! And butane! Camping gas!"

"What's the matter?" Kyle yelled back.

"In your store! In back!"

Just then PJ and Stephen came out, lugging great cans. "Jesus Christ," Kyle whispered. "The whole damn town."

Brian saw Sir Francis trembling in almost uncontrollable excitement, while Prathna's face had set into an inscrutable mask. Terry was screaming from the drugstore: "We're gonna blow up the car, OK?"

"You're crazy!" Kyle shouted.

Stephen began to cackle like a mad scientist. The sound echoed from building to building across the empty street. Terry was coming over to them now, carefully retracing the path that they had made getting to the drugstore. "Come on, Brian," he was saying, "let's get to work. The arcade."

"Aracde?"

"There might be someone there."

"Wait for us," Francis and Prathna said simultaneously.

"Fuck that!" Terry said, and Brian saw a possessed gleam in his eyes. "I've already killed my own fucking brother and a half dozen others while you guys sat around at home."

The wind rose a little; smoke billowed onto the street from below.

Brian went into the arcade. The carnage—

All the games were still on, blinking, flashing, whooshing, booming, demanding quarters in insistent electronic voices. But draped over Ms. Pac-Man was a teenage kid in pajamas with a lunchbox in his hand, blood dripping from his neck; at the foot of Bloodsucker was a middle-aged woman whose hands, peacefully crossed over her breasts, were mottled with congealed blood. On the floor, here and there, were scattered body parts: a row of left feet stacked on a pinball machine, a finger here, a cheek with an attached ear sticking out of the slot of the change machine. Zigzag sprays of blood covered the walls, here and there accented by a skin scraping or a blob of brain tissue.

"Splendid!" Prathna said rather halfheartedly; the Gods of Chaos and PJ's father had followed them in.

"Just come and help me hold the stake," Terry said angrily.

The prince pulled a sharp one from his cache and bent carefully over the woman on the floor. Terry began to pound. The woman's eyes opened; she began to scream, and blood spattered on Prathna's overcoat. "Oh, I say," said the prince.

• "Now we gotta do Alex Evans. I wonder if he has any quarters in his lunchbox." Terry pried the box loose and opened it; a human heart slithered onto the floor. The others gasped, but Terry seemed inured, almost bored by the whole thing. "For God's sake, help me lift this corpse, I'm just a fucking kid!" It was Brian who sprang to his aid now, selecting a stake and aiming it carefully at the dead kid's heart. As Terry pounded, the body writhed like a sack of fish.

"Let me do it," Francis said, breathing heavily. "I bloody well want to do it—"

"Wait your turn," Terry said. "This is our town, these are my friends—and you guys turn up from nowhere and expect the whole town handed to you on a silver platter!"

"What impertinence!" Francis said. But Brian thought it served the man right.

Outside, the sound of an explosion—

"The car!" Kyle said.

They ran outside. A pool of flame in the snow, and the water starting to stream . . . Stephen and PJ had assembled all the flammable things from the drugstore and had made a heap on the other side of the street . . . PJ was saying, "There was a couple stiffs in the drugstore, we staked them already." The flames leaped up, obscuring the drugstore window. An acrid stench of burning plastic made Brian wince. The fire was spreading to the drugstore as fragments of hot metal and burning rubber erupted from the car.

Another explosion. "Duck!" someone yelled, and they sought shelter in the grisly amusement arcade.

"Holy shit," PJ said, looking around, "Ho-lee-shit!"

Stephen began sprinkling the corpses with kerosene. "Excellent, excellent," Prathna said, trying to reestablish control of the situation. He took a can himself and began sloshing it on the floor. Meanwhile, Bloodsucker politely informed him that he needed another quarter. When they had emptied two cans, they filed out quietly, trudged several buildings up the street to the general store with the wig display; Stephen was putting down a trickle of kerosene along the sidewalk as a makeshift fuse, and then he lit it and Brian watched the pencil of flame slice through the snow, he watched it enter the door, and a moment later the fire bursting, the smoke tendriling from the open door, a piercing wail, perhaps from some vampire they had not yet staked, now being consumed by the flames . . . a wall of blazing heat beneath where they stood, and above, still frozen, still snowed under, the train tracks, the general store, the mountain.

"You'd have thought they'd all be up there," Kyle said, pointing uphill.

"Maybe they just couldn't make it home," PJ said.

"Or," said Brian, "they had a need to sleep where they did, in the arcade, or at home, or whatever. They couldn't totally give up what they used to be before the changing." He thought of Lisa, for whom it was all too late.

"Cars!" Stephen said. "Any more cars?"

"My dad's," Terry said, "still in the parking lot. The train station."

"First we'll do the general store, then try to make it to the train tracks, then—"

"By nightfall?" Sir Francis said.

"It's four already. Sun sets earlier every day," Kyle said.

Brian, flinching from the heat, started up the street. Beyond the mountain were the ghostly outlines of more mountains, shrouded in mist and snow, a vast bleak vista. The burning town would just be a tiny oasis of blazing energy in this freezing wasteland . . . and up there, up there? What will I say to Shannah Gallagher? he thought. I was just about to fall in love with her last night. . . .

dissolve

Come out here, on the porch, Rudy. Look. The town. Glowing. Unnatural heat rising. And the sun not yet setting. . . .

Yes, master Timothy. What could it be?

They're here. Quick, call Maria. There are things I must say to you both.

She is still polishing Miss Carla's coffin, master Timothy, but . . . ah, here she comes.

Look. The trees are beginning to smoke. The snow on the road will melt soon and they will be able to reach me.

Shall I fetch guns, master Timothy?

No. Let them come. Let them come. Ah, Maria. Listen. I can already hear their voices, I who cannot shut out the noisome sounds of mortality. The fire has maddened them. They will come here with their stakes and their mallets, and those of my kind who have taken cover here will die, many of them; you will offer no resistance.

What, master Timothy!

In fact, the time has come, Rudy and Maria, my faithful ones . . . you must leave me. For the story will soon end. Oh, Maria, Maria, don't cry. You have loved me the most. And I've needed that love; often it has sustained me even more than the bitter taste of blood. And you, Rudy, always kind, never complaining . . . there have been times when my old promise to you at Auschwitz was the only reason I went on singing.

Master Timothy—

Enough. This is not a time for tears. Rejoice, humans who have loved me . . . if the Fates weave well, if the right trains intersect at Vampire Junction, then I will go forward to something more glorious . . . listen. Soon the roads will become passable for a few hours, before the fires die down and the snow returns . . . I don't know how far you will be able to go, but everyone will assume that I perished in a freak blaze set by a madman. There is a will in the offices of Stupendous Sounds Systems; one of the lawyers will direct you to it. Listen to that crash! Was that a pine tree, collapsing, setting more trees alight? Go now.

Master—Maria and I discussed this last night. We have decided to stay with you even through this. If you wish, we will cross the border with you and join you in eternity. . . .

Oh, Maria, Oh, Rudy, if you only knew, you would not beg of me such anguish. . . .

We're willing, master Timothy.

No! It must not be! Go! I command it!

. . . .

Rudy, I didn't mean to shout—Rudy! Rudy!

Gone already, then? Didn't even wait for sunset? There, the limousine starting up; its roar almost drowned by the roar of the fire below us. I hear the car plough through melting snow. It's not even sunset. There's no one here but corpses. Until they awaken, I'm by myself.

Oh, the scorchbreath of the wind . . . I'll go inside. I cherish the cold. I'll stand by Carla's corpse, make sure her rising is on schedule, I—

I'm alone. Alone.

26

fire

A car tore down the hill, skidding, leaping the train tracks, sliding down the slush of Main Street between the lines of burning buildings. "Stop them!" Kyle cried.

"They're not important, it's still fifteen minutes to sunset," PJ said, looking up from the window of the general store, still decorated with severed heads, which he had been dousing with kerosene. Ahead, Terry and the prince had been setting fire to the train station, and Stephen heard the explosion now, drowning out the rest of what PJ was saying.

Fire slithering from head to head now. Below, the arcade almost gutted; the Ms. Pac-Man, twisted by heat, rolling in the dirty snow . . . streaks of blood gridding the water and ice . . . from the drugstore, black smoke and acrid fumes belching . . . the sun setting, setting . . . the mountain darkening perceptibly. . . .

"Jesus, watch out!" PJ screamed. A half-charred figure shambling from the door of the general store. "Mr. Kavaldjian!" He had Kyle Gallagher by the throat. Stephen and PJ rushed at the vampire with their crosses. "Back into the fucking fire with you, asshole!" PJ cried as he smashed his cross over and over across the figure's face, and it bellowed in agony. Another man in flames was coming up the street. His clothes were on fire, his hair was on fire, his cheeks were

341

blackened and ripped, the teeth shone diamond-brilliant
against the charred lips—

"We're cut off," Kyle said. Stephen saw that the man had
given up. He didn't even try to wipe the blood from his nose,
his cheeks.

"Dad, come on!" PJ said. "The others are all up the hill
now, we can make it—"

"Go on. We're going to die anyway."

"No we ain't. Come on." Stephen saw the look in his eyes,
contempt mingled with terrible weariness. A sooty hand
reached out to seize Kyle. The boy did nothing at first, then
played a perfunctory tug-of-war as his father slipped from his
hands and was consigned to the fire. . . .

"Damn it, Dad," PJ whispered.

The fire danced over the old man's body, and Stephen was
almost bursting with the firejoy, he cried to the boy, "Come,
we've got fires to set," and the boy glared at him, just glared,
and at that moment Brian Zottoli emerged from a building
across the street where he'd been killing vampires, and the boy
turned to Stephen at last and said, "It ain't no game, mister.
You're crazy, you're fucking crazy." And he walked over to
Brian, leaving Stephen alone. He waded uphill to catch up
with the others.

Terry, Francis and Prathna met them at the train tracks.

"They're coming to life," Brian said. "There's dozens of
them down there."

"We'll have to go up," Stephen said. The *fire* music
welled up in his mind, triumphant, all-embracing. Every single
option in his life had been removed; there was only one path
now. He wanted to hasten, to greet the terrible joy, to bring
Valhalla crashing down into the Rhine—

"We got the crosses," PJ said. "They can't harm us."

"That's where you're wrong, boy," Brian said. "Crosses
are no good against the leader. . . ."

"What the hell?" Terry said. "We gotta do something. We
gotta go down fighting—"

"I'm eighty years old," Prathna said. "I am ready to meet
my destiny—whatever it may be!"

"We're resolved then." Darkness was falling swiftly. The
heat from below was almost unbearable, the smoke suffocating. Stephen told the boys to lead the way.

labyrinth

Francis Locke was the first to enter the house. The curtains were drawn; there was only a dull glow from the fire that had begun to rage in the forest outside. This was the moment! He held his cross high.

"I'm going to confront you," he croaked, "whatever you are. I brought you into the world, and I'm going to send you back to hell—"

Silence and dustmotes dancing in the half-light.

"Come out!" Locke remembered it all so vividly now. The plunging knife, the squishiness of the teenage girl's soft belly, the blood and urine trickling down the altar of Saint Cecilia's.

He stepped further into the room. Dark. Dark. And utterly silent. And then, from somewhere upstairs, a seductive, mocking laughter. He saw the staircase, just an outline in the gloom, and he began to climb. I must be young again, he thought, his heart pumping feverishly, trying to force more energy into his weary legs. The stairs stretched upward. How many bloody steps were there? Sometimes they seemed to be worn stone, like the steps at Eton where he and Prathna had played fives when they were children . . . sometimes bare wooden steps, sometimes steps of marble richly carpeted . . . always the laughter, breaking out from the darkness itself, and a sound like the beating of vulture's wings.

"I'll kill you!" he repeated over and over as his steps slowed, as he felt with each footfall the weight of his age and his exertions, and the cross seemed to grow heavier, heavier. . . .

And now, at the top of the stairs, that same altar, that same girl, and he was raising the knife and about to thrust it into her and now the boy-thing, wolf-thing springing out of the darkness in a cloud of incense, and Francis said, "Go back, go back—" and he shook the cross and the wolf thing reached out to touch it and it shattered into two jagged fragments and clattered down the steps, the sound went on and on and on, metal on wood, metal on marble, on granite, on metal. . . .

"Foolish man," the thing said, its voice at once a child's voice and a voice echoing with immense age, "you did not summon me. Your act of violence was senseless; it had no meaning except to satisfy your own sadism. You have tricked yourself these sixty years, built up this notion of a vast con-

frontation between light and darkness, with you one of the
protagonists. . . . Fool! Look at yourself! Are you the kind of
man who plays such cosmic roles?"

"I made you!" Francis rasped. "My killing, my act con-
strained you to come out of hell—"

"No, Francis, you pitiful old man."

And he knew at last that it was true. He had lived a lie, his
nightmares fueled only by self-delusion. In the end it was the
pity in the creature's voice that drove him into the final
despair. And, because he could not live with what he now
knew himself to be, Francis Locke's heart burst, and he col-
lapsed, dead, on the staircase of eternity, and he rolled slowly
downwards, flesh on wood, flesh on stone, on marble, on
metal.

As the others entered, they saw his corpse come thudding
down the stairs, and Stephen and Prathna hastened to drive in
the stake, in case he had been infected by vampirism. And the
five survivors ran up, abandoning the withered corpse, and the
stairs began to branch off and divide, and the house seemed
almost a living thing. . . .

arcade

PJ vanished behind an arcade machine as tall as a house, the
screen showed a giant Bloodsucker sequence but it was real,
the little vampires were perfect holographic Timmy Valentines, the coin slot was bleeding all over Terry as he shouted
PJ's name, ducked behind the machine and saw nothing but
corridors branching off into more corridors—

"PJ!" Terry shouted. The walls reverberated and bled from
thousands of little scratches. They jiggled like vast intestines
or something. Once Terry thought he saw PJ but it was one of
those vampires, he stabbed at it repeatedly with his cross and
sent it fleeing in the opposite direction, where flames were
hissing down the corridors of the doomed house. . . .

And he was *in* Bloodsucker now, it was more than a holographic projection, he was leaping over the gaudy stylized
train tracks that crisscrossed over real scenery that showed
mountains and quaint towns and a volcano and an ancient city
and even a concentration camp. . . .

"I'm lost!" he said to himself at last, slowing down. Trains
whizzed past him, some blurring, some blending into a distant

forest fire. He called PJ's name until his throat was raw, realized that he'd never find him, that he was tangled up in someone else's mind or something, that he'd have to bust through on his own, and—

More corridors now. Zombies, their eyes dripping dark blood, arms outstretched, were shambling about, being pursued by a boysized Pac-Man brandishing a stake and a crucifix. Darkness, funhouse shrieks and shivery evil voices, skeletons popping up from trapdoors. He stopped to demolish a vampire, that Mrs. Halliday who always used to bring over old books and try to make him read them, he cornered her with his cross and silenced her with a stake in the heart, and she shriveled up; fire was racing up the corridor now, and then a huge sign flashing BONUS 20,000 POINTS BONUS BONUS YOU HAVE COMPLETED THE FIRST SCREEN and an inane electronic pingpinging music to the tune of *Vampire Junction*, and—

INTERMISSION! INTERMISSION! The sign kept flashing. A dark room. Someone he knew, standing there. Yes, Prince Prathna. With . . . Jesus God, PJ's mother! Terry hid in the shadow of the arcade machine, but it was a huge gravestone with a video screen instead of an inscription and the words strobing on-off on-off were ALL TIME HIGH SCORE TERRY GISH—VAMPIRE JUNCTION HALL OF FAME, WELCOME TO HELL—and Terry was scared shitless and didn't know what to think, and he heard the prince's voice, nasal, bored-sounding: "I had them all, boys, girls, dwarfs, giants, whippings, chainings . . . nothing moves me, I'm so jaded . . . but a vampire! Someone both dead and alive at the same time! You see, I had to come. Only the prospect of actually getting an erection after ten years of unintentional celibacy could have dragged me away from my nice warm palace and its garden of delights . . . you see, my dear, why I needed to. . . ."

And Shannah Gallagher was saying, in a weird, broken-reed parody of a seductive voice, "Oh, I've never had a real live prince before," and she was slipping out of her nightdress, the same one she'd been wearing the night she came down to see Brian, and Terry had always wanted to see PJ's mom naked ever since he could remember, and even now he was getting an erection and turning beet-red in horror and shame and cowering even further into the shadow of the giant Bloodsucker, and now he saw her toying with Prathna, her hand stroking his cheek, slipping into his shirt, skimming the buttons of his trousers, and she was saying, "My prince, my prince, I'm going to show you things you've never felt before," and the prince was shaking with the chill of her touch and the thrill of his own sexual excitement, and now Terry saw his engorged penis springing from his fly and he was whispering, "This is it, this is the fulfillment of my deepest fantasy, to love a living corpse, oh, your lips are cold, cold as death, oh, I'm going to fuck them now, fuck the searing cold," and Terry saw Shannah Gallagher on her knees now, teasing the penis with her tongue, and now the prince was coming and she howled, wolflike, for a split second she was a she-wolf as she bit down on his penis and spat it out and the prince's eyes were closed in some transcendant pain, some ultimate ecstasy, as his blood fountained, red and steaming, from the stump of his penis, and Shannah was in human form again, sucking greedily at the wound, letting the blood flush her icy lips and the prince screamed again and again in pain or orgasm as she drew the last ounce of life from him, as she raked his corpse with tiger claws and worried the body with slavering wolf jaws, and just then Stephen Miles came in, a cross held high, and Terry snapped out of his shock and advanced with his own cross, and Shannah Gallagher wailed, like a she-wolf giving birth, she wailed and Terry heard Stephen shouting, "Why, Carla, why?" and he thought not Carla but Shannah, the man's gone completely insane now, who the fuck is he talking about any-ways. . . .

Someone tugging at his arm now. He whipped around and saw it was PJ. "Thank God, PJ, PJ," he said, clinging to his friend.

"What happened?" PJ was saying, his voice desperate. Stephen was leaving the room, pursuing Shannah Gallagher with his cross. "Who was that woman?"

And Terry knew that PJ hadn't seen what had happened, and he thought: how can I say I saw your mother biting off a guy's dick, how can I tell my friend something so gross about his own mother, and he remembered that the sight had aroused him even, and his cheeks burned and he said, "I don't know, PJ, I don't know, for God's sake let's stick together from now on—"

And the two friends left the room and were plunged right

back into the living Bloodsucker game and they tried to retrace their steps among the whooshing trains and the fire billowing from miniature concentration camp ovens and Terry tripped over a model castle and saw a man with a blue beard brandishing a dagger, but it was just an illusion, and he clutched his friend's arm tightly as another train hurtled past. . . .

fire

And Stephen saw the staircase, arching, its crystal balustrades sweeping like the flying buttresses of a Gothic cathedral. He could not see the summit; but he knew the steps led both to hell and to Valhalla, both to salvation and perdition.

Now he heard the voice of Timmy Valentine—or Konrad Stolz—singing words from *The Magic Flute*; it was the song of the three boys as they led Prince Tamino into the domain of the enigmatic Sarastro. Yes. He had conducted it once, in Thauberg. The music came from his own past. The past, he realized as he trod the first few steps, is never lost, but co-exists, unchangeable, with the present. The music resounded from an invisible loftiness; for the ceiling of the attic of the mansion on the mountain was so high that it contained the stars themselves.

And now the boy's voice again, spoken, above the music, by some kind of psychic multitracking: *Stephen. Stephen.* And Stephen remembered that brief exchange of glances, sixty years ago, that had sealed his fate forever. And the voice said: *They are all gone now, your silly "Gods of Chaos." But what were they anyway? Self-deluders. Bystanders, never once comprehending the cosmic drama to which they were unwitting witnesses, and all the while thinking themselves the center of the universe, the point from which good and evil emanate, at which light and darkness are one. Such hubris! But, Stephen, we can reject them now, that comic-opera prince, that quack witch, that tired, murderous old man. Come to me now. Up, up, up. The still point of the wheeling cosmos is the hall of mirrors in the vampire's funhouse.*

Stephen said, "I burn my staircase behind me." And, turning back for the last time, he sprinkled the last of the kerosene onto the steps of half-rotten wood and lit it. The flames sprang up, fire-rivers trickled down the staircase, the flames divided, writhed, seethed, the curtains in the room below

caught fire and the fire mated with the forest fire beyond and
fire circled the tombstone in the garden and ate away the snow
. . . heat blasted Stephen's face, unbearable, brought tears to
his eyes, and he turned away, looked only upward now, ran up
two steps at a time, never feeling weighed down by his age or
by the immense distance; the stairs traversed a black forest
where a humanoid red chesspiece king lay snoring beneath an
elm tree, they twisted through barbed wire and Cambridge
streets and medieval castles, and always the flames pursued, a
step or two beneath, so that he couldn't even think of turning
back anymore—

And the voice whispered in his ear: *Welcome, Stephen, to
the topsy-turvy world through the looking glass and what
Carla and Stephen and Timmy found there, welcome to death,
to the land where a mediocre psychiatrist who subsists on the
illusions of the rich can be wise as the Sibyl herself, where a
madman can be a mage, and where a little boy vampire can be
Christ. . . .*

He was suddenly tired now. The fleetness left his feet. How
many more steps could there be? Weren't sixty years of
madness and mediocrity enough, must he now go through
some Olympic marathon just to get to the venue of the final
confrontation?

The top of the stairs, surely, surely—

He fell into an embrace of muscle, ice. Long razor hairs
whisked his face, drawing blood. He smelled decay, saw pallor
in her face, and when he called Carla's name she smiled and he
saw what she had become.

seeker

The fire seemed to know where he was going. When Brian
slipped into a fork of the passageway the flames followed; he
burst into the room where he had killed Lisa. The fire broke
out behind him, the television monitors twisted as they melted,
the glass coffin dissolved into a seething puddle. Brian ran. In
another room his brother was still raping Lisa but he knew
they were phantoms and he passed right through them and
they vaporized as the flames encroached.

A dank room now, cold, conical . . . walls of buffalo hide, a
hole in the ceiling to the stars . . . a tipi, Brian realized . . . a

rattlesnake coiling on the buffalo robes, the fire licking at the tent-flaps. . . .

"The fire will not come in. It will not invade the magic circle. We are safe, Brian." He turned and saw her, reclining in shadow; the walls glowed, translucent in the firelight, highlighting with warm orange the pallid luminosity of her skin. She was clad only in her long hair, swirling, stirring voluptuously with the rise and cadence of her breasts.

"Shannah . . . but you're a. . . ."

"We must finish what we began." Her lips parted; they were moist as if they had been painted with jellied blood. "Do you think even death can separate us?"

She rose. He could not speak. He had been hiding a paper bag with some crosses and stakes, but it fell from his hand. Her gaze, fathomless and death-dark, stole his breath away. She said, "Why is it, do you think, that every woman you've made love to since you started out in pursuit of Lisa has been killed by vampires?"

"I—"

"Don't you think it's some kind of punishment?"

"For neglecting—" The thought, gnawing at him since the beginning, sprang up unbidden. He had tried to repress it before . . . but he couldn't anymore. He had reached the end. "God yes," he whispered, "I always knew I should have taken her away. I always promised her that, even when I knew I wouldn't do it, even after I learned what was going on at their house. Jesus, I can't face myself anymore."

"There is a solution."

"It's not for me." But she had already stretched out her arms to receive him, and he fell entranced into the cold embrace, and the warmth left his body in an instant, like hugging alabaster or marble, he couldn't warm her to life . . . but he couldn't resist either. It was what he had longed for ever since he'd pierced his niece's heart and envisioned himself as Mark, and had known himself capable of the very act he most abhorred.

"Shall I take you now?" Shannah said. Outside, the flames roared. Her eyes glowed, crystalline, implacable. He touched her cheek, trying to trace the line of that subtle iridescence. Always it eluded him. Even her hair was fire, black fire. "Shall I take you?" she said again. "Shall I? Shall I?"

"Yes," he said, despairing.

And threw himself into the awesome cold, and felt the hypodermic pinpricks on his neck, and the tingling invade the holes and push through his veins like an electrified catheter, and the lifewarmth siphoning out of him—

In the distance, beyond the fire, a cry: "Mom, how could you do it, Mom?" And abruptly the warmth was returning, flooding his senses, and the boy stood between them and was burning a crucifix into his mother's face, the boy in loincloth and wolf's hide, red stripes of paint across his face, and his friend beside him shocked into bemused detachment.

Brian saw the red streaming between her teeth. "Who are you?" she was shouting. "I don't know you anymore—"

The stake plunged down, quenching the scream as it wrenched from her lips. She toppled. Already fire had begun to consume her extremities. Her eyes widened, turned imploringly to Brian. He stared hypnotized by their very emptiness; the boys were pulling on his arm, desire tugged at a distant corner of his consciousness. The shield on the wall was a disk of flame. The two boys' images were smudging against it.

"Pull him out!" Terry was shouting.

"He's heavy . . . help me. . . ." The voice of the other boy.

The tautness dissolved from Shannah's face. In death her features took on new softness, new delicacy. He heard PJ's voice again: "Look, Terry, at least she knows who she is again." And Brian became aware, slowly, that he was sinking into a quicksand of fire, and that part of him desperately wanted that final dissolution, and that the boys had him by the arms and were trying to pull him out, but if he didn't help them they wouldn't succeed . . . he strained against burning darkness . . . as they jerked him free he saw snowflakes, one by one, appear beyond the fading flames like sparkling stars, pink and orange in the glow, and for a moment he saw mountains, before the huge darkness seized him.

redemption by love

The staircase swept to a fire-girt mountain peak. The snow was littered with corpses of the heroes who had been rash enough to brave the magical flames. But fire was Stephen's friend; hadn't he played with fire since he was a child? The fire knew Stephen and did not scorch him; it even parted to admit him.

And he stood in a chamber of infinite mirrors. It was the heart of the attic, and therefore the dark heart of human consciousness.

Toy-train tracks crisscrossed the floor. Engines whistled as they hurtled over bridges improvised from leather books, across bedsheet meadows, through plastic tunnels. In exquisite miniature were the Opernhaus Thauberg, the chapel at Saint Cecilia's, even the graveyard that once contained Konrad Stolz. Castles sprouted from padded armchairs. A tundra of hairpin evergeens—all reflected a million times in the mirrors.

He recognized a couch from Carla's old office. And there was Carla. She said: "For an age he's waited for us, Stephen. Look, I've drawn a little chart." She pulled a pad from her pocketbook and held up a hand-drawn diagram—

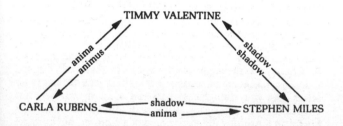

"You see," she went on, "what a complex relationship entwines us."

He didn't speak. The fire—he felt the fire as one feels a living entity, a lover—was already eating out the bowels of the house.

"You remember when we first met? Not at the home, but a chance meeting long before then, when I was a student and you handed me a doughnut at Carnegie Hall? No, of course not. But I never forgot you. You see, we've always been plagued by these mysterious coincidences. It's a conspiracy of fate. Fate prods us, eliminating our options one by one, until we each have only one road left—"

"The way to Vampire Junction." Then, "Are you—"

"Yes. I am a vampire." He saw it in her feline movements, in the phosphor sheen of her face, in the glowering darkness of her eyes. "Listen. It's not what you think. A thousand years ago Timmy Valentine began to change. To feel compassion was only the germ of metamorphosis. It started as . . . an unquenchable yearning for completion. Part of him sought out his anima and his shadow; and since he was himself on the shadow universe, for him those archetypes existed in *our* world . . . though they had not then yet been born. Do you understand? We three were made for, impelled toward, each other. We will now enter a crucible of transformation, we will wrap ourselves in a chrysalis of self-renewal, and we will rise phoenixlike from these flames, transfigured, invincible."

"Hard to believe." He could see this truth just ahead, but he didn't want to grasp it yet. He was afraid. He wanted to cling to the firejoy, to exult in the flamedance of the town and the house. He said, "And the reason our marriage didn't work out before—it was because we didn't have Timmy yet?"

"Something like that."

"And the Gods of Chaos? What was their part in this?"

"Oh, come. You've always known that they weren't important. That moment in your childhood, when you and the Gods of Chaos saw the night-child—what did *they* see? Ghosts, monsters, gibbering phantoms. Personifications of their inner selves. But you, though they had tried to twist you, were not twisted. So you alone saw all the way through the millennial horror to the primal innocence . . . not a monster, but an angel . . . not hatred, but love!"

A fireshimmer in the air between him and Carla . . . the boy's shape wringing itself from the haze . . . at last they stood face to face again. Sixty years dwindled to nothing. The mirror-hall and the chapel with its stone fan-vaulting were the same place. The boy had not changed either, for his was the substance of eternity.

He gazed into the eyes, dark as polished obsidian, yet, like obsidian, forged from a volcano's heart; the eyes framed by a complexion of Dresden china and by the blue-black hair woven from shadows. He trembled with the same emotions the ten-year-old choirboy and acolyte had felt. The tingle of an exquisitely sensual terror. The helplessness. The shock of having recognized an absolute beauty.

He said, "I've set fire to the way behind. I can't turn back."

And Timmy spoke at last, the melody of his voice edged by profoundest melancholy. "I greet you, my shadow. And I'm sorry that, in our previous meetings, I never dared acknowledge this truth."

"And I greet you." They would have embraced, but fear interposed itself, fear of that igneous darkness in Timmy's eyes.

"He's so old," Carla said, "and so alone. Only he has survived the vampire's infancy, with its elemental rage and bloodlust, its childlike superstitious dread of cult objects. He has experienced the first inklings of compassion; and now he is approaching a new threshold. And as he is our spiritual self, so we are his humanity."

"Why do I cast no reflection?" Timmy said. "Because you are my two souls."

Beyond the couch was an iron-barred oaken door. Stephen wondered why he hadn't seen it before. Timmy said, with a twinge of impatience, "It was always there, if you cared to look. You Wagnerians are so melodramatic. You never see *anything* until you hear its leitmotif!" And laughed a bewitching laugh.

"You mean all this could have been avoided if only I'd spoken to you in college chapel—"

More laughter, like windchimes. "Oh, Stephen, always after the simple answers. You want to burn your way through life like a ball of fire."

Somewhere in the house, a clock struck. One . . . two . . . three . . . thirteen.

"It's time," Carla said, her upper lip quivering with nervous anticipation.

The flames had burst through the floorboards and were racing down the train tracks and devouring the books and vaporizing the plastic mountains. In the firelight their fangs flickered.

In utmost bewilderment Stephen cried out: "How can you say I saw love when I saw burning cold and darkness?"

The boy vampire's smile dazzled like the sunlit sea. "I am the dark side of love," he said, "the ocean of chaos upon which the universe is built. Without me love has no meaning. In the darkest heart of universal darkness, I am the memory of light."

He beckoned toward the door.

Rumbling racked the entire house. An earthquake? A

volcano? "Will you step through already?" Timmy shouted,
stamping his foot in a childish tantrum. "I haven't got all
day."

The boy and the woman opened their arms wide to receive
him. The boy was the moon and the woman was the earth and
he would be the shining sun. The door creaked open; behind
it, a slit of blinding sulphurous incandescence. Brimstone
fumes tendriled from the opening, swirling, misting the mirrors, hugging the three in a spectral embrace. Nausea welled
up. He couldn't breathe. I'm dying, he thought, I'm actually
dying!

"Is it the door to hell?" he cried, remembering Don
Giovanni and Doctor Faustus, dragged bodily into the underworld.

"Such hubris!" Carla was smiling beatifically through the
clouds of smoke. "What evil have you done?"

The boy's voice rang out, trumpet-clear over the thunder-
roar: "There is no evil! There is no hell!"

Stephen succumbed then to their frozen embrace. Their perfume, laced with putrescence, pervaded his nostrils. As the
door swung wide, he kissed fanged mouths and caressed snow-
pale flesh, and he seemed to grow young again; the door
palpitated like the vagina of a cosmic earthmother as the three
danced out their love on each other's bodies and he felt the
firewarmth flow from his body and encircle the others, he felt
secure at last in the closed triangle of their mingled passions—

fire

—and now the Mage caresses the Sibyl's wrinkled flesh and
Stephen and Carla are there too, they are conjoined with the
shuddering earth; Sibyl, possessed by Carla, responds, her
shriveled body wakened to violent passion. The earth rumbles.
Outside the window the boy sees brightness and smells death.
A burning wind, glittering with glowing dust-stars, invades the
Mage's sanctum. They have been anointed with a slippery
poultice that contains, among other ingredients, the boy's own
severed and pulverized testicles. The three make love. It is not
the love that Carla and Stephen and Timmy will share in the
future, but a selfish, possessive lust, and the Mage pauses
often to make ritual passes that invoke the sexual magic of the

erupting earth. From somewhere outside the boy hears a column ripped out by the roots and smash into the side of the wineshop. Inflamed now, the Mage rises rampant, his teeth bared; the boy barks in sharp pain as the leopard Mage leaps and satisfies both his lust and his hunger on the boy's body, he exults, he roars over the screams of the dying, while the Sibyl claps her monkey hands and the folds of her eyes quiver and she giggles and croons over her long-awaited death—

fire

—and as Stephen gazes awestruck Carla becomes the earth and her cunt becomes the Sibyl's cave and Timmy and Stephen crawl upward into the tunnel, the hot magma glistening, the passageway glowing redhot, shaking; their feet blister against the searing lava but still they run upward, and now, in the womb that is the sunlight, time shudders to a stop, the fangs tear into him, he surrenders to darkness that is no longer darkness but fierce illumination, he climaxes again and again, they share their orgasms as they shatter the final door in Bluebeard's castle and become one and three and three and one, as hawklike they soar up to the ineffable brilliance, and then—

fire

—the peak of Vesuvius flowers in a thousand colors—

fire

—they are born—

fire

—and they come to the Mage's sanctum, and they see the lava streaming in through the atrium from the wineshop and they are in the boy's consciousness as he struggles to tear himself free from the embrace of the leopard and the monkey and though they are invisible, extradimensional, they feel his terror and the pain from the wounds of fang and claw, they interpose themselves, they try to make themselves real, for a moment they flicker into the reality of Pompeii before the unbearable heat drives them screaming back to the shadowland. The Mage, astounded, has reverted to human form and within the instant that the shadows from the future have impinged upon his consciousness the boy tears himself free from his deadly embrace with a supreme effort and begins to run and sees the smoking lava lapping at the doorway and doubles back to the window and the Mage darts eaglelike at his face, his knifebeak stabbing at his brows, his cheeks, making the blood spurt, hiss as it encounters encroaching lava, and the Mage shouts in his screeching eagle voice: "We must complete the ritual . . . we must . . . or we will be neither dead nor alive nor undead . . . a wisp of our immortality will remain, we will lose our substance yet never acquire insubstantiality, we will haunt the earth as nightmares within nightmares, shadows of shadows, resonances of resonances—" and the Sibyl tries to grasp him in her frail arms, but the boy jumps from the Mage and the Sibyl and the flames lash the walls of the house and the earth trembles and roars as in an agony of childbirth—

fire

—a child's footsteps patter on a splintering mosaic, bitter-toast smell of charring feet, fleeing, mountain thunder, then blood, *spatter spatter spatter* bursting *spatter spatter spatter* boiling on the hot mosaic stones *spatter spatter spatter*

fire

—Stephen and Carla hover ghoul-like over the marble columns that snap like bones over the screaming and the fire running through the streets and fangs glitter in the ash-hail they glitter *spatter* glitter *spatter* glitter *spatter*

fire

—the last vampires stagger screaming from the drugstore and the general store and an arcade machine vaults from the parlor and collides with the charred hulk of Prathna's car, and still dragging the unconscious Brian the two boys look up, the snow has melted from the Main Street and corpses are bounding downhill, slipping and sliding in the dirty slush, and
—white flame fountaining from black Vesuvius—
—and Carla and Timmy and Stephen are borne skyward,

erupting, on the tide of the bursting magma—

—and ash rains on the boy, already half-dead from leopard bites, and Carla and Stephen experience with him the nausea of the brimstone fumes and the lacerations of streaking embers and the suffocating engulfing powder trapping him as he struggles to breathe and his blood *spatter spatter* on the mosaic stones—

—the drugstore roof collapses spraying the street with Coke cans—

—the Mage and the Sibyl open their arms to greet death, the Sibyl rejoices that she has cheated eternity, the Mage's mind is riddled by doubt as he succumbs to the molten lava, and stones from the ceiling crash on top of them and their bones crack and the Sibyl is pulverized under an Ionian column and rubble streams down, burying them completely, and—

fire

—the boy screams, "God is love!"—

—the snow shifts on the mountain peaks. It begins to roll downhill. It streams into the town of Junction, an avalanche set off by the boy's shrill cry—

—the statue of Konrad Stolz tumbles from its gravestone and splits into zigzag halves on the gravel—

—the three spirits of the future fly skyward, sunward from the flames of the city, as an ocean of oozing fire descends to engulf Pompeii and columns poke out like twigs from the lava crests and thousands upon thousands of souls are embedded like insects in the glowing crimson sea—

—they are born, they flower from the bowels of the mountain—

—the fire has reached Valhalla, where the gods, the first constrainers of chaos, sit statue-still on their golden thrones and yearn for death—

fire

Stephen stirs in the arms of the woman and the boy. Touches their faces, their limbs, which have lost their coldness. Thus it is that he knows he has crossed the boundary. In the single protracted orgasm of this troilistic union he has experienced the death and rebirth of universes. He is overwhelmed by wonder. Beyond the fire, his attenuated hearing perceives even the music of the spheres. As the house collapses around them, eternity seeps into him in all its pain and rapture. There is a thirst that can never be slaked, and an absolute beauty that chills the heart.

27

dissolve

—the boom of a distant explosion. And a fireglow on the snow, the color of the encroaching sunrise.

"Don't look back," PJ said to Terry. "Just help me pull this fucking thing."

Terry tugged at the poles and cloth that PJ had put together for the unconscious Brian. "I'm cold."

"I know, I know. Come on, pull."

They heaved, freeing it from the snow. "How did you know how to make this thing?"

"It's a travois, stupid. *Tra-vwa*. The Shoshones use them when they move camp. I know stuff like that. Mom taught me.

"Where are we going?"

"To the reservation, I guess."

"How the fuck are we going to get there? Shit, it's started to snow again."

"My people know many things," PJ said. Terry had never heard him talk this way before. Oh, he was always saying wistful things about wanting to go live with the Indians, but now he had so much certainty. PJ said, "I know how to build snowhouses that conserve warmth. I know how to hunt. I've never done it, but I guess I'll figure it out somehow.

"What about him? What if he's dead?"

"He ain't dead."

"What if he dies?"

"We'll bury him."

"What if . . . I mean, your mom bit him, and. . . ."

"We got stakes, don't we?"

"Yeah. Yeah."

They hunched into the wind and went on. Though it was bitterly cold, his grief seemed to melt away as they thrust onward into the snow. Behind them fire sparkled in the forest, a heartbreakingly beautiful sight. From here it didn't look at all as if a whole town had been consumed by fire and madness.

"We survived," he said, without joy.

And PJ let out a wild whoop, which was lost in the wind's incessant howling.

dissolve

As winter draws to an end, the roads will become passable once more. A train will pull into the charred ruins of the Junction station. It will be a moonlit night, and the passengers, if any, who look out will be able to see the devastated remains of the town. It will be a picturesque, if bleak, sight. The moonlight will glitter in thousands of shards of shattered mirror glass that have blown down from the house on the mountain. It will gleam on naked rivets protruding from blackened posts and doorframes; it will glisten on the marbled innards of arcade games, inexplicably piled up at the bottom of Main Street. There will probably be no passengers at this point; those that might be there will probably be asleep, since Junction is a stop of no significance.

This time, though, three new passengers will board the train. They will take a compartment, first class, all to themselves. One is a middle-aged woman; another an older man; the third a young boy with delicate, androgynous features. Our hypothetical passenger will notice, perhaps, the unusual sheen on their pallid faces; he will naturally attribute it to a trick of the pervasive moonlight.

When they speak to each other it will not be a human discourse at all, but the language of the night, which we mortals perceive as the stridulating of cicadas or the baying of distant wolves or perhaps merely the suspirant sifting of the wind. Even if we knew the meanings of their words, their nuances would pass unperceived. But our hypothetical by-stander, with some glimmering of the nightspeech, might glean by his hypothetical eavesdropping this conversation:

"It was a beautiful story. I wish I had it to experience all over again."

"There was so much more I could have told you, Carla. Like when I exchanged harsh words with Caravaggio in Rome in the piazza in the rain . . . or sucked blood from the bound feet of the Empress of China."

"Lies, all lies."

"Truth, my dear friends, is merely the prevailing percentage of our private illusions. . . ."

"The fire is doused. I am at peace."

"Where are we going now?"

It does not matter to whom we ascribe the voices; in some sense that cannot accurately be described, the three have been translated into one. They have evolved.

But in spite of their progression to another plane, another cog in the wheel of being, they are a far from solemn trinity. They will often laugh. Their eyes will sparkle (not as human eyes sparkle, but as midnight dewdrops in the moonlight); their merry smiles will often reveal the glint of deadly fangs. If sadness falls over one of them for a moment, as he thinks of what has been and the enormity of what may yet come, the others will comfort him gently. For there is still love among the dead.

"Was I the Sibyl in the story? And Stephen the Mage?"

"And Dr. Schweiss? And Bluebeard? And Poitou? And Joan of Arc?"

"Perhaps. Perhaps it is only that the resonances of these people, their echoes in time, have clung to you more tenaciously than to others."

"I think we have them all inside us."

"Even Bluebeard."

"To face the Bluebeard within ourselves—"

"To dare to unlock the final door—"

"Is the beginning of wisdom."

"But where are we going, damn it?"

As to where they are going next. . . .

The train will enter a forest, still hugging the side of the mountain. Not the whole train, perhaps; the other cars will doubtless progress to their preordained destination. But this segment, at least, will pass into an ever-deepening forest. The forest will thicken until it appears an impenetrable darkness. Even the image of the train will be swallowed up in the darkness, and they will seem to roam free in the cool of the forest, basking in the darkness, in the commingling scents of earth, wood, stone, and beast, in the sussurant symphony of forest murmurs. In the darkness they will grow strong. But though time here seems to stand still, it is true that the train must eventually leave the forest, just as the boy left the Sibyl's cave to become a vampire in a dying city, just as Carla left the lucrative practice of soothing the neurotic rich, just as Stephen breached the wall of his own mediocrity to conduct one brilliant performance of *Götterdämmerung*. Even death must end. But to tell of our protagonists' rebirth is beyond this story's provenance.

And the town of Junction? There is little to tell. It has been abandoned. No one will live there, and few will even visit. Though an aura of unease will hang over the town for many years to come, even that will pass. But the natives of Highwater, the neighboring town, will sometimes refer to the street of gutted houses as Vampire Junction. If you ask why, they will say it's an old song, and they'll laugh, a trifle nervously. But no one will understand the joke. No one will even remember the tune. They are so ephemeral, these pop songs.

—Alexandria, New York, Rome, Geneva
1980–83